There were safer ventures than loving Jane . . .

Keller didn't move or breathe as Jane walked into the hot spring and lay down, her eyes closed.

Keller had seen his share of naked women. It wasn't the bare female skin that startled him so thoroughly as he sat there on the hot stones. It was *Jane's* bare skin that rendered him speechless. Surely he was dreaming . . .

She opened her eyes and studied him. In a husky whisper she said, "You know, with a few bumps and bruises on you, Keller, you look sort of dashing."

"Dashing," he repeated.

"Your first battle scars." Jane smiled. "And they're not bad at all."

That was a cue if he ever heard one . . .

BLACK BRIDGE TO CHINA

NANCY MARTIN

POCKET BOOKS

New York   London   Toronto   Sydney   Tokyo

Another *Original* publication of POCKET BOOKS

POCKET BOOKS, a division of Simon & Schuster, Inc.
1230 Avenue of the Americas, New York, N.Y. 10020

ISBN: 0-671-63841-6

First Pocket Books printing April 1988

10 9 8 7 6 5 4 3 2 1

POCKET and colophon are trademarks of Simon & Schuster, Inc.

Printed in the U.S.A.

"Do not take life too seriously. You will never get out of it alive."

—Elbert Hubbard

BLACK BRIDGE TO CHINA

Chapter 1

HE LOOKED LIKE A BOUNTY HUNTER. WITH STEELY EYES FASTened on the horizon, his lean body coiled for action as he stood alone on that sunbaked stretch of Third World runway, he could even have been a CIA operative poised for adventure and intrigue. He probably kept a sealed envelope in one pocket and a cyanide tablet in another. A man from the CIA, yes, perfect. Paul Keller squared his shoulders to fit the part.

To make the scenario complete, one of the local people peering out from the louvered windows of the terminal building ought to intone, "He is a man to be reckoned with."

That's the way it would have happened in the movies, anyway. But the fantasy disintegrated before any such words could be pronounced. As Keller stood on the runway with his split-open suitcase at his feet and the pieces of his ruined camera cupped in his hands, he drew no respectful glances from the other passengers getting off the plane. He got no awed stares, no attention at all, in fact, except from a swarm of round-faced, bare-bottomed children who crouched just three yards away on the other side of a chain link fence and grinned at him like scavengers.

They recognized Paul Keller for what he was—a tourist. Tall but not too tall, lean but not too lean, wearing clothes direct from Banana Republic. Keller kept himself trim and ate bran cereal regularly, but no Nautilus muscles rippled beneath his buttoned-down shirt. His hair was thick but dusty colored, his nose was straight but characterless in spite of a basketball injury in high school, and his blue-gray eyes were not piercing, but rather puckered at the corners. He wore glasses most of the time, only they were lost with the other part of his luggage. No, he was not a bounty hunter. Even the children knew that.

A gnarled old Hindu man shuffled out of the terminal past the pack of kids and stopped expectantly in front of Keller. He cast a look down Keller's airplane-rumpled clothes, past the bits and pieces of his Nikon to the broken suitcase at his feet. The once spiffy Hartmann had been rent apart between Hawaii and Bangkok by a baggage handler who clearly had no respect for fine labels, and more of Keller's belongings were scattered on the ground. The profligate display they made for the gap-toothed Hindu man caused Keller to actually blush. The hair dryer, his tube of plaque-fighting toothpaste, and a pair of Timberland boots that had yet to see timbered lands beyond the grounds of his Georgetown condominium were hardly the trappings of a hero.

With the last shreds of his self-respect, Keller glared at the old man. "Go away," he snapped. "I don't need your help!"

The Hindu shrugged amiably and headed back to the terminal, empty-handed but smiling. The children giggled some more, which thrust Keller out of his bewildered funk and into an action mode. He threw his smashed camera to the ground, snatched up his suitcase, and stuffed the contents back inside. Dodging the wave of chattering children who boiled over the fence and fell upon the remains of the Nikon like starving hyenas, Keller hugged his belongings to his chest and headed for the terminal.

The pressure of the suitcase against his chest helped him

feel better as he stepped into the crowd. A phalanx of more experienced travelers pushed past him toward customs. Not wanting to subject himself to official scrutiny yet, Keller hung back. What on earth had possessed him to come, anyway? To blow his vacation time on a errand such as this?

It was Nina's fault, whined a small voice in his inner ear. Nina's disdain had stung him into doing something totally out of character. She had goaded him into coming to Nepal. He was already out of his element, and it was her fault.

It wasn't the first time he'd done something to impress her, either. An ambitious administrative assistant to a rising humbug on Capitol Hill, Nina Orrinfield had early on convinced Keller that he'd better measure up to her upscale standards. He went to her aerobics class, but nearly died from cardiac arrest. At her suggestion, he bought season opera tickets—the kind of seats she wouldn't be ashamed to be seen in but cost a hell of a lot more than box seats for any Super Bowl. After a while, he was even eating pasta and goat cheese to please her. All these ventures were far from Keller's usual activities. He followed college basketball with a passion equaled perhaps only by his love for tortilla chips with Bartels and Jaymes. Nina was on the A-list to parties on the Hill, though, and she was good at the horizontal sports, too—even showing a formidable imagination there from time to time—so Keller wanted to stick with her. Things had gotten out of hand, that was all.

It started when he broke his own vow to keep her away from his family. He should never have taken her to the send-off party for his father, but lately his mother had been hearing a lot about AIDS and wanted proof that Keller was actually dating one specific woman, so he produced Nina.

Nina had been dazzled, of course. Not by his mother, either.

As they drove back to her place after the party, Nina had positively gushed. "Your father is fabulous, Paulie! I can't imagine why you said I wouldn't like him."

"He's not interested in politics," said Keller.

"Politics isn't everything," she replied, which would have astounded Keller if he hadn't been bracing himself for what was sure to come next.

"I hadn't realized how famous your father is," Nina said.

"You've been keeping secrets. His stories are so fascinating! Did you hear him telling about the Amazon expedition? He's marvelous. You're attractive too, of course. That goes without saying. But your father—well, he's so *dynamic,* isn't he?"

Yes, a brilliant cartographer, a daring adventurer, a womanizer of awesome experience if you believed everything he said, Professor Randall Keller possessed the kind of reputation over which movie producers salivated. Sure, his son could admit that. But Paul was above trying to compete with his own father. It was such a cliché, anyway, wasn't it? So ridiculous. He shrugged off Nina's remarks. Tried to, anyway.

But Nina spouted on enthusiastically. "Oh, you're intelligent, moneyed—all that usual stuff. But that's so *ordinary* now, Paulie. Compared to him, anyway." She sighed. "He must have been an animal in bed!"

She was sitting behind the wheel at the time, and Keller didn't usually mind letting her drive his BMW. In fact, he frequently allowed Nina to bully him into the passenger seat. She liked the feel of the steering wheel, the quiver of the powerful engine, and the ease with which she could control the car. For Nina, driving was foreplay. If only she didn't wax so damned philosophical.

His annoyance must have shown.

"Oh, don't be offended, darling," she said, smiling across at him in the light of the dashboard and looking about as innocent as Lauren Bacall. "You're a pretty good screw yourself, you know, but your father's a legend."

To heap disgrace on indignity, that night was the first time during his thirty-five years that Keller experienced a sexual nonperformance. Terrific timing.

It was supposed to be normal once in a while, Nina soothed. Especially after a few drinks. Rest, darling. Don't think about it. She was nice about it. Too nice, maybe. There was no doubt in his mind who Nina went to sleep dreaming about, anyway.

Keller slept off the booze, but in the morning Nina only wanted to talk.

"I think it's time we started seeing other people," she said while rolling up one leg of panty hose. He watched from the opposite side of the bed while she recited the lines as if she'd practiced them in the bathroom. "Not that I don't enjoy our time together, Paul, but some variety can only enhance what we've got."

Keller took it badly and resorted to sarcasm. "Where did you pick up your dialogue? *Knots Landing?*"

She ignored him prettily. "Think of what we can bring back to this relationship if we have a little freedom."

"I'm not exciting enough anymore, is that it?"

She pretended not to hear that either. "I need some space, that's all I'm saying. I *like* you, Paul. You're cleverer than most men I meet, and you don't play around enough to pick up anything contagious, but I'm just not ready for monogamy."

"Especially not with me?"

"Especially not with any man who makes his life's work out of studying musty maps of Peru, for God's sake, and never has the urge to get out in the world!"

Keller, who was proud of his job at the Library of Congress, promptly said, "They're not musty. I work in a goddamn vault, you know!"

"That's not the *point!*" The dam of her self-control must have broken, because she swung around and lectured him. "You're wasting yourself, Paul. Young men are supposed to have passion and courage and—and all that dashing stuff! Why don't you get out and *do* something now and then? My God, pretty soon you'll want to spend Saturday nights home *reading* or something! You're going to be middle-aged any minute!"

He said, "You were really sucked in by my father, weren't you?" He got out of bed. "I should have introduced you when he was still young enough to do something about that look in your eye."

"Maybe you should have!"

"For crying out loud, he's a dotty old man now!"

"Well, he still knows how to live," she retorted. "He's not sitting around waiting for his investments to mature. He's got more style than that!"

"Style?" Keller halted in the bathroom doorway. "You think he's got *style?* Did you know he doesn't even take clean underwear on those trips of his?"

Nina flushed. "He's still got something—panache, maybe, or—oh, you know what I mean! Why don't you do something like he does once in a while? Isn't that part of being a—whatever you are?"

"Cartographer."

"Well, cartographize or something! Go on an adventure!"

"An adventure?"

"Yes, exactly. Why not?"

He sputtered. "Be-because I like my job for one thing! And I want to keep it, thank you. I'm up for one hell of a promotion soon, Nina."

"*He* takes trips," she said. "*And* keeps his job at the university."

"That's out of kindness. Everybody knows the old coot's great expeditions no longer have any scientific purpose. The university won't even fund him anymore. He's just gallivanting now, trying to relive his old glories. It's embarrassing."

"I think it's romantic."

"An old man doddering around on mountain trails in Tibet? Oh, sure, very romantic, all right! Let's hope he doesn't trip over a goat and drown in yak shit."

"You're being immature," she said, getting off the bed. She chose a red-and-white printed dress from her closet and took it out by its hanger. "You're still a little boy in the throes of the oedipal stage and talking about bodily functions." She blinked at him in the mirror on the closet door. "What's the matter, Paul? Did you catch a glimpse of Daddy's dickie in the YMCA and decide you'd never measure up?"

"Jesus Christ."

"Don't be such a baby." She held the dress against her body and studied herself in the mirror. "I think he's exciting, that's all," she said. "No reflection on you, of course."

She wasn't looking at the dress, Keller noted. The dreamy expression in her eyes as she gazed into the mirror gave her away. She was miles off, fantasizing about the one man he couldn't compete against. Before he could think, Keller was across the room and grabbing her arm. He spun her around, determined to at least get the look off her face.

"Oh," she said, and dropped the dress over the side of the bed.

With the adrenaline of oedipal rage seething in his bloodstream instead of alcohol, Keller managed a performance that quite made up for the previous night's misfire. Nina responded accordingly. When it was over, he felt much better. Giddy, in fact.

While he dressed, Nina lay languidly in the tangled bedclothes and watched. She read the signs correctly. "Is this the end for us, Paulie?"

"Yes," he said, zipping up.

Undismayed, she snuggled down for more sleep. "With a bang, not a whimper. Thank you, darling."

"You're welcome," he said, and left with dignity.

His postcoital euphoria didn't last, though. Nina was right, of course. He was going to be middle-aged soon. He was a nice guy, all right—well-read and well-paid—but everyone knew where nice guys finished in a time when the likes of Rambo and Dirty Harry Callahan were still generating positive public sentiment.

Paul Keller started to figure he was a lost cause.

Then his father called. It was a week or so later and late at night, of course. Suitably melodramatic.

"My boy," boomed Professor Keller over oceans of static, "you know I'm not a man to ask favors."

Keller stayed under the covers, but tried to wake up. "Hello, Dad," he mumbled.

"I'm self-sufficient and always have been!" The old man streamrolled ahead, saying, "In my business, I can't risk depending upon anyone but myself—it's just too dangerous most of the time. It's a sad state of affairs when you can't trust even your own family to come through, but—"

"Dad," Keller called. "What do you want?"

"What time is it there? Are you awake?"

He squinted at the clock radio. "It's twelve-fifteen."

"You've had an hour's rest at least. Good. Get up. I need you here right away. Something tricky's come up."

"Tricky?" Keller knew all the family euphemisms, and he was immediately on his guard. He didn't have to close his eyes to imagine what the old man looked like at that very moment. He'd be pacing around a pay telephone, his tall stringy body hunched, his skinny legs dusty, his clothes caked with trail mud. His hair would be dazzling white—a shock of snowy locks that could be seen for miles in a desert sandstorm. In Keller's mind, the picture was as vivid as if the old maniac towered over the bed with wild eyes and waving fists. At least he was at a safe distance this time. "Dad, start at the beginning, will you?"

The Professor made a growling noise full of exasperation. "I'm in Kathmandu. You do know where Nepal is, don't you? To think that a son of mine doesn't—the government spends perfectly good money for dandified schoolboys like you to moon over maps in a library! I'll never understand what good it does to—"

"I know where Nepal is, Dad. What's going on?"

"Quit asking damnfool questions and I'll explain! I've got a job for you."

With a great deal of patience, Keller said, "I've already got a job, Dad."

"And God forbid anyone should drag you out of that cellar you call an office! A *librarian,* for God's sake! No, no, I won't ask you to leave that!"

An old argument. Keller forced himself not to raise his voice this time. "We've got several important projects going at the Library right now, Dad—I'm up for a promotion soon as a result of them—but if you need me to—"

"Promotion to what?" the Professor exploded over another rush of static. "Chief tour guide? Good God, this is an emergency!"

Keller plugged his ear so he could hear better. "Dad, are you all right?"

Another growl. "Just listen to my directions! Do you have a pencil at least? Write this down so you don't miss something. There's a thing I need from home. I'm—It's a map, all right? A drawing. It's in my safe at the house."

"What map? Dad—"

"I want you to send it to me. You may have to catch the earliest plane to the West Coast yourself to get it here in time—"

"I can't do that! Not till Saturday, anyway. I—"

"Find the most dependable international carrier you can and put the map on their next flight to Kathmandu! It'll have to go through Thailand, so make damn sure it doesn't get held up there. Bribe somebody to fix the paperwork if you have to. I want that map here in forty-eight hours, boy. Understand me? Someone will pick it up when it gets here. Got all that?"

Still frantically scrabbling in the bedside drawer for a pencil, Keller said, "Dad—"

"Listen!" his raspy voice insisted. "This is important! Go first to my study at home. The map's in the wall safe—your mother has the combination. Pack the map so it won't get damaged and send it *immediately* to Kathmandu in my name. I'll pick it up at the airport myself. For God's sake, don't wait! I need it right away."

"Why? Dad, if—"

"Don't ask questions! You might not like the answers. I need that map as quickly as possible, that's all."

Completely caught up by the urgency of the moment, which was something he knew he should never do but couldn't seem to stop himself this time, Keller heard his own voice say, "Look, if it's so important, I'll bring it myself."

"Jesus Christ," said his father. "You think this place is some kind of country club? Just send the damn map and no funny business, you hear me? I'm in a mighty uncomfortable place until it gets here!"

Chapter 2

KELLER CRADLED THE PHONE AND LAY THERE THINKING. OH, THE idea of hurrying some tattered bit of paper off to the Professor wasn't anything new. During Keller's sophomore year in college, for instance, the old man had called him away from midterms and sent him to Uruguay to photocopy an entire collection of maps belonging to a young, wealthy, and extraordinarily beautiful widow. That particular trip had resulted in Keller's first one-night stand, so he had considered repeating Geology 371 no great punishment. Now, however, with heaven knew what forms of God's wrath lurking in the bodies of nubile maidens, Keller wasn't lured by the possibility of short-term sex under exotic circumstances.

No, something else made Keller consider running off to Nepal. The Professor always sounded like he was in a manic frenzy, but this time there was desperation in the old man's voice. It was almost like his father was asking for help. *Really* asking.

Keller sat up in his bed. He'd go to Kathmandu himself, by God! It would only take a few days, and the look on Nina's face when he'd casually mention his little jaunt would be reward aplenty. He had some vacation days stacked up, so dammit, he'd go! He climbed out of bed and began to pack.

At six A.M., he arrived at his mother's house and declared his purpose.

Charlotte Keller was not keen on the idea of her son's trip. In fact, it might be more accurate to say she was horrified when he announced his plan to deliver the map to his father personally.

"Darling!" she objected, thoroughly alarmed. "You can't be serious!"

The house was a Victorian pile near DuPont Circle, and he still had a key to the back door so he'd walked in unannounced. His mother had passed from the country phase into some other fashion in home decorating and was in the process—being an early riser and a vocal proponent of not wasting a minute of the day—of sanding a parade of stenciled ducks off the kitchen baseboards. On her dimpled hands and knees, swathed in a paint-spattered smock from her watercolor days and with her wild blond hair bound up in a batik scarf, she looked like a kind of elfin harridan. An aging Bette Midler.

Keller helped her off her knees and put her sandpaper block pad in the sink. "Of course I'm serious, Mother. Find the map for me, will you?"

"Darling, you can't go running off like this! It might be dangerous. This isn't like you at all. Why do you have to go?"

"He said it was urgent."

"He always says that! Why listen this time, Paul?"

"I want to. I have to. Help me find the map, Mother. I want to get on a plane as soon as possible."

"But, Paul, if he told you not to go—"

"I'm going," he said.

They argued like that for a while, but in the end she shut up and just studied him curiously. Because he'd been her only child, they had good communication, and whatever she saw in his face was enough to silence her protests.

Mumbling, however, she led the way to the safe in the den where the Professor kept all his most valuable materials. Naturally, she couldn't find the combination to the safe. "How am I supposed to keep track of such things?" she asked in a fluster, pawing through the desk drawer. "I'm an artist, not a housekeeper. I write poetry, not grocery lists! Can't he remember that?"

Yes, Charlotte Keller was a poet, all right, but only in the sense that she wrote verse that rhymed. It was mindless stuff, and when asked years ago to give his opinion, Keller had hit upon the ideal remark to please his mother. "It's esoteric, Mom," he had told her, manufacturing a scholarly frown. "Really esoteric."

That kind of praise from her son delighted Charlotte immeasurably, and she often dredged up the same word when the subject of her forays into various realms of the art world came up. "Why do I have to keep track of the combination?" she fussed. "I'm an esoteric person, Paul. At least you realize that."

They spent that first precious morning of vacation time ripping the den apart to look for the numbers that would unlock Randall Keller's safe. The map was indeed inside. It looked ordinary to Keller, who was accustomed to artifacts —the rice paper was in relatively good condition, a clue that the markings were simply a modern copy of an older map. If a penciled note in the top right corner could be believed, the map was dated 1801 and depicted a place Keller did not recognize except that it appeared to be mountainous and was landlocked. More than likely, the land was Nepal. Nothing extraordinary, no writing, no skull and crossbones to mark treasure, no drawings of naked women to suggest a hidden harem. Nothing exciting. Unless he had some other research materials to go on, Keller couldn't draw any conclusions from the map alone. In disgust, he rolled it up and stuck the map into a fancy brass-and-leather tubelike case he found in the study. Maybe he'd study it more carefully on the plane.

"Now," said his mother, "let me get my purse. I'm taking you downtown."

"What? I can't. I've got a plane to catch—"

"You can't go to Nepal dressed like it's your first day at prep school. I know the shops where your father buys his equipment. We'll get you some decent things, and you can take a later flight."

"Mother—"

"I know what I'm talking about," she said sternly. "I won't have my darling boy go chasing off unprepared this way. You never know what you'll run into."

Truer words were never spoken.

"You'll be careful, won't you?" she asked when the shopping was done.

"Of course, Mother," he promised, and kissed her.

She tucked his jacket lapels around his neck, fussing as if she was unwilling to let him go. "And if he—if your father needs help, you'll—"

"I'll do my best, Mother."

His best did not include bullying airline ticket agents. He missed the first flight to San Francisco because of a lack of seats, and as a kind of harbinger of misfortunes to come, his baggage went on ahead. He caught up with one suitcase in Bangkok, but Lord knew where the other came to rest. By way of India, Keller finally arrived in Nepal clutching his father's map case under one arm and wondering what the hell he was supposed to do next. He endured an inspection and interrogation by a customs clerk with the instincts of a proctologist who reluctantly allowed him to cross the barricade. Then Keller went looking for his father.

He didn't expect to be met, of course, but Keller thought the old man might possibly have been hanging around waiting for his precious map in the thronged terminal. There was no sign of him, however, and the Professor was hard to miss.

"No," said the clerk in the baggage claim area whom Keller had finally approached for information. He shook his head and folded his hands on the top of his enormous desk as if to absolve himself of any responsibility. "There is no Professor Keller here. I have orders only to forward his packages."

"Great! I've got his package right here. See? Where am I supposed to take it?"

"To American Express," said the clerk. He pointed out the doors to a dusty road. "Kathmandu that way."

Keller hailed one of the two waiting cabs for the trip into the city. The car was a rusty, windowless yellow Renault that was driven by a masculine old woman who spoke no language at all. She smiled and nodded and seemed to know all about "American Excess."

The city was a jumble of images to Keller. Humid, oppressive air hung in the dismal streets, but above the rooftops loomed the awesome and luminous white peaks of the Himalaya. The distant glaciers were cloaked in soft white clouds and looked like another world. The land below was gray and dusty. A mishmash of cultures clashed on the rutted streets. Ancient shrines stood in urban, squalor. Hindus, Buddhists, and Christians mingled in the usual kind of city noise. Buildings ranged from concrete-block hotels and houses to ornately trimmed miniature palaces.

Keller's cab arrived at the American Express office. He paid the woman, ducked a couple of leaflet distributors lurking on the steps, and approached the main desk.

"I can hold the package for you, but we can't deliver it since we don't know where he's staying," explained the fresh-faced California girl who listened to his situation with sprightly interest. Her name tag read, "Marci," and she delivered bad news like a perky weather girl. "We'll just have to wait for your father to pick it up, I'm afraid. Meantime, you could leave a message for him to get in touch with you at your hotel."

Keller, already thinking up alternatives, snapped his fingers and said, "Or I could go around to a few hotels and look for him myself, couldn't I?"

Marci nodded, her hair bouncing. "That might be faster. Believe me, doing things yourself is probably the best way around here."

"Oh?"

"Yep." She leaned companionably across the counter and proceeded to confide her life's story before Keller realized what was happening. "I came here two years ago, you know? As a stewardess. I had a relationship with this guy who was going to build a ski resort here and I was going to do public relations, but that fell through. Then my boyfriend from home—he's this actor on one of the soaps, right?—wrote me and wanted to get married. You know I'm *still* waiting for the Embassy to process my papers so I can leave?"

"Wow," said Keller, a little dazed. "Two years?"

"It's okay." She shrugged. "This job might be better than being married to an actor. I meet a lot of nice guys here." She blinked at him and smiled.

"Uhuh," said Keller, suddenly reminded of sexually-transmitted diseases. "Well, any suggestions about hotels? For me, I mean. Where should I look for my father?"

She wrote down the names of several hotels and passed the slip of paper across the counter to him. "Try these. They're the hotels that the Americans seem to like the best. The one on top is my personal favorite."

"Right," said Keller. "Thanks."

Outside, he looked at her list and saw that she had written down her name and a telephone number. He also noted that instead of dotting the "i" in her name, she had drawn a little heart above the letter. Prudently, he chose the last hotel on Marci's list and went looking for it on foot.

The town was crowded with tourists, all easily distinguishable. When Keller needed directions, he spotted a fellow wearing a "Mets #1" ballcap and received his instructions to the Hotel Asia in Brooklynese.

The Hotel Asia had no Professor Keller booked there, but needing a base of operations, Keller took a room for himself. He went upstairs to unpack what was left of his luggage.

The room was Spartan, to say the least. It contained an army cot with a single wool blanket, in fact, and no bathroom—unless he was supposed to recognize a closet with a drain in the floor and a hand-held shower spray as civilized facilities. Upon inquiry, Keller was assured that the closet did indeed function as toilet, shower, and washbasin. Should he have risked an encounter with Marci and avoided such dismal quarters? No, he reasoned, the room was just for one night, and a disease was forever.

With a splitting sinus headache starting, he staggered out into the blindingly bright street to begin his search for his father. Although the sun shone with the intensity of desert light, the streets were so chilly that Keller kept his new mountain parka on. He'd have to remember to layer a few shirts underneath from now on.

Nepal was nothing like Keller imagined. He thought the city of Kathmandu was supposed to be populated with bearded gurus and bliss-faced hippies looking for the meaning of life and maybe scoring a little smack from Afghanistan. He remembered newly turned-on Beatles who spouted Kahlil Gibran for *Life* magazine and posed behind sitars for the international paparazzi. But modern-day Nepal was mostly overrun with mountain climbers and shaggy health food advocates. The local people were practically outnumbered by the foreigners. The central town was still flocked with expatriates looking for Shangri-La, but now they wore Thinsulate instead of flowers and love beads.

Nepalese people stood around and grinned a lot at the ongoing sideshow. While dining on western food and bottled water from other countries, the tourists appeared to sit around tables and either exchange lofty philosophies, describe near-miss climbing accidents, or the condition of their digestive systems. The conversations Keller overheard most often concerned world politics or dysentery. One Australian woman had plastered a bumper sticker across the back of her knapsack that read, "One nuclear bomb can spoil your whole day." Perhaps as an indication of her real concerns, however, was her discussion of the virtues of Lomotil over Kaopectate—a treatment only for sissies, not serious travelers, she assured the man she was sitting with, an emaciated tofu-type who looked as though his hospitalization was imminent.

If he had been in a different mood, Keller might have tried to insinuate himself into one of the groups of foreigners. He felt absurdly lonesome, and they looked as if they could use someone with his ability to separate the sublime from the ridiculous. Yes, Keller might have dazzled these lesser beings with his sophistication.

But Keller found himself feeling depressed as well as lonely. Like a disobedient spaniel, he'd dashed around the world when his father whistled, and already he felt like a fool. He walked into three hotels asking for the Professor, but nobody had ever heard of him. Keller realized that the odds for locating his father without expending any real effort were low. Yet he just wasn't sure what to do next.

He returned to the Hotel Asia well after nightfall, and by then Keller was too exhausted from just breathing the thin air to care what the place looked like.

The desk clerk hailed him. "Sah! Mistah Killa! A message!"

Keller eagerly snatched the paper from the man and then couldn't read a word written there. He thrust it back. "What does it say?"

"A lady call, sah. Mar-see. Here is her telephone, sah. You go call the lady."

Marci, the clerk at American Express. Keller's hopes fell. "Is that all? She's the only one who called?"

The clerk admitted that Marci was the only person to leave a message, and Keller dragged himself up the stairs to his room. The altitude affected him so that he was wheezing when he arrived at his room. He lay down on the bed with his clothes on and tried to breathe evenly. Finally, he just lay still and let lethargy take over. He wasn't sleepy, but paralyzed—rendered stuporous by the dawning realization that he was terribly unsuited to the situation in which he found himself. His mother and Nina had been right—he didn't belong in Nepal. Keller didn't belong dashing to anyone's rescue or delivering important papers. He belonged in his own niche—the savvy set in Georgetown. He certainly didn't belong in the Hotel Asia.

"I'm not cut out for this," he said to the ceiling.

Hearing the words spoken aloud shook him. Keller sat up, sweating. He dug into his coat pocket and found the crumpled paper with Marci's phone number on it. There was something he could do to bolster his self-esteem. In the downstairs hallway, he found a telephone.

"Marci? This is Paul Keller. We met at the—"

"Oh, Paul!" Marci cried on the other end of the line. "I'm so glad you returned my call! I tried every hotel before I found you! Listen, something came up. I thought you should know."

"What? Something—"

"About your father. We got a message after you left today. We were supposed to save any packages addressed to Doctor Keller. He'll send someone soon to take packages to a place called Kol. You didn't tell me your father was a doctor, Paul."

"He's not. He's—Listen, to Kol, you say? Is that a hotel?"

Marci giggled. "No, silly. It's a town. Or a place like a town. It's up in the mountains. If you want to take the package yourself, you'll have to hire a guide."

Already in the act of wrestling his jacket back on, Keller stopped and asked, "A guide? How far is this place?"

"A long way," Marci said, and she sighed. "You'll probably have to hire a pilot, in fact. Come around to the airport tomorrow, and I'll help you find one. You'll need supplies, too."

"How about tonight?" Keller asked, inwardly praying he could avoid actually sleeping in the Hotel Asia. "Can't we go tonight?"

Marci giggled again, sounding playful. "I can't, Paul. I'm tied up at the moment with a—a friend. When you didn't call, I went ahead and made other plans for tonight, so—"

"All right, all right," he said. "If I go to the airport myself, who should I ask for?"

"You *can't* go tonight. Nobody'll be there! My shift starts at noon tomorrow, so just wait—"

"Listen, Marci, I'll have to get an earlier start than that. If I haven't got a guide by noon, I'll check with you, but—"

"What's this?" she asked. "A brush-off?" Sounding muffled all of a sudden, as though she had cupped the receiver close to keep their conversation private, she whispered, "I thought I sensed a spark between us, Paul."

"What?"

"A spark," she said. "You know. A specialness."

"Uh, Marci," he began, "look, I'm just not interested in any kind of—"

"I guess I was wrong about you!" Marci cried. "Get your own guide!"

18

And she hung up.

Somewhat dazed, Keller went into the bar connected to the Hotel Asia. He sat at the first table and tried to think. The final blow of the day came when Keller learned that the Hotel Asia did not stock wine coolers.

Things were not shaping up well at all.

Chapter 3

MINDING HIS OWN BUSINESS FOR ONCE, NEPALESE NATIVE BILLY Bhim began his Tuesday morning by taking a short meditative snooze in the sun beside a single-engine deHavilland Beaver that was his very own. He sat on a spanking new swivel chair wangled from a night maintenance man at one of the embassies, and he propped his feet on a discarded tea chest he'd covered with a pretty rug his mother had made, but it was the presence of the plane—his very, very own— that made Billy feel like a professional.

He linked his fingers behind his head and doodled a toothpick around in the corner of his mouth to complete the picture of rugged nonchalance. He felt like Cary Grant. He looked more like a Chinese Peter Lorre, to be accurate, for he was short and stocky and his face seemed forever set in an expression of sly amusement, but he admired Cary Grant greatly and liked to emulate him. Billy had seen *To Catch a Thief* four times in Hong Kong. A few years of military service in the Gurkha regiment—the only financially rewarding profession for a young and unconnected Nepalese man—had given Billy the money and opportunity to indulge his love for western cinema.

Billy had chosen to retire from the Gurkhas at the age of thirty-eight, however. He had good instincts for self-preservation and in his heart didn't like answering to anyone. He was too old for the big risks anymore, he decided. Putting his force-fed military know-how to good use, he had bought a plane and opened a charter service. People were always looking for quick and easy air transportation around the Himalaya, and since the government had clamped down on drug-running, there wasn't much danger in ferrying human cargo.

But a recent error in character judgment had cost Billy his first plane. He had a few other assets, but the loss of Grace—who had been more like a pet than a machine—aggrieved him terribly. A slick-talking American who looked like Chuck Norris had stolen the plane and crashed it somewhere in the western mountains. Billy took to his bed for three days, and for several months after the disaster, he had avoided his friends at the airport.

Fortunately, however, Billy had recently become the beneficiary of a generous American woman. He had a new plane *and* a client with money in her pockets. All he had to do was hang around and wait for her.

So Billy wasn't really looking for more business that morning. If he had needed income, he could have sauntered up to town to fleece a few tourists with delusions of drug-trafficking. But he didn't need extra money at the moment. He was content. He was sitting in the sun minding his own business when another client just happened along.

He was an American, Billy saw right away. Having taken a recent scunner to American men in general, Billy became alert immediately. This one looked safe as he wandered around the side of the hangar, stopped, and glanced around, blinking several times as if he hadn't slept well and didn't trust his eyes. The man was good looking and had an air of sophistication, which Billy recognized in spite of the fellow's hesitancy. His clothing was top quality. His hair was expertly cut. Billy saw that he also carried a recently purchased knapsack and some kind of long, skinny purse that he had slung over his shoulder like Robin Hood's bow. A tripod, maybe, Billy decided, since he knew many tourists carried camera equipment. Judging by his gear and as-yet undamaged boots, this American was rich.

"Mister Bhim?"

Billy stood up grandly and removed the toothpick from his mouth. Cary Grant would never speak with a toothpick hanging on his lip. Billy knew he could dazzle nearly anyone with his cosmopolitan aplomb. Smiling his best Cary Grant amused-with-the-world smile, Billy replied, "Very good, sah. Billy Bhim, I am. And you, sah?"

"Oh, I'm Keller. Paul Keller." The American extended his hand. "Am I glad I found you."

To himself, Keller had to admit that Billy Bhim, the man recommended by the English-speaking clerk in baggage claim, did not look like the kind of pilot with whom one ought to trust one's life. Untrustworthiness oozed from Bhim and then seemed to hang around his person like a smog.

Like most Nepalese men, Billy wore white cotton jodhpurlike trousers, but also a frayed military shirt, unpressed and stained down the front, and a little hat that looked like a cross between a sultan's turban and the cap of a boy manning the take-out window at McDonald's. There was dust in the tufts of matted black hair that stuck out around his ears. His face was catlike, round with a curving mouth and pug nose, and his eyes were Mongol almond-shaped. Above his right cheekbone lay a scar in the shape of a scimitar, the result of a back-alley knife fight, Keller was sure. On the other hand, Billy's English was beautifully enunciated and certainly enthusiastic, and he bore himself with the bravado of a bantam rooster.

Keller said, "You speak English very well."

"Yes, sah. Very well. I am," he explained, taking a modest bow, "not long retired from the Gurkha regiment, sah."

"The Gurkhas?"

After reading the only magazine on the plane that brought him into Kathmandu, Keller had learned enough history of

Nepal to know the significance of the Gurkha regiment. Nepal's economy depended primarily upon tourism, for the Himalaya drew hikers, serious climbers, sightseers, scientists, and still a few seekers of the truth, all of whom required supplies, labor, and guides. The second source of national income came from the British Army, which drew from the tribesmen of Nepal to keep the ranks of the famed Gurkha regiment full. Gurkhas had fought beside British troops for nearly one hundred years and were renowned for bravery and survival skills.

The East India Company first recruited Nepalese men, and since that time the Gurkha Regiment had been hailed as tenacious and loyal—soldiers *extraordinaire*. Keller knew the stories. During World War II, a British officer once lined up a group of Gurkha paratroopers and asked for volunteers to drop behind enemy lines. Without hesitation, about half of the assembled troops bravely stepped forward for the risky mission. The rest hung back. The officer began to explain the logistics of the drop to the volunteers, but he was suddenly interrupted from the ranks of the less courageous. "Oh," cried a voice. "Do you mean we can use *parachutes?*" When the officer hastily answered in the affirmative, every Gurkha soldier promptly stepped up for service.

For pluck, a Gurkha guide could only be the best, Keller reasoned.

If only Billy Bhim didn't look so disreputable. His headquarters consisted of a hangar that was nothing more than a sorry three-sided lean-to made of scraps of corrugated tin. The boxy bulk of a single-engine, high-winged airplane lurked in the shadows, but it was dented and splattered with mud, then lightly coated with a layer of runway dust.

The whole Tribhumvan Airport wasn't much better, if the truth be known. The sad buildings of terminal and hangars looked like a bus station that had been relocated to an Ozark turnip farm by a tornado. The landing strip alone would have set inspectors to swooning, and the smell of burning cow dung overpowered the stench of jet exhaust.

Billy, perhaps understanding that Keller was making

unfavorable judgments about his surroundings, stepped forward smartly and sketched a salute. "Sah, I am bloody happy to meet you. You are looking for something?"

"Yes," said Keller, setting down his new knapsack. "A guide. I need a guide, and I hear you're a good one."

Billy smiled, and the resulting expression reminded Keller of an alerted fox terrier. Confidently, Billy said, "A good one, yes, I am, sah. A bloody good guide. And a pilot also, sah." He put out a hand to acknowledge his plane.

"So I hear," said Keller, careful not to look at the filthy aircraft. "I need somebody to take me to Kol, Mr. Bhim."

"Please, sah. I am Billy to you."

"Billy, then. I need a guide to take me to Kol, Billy."

Billy sucked his lower lip and frowned. "Bloody long trip to Kol, sah."

"You could take me, though?"

"No, sah," said Billy, sighing, "I do not think that is possible."

Well, if Keller had found himself in a buyers' market, he would have thanked Billy Bhim then and there and gone on his way. An entire morning's investigation, however, had turned up nothing in the way of a native guide. It seemed that Keller had arrived in Nepal at the very beginning of the trekking and climbing season, and all the reputable Sherpa guides had been snapped up on a first-come, first-served basis. Billy Bhim was the last pilot available, and if Keller didn't convince Billy to take him to Kol, he was doomed.

Smiling in his most friendly and beguiling fashion, Keller said, "I'm willing to pay."

"Hmm," said Billy, his interest clearly piqued. He shook his head as if to chase out the temptation. "A long way to Kol, sah. You need more than pilot and guide." He counted items off on his fingers. "You will need supplies, climbing gear, porters—"

"Porters?" Keller interrupted. "No, no. Look, I have one bag and I can carry it myself. I won't need any porters. This is a simple trip, honest. It won't be hard."

"Without bloody porters, it will be very hard, sah. Much gear needed for a trip as far as Kol. Many things are needed for your comfort."

"I travel lightly," Keller promised. "We won't need any luxuries."

Billy looked up and down Keller's sportswear, and his expression of doubt deepened.

Hastily, Keller said, "I've done this kind of thing before, really. Not here, of course, but I've hiked in the Smoky Mountains. I was a Boy Scout, for Pete's sake. I'm not an amateur."

Billy shook his head. "Very long trip, sah. Expensive trip. Cost you very much money."

Prepared for that, Keller asked bravely, "How much?"

Billy continued to shake his head. "Five—six hundred dollars at very least, sah. And that leaves bloody little profit for me. I would be giving my services to charity. If it is a cheap trip you want, sah, you should go see one of the tour offices in the city. They will—"

"I don't want a tour. I need to get to Kol. I—look, Billy, I can go to the American Express office and get some more money wired here. I'll pay you five hundred American dollars to take me to Kol—"

Billy turned away. "No profit for me in that deal, sah. Five hundred dollars hardly pay my expenses. I will have to hire tents and—"

"All right, all right, how much *will* you do it for? Seven hundred? Eight hundred?" Keller followed Billy under the belly of the plane. "Hey, I can raise a thousand dollars for you, Billy."

"All in advance?" Billy asked, quick as lightning.

"In advance?" Keller straightened and bumped his head on the plane. "Well, not all of it. Half, maybe. Yes, half. Five hundred now and five hundred when we return. How does that sound?"

Billy sighed, frowning.

"A thousand dollars," Keller repeated, wheedling unashamedly now. "An easy trip. We can fly in and out and be back here in a couple of days."

"Days?" Billy protested. "Sah, it cannot be done!"

"Why not?"

As if explaining the facts to someone who had never set foot outside the confines of an asylum, Billy put his face close to Keller's and spoke very clearly. "My plane cannot go just anywhere, sah. I need landing strip, see? No bloody place to land in the mountains! We land in Jumla and walk. Three days walking up, two days walking back."

"Jeez," muttered Keller. In his mind's eyes he saw the last of his plans disintegrate, including his strategy for avoiding dysentery. He had hoped to simply not eat during his time in Nepal, assuming he could be in and out of the country in a day or two. Now what? Things looked worse and worse.

"You're sure we have to walk?" he asked. "There isn't a bus or something?"

"No other choice, sah," Billy said, full of sympathy. "In Nepal, everybody walks."

Keller's heart sank. He felt a great urge just to forget the whole idea and go home. Coming to Nepal had been a bad idea to begin with. To hell with his father. To hell with Nina. Neither one of them was going to be that impressed that he'd come this far, anyway.

Billy must have seen his determination waver. Suddenly accommodating and full of kindness, Billy said, "Sah, you have an unhappy look. I will take you to Kol. Yes, I will."

Keller blinked. "What?"

"For reduced rate, even," Billy added generously. "You have bloody unhappy look, sah. Only nine hundred dollars to Kol. We fly plane most of the way, then take just a few porters. And no waiting, sah."

"No waiting?"

"We leave today, if you like. Soon."

"You mean it?" Brightening, Keller said, "How soon? I mean, I've got to get up there fast, Billy. My father's on some kind of expedition, and if he gets too far ahead of me, I'll never find him."

"You looking for father, sah?"

Keller nodded and bought up the map case, which he had worn slung over his back like a quiver of arrows. He held it out. Exhibit A. "I have to take this map to him."

Billy's eyes immediately and glitteringly fell on the narrow leather case. "What kind of map is that, sah?"

"One he wants to study, I guess. He's a cartographer."

"A—?"

"He studies maps," explained Keller. "And he explores a little. He asked me to bring this map to him."

"The map is for this country, sah?"

"I don't—I'm not sure. But probably." Smiling, Keller tapped the case into the palm of his hand and looked at it. "Whatever it is, the old man has got something up his sleeve, I'm sure."

"He does?" Billy asked. "Do you mean this is a bloody treasure map?"

Keller laughed. "Hardly that! No, don't get excited, Billy. I'm sure my father doesn't care where the map leads to exactly. He's not looking for riches, Billy. It's laurels the old coot's after."

Billy considered that, filing through his vocabulary for a definition that made sense. Finally, he peered at Keller and asked, "These laurels, sah, are they worth a great deal of money?"

Smiling, Keller patted Billy's shoulder. "To some people they're worth a fortune, Billy."

Billy grinned broadly. "Then I am bloody pleased to take you, sah, to find Papa."

They shook hands, and then Billy dusted his off together as if getting down to business.

"Now, sah," he said, "I have everything ready. You have warm coat? A hat? Very nice new boots, I see. That is all you need to bring. I have all the gear you need. Anything else you want? I can get whiskey, cigar. Oh, I take bloody good care of you, sah!"

"That's great, that's great," said Keller, delighted with the turn of events. "No, I'll be fine. When do we leave?"

"When Missus Jane comes, sah."

Keller stopped. "Who?"

"Missus Jane, sah. She hired me to take her up today. You come, too."

"What?" said Keller. "You mean you already have a customer?"

With a huge smile, Billy said, "To Jumla, yes, sah. Missus Jane wants to go today also. Two trips combined into one!"

"And you," said Keller, "get double the money?"

"Yes!" Clearly delighted with the way things had turned

out for him, Billy said, "Bloody good deal for Billy Bhim today, right, sah?"

Keller was saved from having to make a civil response to that observation. Billy obviously figured he could bulldoze Keller into anything, but they were interrupted. The sunlight wavered suddenly as two people strode around the open side of the hangar. They stopped, two dark figures against a blazingly bright backdrop. Both carried knapsacks.

Billy jumped forward like an eager bellhop to greet the new arrivals.

"Aha! You have come—just on time! *Namaste.*" He delivered the traditional Nepali greeting while bowing, and then gushed in English, "Hello, hello, Missus Jane!"

In silhouette, she looked like a man: spare and hipless with square shoulders and a firm stance. Some men might have described her as slender, but to Keller that word implied gentle curves and feminine slimness. This woman was lean and strong. Her breasts were nonexistent. The jeans she wore rode low, slipping down squarish haunches and bunching loosely at the knees. Her cotton shirt was unbuttoned enough to show a nice long throat, though. Her hair, drab blond in color, had been skinned tightly against her head, then braided into a long ponytail that fell down the middle of her back. She wore double-laced boots and carried a khaki mountain parka.

Keller was sure that she was over thirty, but just. Her face was fine-boned with a serious mouth, not a fashionably pouty one, grayish eyes, and level, sandy brows, all without makeup. Her expression was no-nonsense, her gaze direct. She measured Keller without a flicker of sexual interest, one hand plunged deeply into a front pocket of her loose jeans. Keller steeled himself to return the look she gave him, but he wavered under the intensity of her stare and pretended to turn his attention to the man beside her.

Her sidekick, for it was somehow apparent that she was the leader and he the follower, was a tall and skinny chap with an unmistakably British air about him: scrawny neck, blond pencil mustache, knobby knees sticking out from under Bermuda-length khaki shorts, and perfect posture. He even sported a pair of ears that surely had been patriotically altered to match those of Prince Charles. As he looked down the length of his nose at Billy Bhim, his expression was ever so British—a little surprised, a little repulsed. The word *prig* sprang immediately to Keller's mind.

"Good heavens," said the gawky Englishman in exactly the tight-jawed musical accent that the Monty Python troupe loved to mimic. "Is this the guide you hired, Jane?"

"Yes, Dennis," said the woman, and her voice was surprisingly pleasant.

"And this is the airplane?" Dennis asked, as if the mud-splattered plane behind the beaming, but unkempt Billy Bhim could belong to anyone else. Aghast at the whole picture, the Englishman suddenly blustered, "My dear Jane, are you quite sure you know what you're doing?"

"Yes," she said again, just as patiently as before. "Hello, Billy."

"Hello, hello, Missus Jane," Billy crowed again, seizing her outstretched hand. "You come just on time. Bloody good show! You like the plane?"

"Looks fine to me."

"Fine, yes, very fine. Very good for me, Missus Jane, to have another plane."

"I'm glad," she said, and smiled.

The woman was not a beauty exactly, Keller decided. And she had made no effort to put forward a sparkling personality as she shook the Gurkha's hand. But she possessed an unmistakable presence, a regal air like that of an Amazon priestess. Even Billy recognized it, Keller could see. Her serenity looked as if it sprang from the knowledge that her world was whole.

"See here," the hemorrhoidal Englishman said. "Are you qualified to fly that plane, Mr. Bhim?"

"Oh, yes, sah. Quality flight, sah."

"Is this your copilot?"

Keller walked out into the sunlight and extended his hand to the Englishman. "No," he said, drawling a little, "I'm another paying customer, that's all. My name's Keller."

"Ah," said the Englishman, grasping Keller's hand and pumping. Crisply, he introduced himself. "Ogden-Helms, photographer, *National Geographic.*"

Keller shook the man's hand. He suspected that Ogden-Helms was terribly proud of landing a job with the *National Geographic,* for he included the magazine's title as if it was the third part of his own hyphenated name. And the man actually wore a light meter around his neck, too. How many field photographers, Keller wondered, displayed their light meters at all times? Maybe Lord Snowden did so he wouldn't be mistaken for idle royalty as he strolled around Balmoral. This fellow seemed equally concerned that he might be improperly identified.

Keller smiled. At last here was someone to whom he could feel superior. "How d'you do?"

"Going on a trek?" Ogden-Helms inquired, careful not to appear too interested.

"In a manner of speaking."

"I see. You're in magazine work, maybe?"

"No, I'm employed by the Library of Congress in Washington."

"Oh, well! I see, yes!" Ogden-Helms looked a little more pleased and folded his arms across his chest, smiling in a comradely fashion. "On assignment in Nepal, are you?"

"It's more of a personal jaunt than a professional one."

"Oh." The animation drained out of Ogden-Helms' face at that disappointing news. Just another tourist.

"Billy," said Jane, her voice full of sternness. "What's this about a paying customer?"

"Oh, Missus," Billy said swiftly, "I knew you would not mind. Poor Mister Keller is looking for his papa. He must go to Kol and needs a plane to take him to Jumla first. I thought—?"

Jane looked at Keller once again. He did his best not to look like a mad rapist during her scrutiny. "I didn't realize Billy had been hired already. I wouldn't have asked him if I thought he was booked. I'm just hoping to make a quick trip. To deliver this." He held up the map case.

Jane regarded the case, then nodded and turned back to Billy. "All right," she said. "I'll split his fare with you. Is everything else ready?"

Relieved, Billy said, "Bloody good and ready, Missus. You want to check?"

"I think," snapped Ogden-Helms, "that we should check your credentials first, Mr. Bhim."

"You would not find any to check," Billy said cheerily. "Bloody sorry for that, sah."

"So you admit to being a confidence artist?"

Billy blinked, bewildered. "Sah?"

"Oh, never mind!" Ogden-Helms swung around, frowning importantly. "Keller, have you investigated this man's reputation at least?"

"No," Keller admitted.

"Heavens!" Ogden-Helms shook his head. "I have a bad feeling about this. See here, Bhim—"

Serenely, Jane walked away. Ogden-Helms pitched in on Billy again, but she ignored the squabble like a parent who was accustomed to such noise and didn't interfere unless bodily injury was about to be inflicted. She ducked under the plane, stepped over the coiled rope, and straightened up to survey the gear that was spread out there on the hangar floor. She crouched down and proceeded to fold up her parka. Her hands were small, Keller noticed. She packed the jacket into her knapsack, then pitched the sack onto the rest of the stuff without any wasted energy.

Ogden-Helms gave up trying to intimidate Billy and trailed after the woman. "See here, Jane," he bleated again. "Wait a week and I'll take you up myself. The magazine won't mind too much, and I might even get some usable photos if the weather's not too horrid. This chap Bhim has been involved in the sordid mess since the beginning! How do you expect to trust him now? Why, he must be as disreputable as they come!"

"Don't fuss, Dennis," she said, and gave him a rather sweet smile, one that transformed her face. "May I have the other pack now?"

Her smile melted him completely. Ogden-Helms rushed to supply Jane with the second knapsack, and Keller was reminded of a panting puppy grabbing his leash to go for a walk with the mistress he adores. Ogden-Helms was smitten, it seemed. Keller, however, viewed the existence of Missus Jane as another unexpected hitch in his plans. As she began to pack her things into the plane's cargo hold and turned a deaf ear to Ogden-Helms, he decided she could be a formidable enemy if she changed her mind about him. While she worked, her braided hair swung around her elbows like a length of sisal rope.

"Billy," Keller murmured as Ogden-Helms doubled his effort to be convincing, "who is this lady?"

"Lady?" asked Billy.

"Her. Who is she?"

"Oh, Missus Jane?" Billy laughed, much surprised that anyone should mistake that particular female for a lady. "She is Jane," he said simply. "Very fine American woman. She hire me, too, sah. She is going to Jumla, so I will take both at the same time. You pay half in advance now, right?"

Resigned and a little amused, too, Keller dug into his pocket for his wallet. "Right. So what's she going to do in Jumla? She on a vacation or something?"

"Oh, no, sah, Missus Jane goes to find her husband."

That was interesting. "You mean she's joining him somewhere?"

Billy Bhim pried the money out of Keller's hands and began to count it, thumbing through the notes. "Her husband is gone many months, sah. He crashed my airplane into the mountains and—"

Startled, Keller looked up at the craft parked beside them. *"Your* plane?"

"My *old* plane, sah, not this one. Now she goes to look for him. Her husband, sah, not the plane."

"Jesus," said Keller. "You mean the guy might be dead?"

"Oh, bloody likely, yes, sah."

"And she's going to look for his remains?"

"Remains, sah?"

Keller decided not to explain. The Nepalese, he remembered, used any number of methods to deal with their dead, ranging from floating the body down the nearest river to hacking the corpse into bits and feeding it to birds. Keller studied the woman as she worked under the belly of the plane, oblivious to his observation as well as Ogden-Helms' pleading. She looked capable and determined, all right. Automatically, Keller began to wonder what kind of man her husband must have been.

Billy misinterpreted his silence. "Missus Jane will not be

any bloody trouble for you, sah. She knows where she is going and will not interfere."

"How do you propose to guide both of us, Billy? I mean, if I'm going on to Kol, she—"

"Oh, no problem, sah. You will both go to the same place, sure."

"You mean her destination is near where my father is?" Billy laughed. "Near enough, sah."

Chapter 4

Chapter 4

JANE PARISH SAID GOODBYE TO DENNIS OGDEN-HELMS, WHO wasn't a bad fellow really. He was just a pest at a time when she hadn't any patience for more obstacles. She felt a little sorry for him when he kissed her cheek and clasped her hand in his two damp and feverish ones to bid her a heart-wrenching farewell.

"You'll come back?" he asked wistfully.

"Sure," she replied, before realizing what he really wanted. Then Billy arrived before she could set Dennis straight.

"All set, Missus Jane?" he inquired, his eyes sliding hopefully from Dennis to herself and back again.

Billy wanted her to forget the trip, Jane knew. Already he seemed to perceive that there was more to her mission than she had told him, and Billy didn't like secrets. Not knowing all the angles made him nervous. Billy would be delighted if Dennis swept her away and left Billy to keep the new airplane in peace.

Firmly, Jane said, "All set, Billy. Let's go."

He exchanged a sorrowful glance with Dennis and sighed.

Jane climbed into the plane unassisted and sat in the back seat. The American man got in after Billy and chose to remain up front. What was his name again? Keller. Jane eyeballed him while he strapped himself in. He looked unassuming enough. Earnest, even schoolteacherish. He was definitely out of his element. As a matter of fact, he looked as if he'd rather be anywhere else in the world as long as there was indoor plumbing. He even displayed a certain wish to keep his business separate from hers. Good thing.

Jane sat back and closed her eyes. Meditation was in order. Lately she had been trying to store more and more energy inside herself for use when she would truly need strength. Now that her journey had begun, she needed to stretch out her senses. Her mentor, Lana Briskine, had often taught that the success of a quest depended not on actions.

"Use your intuition," Lana said. "Think you will succeed and you will. Norman Vincent Peale had the right idea. He was just a couple of thousand years behind Buddha."

Jane had been at her most vulnerable when she'd met Lana. She'd been lonely and frightened—spending most of her days alone in the depressing apartment supplied for servicemen and their families. Lana ran a weekly seminar that Jane attended out of desperation, and at that first meeting she realized there was a whole world of knowledge she hadn't discovered yet. Lana had shared Jane's joy in finding out about books and music and even herself. With Lana's spiritual guidance, Jane had started on a road to enlightenment. Now she needed to tap that inner strength, and Jane was thankful that it was there to use.

Concentrating on Lana's positive message, Jane sank into the gentle swirl of images she used to bring on her trance. When the plane lumbered out onto the runway and shrieked its way down the tarmac, Jane hardly felt any of it.

Though the takeoff jolted Keller's stomach to a location somewhere closer to his tonsils than normal, he decided that Billy was not a bad flier. The Gurkha appeared to be conscientious in the air, keeping a vigilant eye on his dials and scanning the horizon. Relieved, Keller sat forward in his seat and took his first real look at the scenery.

From the air, Nepal was made up of the small green patches in the lowlands where tea and rice were grown, rising to the smudged-brown slopes of essentially barren land where both wild and domestic animals supposedly grazed on minuscule plant life, and humans terraced the slopes into meager plots for raising who-knew-what pathetic crops. The mountains rose from there, obliterating even the sky at times.

The plane swung northward, away from Everest and Annapurna toward the wilder, even more remote western reaches of Nepal. Few trekkers chose to hike in the districts nearest Tibet and the Chinese border, and Keller knew that only a few scientists explored there. Kol, buried high on a nearly inaccessible mountain, was a place Keller couldn't help feeling that his father had chosen on purpose.

Since entering the country, Keller had never been out of sight of the misty peaks of the Himalaya. But like a Hollywood painted backdrop, they had seemed too beautiful to be real. Only when the plane banked and began to climb over the foothills did Keller begin to sense their reality. The highest summits in the world were jagged mountains thrust skyward by the forces of an Ice Age long past, but forever remembered in stone.

They were beautiful. But Keller felt his stomach quiver, and the sensation did not result from an appreciation of the landscape. The mountains held his father, and the higher the plane flew into the Himalaya, the more uneasy Keller became.

Unaccountably, he found himself associating the queasy feeling in his stomach with an experience from his teenage years. At thirteen, he had spent a week hiking along the wild and beautiful Appalachian Trail with the Professor. It was supposed to have been a happy-go-lucky father-son outing, but like most adventures thrust upon the participants by the mother-figure who envisioned great fun and heart-to-heart talks around the evening campfire, the week had turned into an appalling contest of wills.

The Professor had spent most of the waking hours complaining about park rangers. "These sissies," he shouted over his shoulder as they marched along a mucky trail, "they don't know their asses from holes in the ground! Why, you know a hell of a lot more about these forests just from listening to me, boy!"

During a cloudburst, the Professor found a bedraggled ranger crouched in a stick-built shelter, and he'd lectured the poor slob nearly to the point of tears. Keller had been embarrassed as only a teenage boy with an overbearing father could be.

During that loathsome week, Keller worked his stomach into exactly the same sour and roiling condition that he experienced now. The mountains looked a hell of a lot like the Appalachian Trail.

The hills slanted into cliffs rutted by washed-out gullies. As they flew higher, the gullies turned to gorges, the steep inclines to solid faces of snow-blasted rock. The mountains surged upward toward the white glaciers. Often, the plane dodged in and out of clouds, and ice formed on the windshield.

From his own studies as a cartographer, Keller knew a little about the Himalaya. The regions surrounding the mountains had first been mapped by Englishmen—mostly officers of the East India Company who were always looking for cheaper and more convenient ways of getting tea out of India and China. Mapmakers braved poisonous snakes, jungle fevers, an occasional marauding tiger, and even battles with fierce Tibetan warriors who screamed down out of the Himalaya with weapons flashing; but they dared not venture into the mountains themselves. Nearly a century later, George Everest took it upon himself to press into the hills. He spent a decade camping in tents and made his measurements with the aid of flashing mirrors and fires that could be seen through the constant Himalayan haze. He made progress, but it wasn't until long after Everest's retirement that Europeans discovered the highest mountain in the world, a peak that the Tibetans still called "Goddess Mother of the World." The English couldn't resist naming the mountain after one of their own, and called it Mount Everest.

Everest was not the end of the matter, of course. Intrepid Brits continued to explore the Himalaya and to suffer the pains and disasters of surveying a hostile country. One determined British surveyor recruited and trained the local

Nepalese for the purpose of clandestine ventures into the forbidden Chinese territories. Disguised as Tibetan horse traders, their faces darkened with walnut oil, they stole over the guarded boundaries, concealing their survey equipment in the false bottoms of boxes. Every step was measured by an ingenious length of Buddhist rosary beads—only 100 beads long rather than the standard 108—every tenth bead larger than the others so exact measurements could be made. These men were often viewed as spies by the mountain villagers and more than a few times were forced to make furtive escapes into the night. Another expedition disguised itself as a religious pilgrimage, complete with a real lama. Unfortunately, the holy man lost his head. He drank liquor and dallied with married women along the way, much to the anger of his employers and cuckolded husbands. To prolong his pleasures, the lama sold the head surveyor into slavery, from which the poor fellow eventually escaped, but he spent several years holed up in a monastery as a novice monk before he could bolt for India.

Keller chuckled at the thought.

From the back seat, Jane brought him out of his daydreaming by suddenly asking, "Is that Jumla?"

Billy turned the plane up on one wing to take a look at the ground. "Yes, that is Jumla, Missus Jane. We will go down now."

And down he went. In fact, the plane plunged so quickly into a dive that Keller grabbed for his seat and hung on.

The community of Jumla consisted of a handful of low, colorless buildings cuddled against an arid hillside. The two- and three-storied houses were built overlapping each other, one flat roof providing a kind of outdoor living space for the dwelling above it. It looked like a movie set for a medieval village, with decrepit stone buildings crammed together and further off a herd of scraggly cows hopelessly snuffling the bare ground. The airstrip was a rutted stretch of road that was long enough to accommodate Billy's exuberant landing, but just barely. A flock of chattering children engulfed the plane even before it rolled to a stop. Just the sight of the place set off a tremendous ache in Keller's sinuses.

"Come, come, Missus Jane," Billy called, unstrapping himself. "We go talk to the bloody porters now, right? We get started today."

Jane set off towards the nearest building, a low structure built of hard-fashioned bricks.

A group of scruffy-looking men were crouched in the lee of the shack. The villagers were a stocky, sturdy, ill-clad lot, with a hairy orange cow dozing in their midst and a mangy black-and-white goat snuffling around their boots while they gossiped.

When Billy and Jane approached, the men stood up and shoved the goat away. Keller stopped a few yards back, clearly not wanting to give the impression that he intended to assume any responsibilities.

Billy greeted the gathered Sherpa men like Napoleon must have addressed his troops in Russia. He struck a dramatic pose and delivered a speech that—despite its panache—left the Sherpas unimpressed. They glowered at Billy at first but gradually warmed as he talked and paced up and down. Finally, they began to elbow each other, amused by Billy's martinet routine. One fellow whose face was swaddled in a filthy rag cracked a joke behind his mask, and all the men burst into snickers.

The goat was the only one who took Billy seriously. The little animal scampered right to the front of the Sherpas and gazed intently up at Billy until the speech was over. Then the goat let out a long and impressive, "Baaah!"

The Sherpa men burst out laughing, even the American called Keller.

Not a good start, Jane decided. Not a good start at all.

Jane decided to hold back, however. To undermine Billy's authority right away would be a mistake. In the meantime, the goat cantered over to her and rubbed its knobby head against her jeans.

Billy shushed the Sherpa men and tried to make them see reason. While she waited, Keller sidled up to Jane. He seemed torn between making the usual polite introductions and the diffidence he so clearly wanted to maintain. When the Sherpas began to argue with Billy, Keller asked, "What's going on?"

Jane didn't glance at him. She scratched the goat's ears. "The usual squabble over money, I'm sure. They want to be paid more for hazardous duty."

"Uhm," he said, "is this trip more hazardous than any other?"

"They claim it is, as long as Billy's in charge." She pushed the inquisitive goat away. "Don't worry about Billy, though. He'll take care of things if it suits him."

The goat butted her leg, and the American man stewed for a while. Then he said tentatively, "They don't seem very confident in him."

Jane shrugged.

"I mean, this trip isn't exactly cheap for me. I assume— well, I'd like to get my money's worth. Do you know Billy very well?"

"I know him well enough," she said. "I trust Billy. He knows what he's doing, I think, in spite of the hard time they're giving him. He'll be discreet, and that's what concerns me."

"Discreet?" he echoed, puzzled. "Oh, yes, I—well, Billy mentioned that you were on a search for your husband."

Jane let out a sigh. Terrific. She shook her head and muttered, "Maybe he's not as discreet as I thought!"

Keller grinned and said ingenuously, "I guess not. Listen, we haven't been introduced exactly. I'm Paul Keller."

She rubbed the goat smell off on her jeans and accepted his handshake. "Hello. Jane Parish."

"Yes. Hi."

"You're looking for your father."

He gave a huff of self-conscious laughter. "Well, we can certainly write off Billy's discretion, can't we?"

She smiled again and withdrew her hand. Keller had a nice face—snub nose, round chin, a shy but scholarly gaze. He looked like a friendly accountant, but there was no sense getting buddy-buddy. Rubbing her palm unconsciously down the side of her thigh all over again, she glanced toward Billy, where he dickered with the Sherpa men. "Well, I hope you have good luck."

"Yeah, right." Paul Keller put his hands into his trouser pockets. "The longer I'm in this country, the more worried I get. About my father, I mean. There are lots of possibilities for getting into trouble. He could—well, you don't want to hear about him. You must have a lot invested in this trip yourself."

"Yes," she said absently, trying to follow Billy's discussion at the same time. Without thinking, she added, "I've been training for half a year."

"Training?" Keller repeated.

She nodded. "And studying. The preparation was tough, but I think it will pay off. Especially if this drags on for several months."

"Several—" Keller caught himself before his voice squeaked. In a moment, he had himself under control again. Casually, he asked, "Several months, huh? I guess you're serious about this trip. I had a feeling you were very—focused."

"I am," she said. Then, before she could stop herself, she broke her own rules about making overtures that could be perceived as friendly. "I sensed some things about you, too."

"Oh?" He smiled, looking pleased, and Jane realized that his nose was sunburned already. He asked, "Like what?"

She frowned. Maybe he'd take it the wrong way. On the other hand, maybe it would put him off. "Nothing concrete," she said finally. "But I think we knew each other before."

"Oh, I don't think so," he replied, wagging his head. "I'd have remembered you."

Better say it straight out. "It was in another lifetime," she told him, matter-of-fact. That was the way to reveal these things. "I feel we might have been acquainted a long time ago. So far it's just an impression. I'll have to explore the concept during my next meditation."

That rendered him speechless. Jane decided to leave things as they were and walked away. The last thing she wanted was to get into a spiritual discussion with a tourist. The goat followed her. Approaching the men, she asked, "What's the trouble, Billy?"

Billy looked nervous, clearly unwilling to share the mantle of leadership. "These men, Missus, they want more money, and a promise that loads will not be so heavy, but—"

"Tell them we agree," Jane said. "Add twenty percent to the usual wage, and we'll take two extra porters to share the loads. Anything else?"

Billy's eyes bugged out. "But—"

"What else?" she asked. "I'll agree to all their terms."

"They do not want to go to the north, Missus. The Forbidden Land is not a place for them to go."

"What? They're afraid to get close to Tibet?"

"No, no," Billy said hastily. "Not afraid, Missus. It is too bloody far, they say. They want a promise we will not ask them to go there."

"I can't make that promise, Billy," Jane said steadily. "I want to be honest with them. I may have to go into the Forbidden Land, and I must have their assurances that they will go with me."

Billy looked pained. "Missus—"

Quietly, Jane said, "Double the wage, Billy."

His eyes got wider still. *"Double?"*

"Yes. We'll pay them well, and in return, we expect their loyalty. I know they are honorable men. They are Sherpas, known for their fairness. I want to be just as fair. Double wages, extra backs, but they must go where we ask them to go. Tell them that, Billy."

He seemed glad to be the one to make the speech, at least. He relayed her message, and the Sherpas listened politely.

"What do you say?" she asked them when he was finished.

They looked at her, but appeared unwilling to take her word for truth. Billy repeated the question and as a group, they all nodded, murmuring. The head Sherpa stuck out his hand American-fashion and Billy pumped it once. Then the Sherpas turned away and dispersed to collect their own gear.

"What about the other supplies?" Jane asked Billy, following him as he retreated to his plane. "Do they have enough food for us?"

"Missus Jane," Billy begged, "Billy Bhim does a good job, right? I will be the boss now. Please!"

"All right," said Jane. "But is there going to be enough food if we take extra men? And what about your pal Keller? How far is he going?"

"Not far, Missus. A day or two maybe. There will be food aplenty. Cheese and bloody lentils and the goat, of course."

They stopped in front of the cargo hold, and Billy began to wrestle with the door latch. Jane waited for him to get the thing unfastened. "Okay," she said. "Plenty of protein, that's good. And fresh goat's milk, too. Good idea, Billy."

He stopped fiddling with the latch and eyed her cautiously. "No fresh goat milk, Missus. Fresh *meat.*"

"*Meat?*" Jane couldn't control her voice. "Billy! I will not permit that goat to be slaughtered."

"You want us to leave the goat here?" Billy asked.

"Yes, absolutely."

Billy shrugged. "Here or there, the goat will be eaten, Missus."

"They'll eat it if we leave it here?" Jane demanded, looking around the squalid settlement.

Billy said, "Oh, yes, Missus."

"Then we take it with us," Jane declared.

"*With* us!" Billy cried, totally unprepared. "For a—a bloody pet, you mean? Missus, the animal will be useless! We—"

"I take responsibility for everything I eat, Billy. I won't allow an innocent animal to be killed just so I can have a full stomach. We're wasting time," Jane said. "Let's get going."

43

Chapter 5

KELLER SYMPATHIZED WITH BILLY. THE LITTLE GURKHA looked beseechingly at Keller, so Keller sketched a commiserating shrug. *Women.*

Billy smiled again. "We will be ready in bloody few minutes, sah. May I introduce the porters before we go? They will be pleased to meet you."

"Sure," Keller said, game for anything. He followed Billy to the shack.

The porters formed a line and stepped forward one at a time when their names were called. All smiles, they put their palms together prayer-fashion, bowed their heads slightly, and said, *"Namaste."*

Doing his best imitation of the Great White Hunter, Keller bowed back and murmured assorted pleasantries, including, "How do you do?" and "Pleased to meet you."

When the introductions were complete, Billy clapped his hands and exhorted the porters to hustle the gear out of the plane's cargo hold. Then Billy became the tour guide. He presented Keller with a gift. "Take this whistle, sah."

Keller accepted the lanyard and shiny referee's whistle. He held it up to the sunlight and grinned. "What's this for?"

Seriously, Billy said, "In case you get lost, sah."

Keller laughed. "Lost? Did you give one to the goat, too?"

Behind him, the Sherpas laughed, too. They understood little English, but they must have heard the derision in his voice. They chortled merrily at Billy's expense while hefting their packs. Billy glared at them over his shoulder, then turned back to Keller. With a lowered voice he urged, "Keep the whistle, sah. Even if you do not need it."

"Billy," said Keller, "I'm not a complete baby. Don't worry so much about me."

The porters argued with Billy for a while after that about who should carry what and for how long. Keller ignored the squabble, but Jane watched the men coldly until they began to throw her wary looks and finally divvied up the gear. In less than an hour, all fifteen Nepalese men were laden with baggage. Each man carried a pack on his back secured by a strap that wrapped around his forehead and balanced the load. Though they had argued bitterly about the weight of each pack, they seemed cheerful enough as they set off in a line toward the foothills. Billy and Jane took the lead.

Keller entrusted the map case with the least objectionable of the porters and followed the procession.

The goat tagged along with Keller, baa-ing cheerfully and prancing like a palomino in the Rose Parade.

"Come on, Lambchop," he said to the beast. "Looks like we're bringing up the rear."

The rear position had its advantages, Keller soon discovered. As Jane started up the hill with the others, he had a perfect view of her backside. Her jeans were loose except across her bum, and the effect of her long-legged stride and snugly-fitted posterior was almost enough to have come around the world for. He found himself startlingly attracted by the sight. Jane had an attractive smear of dust across the most rounded part of her buttocks, and Keller wondered if someone ought to do her a favor later and brush it off.

With that thought in mind, he set off up the hill, smiling.

The afternoon was sunny. After a mile of steady uphill walking, Keller shed his mountain parka. His sweatshirt followed, and he was soon hiking along after the expedition in his cotton shirt and trousers, enjoying the fit of Jane's jeans in the glow of afternoon sunshine. She marched along purposefully, her braided hair glinting in the sunshine, her hips moving in an easy rhythm. Keller's own boots were stiff, but he decided not to stop the whole procession to dig an extra pair of socks out of the backpack that some Sherpa porter was carrying. Things were going well. Maybe he had worried for nothing.

The euphoria didn't last. He hiked for several hours, moving constantly upwards. The countryside was barren, for the most part. There were no trees, and the ground was rocky. Tufty weeds grew haphazardly in meager gray-brown soil. The place was desolate. Except for the sounds of their porters, the air was uncannily silent, the hillsides eerily devoid of life. Only mountains interrupted the bleak landscape, and they were spectacularly beautiful, lit by the sun from an acute angle Keller had never witnessed before.

Steep, he decided, did not describe the trail. It ran along a series of ridges, and in places the walking space was no more than a few inches wide before dropping off into empty space. Each step took Keller higher and higher, and in an effort to keep dizziness at bay he began to avoid looking behind himself and down. He quit watching Jane's backside, too, and concentrated on setting his feet down in safe footholds.

The air was unbelievably thin. It took Keller a while to realize what caused his chest to ache and his head to feel light. The altitude affected him more than he imagined it might. The Sherpa guides stumped along at a steady pace and didn't look back, thank heaven.

By late afternoon, Keller was sucking in each breath as though it was his last and staggering after the others, terrified that one misstep might put him over the edge of an abyss. The goat dashed on ahead into the safety of the larger group, clearly afraid he was going to stumble and knock her into eternity.

The trail petered out finally, and the going became truly miserable. Keller tried to concentrate on the scenery, but eventually he could only think about his own suffering. His muscles ached. His feet felt swollen. Even his arms were heavy and tingled with increased blood supply. He had prided himself on the ability to jog a few miles twice every week, but this kind of exercise was excruciating. And his sinus headache had intensified to phenomenal proportions. As the afternoon wore on, he lagged farther and farther behind the procession of porters.

Billy came back to him finally, looking annoyingly perky. He bounced to Keller's side. "Sah, are you feeling okay?"

"Sure," said Keller, trying to keep his breathing under control. There was no sign of the intrepid Jane, but he wanted to keep up appearances anyway. "I'm just enjoying a look at the countryside, Billy."

"Should we slow down for you, sah?"

"Of course not." Keller stretched out his arms at shoulder-height and took a deep breath of invigorating air. Heartily, he said, "I'm enjoying myself, that's all, Billy. Don't concern yourself."

"Very good, sah." Billy looked just slightly doubtful. "Trail like this can be bloody dangerous, sah. I fell myself once, sah, and it was such a bloody bad thing I never want to do it again. Broke my ribs, sah. Damn near every last one of them."

Keller tried a laugh. "Well, you're back out here again, though, right? Back home, if you fall off your horse, you should get back on again."

Billy said, "I do not know a bloody thing about horses, sah. I only know that money from you and even more from Missus Jane is what brings me to these mountains again." He glanced around at the jagged peaks around them and appeared to shiver. "I do not like coming back, sah."

Great. Even the guide was scared.

Billy pulled himself together, however, and flashed his big smile. "But if you need help, sah, I will be ready! You call. Or use whistle."

"Nonsense!" said Keller. "Keep up the pace, my man."

With another smile and a few more bows, Billy marched

off to rejoin Jane at the head of the line, leaving Keller to his miseries.

He limped into the campsite late in the afternoon. Billy had managed to find a few square yards of flat ground, and the porters were busily setting up tents and starting a cook fire in the center of everything. A thin wisp of smoke rose from the pathetically small pile of fire wood. Jane was nowhere to be seen. Keller hoped that she had collapsed into some bushes and was whimpering over blistered feet, but no evidence suggested that his fantasy was true. Jane had outlasted the porters. No doubt she was scouting ahead, perhaps hoping to encounter a snow leopard she could wrestle.

Keller felt like a fool standing around with nothing to do while everyone else was occupied. Billy must have noticed his unease.

"Sah," he said sympathetically, approaching Keller with a porter's basket in hand. "Why do you not go watch the sunset? It is very beautiful, and we will have some food ready when you get back."

"Sure," said Keller, pulling himself together. "Sounds good."

"Bloody good, sah." Billy smiled. The basket held Keller's own belongings, the map case was on top. He tipped the load to show the contents. "I will take care of your things, sah. Go up the trail, see? Just a few more steps, though. It is very narrow. And remember your way, sah. Very important."

"You'd make a good Eagle Scout, Billy."

"Sah?"

"You're a good man, Billy, that's all. I'll be back in a short while."

"Yes, sah."

Keller strode manfully out of the camp. He hoped he could keep from hobbling until he was out of sight. The trail narrowed, then curved uphill, with a cliff rising to supply a little privacy. Keller was soon out of the porters' view.

The trail narrowed and became a ledge, but he continued to walk, only half aware of what he was really doing. To Keller's left rose an escarpment of lichen-coated stone. To his right fell a steep slope. He hesitated suddenly, not sure he wanted to proceed along such a goat path alone. A voice called out behind him, however, and he heard the porters laugh merrily in response. That was enough. Keller limped out onto the ledge and kept going until the trail was nothing more than a cutout of stone above a chasm. His boots slipped on the crumbling rock, and a tiny shower of pebbles skittered down the cliff.

A screech from the sky startled him. Keller stopped, shaded his eyes, and spotted a black bird, a raven, he supposed. It hung in the air, then shrieked again and plunged downward, swooping past Keller's shoulder and into the darkening gorge while emitting a terrifying primal sound. The bird tumbled for an instant, then caught the downdraft and plummeted out of sight, screaming a war cry. The sound was almost human. Keller's stomach rolled, and he stepped back, colliding with the rock face. He took a deep breath and closed his eyes. Heights usually didn't bother him, but this was extraordinary.

Remembering himself, Keller plunked down on a stone and glanced around to make sure he was alone. Reassured, he set about untying his boot laces. His fingers were almost too numb to manage the job, but at last and with a groan of relief, he drew off both boots and slumped back against the rock face. Eyes closed, he agonizingly attempted to flex his toes.

"I'm not cut out for this," Keller mumbled. He'd always thought he was in good physical shape, but this was altogether something different. Keller was out of his element in many ways, and that was clear to him now. There was nothing to rely on but his own body and his brains. Next to Jane's cool determination and uncomplaining execution of the task at hand, Keller felt extremely inadequate. If he was given a chance, he might be able to show everyone he was made of stern stuff, too. If Jane fell off a cliff and he pulled her to safety just in time, that would do it. All he needed was a crisis to prove he wasn't a loser. For a few minutes, Keller sat still and fantasized.

He should have been paying attention to the sunset instead of letting his imagination wander. The colors were brilliant and the mountains were spectacular. But all Keller was really aware of was how suddenly cold it was. Forgetting his fantasy, he opened his eyes. Nepal had the shortest sunsets on record. The sun had simply disappeared.

He sat up in the utter darkness. He couldn't see his hand in front of his face. He couldn't believe how fast it happened.

And the silence was absolute.

"Hello?" he said tentatively.

No answer, of course. The breeze ruffled his hair, but made no sound. The night was so black that a blanket of velvet might have been draped across the mountains.

Hastily, Keller thrust his feet back into his boots. He skipped the laces and got into his parka, teeth chattering. He squinted to see through the darkness. "Christ," he said, and zipped his coat. The sound was loud, intensifying his impression that he was absolutely alone.

Now what?

He'd come a few hundred yards from the campsite, and yet he couldn't hear a sound from that direction. The huge chasm fell at his feet, and the escarpment at his back was two stories high, impossible to climb even in daylight. The trail had been rocky and rutted underfoot. The loose stones of the trail could cause even a mountain goat to slide right into the mouth of the gorge.

"Hello?" he called again, but very softly, of course. He fingered the whistle that hung around his neck, then dropped it. It would be too humiliating to have to be rescued.

Keller edged off of his sitting place and stood up. Like a blind man, he stretched one hand in front of his face and laid the other palm against the rock of the escarpment. With his back pressed against the cliff wall, he slid one foot sideways, then the other. Slowly, he made his way a few feet down the ledge. Pebbles slid away from his boot, and the rattle echoed down the hillside.

Keller stopped. To go a step further would be suicide. His mouth and throat were suddenly very dry. The only sound he could hear aside from his own heartbeat was the wafting whisper of empty air.

"Sah? Is that you, sah?"

Instantly relieved by the sound of a human voice, Keller expelled a sigh. He couldn't respond at first and struggled to regain his self-control. "Billy?" he finally croaked.

"Stay where you are, sah," Billy called back, a disembodied voice in the darkness, but sounding wonderfully close and encouraging. "A bloody big gorge is here."

"Yes," Keller answered, laughing unsteadily. "Bloody big, all right."

Good old Billy. For the right price, he'd even rescue a stranded city slicker. A pencil-thin shaft of light preceded the old Gurkha as he edged his way closer. His footsteps echoed eerily in the chasm below.

Keller felt as if he was standing on the rim of a gigantic crater, and the meager light affirmed that impression. The hole loomed like the maw of darkest hell. Keller felt his body lean involuntarily toward the empty hole, and he had to catch his balance by putting both hands on the rock behind himself. Each of his senses registered the vast void below. Cool air rose to touch his face like ghostly caressing fingertips. The darkness was thick, the silence terrifying.

"Billy?" he called again, hushed to keep his voice from cracking. "Billy?"

"I am here, sah." The light flashed into Keller's face, then down toward his feet. Billy's steps halted. He cleared his voice to make it work properly. "You . . . you are very on the edge, sah."

"Close enough, yes. The trail narrows up here."

Billy was silent. Then, trying to remain polite, he asked, "How did you get up there, sah?"

"It—it didn't seem dangerous in the daylight."

Perhaps Billy heard the quiver in his voice then. There was a pause, and Billy said gently, "I get you out now, sah. Can you see me?"

"Yes, I—" Keller squinted toward the light source, and his facial muscles were so tense that a spasm shot down his cheek. He put his hand there to quell it. Slowly, he said, "Yeah, I can see. You're sort of a shadow, though."

"Very good, sah. Now stretch out your hand. I'll come up."

Keller put out his arm as Billy crept closer up the stone-slippery trail. Hugging the face of rock, Billy slid one foot in front of the other. Though the trail was at least eighteen inches wide, that space seemed horribly inadequate in the dark.

Keller thrust out his hand to Billy and held his breath.

He wasn't sure how it happened. Billy made a swipe to grab his hand, missed, and lost his balance. The light bounced, then cut a flashing arc against the black sky. Billy flung out both his arms. He twisted, slipped in the stones, and went down. He cried out.

Or maybe it was Keller who made that sound. The flashlight disappeared down, down into the chasm.

And Billy fell, too. He scrabbled in the stones for an instant, desperate for a handhold. Then he plunged over the edge of the trail. "Sah!" he cried.

Keller couldn't move. At his feet in the darkness, he could hear Billy struggle for his life.

The Gurkha didn't disappear down the yawning mouth of the chasm. Billy must have caught a hand in the rocks at the gorge's rim, for he hung there with his legs dangling helplessly. He panted, struggling to find a knee- or foothold. Keller could not move. "Jesus, Billy."

"Sah?" Billy pleaded. "Sah, if you could reach your hand down—"

Keller couldn't catch his breath. Maybe he was hyperventilating.

"Sah, please—"

It was cold. So cold that Keller could hardly make his muscles obey. He had to force himself. He tried edging downward into a crouch. Not enough room. He stood up again, sweat streaming down his face. Fumbling, he unfastened his belt, galvanized by an idea. He pulled the belt out of the pant loops and wound the buckle end once around his hand. He closed his eyes and extended the belt. It swung back and forth in the breeze, the buckle giving off a tiny spark of reflected light. Back and forth it went, like the pendulum of a grandfather's clock.

He could hardly whisper. "T—take it, Billy."

Billy gasped a huge breath and lunged. He grabbed Keller's belt, crying out in relief. But his palm must have been slick with sweat. For a heartbeat, he hung on the end of the belt. Then his grip began to slide.

And the ledge shifted. Under his boots, Keller felt the ground move. Stones loosened, and the trail began to give way. Keller's eyes flew open and saw the terrified glint in Billy's gaze, too. They were both going to die.

So Billy let go.

He released Keller's belt and fell. The chasm sucked him down, and he screamed as he went. He sounded like the diving raven, only louder. Much louder. The sound hung in the air for a moment, and then disappeared downwards into the hole. Even when Billy's voice was stilled, his cry reverberated in the night. Keller did not hear his body strike rock far below. Like the tumbling crow, he simply vanished. Keller flung himself backwards against the face of the cliff and held on.

More lights came after that. Keller wasn't sure how many minutes passed before the Sherpas came to investigate. He was still standing in the same spot when they scrambled up the trail. They waved the flashlights that he'd paid Billy for in advance. The head Sherpa glared one of the lights directly into his eyes and demanded something in Nepali.

Keller still could not speak. He saw their faces. He knew what they thought, and he couldn't defend himself.

Later in the camp, Jane pushed a cup into his hands and forced him to hold it. "Drink this," she said.

Keller couldn't obey, even then. The Sherpas watched, sitting a few yards away and looking at him in the firelight. Not one of them blinked, and the reproach in their eyes glowed like embers.

Dazedly, Keller said to Jane, "I could have pulled him up, you know." The ledge just couldn't support both their weights, that was all.

"Be quiet," Jane said. "Just hush."

He wanted to tell her about the broken ledge. About how he had tried to help Billy. But that seemed so foolish. His reputation wasn't important. Billy was gone, that's what mattered. He had come close to death himself.

"I was afraid," Keller whispered.

"Shut *up,*" said Jane, and this time her teeth were clenched. Under her breath, she muttered, "You're not going to blow this for me."

Chapter 6

JANE WAS THE FIRST TO WAKE UP THE MORNING FOLLOWING Billy's death. She walked away from the camp to rethink her plan in the aftermath of disaster. With Billy gone, things were different.

Up until now, her journey had been on paper, of course. It had looked smooth and uncomplicated. Oh, Billy had been a questionable variable all along, but he hadn't posed a serious threat to her plans. In fact, he had made the whole thing a little more bearable with his clever attempts to squeeze an extra profit for himself whenever he could get away with it. Now, though, his death brought the reality of her trip into focus. Though Jane felt terrible about losing Billy—he had been a friend in his own peculiar way—she knew she had to keep going. Billy's dying had to be a lesson for her.

She sat down and tried to meditate, but today the relaxation technique numbed her emotions. Jane wanted her emotions to be sharp. She intended to use the anger when the time came. No, she'd have to puzzle through the lesson later.

When she smelled the cooking fire, she got up from her cross-legged position and slowly returned to the campsite.

The barren landscape was shrouded in morning fog that the rising sun had only begun to burn off. Birds cackled, as the Sherpas busied themselves with ordinary tasks. The fire, no more than a few broken twigs and the usual cow dung, gave off a little heat, and the group of men huddled as close as they could get without singeing their swaddled boots. One of the bundled-up porters absently stirred the contents of a single pot, waiting for it to heat. While the rest of the porters stolidly awaited their meal, steam rose from them as though from beasts in a barnyard. Vapor curled from their flared nostrils.

Beyond them was Paul Keller's sleeping bag, half-in and half-out of his tent. He was upright and hugging the sleeping bag against himself, staring at the ground. His face was gray, and his ash-brown hair, ruffled by the breeze, was the only part of him that moved. The sight of him stirred Jane's maternal instincts. He looked young and miserable, a little lost boy who'd wandered upon a scene of terrible trouble. His belt lay on the ground in front of him.

At the fireside, Jane elbowed the hunched Sherpas aside and used a rag to grab the blackened kettle from the licking flames. Keller hadn't had any food or drink since yesterday. She poured hot tea into a crockery cup and set the kettle back down into the coals. With the cup, she advanced toward Keller, her unlaced boots clomping as she walked. He didn't even hear her coming.

She crouched on her haunches beside the open tent and thrust the cup at him. "Morning."

He raised his head. His voice was toneless, but not weak. "Hello." At least he wasn't catatonic. He wrapped both hands around the hot cup and hunched to keep the sleeping bag from slipping off his shoulders. Even his posture looked guilty. He cleared his throat. "Everything under control?"

Jane shrugged. "As much as can be expected."

Keller glanced toward the Sherpas, who were pointedly ignoring him. "Has anyone—have they found him yet?"

"Billy? Nope." She jerked her head toward the site of the accident. "The gorge is too steep to climb, and we haven't got the equipment for getting down there to look. Yamdi went back to Jumla last night."

"Yamdi?"

"The boy." Jane decided against telling him that Yamdi had been Billy's cousin. "Little guy, remember?"

"Oh, right." Vaguely, Keller sniffed the liquid in his cup and apparently decided that it was no substance he recognized. Maybe the lack of food had made him delirious. Out of the blue, he asked, "Where's Lambchop?"

"What?"

"Your goat. It didn't run away? Or fall?—"

"Oh," said Jane, understanding. Definitely delirious. "No," she soothed. "The goat's around somewhere. She's okay."

Jane was tempted to reach out and pat him, to caress Keller's hair and comfort him. But she refrained. "Listen," she said, "Yamdi will bring help, you know. Somebody from the government, no doubt."

He nodded.

"I mean," said Jane, "somebody official."

Keller looked at her. "Okay," he said cautiously. "So?"

"So," Jane said, "they'll ask a bunch of questions, you know."

"That's—well, it's to be expected, don't you think?" He blinked. "I'll have to—there will be a lot of things they'll need to know."

"Uhm," said Jane. "They'll want to take you back to Kathmandu."

"Just as well," he said, sighing. "I'm in over my head."

"I wouldn't say that. Not exactly—Look, I feel bad about Billy too, believe me, but—" She sighed. "Oh, hell. I might as well tell you before it all hits the fan. Billy was—well, among other things, he never got a permit for this trek."

"A permit?" Keller repeated.

Jane touched him then. She patted his arm gently. "Yes, you're supposed to get permission before you go hiking around in the mountains. It's a rule. The Nepalese government doesn't want to lose anybody, I suppose, but I asked Billy not to get one."

His face suddenly seemed a little slack. "Why?"

"Because I didn't—" Jane stopped, considering a lie. But Keller deserved the truth. At least part of it. "There's a lot of red tape," she said slowly, "no matter what country you're in. And in Nepal I've gone through it all a hundred times, it seems. I've been a pest to the government."

"A pest?" he asked.

"Yes, a royal pest. They know me, and by now they certainly don't like seeing me come through the door to pound on their desks. They react with hostility. I can't get any help anymore. I've been hassling everybody about my husband—I mean *everybody*."

"Uhuh."

"Now with Billy dead, I . . ."

Keller was no dummy. He said, "You're worried that this will jeopardize things?"

"Exactly. Billy told you some of this, didn't he? About my husband crashing the plane?"

"A little."

Jane nodded. "Okay, here's the story. When I heard my husband was missing, I spoke with embassies and policemen—everyone I could think of to try to find out what had happened. I got nowhere. The Nepalese government claimed his disappearance was not their responsibility, so—"

"Was it?"

"Their responsibility? No, but I had to start someplace." Jane folded her legs and grasped her ankles. "I'm getting the story all backwards, I'm afraid. The crash happened eight months ago, and since then I've fought every bureaucrat between here and Washington to get help finding my husband. As you can see, I've decided to look for him myself. I figured I'd avoid another bureaucratic go-round and skip the permit thing for this expedition." She paused, eyeing Keller. "This means, of course, that Billy probably didn't get a permit for you either."

Faintly, he said, "I see."

"I had to do it this way. They're touchy about who's

allowed up here and who's not, and I couldn't risk asking. I hired Billy to bring me up because he promised not to tell anyone what I was doing."

"And you bought him a new plane."

"And that," she admitted.

"I'm getting the picture," said Keller finally. He looked paler and sicker than ever. "Billy bent the rules for you."

Jane nodded. "Now he's dead—and there's going to be hell to pay."

There should have been tears of woe, she supposed. Some handwringing at the very least. Keller was even looking at her as if he expected some kind of female outburst. But Jane could not let herself. She'd kept a cool head so far, and that was the way she was going to continue.

Jane stared up at the mountainside and narrowed her eyes against the first shards of sunlight that penetrated the mist. Above them, the snow was glaring white against the silver-gray of rock. If she thought things through, this setback wouldn't ruin everything. With care, she said, "It would certainly be nice to just get out of here before the officials showed up."

Keller splashed tea. "You're not thinking of it, are you?" He sat up straighter, staring. "I don't—I mean, running away's not sensible. Not really."

Jane turned to him, maybe too eagerly. "But it would be easy, you know. We could take half the Sherpas and as much gear as we could carry between us—clear out now and have a head start on them."

"We!"

"Yes, us. I figure we could be out of here in an hour."

"Jeez!" he said. "But if we leave the scene of a—a death before—well, it's impossible, that's all. *I* can't go, anyway."

"Why not? What can you tell them that they won't be able to see for themselves?"

"Jesus Christ, everything!"

"Everything speaks for itself," Jane snapped. "The man fell!"

"I have to stay," Keller repeated. "I can't run off. I was—my responsibility is—well, no matter what happens over Billy, I just—I want to get out of here, that's all. I've had enough. I came up here on a kind of wild-goose chase, and I think I've proved that I'm not enough like my father to—well, I don't belong here."

"Oh," Jane said generously, "that's exaggerating. You're not so bad."

Keller blushed, a thoroughly charming act for a man of his size and obvious cosmopolitan nature. "Oh, yes, I am," he said unsteadily. "Look, that doesn't mean you can't go on, though. Sure, go ahead, if you like. Take a few of the guys and clear out before the hassle starts."

"That's just it," said Jane. "They won't work for me."

"Who? What?"

"The Sherpas. They want a man."

"What do you mean?"

"It's amazing, I know." With a murderous glare sent in the direction of the unsuspecting porters, Jane said, "We talked last night. They won't take orders from me, pure and simple. It's prehistoric! With Billy dead, I'm back to square one. I can't go up there by myself, though I'm certainly tempted to try! I need help."

Keller steadied his nerves with an effort. "I'd like to be of service," he said firmly. "But I can't, you know. Billy died because of me and—"

"Look," she cut him off, "accidents happen, Keller. But if you start moping around about how it's your fault that he's dead and you haven't got a permit for being up here in the first place, the government types are going to think this whole thing is *very* fishy! Don't slit your own throat." She jerked her head toward the guides crouched by the fire. "The Sherpas already have a few opinions, you know. You didn't exactly pull yourself together very quickly last night. Some of the men have run off already."

"I can't pretend last night never happened!"

"Yes, you can!" said Jane. "And it's best that way, believe me. Both of us could land in jail if we screw this up. I can't get arrested at this point, Keller. I have to keep going."

Keller stared at her. He seemed incapable of speech.

Jane had stopped short of telling Keller the whole story, of course. In case he really did bolt, she didn't need somebody else floating around who might cause trouble later. The time had come for a little creative manipulation.

She began to tie the laces of her boots. "This whole thing

must have started pretty innocently for you," she said after a moment. "You're just taking something important to your father, right?"

"Yeah," he said, increasingly morose. "That's all it started out to be."

She finished the laces and sat back. "What is it exactly? The thing you're taking to him, I mean."

"A map." Keller raked his hair, sighed, and said unwillingly, "My father's a cartographer, you see. So am I for that matter. But he studies old maps and then explores the places depicted by the original mapmaker."

"And what place is on this particular map?"

"I don't know. I've looked at it and don't see anything special. It's probably a forgotten village or something."

"A forgotten village?"

"Something like that, I'm sure. That's always been his specialty, you see. Finding lost civilizations."

"Lost—? Like Atlantis or something? He must be famous."

"Sort of." Keller rubbed his arms to keep warm. "That kind of work has been his claim to fame since the beginning. Crumbling cities in the jungles have always been a favorite of his—since the fifties. Remember Kalang? The palace in Cambodia? He studied the maps for that and found the place in 1958. Now he's—well, this map I've got is something else he's working on, I guess. No doubt he's hoping to make one last fabulous anthropological discovery and retire in glory."

"You sound like you want him to fail."

"Me? No. No, not really."

Linking her fingers around her knee, Jane rocked back and said, "I can imagine how tough it must be having a father like that. Really frustrating." She rocked some more and said, "What happens if you don't deliver the map to him?"

"Who knows? He'll probably lose his big chance at immortality."

She nodded seriously. "I see. If he doesn't get the map, his dream will be spoiled. You get the last word, I guess, huh?"

When she glanced up, Keller was looking at her, wryly.

Jane grinned at him. "Too obvious a ploy, huh? How

about 'your father's last expedition will be in vain because you got into a snit and couldn't deliver'? He'll hate your guts."

"He probably does already."

"Look, I'm desperate, Keller," she suddenly implored. "Don't you see? I'll do anything to get up there."

"I got that impression, yes."

Urgent, she leaned toward him. "I understand how you must feel about Billy. And it's noble of you to want to stick around this morning and try to make it up to him. But it doesn't matter now! Think about it. Billy isn't going to come back and give you a second chance. You've got to keep going!"

"I—"

"Look, maybe your father's thing is no big deal to you—but I *must* find my husband, Keller. I've come this far, and I won't turn back. If you want to stick around here and mope, that's your business, but it's damn stupid in my book! I'm going ahead no matter what. And I really need you."

Keller noted that women didn't often say that kind of thing to him and really mean it. But Jane wasn't lying, Keller could see. The intensity was back in her face, tightening the flesh around her mouth, sharpening the color of her eyes.

She was strangely beautiful at that moment. There was more than strength in her expression, more than a glow induced by adrenaline or the chill in the air. There was wildness and beauty. Her face was tight, but shining. Even her voice had turned husky with suppressed urgency. Keller knew he shouldn't stare at her, but he wanted to absorb the look she had, the power she exuded. He wanted to forget what had happened and concentrate on this woman.

Fair wisps of her hair clung to her temples, and her cheeks glowed from the chill in the air. Her eyes were blue as cornflowers, but packed the power of laser beams. The rest of her appearance was almost fragile, though. Her fingers were slender, her hands almost childishly small. He could see her pulse as it beat in the exposed flesh of her throat. And not an ounce of excess weight marred the symmetry of her limbs. She was delicate. Her little girl's braid fell over one shoulder and brushed the breast of her parka. She looked pretty. And she was asking for his help.

The idea came to him like a dart spiked with adrenaline. There might be benefits to this hero stuff. Benefits indeed.

Finally he swallowed and asked, "Where exactly are you headed?"

"To the temple at Kol," she replied, no hesitation. "Billy thought that he and I could use it as a sort of base camp. We'd go out in a series of one- or two-day searches from Kol to look for plane wreckage. Wasn't your father last heard from at Kol, too?"

"Yes."

"Okay, then. Kol's just another couple days' hike from here. Lord, you've come around the world, Keller! You're not going to quit less than a hundred miles from your father, are you? I'm not. I'm asking you for help, too. I need you to get me up to the temple."

Keller said nothing. She had fixed her luminous, glowing eyes on his and the effect was mesmerizing. He felt a dryness in his mouth and couldn't respond. She was a huntress, her wild animal beauty tempered by just the right touch of defenseless femininity. Oh, he wanted to say no. Really, he did. But her eyes were smoldery and the feather-like strands of hair looked as soft as dandelion puff. Her appearance and the scenario playing in his head rendered Keller wordless. The rest of his body was not so quiet.

She paid no notice to his silence, and must have assumed he'd agreed to help. She nodded once, then stood up and dusted off the seat of her jeans. She used her own hands to do exactly what Keller had spent the previous day envisioning. He almost made a noise of pleasure.

"Drink your tea," she said, and allowed a quick smile. "We'll get going as soon as possible."

In a confusion—the head-buzzing, crotch-warming kind that only indecent lust could kindle so swiftly—Keller picked up the cup and looked into it dazedly. When he found his voice, he asked with a squeak, "This is tea?"

"*So-cha.* Tea mixed with butter. Hot and very nourishing."

He sniffed the concoction and had his suspicions confirmed. "The butter's rancid!"

Jane shrugged. "It's still good for you. Drink up," she said heartlessly. "And then finish getting dressed. Yamdi could be back very soon with the cops, and I sure as hell don't want to be around then. Got to move on, Keller!"

She strode away at that, without a backward look.

Watching her go, Keller collected himself abruptly. Jesus! What had he been thinking of? Sex with Jane Parish? He suddenly shivered at the thought. This was a woman who found Billy's death inconvenient, for crying out loud! Spending the next few miserable days slogging along behind Jane Parish while she marched up the mountains into Tibet sounded horrible enough. Sex with her would probably be like poking his most prized bodily part into a shark tank during a feeding frenzy. The idea disintegrated as quickly as it had come, leaving Keller weak. Close call.

Without thinking, he sipped the tea, and it was horrible. Not just horrible horrible, but disgusting horrible. That helped settle things. Rancid butter and a woman who looked as though she had trained at Parris Island were not Keller's idea of a worthwhile expenditure of vacation time. The hell with being a man. He had to figure a way to go home.

Chapter 7

KELLER WAS JUST STARTING TO THINK UP A WAY TO GET THE hell away from Jane Parish when the law showed up. Naturally she had chosen to make herself scarce at the exact moment the government officials appeared. Keller manfully buckled on his belt and went out to meet the newcomers. He hoped he didn't look as scared as he felt.

The Nepalese official, a scuttling little fellow with a spanking-new green plastic clipboard of which he seemed very proud, arrived in the daunting shadow of a man who was unmistakably American.

He was a big, swaggering brute dressed in complete safari kit, including an Australian bush hat that sported a snake-skin band and a bristle of erect feathers. He also wore mirrored aviator sunglasses, a Gore-Tex vest with epaulettes and numerous zippered pockets, and a sidearm. The gun looked almost as lethal as the jut of its owner's jaw. The Nepalese official, with an understandably frightened look on his round little face, heeled like an attentive sheepdog.

Keller greeted the two of them on a rocky knoll about twenty yards from the campfire. Jane was no help. At the first sign of trouble, she had disappeared like a puff of smoke.

The beefy American crushed Keller's hand in his own and pumped once solidly. "My name's Pompowsky."

"Glad to meet you." Trying not to cradle his injured hand, Keller said genially, "I'm a little surprised that someone like you showed up today."

"American, y'mean?" Pompowsky took off his sunglasses and grinned, a good Jack Nicholson smile complete with a slightly fanatic gleam in his eye. "Well, young fella, let's just say I'm here on semiofficial duty. State Department."

Keller had lived in Washington long enough to feel confidence in his ability to recognize the common characteristics in employees who worked for various government branches and bureaus. He was immediately certain that Pompowsky was not State Department–connected. No, the State Department attracted painfully polite Yalies who wore tie pins through the starched collars of their shirts, talked like William Buckley, and played squash on the weekends. Pompowsky looked like the sort of man who spent his off-hours reading the memoirs of George Patton and reenacting maneuvers.

Pompowsky was big. His forehead was broad, his jowls were massive, and he had a jaw like a Panzer tank. His belly was hard and big as a keg of beer, but it did not look like the kind of stomach achieved by munching too many jelly donuts. Rather, Pompowsky looked like the kind of man who kept up his strength by eating raw beefsteak. His veins were no doubt packed with cholesterol, and he would die, Keller was sure, by a stroke of the magnitude of Mauna Loa. He was chewing gum, and the muscle in his thick neck flexed with each powerful chomp.

Pompowsky skipped introducing the Nepalese official, steered Keller aside, and took control of the interview himself. "You folks had a casualty up here, I'm told."

"That's right. Last night."

"Not a U.S. citizen, correct?"

"Uh, correct," said Keller. "Nepalese. A man I hired to guide me—us—up here."

Pompowsky clucked his tongue and shook his head in a pretty fair imitation of sympathy, though it was brief. He dug into the hip pocket of his twill trousers and came up with yet another stick of chewing gum. "These yo-yos," he confided, jerking his head toward the Nepalese porters who remained just out of hearing range, "they figure they know how to walk up the side of a hill, so they set themselves up as trained guides. Burns my coconuts. The American public shouldn't be subjected to this kind of shoddy—gum?"

"Uh, no. Thanks."

Pompowsky peeled the wrapper, jammed another stick between his teeth, and began to chew harder. "Altitude," he explained. "My ears are popping like artillery fire. Gum helps, so I'm told, but so far, zilch. Oughta be getting combat pay. So what happened last night? Sketch out the scenario for me."

Keller nodded and strove to be concise. "Okay. We came up from Jumla yesterday and stopped here just before nightfall. I took a short walk to see the sunset—"

Pompowsky looked as if Keller had messed on his foot. "The sunset?"

"It was a chance to be alone while the porters set up camp, that's all."

"I see. Of course." Pompowsky's gaze traveled over Keller's shoulder, and he frowned at the Sherpa porters. Clearly, he could understand why Keller didn't want to associate with the likes of them. The glitter in his eye hinted that he'd like to frisk the lot of them for concealed weapons. "Okay, then what happened?"

"Perhaps I'd better show you. The accident happened over here." Keller pointed. "If you'd step this way, Mr.—uh —Pompowsky—"

"Colonel."

"Uh—yes. Colonel. Over here."

"This is the place, eh?"

Keller stopped a yard from the edge of the chasm and he avoided looking down. "Yes. I walked along this ledge, you see. It runs up the side of the hill for twenty or thirty yards, getting narrower as you get higher."

Colonel Pompowsky stepped to the rim of the gorge and

peered over the tips of his boots into the hole. "You came up this way in the dark?"

"No, no, it was daylight then, but it got dark fast. Billy followed me."

"Billy. That's the dead guy."

"Right," said Keller. "Billy Bhim was his name."

Pompowsky's jaws worked the gum like pistons. He nodded. "Bhim. Got it. The two of you were standing right here, correct?"

"Yes. Nightfall came. It happened very fast and caught me off guard. The altitude must have something to do with it. One minute the sun was shining and then—"

"It got dark, and the son-of-a-bitch fell. Slipped over the edge out of simple clumsiness." He glanced at Keller sharply. "No foul play, just an ordinary klutz at work. Am I right?"

Keller gulped. "Well, I guess. There was no foul play, certainly."

Pompowsky grunted, taking a last look down the gorge. "Glad to hear that, I'll tell you." Abruptly, he turned to Keller then, glowering. "Okay, let's cut the shit now, son. I'm not here to listen to a story about some poor slob who bought the farm on a hiking trail."

"What?"

Pompowsky continued to eye Keller with suspicion and came to his point quickly. "I want to know what you're doing here."

"Me? Oh."

"Well?"

"I'm looking for my father, actually. I—he asked me to bring him some information."

"What kind of information?"

"A map. He's a scientist and—"

"An archaeologist?"

"No, a cartographer. That's maps, you see, and—"

"We'll come back to that," said Pompowsky. "Did you know this Bhim character before you hired him?"

"No, I was in a hurry and looking for a guide. Billy was the last one left in Kathmandu, so I took him."

"Okay," said the Colonel. "You ever hear of a guy called Roger Parish?"

"Parish?" Startled, Keller repeated, "Roger Parish? N—no, I don't know anyone by that—"

"Or his wife?"

"His wife?"

"Yeah," Pompowsky said testily, impatient with the stalling. "She's a blonde. Spouts a lot of ashram malarkey, but a good-looker, I hear. You seen her?"

Keller cleared his throat and tried to formulate a cautious reply.

"I'll tell you why I'm asking," Pompowsky said, suddenly oozing craftiness. He took off his hat and fanned his face with it. His hair was black around his ears, but the top of his head was bald and shining in the sunlight. He said, "We're looking for this Parish character, Keller. He's Navy. A pilot. Fighter pilot, in fact, or was. Now he's disappeared. You with me? Naturally we want to make sure he hasn't gone someplace unsafe."

"Unsafe? Like where?"

"That's classified."

"Classified?"

"You know what classified means, don't you?" Pompowsky's eye contact intensified to a glare. "You're a smart boy, Keller. And you've kept a clean nose up till now, I'm told. So I'll spell it all out for you, if you can keep your mouth shut."

Faintly, Keller said, "Sure."

"Okay. Parish knows a hell of a lot about planes, see? Not ordinary planes, but the latest Navy fighter jets. Plenty of classified stuff. Now he's hanging around a part of the world that's damned close to China and the Russkies."

Aha. Enlightened, Keller murmured, "I see."

"His wife is already some kind of communist fruitcake. Belongs to funny clubs, gives money to weird charities, that kind of stuff. We don't know how much of her politics got rubbed off on him. Naturally, we want to be sure Parish doesn't get—" Pompowsky found the right euphemism and smiled. "So he doesn't get hurt."

It was as good a story as any, Keller supposed. He wondered what kind of charity Colonel Pompowsky would consider "weird." UNICEF? All that money pouring into the Third World could only undermine the foundation of capitalism and democracy.

"You want the whole story?" the Colonel demanded, still chawing his gum as if Sousa was conducting. "Okay, Keller, Roger Parish retired from the Navy, see? He went a little nutty toward the end—the fly-boys sometimes do. He buys himself a big plane and starts around the world—billed it as some kind of sightseeing retirement trip for himself. He lands in Kathmandu and hires this Bhim character to take him up into the mountains—we don't know why—in some itty-bitty death trap that Bhim owns. But before they can take off, Parish bumps Bhim on the head, takes the plane up himself, and manages to crash it someplace godforsaken. You still with me?"

"Sure."

"So Parish is never heard from again, and Bhim is left high-and-dry with no plane. No plane, no expeditions, no income. Bhim is broke. Now eight months later he's suddenly in business again with a new aircraft that's obviously been bought and paid for by someone other than himself." Pompowsky paused significantly. "Any ideas, Keller?"

"Me? No."

"You sure?"

"*I* didn't buy any airplanes, if that's what you're getting at."

"So who was it?" Pompowsky began to stroll, signaling Keller to follow. "That's what I want to know, Keller. We're concerned about Parish. We've been asking questions around this hole-in-the-wall country—in our own cautious kind of way, of course, but, at the same time, there's been this crazy wife of his running around like a typical hysterical female asking pretty much for the same information. Only she's not cautious. She's blabbing to everybody—things she's got no business knowing in the first place. Still follow?"

"Yeah, I follow."

"This Parish woman has been a pain in the A around Kathmandu ever since her old man went down. There must be a doozy of an insurance policy at stake here, let me tell you. By now, she's probably desperate enough to buy a new airplane for Bhim and go looking for her husband alone. Make sense to you?"

"Well, I don't know."

"Well, I do." Pompowsky stopped walking and faced Keller. Slowly, he smiled, his eyes narrowed. "What's funny is you, Keller, my boy. I think Bhim and the wife were in cahoots. They were hot on the husband's trail together—maybe even all the way to Moscow in the new airplane. And who should be along on the maiden voyage? You."

Keller only just managed to keep panic at bay. Inside he was holding back terror, and only just. "I don't know anything about this stuff, Colonel," he said. "Honest, I don't."

"No?"

"No, really. I'm taking some papers up to my father, that's it, I swear. I hooked up with Billy because he was the only guide I could get. I'm just along for the ride. That's the truth."

Pompowsky's smile remained, but the look in his eyes was hardly amiable. "What do you know about the Parish woman?"

There had to be a way to deflect the question. But Keller couldn't come up with one. He was caught flat-footed.

Pompowsky's smile grew. "Let me make this easier for you, son. I know you've got a woman with you up here. The twerp who came down to Jumla to get us said there was a blonde along on this expedition."

Keller cleared his throat. "Colonel," he said, "there's no woman here but my sister."

Pompowsky blinked. "Your what?"

"My sister. That's all. I swear."

Pompowsky didn't look convinced. "What's her name?"

"Charlotte," said Keller, pleased with how quickly he had come up with something that sounded just unusual enough to be the truth.

"Charlotte, huh?" The Colonel's belly tightened, and his face grew stern. "Boy, do you know how long it will take for me to have your nice sister's papers looked up? It'll take four days to make sure she is who she says she is, and during those four days, I can make the both of you real comfortable at the local hoosegow."

Keller said, "Hey—"

"You think I'm bluffing, boy?"

"No, no, of course not. I just—"

Pompowsky put his arm around Keller's shoulder. "Yeah, I know, son. The Prince Valiant thing to do is to protect the lady, right? But not this time. She's not your sister any more than I am. You don't exactly have all the facts, my boy. If you did, you wouldn't be standin' up for her. Son, this Parish babe won't do you any good."

"I never said—"

"This whole Parish situation has turned into a question of national security. You wouldn't want to get mixed up in that kind of show, would you, son?"

Truth was, Keller was starting to regret a hell of a lot of things. He did not want to add treason to his list of transgressions.

Pompowsky thumped his shoulder good-naturedly. "Let's do business, Keller. I only want the girl. Not you, and not anyone else, now that Bhim is dead. Give the girl to me and run along. I won't even mention your name in my report."

Keller squeezed his eyes closed. "Jeez."

Pompowsky tongued the wad of gum into his cheek and chuckled. "Oh, Keller, you'll be glad to get rid of her, believe me! You've got your own thing going here. You don't need to get mixed up in her mess. She is here, isn't she?"

Keller gave up on gallantry and sighed. "Yes."

Pompowsky patted his shoulder. "That's a good boy. You're sure it's her?"

Keller nodded reluctantly. "Jane Parish."

Smiling broadly, Pompowsky said, "Don't feel bad, son. Turning her in is the sensible thing to do. We'll be able to do Mrs. Parish a lot more good than you can. We're trained in this sort of thing, right? We'll find her husband for her."

Keller figured he probably could convince himself of that argument, given time. Jane needed expert help, that was it. She couldn't find her husband alone. She was a capable person, certainly, but she wasn't Wonder Woman.

"One last thing," said Pompowsky.

Keller almost held his breath.

"Your old man." The Colonel brought out his pack of

gum again and began to extract another stick. "He's some kind of explorer, is he?"

"Well, sort of, yes."

Pompowsky nodded. "I heard something about him."

All attention, Keller demanded, "What? You've seen him?"

Pompowsky shook his head. "Nope. But I hear he's got himself a passel of trouble somewhere."

"Where'd you hear that?"

Pompowsky endeavored to look kindly. "Son, I don't give away my sources. Let's just say I think you'd better look him up."

"I *have* been looking him up," said Keller. "I don't know where the hell he is. This whole trip isn't—well, I've run into some trouble, as you can see."

Pompowsky huffed. "Don't let this Bhim business stop you. You just run along, son." He waved at the Sherpas and said, "Take the rest of these boys with you and keep going."

"But," Keller said.

Pompowsky had turned to go, then reconsidered. He swung around and said, "One more thing, my boy. Let's take pains not to see each other again, all right? Nothing personal. I just don't want to hear of you in connection with this Parish affair anymore, okay? Go about your business and stay out of my way and away from this Parish babe."

No problem there. As Pompowsky strutted off, Keller figured if he ever ran into Jane Parish again, she was going to kill him.

Chapter 8

POMPOWSKY MUST HAVE RUN JANE TO GROUND JUST OUTSIDE the camp, because Keller heard her bellowing and screaming in a matter of minutes. How Pompowsky subdued her, Keller couldn't imagine. He did not go looking to find out. After a while, Jane's noise faded, and Keller figured he was alone. He sat on the rocks and looked at the scenery and tried to tell himself he wasn't a fink.

And after a while, he must have convinced himself because things didn't look so bad. Jane was out of his hair, he had a lead on the old man, and he hadn't broken any bones yet. The worst was over, surely.

Three remaining Sherpa guides apparently believed that Jane had been a source of bad luck all along, for when Keller was left alone with them on the hillside, he discovered that he had been absolved in their eyes of any wrongdoing concerning Billy Bhim's death. The Sherpas smiled and bowed and did their best to communicate with him in

English. They expressed their willingness to do his bidding and seemed genuinely sorry that his father was missing.

In very broken English, the spokesman introduced himself as Yamdi. He was the youngest of the three, a robust teenager dressed in an enormous pair of shorts over some sort of wrapped leggings and woolen boots soled with what Keller was later to recognize as twine made from yak hair. Yamdi's vest looked as though it had been cut from an elegant multicolored carpet. His cap was set at a rakish angle, and he approached Keller tentatively.

"Should we break our camp now, sahib?"

Which brought Keller to a crossroads. Should he go ahead? Or forget the whole thing and go home to clean sheets, fresh socks, and Lean Cuisine?

Yamdi didn't look like he'd studied at Oxford, so Keller stalled him without bothering to be subtle. "Oh, it's afternoon already, Yamdi. If we broke camp, we'd hardly get a few miles before nightfall. Let's just have a day of rest, shall we?"

Yamdi smiled and bowed, hands clasped reverently. "Very good, sahib. We rest before our terrible journey. But if the sahib likes, there is inn six miles up road."

Keller did not see anything that resembled a road, but the idea of an inn sounded like heaven in the face of a "terrible journey." "An inn?" he asked, with visions of a shower and comfortable bed immediately dancing in his head like sugarplums. "You mean a hotel, Yamdi?"

"Yes, sahib, very good one, sah, if you do not mind Pirim."

"What's that?"

"Pirim is the keeper, sahib. We know he was once a bandit, a fierce man who stole from the trekkers. But now he is stealing differently, eh, sahib?" Yamdi laughed at his own joke. "We could stay there one night and be gone before his old companions hear of us."

Having seen the childishly hopeful expressions on the faces of the three Sherpas, Keller decided not to demonstrate his own cowardice again. He dismissed the warning about mountain bandits. "By all means, gentlemen. Let's find the inn."

The Sherpas cheered and broke camp quickly, showing their familiarity with such work. The feeble fire had long since gone out, but they were careful to be sure, and even took out the bits of charred wood that had not yet been burned completely. Firewood was hard to come by. With their baskets once again loaded, they fixed the straps around their foreheads and set off up the slope with surefooted energy. They chatted, laughing together, leaving Keller the only one who regretted the loss of Jane. Already he wished she was still with them, capably setting off up the mountain and looking noble and solemn and completely unattainable.

As he was about to leave the ill-fated scene, Keller was startled by Lambchop. The little goat dashed into the deserted campsite and bleated forlornly.

"Oh, hell," said Keller, looking down at her. "Don't tell me you miss Jane, too?"

Lambchop cut a caper and tilted her head at the sound of his voice.

Keller sighed. "All right, come along. Just stay out of trouble, will you?"

With a twitch of her tail, Lambchop appeared to agree to his stipulation.

As the goat galloped after the departing porters, Keller glanced down the hill in the direction Pompowsky had taken Jane. No sense regretting what he couldn't help. His father had to be Keller's first priority. Without quite convincing himself of that idea, Keller hurried to catch up with the porters.

Above the next ridge they came upon a *stupa*. It was a religious shrine, Yamdi explained, but the thing gave Keller the creeps. Even the goat steered clear of the shrine. It was nothing more than a mound of packed clay upon which had been painted a pair of black slanted eyes, nothing more. The eyes of Buddha, Yamdi explained, could see everything. Keller had a pretty good idea of what this particular set of eyes had seen already, so he hurried past the stupa and avoided returning Buddha's stare.

The afternoon was sunny. The air was warm. With extra socks, his feet no longer hurt so horribly, and Keller stepped along, determined to take in the sights. The ache in his sinus passages wasn't so bad, either. Maybe things were looking up.

He discovered that their first night's camp had not been so isolated as he first thought. Perhaps the news of Billy's death had spread quickly and kept the local inhabitants away, because just a few hundred yards up the trail, a pack of children bounded up from nowhere. Half-dressed and unwashed, they tagged along like coyotes, alternately badgering Keller and shyly whispering among themselves. Yamdi ordered them off once, but they reappeared soon with reinforcements who sang ditties and giggled. Amused, Yamdi didn't bother chasing them away again, and the children followed for the whole six miles.

The countryside, Keller saw, looked just as wild as the children did. There were no flat places in the mountains, no plateaus, no terraces for grazing. The people lived their whole lives on a slant. The jagged slopes of rock climbed relentlessly upward, with very little vegetation to keep the skiff soil in place. Grass did not grow except in small clumps, and no trees provided shade from a glaring sun. Anything that could have been used as firewood had been cut down and carried off. The landscape had been left desolate. The ground was dull gray or mud brown, but those colors looked warm against the dazzling blue sky and distant white snows. The palette of nature's hues looked unusual and foreign to Keller, but oddly beautiful.

He could not get accustomed to the altitude, however. Constantly, he was aware of the steep slopes above, and the sheer drop of the hillside below. He couldn't shake the sensation that one false step might send him tumbling down the mountainside. Queerly, he felt very tall, and as if he was always teetering on the edge of a chasm. He was too big and too clumsy. The sturdy, surefooted Sherpas were much better suited to the terrain than he was. They stumped along the trail without apparent concern for their lives, and the goat was even more casual about her footing. The dizzying heights did not bother any of them.

The trail hardly resembled those wide, well-tended paths in American parks. A ditch lay to the left of an eighteen-inch-wide trail, and, on the right, the hill fell away to a several-hundred-foot gorge complete with a swiftly gurgling creek at the very bottom. The going was narrow and so steep in places that Keller often climbed on all fours, using his hands to grasp a hold before risking a move with his feet. A slick of mud covered the rock, but a scattering of pebbles and stones improved the footing a little. Keller sat down and scooted across the most dangerous places. The higher they proceeded, the more extreme the depth of the gorge became. After a time, they could not even hear the rush of water. Keller was not normally afraid of heights, but the constant steepness of mountain hiking was breathtaking.

At last the trail widened, and in a flattened-out space, Keller saw the rubble of some sort of building that was couched against the cliff. The building's slat roof was whole, but one wall had crumbled badly, and the stones were spilled out onto the dusty ground. Perhaps the building was a religiously significant ruin, because a nearby tree had been wrapped with Tibetan prayer flags, scraps of cloth left by introspective passersby. In the breeze, the tattered flags snapped cheerfully, pointing the way toward the ruined shack.

A grimy dog slithered out the doorway of the building, took one look at Lambchop, and yapped heroically. The goat kicked up her heels, though, and the dog drew back, tucking its tail. The barking had alerted someone within, however, for the doorway was next darkened by a stout frame swaddled in loose jodhpurs, a shirt or two, and a fringed apron. The portly Nepalese man spread his hands like a German brewmaster and called a jolly greeting to Yamdi.

The Sherpas shed their loads and turned to Keller expectantly, their faces aglow with smiles.

"Well, sahib? This inn good for tonight?"

The hovel was no Sheraton. Keller halted in his tracks and suppressed a groan.

Pirim, the innkeeper, was a swarthy, jolly fellow with bad teeth who made up for the ramshackle condition of his establishment by bowing and shouting effusive greetings. Yamdi made introductions, and Pirim strode out to shake Keller's hand. "I am so pleased to make you comfortable, Killer-sahib!"

"That's Keller."

"Yes, yes. Come inside, please. May I get you a drink after your long walk? A meal, perhaps?"

Keller's only nourishment so far had been the single cup of buttered tea. By afternoon he was famished. There had to be some alternative between starvation or dysentery.

"Is there anything bland?" he asked the innkeeper, hoping in vain for toast or even saltines.

"A fine meal will come!" crowed Pirim. "We prepare it at once! Be comfortable, Killer-sahib. Food comes—the very best!"

Keller decided against entering the primitive inn before it was absolutely necessary, so he settled himself on a rock near a pen where a pair of flea-bitten yaks dozed. Lambchop butted close, but Keller was immediately surrounded by the throng of children who were much stronger and pushed the goat out of their way. They picked at Keller's clothing with their dirty fingers, laughing among themselves and nattering in their own language.

A little girl asserted herself. She was perhaps five or six years old and was dressed in a black woolen smock. Huge dangling earrings decorated with pretty polished stones hung from her ears, and from the way she tilted her head to show them off, Keller could see that she was proud of them. She clung to Keller's trouser leg, then tugged on his belt for attention. Her upturned face was chubby-cheeked, with beautiful slanted eyes and a clever smile. "Sahib!" she lisped, flirting like a starlet. "Sahib?"

Yamdi, watching benevolently from a yard away, translated. "They like you, sah. These are the children of Pirim."

"All of them?" Keller counted nine children. He tousled the head of the little girl and couldn't help but smile down at her impish face. "What do they want, Yamdi? Coins?"

"Coins, yes, sah, always welcome. But also ballpoints."

"Ballpoints?"

"Pens, sah. For writing with ink. You have any ballpoints?"

Automatically, Keller began to pat his pockets, though he was sure he hadn't even the stub of a pencil on his person. "Sorry, no. How about a penny instead? Here—I've got twelve, no, thirteen cents. Will this do?"

He had just enough for each child, and a nickel for the little girl with beautiful eyes. She had a gaze that was direct—a lot like that of Jane Parish. When she took the nickel from him, she at once popped the coin into her mouth like penny candy and grinned. Before Keller could protest, she skipped away as lightly as a woodland sprite, laughing with her siblings. With a sappy smile on his face, Keller watched them go.

Pirim returned with coffee mugs that were filled to frothing with lukewarm liquid. *"Chang,* sahib. My own, made here. The best in many miles, I am sure."

Well, if he was going to suffer through dysentery no matter what, he might as well get started. Keller accepted the pottery cup and was startled by the weight of the thing. With both hands, he bravely tilted it and sampled the drink. It was beer, sort of, and it went down harshly. The aftereffect was not unpleasant, however. Keller took a second swallow, savored it, and looked up to see the three Sherpas and Pirim smiling broadly at him.

"Very good, Killer-sahib?"

"Very good, indeed, Pirim. Pour some for the rest of the fellows, would you?"

The Sherpas laughed and jostled each other to get to the chang. In moments, they were all guzzling the stuff like the brothers of Theta Chi on homecoming weekend. After refills, they hunkered down for some serious drinking.

Taking that first cupful was the fatal mistake, Keller decided later. The alcohol combined with high altitude and caused a drunk like he'd never experienced before. He was loaded in minutes, dizzy and smiling foolishly, having a hard time balancing the heavy cup on his knee. Lambchop scuttled forward and poked her nose into the cup. Keller didn't bother to shoo her away.

"I have food ready," Pirim announced when it was time to fill the cups a third time. He took care to refill Keller's drink completely. "Plenty to eat, sahib."

"That was fast work, Pirim."

"Oh, I have more guests coming soon," he explained. "We cook for them for two days."

"This is a busy place, then. Am I going to need a reservation to stay here?"

Pirim didn't understand, but was not going to admit it. "No, sahib," he said seriously, "you just need sleep bag. You bring one, yes?"

"Oh, yes."

Pirim nodded importantly. "Then plenty of room. The others have many animals, but not many peoples. They come once every year from great distance to sell. Maybe you buy from them, sahib?"

"What are they selling?"

"Wool, the finest. And some rugs. Beautiful rugs, sahib. The wife of my relation—she is very good rugmaker—"

Keller sensed a sales pitch coming and put up his cup for more chang. "I'm sure she's excellent, Pirim, but I'm not looking for rugs."

"No?" Pirim tilted his head and frowned, inviting an explanation.

Eagerly, Yamdi inserted himself into the conversation. "Mister Killer goes searching for his father," he said. "A great man, the sahib's father."

Pirim's bulbous face brightened. "A great man?" He blinked hopefully at Keller. "A wealthy man, too?"

Remembering Yamdi's warning about Pirim's thieving relatives, Keller played it safe. "No, not wealthy," he said with a self-deprecating laugh. "He's a man of learning, that's all. He studies ancient maps."

Yamdi and Pirim nodded, exchanged a significant look. "Ah," said Pirim finally. "This great man looks for treasure?"

"Well, he looks," Keller willingly agreed, smiling, "but I don't think he'll find anything, do you?"

Pirim stroked his chin. Helpfully, Yamdi said, "I have warned him about bandits hereabouts, but he is not worried."

Pirim nodded in agreement. "No bandits here," he declared.

Expansively, then, the innkeeper poured more chang into the cups. "We will have food now," he announced. "My relations come soon and will eat it all. Come, Killer."

A woman appeared from inside the hovel. She was skinny, bent, with a broad, wrinkled face and her bony body swathed in funeral black, but her step was quick as a girl's.

She carried a stack of hardened pancakes in her gnarled hands. Following her came two of the older children, who carried more food. Yamdi had directed the erection of a camp table, and the innkeeper's family made use of it. The younger children flocked to the table, elbowing each other to snatch the first portions of the food. Keller, starved, waded in with them.

The cheese seemed relatively safe. It was chewy, but filling. The greasy pancakes turned out to be surprisingly lacking in any flavor whatsoever. Potatoes were in abundance, having been fried in some sort of fat that smelled, well, unusual, to say the least. Keller was beyond caring and inhaled his portion, then wondered if going back to the buffet was considered bad form.

While plotting a stealthy return trip, Keller was interrupted by the arrival of Pirim's extended family. First the distant jingle of bells announced their approach, and soon a procession of shaggy ponies appeared, their heads encased in feather-bedecked harness, their curved necks wet and foamy with sweat. On their backs were strapped wildly colored assortments of bound-up fabrics. On matchstick legs, they were agile little beasts, full of spunk even at the end of the day. Each animal was tied to the one in front and behind it with braided rope, and they bumped and hustled each other like quarrelsome cousins. Keller watched them with amusement.

Pirim shouted to the new arrivals. "Mohan! My friend!"

The traders walked beside the caravan of ponies, and none of them looked very friendly. There were three men, all long-haired and clad in colorful leather; all with expressions uncharacteristically hostile for Nepalese. They wore amulets around their necks, and one sported a silver-handled dagger in his belt. He looked familiar. Keller pegged him a minute later. He had a face like Edward G. Robinson. His slightly western look included longer limbs, rounder eyes, and even an American swagger.

The traders thumped down the last yards of trail, already slinging off their packs, apparently glad to find their destination after such a long trek.

The children had heard the bells first and leaped up from their food to greet the new arrivals, chattering with excitement and laughing. At the head of the swarm ran the small girl. With cries of delight, she flew toward the ponies. Lambchop dashed after her, cavorting.

The little ponies snorted and threw up their heads, bells jangling. The lead man sketched a quick, warning motion with his arm, but the girl did not heed him. She raced past Keller and up the path, Lambchop just half a step behind.

Keller hadn't seen the dogs at first. They padded along behind the pack ponies, snuffling the ground and alert for danger. They were the size and configuration of mastiffs, thick-headed, heavy-jowled, and enormous, their black skins scarred by numerous battles. Both dogs must have spotted the little girl before she saw them, for they stiffened. Then they flung themselves down the trail toward her, snarling with lips drawn back from horrifying teeth.

Whether the dogs were after the girl or Lambchop, it was impossible to tell. Lambchop—with better instincts—bolted for the nearest rocks. The little girl froze.

The other children shrieked and scattered, but she stayed still, poised on her toes and terrified.

The wool traders all shouted and moved, but it was clear the dogs were going to be a hell of a lot faster.

Before he could think, Keller acted. As the dogs charged, he got up and hurled his cup directly at them.

It worked. The heavy cup hit the first dog straight across its forehead and smashed. Keller shouted and swung a kick at the second dog. Snarling, it dodged aside. Keller spun around to ward off the first dog again, but it lay still on the ground, stone dead.

Pirim's young daughter looked down at the inert dog and burst into tears.

Everyone moved then: Pirim to snatch up his daughter and Yamdi to chase the second dog into the brush. The wool traders crowded around the corpse of their watchdog, shouting at each other, brandishing their arms.

Keller found the nearest rock and sat down. He could feel the cold tingle of adrenaline in his fingertips, but his head was numb. He was sweating.

"Sahib," said Yamdi, hustling back to Keller. "Sahib, you very quick!"

"Is it dead, Yamdi?"

"Dead, yes, sahib. Killed in one blow!"

"I'm sorry about the cup. I didn't think." He ran his hand through his hair. "I just—well, I threw it before I thought."

Yamdi grinned, whacking Keller's shoulder boldly. "No worrying about cup, sahib. You save Pirim's daughter very quick!"

Sheepishly, Keller looked up at the Sherpa's broad face. "I did, didn't I?"

The wool traders were not so pleased. They advanced on Keller with thunderous expressions, and at the head of the pack was Edward G. Robinson. They proceeded to chew him out in a ferocious babble of voices. Yamdi joined in the argument, apparently coming to his defense. Pirim rushed over to lend his shouts to the din of his relatives. They quarreled, all bellowing furiously while Yamdi begged for order.

Suddenly Edward G. Robinson drew his dagger and flashed it toward Yamdi's throat.

Keller got to his feet. He grabbed Yamdi's arm and hauled him to safety. "Jesus Christ!" he exploded. "Cool down for a minute, will you? I'll pay for the damn dog!"

It was his size that did the trick. He was half a foot taller than any of them. That combined with the sharpness of his voice ended the squabble abruptly. They had no idea what he'd said, but the Nepalese men gaped up at him, struck silent by his command. Nobody moved.

In that instant, Keller felt what it was like to be the boss.

Their thoughts were written on their faces, painted in universal body language, sung in silence. They stopped and gaped at him, ready to receive the next command. He had slain the dragon and saved the princess. They were ready to listen to him now. Sullenly, the leader sheathed his dagger.

It felt good. Like a fool, Keller began to grin.

Pirim laughed and clapped him on the back. "I will bring more chang! Come, my many friends!" He added a sentence in Nepali, which was greeted by a chorus of manly chuckles from the porters. The wool traders were not so cheerful, but they turned away from the fight. At a distance, they muttered among themselves until the cups were brought and filled.

All the porters turned to Keller expectantly, cups in hand.

Keller lifted his cup in a toast, and smiled, hoping that communication was enough.

The Tibetan traders raised their cups, and while still glowering, the servings of chang seemed to soften their mood. They looked at each other. Then in unison, they chanted, "Screw the Army and fuck the Marines!"

Without drinking, Keller lowered his cup. He stared at the men as they guzzled the chang. "What did you say?"

"Sahib?"

"Yamdi, what did they just say?"

"A talk, sahib, that is all. A—a toast."

"Yes, but where did they hear it?"

Yamdi shrugged, but turned willingly to the assembled wool traders. They talked back and forth, and Yamdi translated to Keller. "From a man they met, sahib. A man from America."

"A trekker?"

Yamdi again relayed the question to the traders, who began to sense something was afoot. They looked coldly at Keller and spoke at length to Yamdi, each man adding something to what the others had to say. Eventually, Yamdi turned back to Keller. "No, sahib, the man from America who lives in the mountains now. Not a trekker, this man. Mohan say he is big like you, but with yellow hair, and he laughs very much, they say. He teaches the fuck toast. These men should be very sorry if you are offended, sahib."

"I'm not offended, Yamdi. Just surprised." Keller hesitated. Then, uncertain whether he really wanted to know the answer, he asked, "How long has this American lived in the mountains? Ask them, please."

Yamdi did as commanded, and Keller could see that the wool traders did not know. They shook their heads and lifted their shoulders, pantomiming innocence as well as ignorance. They obviously did not want to take any blame for anything this American had done. Soon Yamdi said, "These men do not know how long this yellow man is there, sahib. They never see him before."

"Could he have arrived recently? Like in the past year or so?"

Yamdi asked the traders, then turned back to Keller with the reply "They think maybe one year, sahib. The man from

America has not lived here long. He does not know the mountains yet."

Wonderingly, Keller murmured, "Good Lord."

"Sahib?"

He shook himself out of his reverie. "Nothing, Yamdi. I think I know who this American is, that's all. Someone's looking for him."

Yamdi grinned, eyes sparkling. "They will look for a long time, sahib. Mohan lives near the border, you see. That is very far."

"Which border?"

Yamdi's smile faded. "The Forbidden Land, sahib."

"You mean Tibet. There's nothing forbidden there, Yamdi. That's propaganda. Tibet's a part of China. They just don't want you strolling over there."

"No strolling, sahib," Yamdi said seriously. "Very difficult walking. These men come only once a year from that place. Snow will come there, even now. Very difficult."

Looking very troubled, Yamdi asked in a rush, "You do not look for this man, sahib?"

Keller laughed. "No, Yamdi, you're in luck. I'm not looking for that character."

Yamdi was relieved. "You make me happy, sahib," he said, sighing. "The border is too far for me to go from my family, you see. They would be very sorry to see me go so far."

Keller patted Yamdi on the back and turned away to think.

So Roger Parish was alive.

There was probably a way to get that information to his wife. Keller didn't consider trying to give the information to Pompowsky. Somehow, it seemed like a better idea to tell Jane first. On the other hand, he did not want to deliver the message personally. She was liable to kill first and ask questions later.

"Yamdi, where are these men going?"

Yamdi willingly relayed his question, which was promptly greeted by surly looks and a single-syllable reply. Yamdi said, "To Kang, sahib."

"Where is that? Far from Jumla?"

"Very far, sahib." With his arm extended, Yamdi pointed

eastward, indicating that Jumla, Kang, and their present position represented the three sides of a triangle. He looked apologetic.

Keller let the matter drop. If Pompowsky got wind that he knew anything about the Parish business, he'd be in deep shit all over again. He drank some more chang.

The chang helped, too. Not only could Keller feel himself getting loaded, but the others appeared to be losing their senses, too. By nightfall, it could have been safely said that everyone was plastered. One of the wool traders chased Pirim's wife out into the darkness, where she could be heard howling and screeching at him. She must have won the scuffle, for the man gave a yelping cry and fell silent, and the woman came triumphantly back to the camp. She halted at the fireside and spat hugely into the embers. The remaining men laughed heartily at their companion's misfortune.

One by one everyone climbed into their sleeping bags. Keller forced himself to be among the last. Stumbling with exhaustion, he finally made his way to his tent. Fearing fleas, he had shunned the shelter of the inn and fell asleep in the warm cocoon of his thermal bag. The dreams that came after that were such grim, blurred images that he might have been on some kind of hallucinatory trip.

In the morning, he climbed out of his tent to discover one of the wool traders holding a knife to Lambchop's throat. Keller yelled and dashed across the campsite.

He chased the would-be butcher out into the flat ground and ran him down. When the trader landed, a welter of Keller's possessions spilled out from inside his clothing. With Yamdi's help, Keller managed to retrieve his pocket-knife, wallet, and toothbrush. Enraged with the thief, he refused to pay for the dog he'd killed.

The wool traders left Pirim's place soon thereafter. They were furious with Keller and shouted vindictive threats over their shoulders as they went.

When the incident was over, Keller was glad to hit the trail for the lonely outpost at Kol. The farther from humanity he could get, the happier he'd be. He whistled, and Lambchop obediently traipsed after him.

With Yamdi in the lead and the two porters close behind him leading a yak they'd leased from Pirim, Keller followed the expedition at a distance. For that day and the following, he kept up without keeping company with the others. Only at noontime and again at nightfall did he join the rest of the expedition, usually at a teahouse run by a solitary family that eked out a living from the occasional travelers. He knew the porters were taking advantage of him by stopping frequently, but Keller didn't feel like pushing them. He preferred being alone when he encountered more of the eerie stupas and the lonely trees that had been swaddled in prayer flags, signs that other soul-suffering human beings had come that way. Keller drank chang with the other men every night, and judging by how he felt every morning, he drank too much.

Finally, on the fourth night, they arrived at the temple of Kol.

Keller had been prepared for something spectacular. A fabulous house of worship with statues and incense and monks, maybe. He'd been hoping for a town, at least. But Kol didn't look any different from the rest of the barren mountain they'd just spent days clambering up. There were no buildings, no people, not even any birds. The place was desolate.

The temple was a poor excuse for a hovel, in fact. By twilight, the crude place looked more like a ruined cave than a religious shrine. Keller stumbled in anyway, too tired and depressed to care. He skipped the meal that Yamdi offered to make and instead drank a portion of the chang he'd bought at the last teahouse. With the cup in hand, he climbed into his sleeping bag and fell deeply asleep.

Chapter 9

THERE WAS SUNLIGHT STREAMING THROUGH THE SLATTED ROOF of the temple when Keller regained consciousness that morning in Kol. In that golden dazzle, he realized that a huge figure towered over him, straddling his inert body the way the sword-wielding god of war must stand over the corpses of battle-mangled mortals. Keller flung up one arm to deflect the blinding light and get a better view upwards, but the god bent and grabbed him by the jacket. Keller yelped in terror.

"You son of a bitch! You double-crossed me!"

"Jane! Jesus! What are you doing—"

"I'm here to slit your slimy throat, you sneaky rat!" Jane Parish dumped him back down onto the ground, then stared at her hands as if they'd been contaminated. With revulsion, she wiped them on her own jeans, and the look she sent down at him was filled with loathing. "You're the most disgusting excuse for a human being I've ever met, Keller. You betrayed me!"

He threw up his hands to deflect the blow he was sure she was aiming at him, then scrambled to his feet. "Honest, Jane, I didn't mean to be such a jerk. It just happened, that's all. I'm glad to see you—"

"You were a chickenshit, Keller! Admit it! You turned me in!"

"What the hell else could I do? That Colonel Pompowsky already knew you were there! Was I supposed to lie to him? To an agent of the United States government?"

Seething, she muttered, "My God, I wish I'd kicked your head in while you were snoring just now! *Yes*, you were supposed to lie!"

"I'm *sorry!* I should have helped, I know. But I couldn't think! And there wasn't anything else I could do to—"

"Don't give me lame excuses! You're trying to weasel out of feeling guilty, and I'm damned if—"

"I *feel* guilty, for crying out loud! Jeez, that's just about the only way I've felt since—"

"Just shut up! Do you have any idea what I've been doing for the past four days?" With teeth clenched, she commanded, "Go on, take a guess! Can you imagine what I've gone through?"

She looked wild and furious, her long hair coming out of the tight braid in tangled wisps, her chest literally heaving with anger. Her face was white with exhaustion except for her right cheek, which was smudged by the beginnings of a bruise. Her hands were dirty, and her clothes were rumpled and splotched. But there was fire in her eyes, and adrenaline had turned her mouth the color of dusky wine. Cleaned up, she'd have been magnificent. The sight of her filled Keller with an absurd bubble of pleasure.

But Jane jammed her forefinger into his chest. "I spent a day and a half being browbeaten by your friend Colonel Pomposity, and believe me, he enjoyed every minute of it! Then I engineered one very illegal escape and came up here with just one porter—and only enough food for a mouse, by the way. And all the while you and your pals have been enjoying one big fraternity party! You've been doing nothing but drink beer since I left, haven't you? I've been following puddles of piss like they were bread crumbs, Hansel!"

"I—we—everyone was being hospitable, that's all." Trying to explain, he said quickly, "These people are so poor, and selling food and supplies and things is at least an honest way to make a few dollars, so I was only trying to—"

"Oh, join the Peace Corps! Do you think you can change the economy by buying a six-pack at every shack in these mountains? Are you that much of a moron?"

"I don't think it's wrong to want to help these—"

She exploded. "What the hell do you know about wrong and right? Christ! You'd feed these people to the Abominable Snowman if it would make this trip easier for you! You're a thoughtless, self-centered—a stupid—I suppose you've even eaten my goat!"

"No, no, I took good care of her! Honest, she's around here somewhere, Jane. I—"

"Oh, shut up! I should have known better! I started this by myself, and I should expect to finish the same way! I just didn't—I only—"

Keller said, "I'm sorry you were alone."

Her taut face quivered suddenly, and for a split second her eyes glistened. Maybe he imagined it, but Keller suddenly wondered if Jane Parish was about to cry.

But she pulled herself together. With a monumental effort, she clamped her teeth tight and forbade the tears to fall. She swayed for a moment on legs as unsteady as a colt's, then she spun away and stalked out of the temple and into the sunlight. Without a good-bye, she started down the path past the prayer flags.

Keller trailed after her, wincing as the clear light of day pierced his eyelids. The pain was excruciating, but he forced himself to keep going across the terrace and down onto the path. "Hey!" he called, trying not to stagger, but clutching his head to keep the pounding at bay. "Look, I admit I wasn't exactly gallant before, but I can make it up to you, Jane. Really."

"Don't even bother," she snapped over her shoulder. "I just wanted to see your miserable face when I got up here, that's all. With all these witnesses around I won't commit cold-blooded murder!"

"Come on, I mean it, Jane! I'm really sorry."

"Save your breath."

"I *am* sorry." He chased her down the stony slope. "I can prove it! I can help you now."

"Forget it!"

"I know where your husband is!"

That stopped her. She wheeled around and glared at him.

"It's true," he said, halting at a safe distance in case she decided to throw a rock. "I heard about him from some wool traders."

Jane's expression did not change, except that her eyes narrowed coldly. "Are you lying?"

"No, I'm not. Really. On my honor."

She snorted at that. "You haven't got any honor, Keller. What did you hear?"

"That there's an American living up near the border. He's got blond hair. That's what they said, anyway. Does your husband—"

"Where near the border?"

"I don't know," he admitted. "But it shouldn't be hard to find out. The traders knew about him. Surely other people will, too. It could be him, couldn't it?"

Jane came back up the trail, her boots ringing on the stony ground. She eyed him suspiciously, not ready to believe a word yet. "Where are the men who told you this?"

"I don't know. They had a bunch of ponies loaded with rugs and things. They were headed down to someplace where there's a market. Not Jumla, but I forget where."

"What about the lama?" she asked, glancing around the temple for signs that the holy man might have materialized. "Does the lama know anything?"

Keller stepped down the path to her level. "I don't know. I haven't met him yet."

She backed up a pace, and her face registered disdain. "You slept in the temple without meeting the lama?"

"Well, it was late when we got up here and—"

"No doubt you were all drunk!" she burst out. "You're a prince, all right, Keller, a real example of what the civilized world can do with raw material."

"I learned something about your husband, didn't I? Isn't that worth something?"

"Not my undying appreciation, if that's what you're looking for."

"Jeez, lady, what do you want?"

She appraised him and answered at once. "I need porters, for one thing. And food. And equipment. I lost all my gear, I'll have you know. I spent months picking out just the right stuff, too. Shur and I only brought the clothes on our backs and sleeping bags."

"I see," he said slowly. "Well—"

Her laugh was short and full of scorn. "Where's that heartwarming generosity of yours now, Keller? You'll toss coins to the Nepalese—yes, I talked to the people you ran into—but you're not about to suffer a little discomfort yourself, are you?"

"I've got a few troubles of my own, you know." Trying not to sound plaintive, he said, "I'm still trying to find my father, remember."

"You want me to play the violin now? If you hadn't been plastered last night, you could have asked the lama and delivered your precious map this morning. Don't give me the soft soap! But now you've probably scared away the poor man and—"

"He'll turn up. Look, do you want some porters? My job should be over with today, and I can spare a man or two now that—"

"I don't want a man or two, Keller. I want them all. And I want you, too."

"Me?" That shook him. "For crying out loud, you want *me?*"

Lest her request sound remotely like a sexual come-on, she said hastily, "I want your stupid map, that's all, and your ability to read it, if it's true that's what you do for a living. I don't have any of the things I had packed before, maps included. Billy didn't have any, and now Pompowsky's got mine. I need to know where I'm going."

"That's all?"

She glared. "Of course. What do you think?"

Before he got into more trouble, Keller said, "Okay, okay. I'll get the map and you can look at it. We'll make some kind of copy if it's something you can use. Come on."

Jane followed as Keller hurried back up the path to the

temple. He crossed the terrace and nearly stumbled over Yamdi, who had toppled over and lay snoring in the doorway. His mouth was open, his eyelids were twitching, and he'd obviously urinated during the night without waking, because his baggy jodhpurs were soaked and reeking. He didn't budge when Keller's boot dragged across his chest. Jane halted, clearly unwilling to subject herself to the stench that a few drunken men had created in the temple during the course of one night. It was a wise decision. When Keller ducked into the place alone, the stink hit him in the face. He wondered if he smelled and looked as bad as the rest of the men.

The baskets had been left along one interior wall of the temple, and he found the map case sticking out of one. He picked up the case and returned to the sunshine and fresh air, unfastening the catches as he went.

"Here. It's a copy of an old map, but around here things can't have changed much in two hundred years."

Perhaps he did smell. Jane backed away from him. "The map is two hundred years old?"

"At least." Opening the case, he began, "Now, if you—"

But Keller's words died in his throat. For a hideous moment, he felt his whole bloodstream fill with ice. He stared into the map case and could not move.

As if from a faraway planet, Jane's voice said, "What's wrong?"

"It—it's not here."

Roughly, Jane wrestled the empty case out of his hands. "What do you mean? Where's it supposed to be?"

"The map—I put it there myself."

"What happened?"

"I don't know—I—"

Jane grabbed the sleeve of his jacket and jerked him around to face her. "When did you see it last?"

"It—in Kathmandu—before we got onto the plane. It was right here—"

"And you haven't seen it since then?"

"No."

"Christ!" Jane muttered. "Somebody's stolen it."

Chapter 10

COLONEL POMPOWSKY WAS IN JUMLA EATING A LEMON PIE WHEN his liaison from the Nepalese government interrupted him. *Liaison* was the official word. Pompowsky preferred to think of the man as his stooge.

"What is it?" he demanded when he caught sight of Stooge lurking in the doorway of the pie shop. "What do you want?"

Stooge entered nervously, clutching his clipboard with both his hands and hugging it to his chest. Pompowsky was not worried. Stooge always looked nervous.

But Stooge said, "The lady, sahib. She is gone."

Pompowsky, his wits momentarily dulled by the aftereffects of a splendid sugar high, demanded, "What lady? Gone where?"

"Missus Parish, sahib. She has run away."

"Christ on a crutch!" Pompowsky heaved himself to his feet. He snatched the paper napkin from around his neck and flung it down on the table. He was too much of a professional to scream.

"Goddamn," he said, shuddering with fury. "Goddamn! Which way did she go?"

Stooge stumbled back as far as the shop doorway. "We do not know, sahib. Perhaps back to the mountains. She wanted to go to Kol—"

"I know damn well where she wanted to go! Get some troops ready, Stooge!"

"Troops, sahib?"

"Troops, men, anything! I want action!"

"We have no troops, sahib. Just my own men—"

"Tell 'em to saddle up. We're leaving." Pompowsky led the way out into the street, oblivious to the unpaid shop-keeper who trailed after him, bleating.

Stooge caught up half a block away. He panted. "I know a man who could save us trouble, sahib."

Pompowsky stopped dead in the street. "What man? Spit it out, Stooge!"

"He is Pirim, sahib. He knows everyone who—well, who participates in criminal activities. There are few criminals in Nepal, sahib, but Pirim has spies and knows all. It is said that he even has a connection to the worst of bad men— Mohan Dok. Pirim can help us, maybe."

Pompowsky found a cigar in his pocket. When he got it unwrapped and into his mouth, he felt much better. "All right," he said. "Let's look up this Pirim character. I like the sound of him. He's going to lead us to the Parish woman."

Stooge said, "Or live to regret it, sahib?"

Pompowsky grinned. Stooge was learning. The Colonel put on his hat and led the way down the street.

Chapter 11

CONTROLLING HIS RAGE WITH EVERY OUNCE OF REMAINING strength, Keller said, "Jane, this whole thing—this whole fucking thing is getting out of hand."

"It's a mess, all right," Jane agreed. She sat down on a rock outside the temple and turned businesslike. "Did anyone act particularly interested in the map since you last saw it? Who wanted to look at it? Did you talk about it?"

"Sure, everyone seemed interested. They weren't supposed to *take* the damn thing!" He flung himself into a spate of pacing.

Jane watched calmly. "But you told everybody all about it. Very accommodating, Keller. You're such a gentleman."

"Well, this is it!" he declared, and he threw the empty map case to the ground. Vibrating with fury, he shouted, "This is the limit, Jane! This is where I stop acting like a fucking tourist. Goddammit, I'm not going to take this lying down!"

"Uh-oh," said Jane, nonplussed as ever. "I think I'm starting to hear theme music."

Keller began to pace. "I'll have to go back and find those wool traders," he muttered to himself. "They hate my guts, but that's just—"

"They hate your guts?"

"Yeah, we had—there was some trouble."

Jane folded her arms. "You're just spreading good cheer wherever you go, Keller."

He stopped short and grabbed Jane by her shoulders. She didn't flinch, so he gave her a shake. "Look, I've got to get that map back, lady! I've got no choice. You don't know what's at stake!"

She didn't get excited even though his fingers bit deeply into her flesh. Jane didn't move a muscle, in fact. Her eyes, Keller noticed suddenly, were very blue with flecks of dark gray in them. Serious eyes, but pretty ones. Her lashes were sandy, but very thick and curled. There were laugh crinkles at the corners of her eyes, too, but he'd never seen them in action. No doubt they were quite fetching. Her mouth would look different if she smiled, too. Softer. Suddenly, Jane disengaged herself from his grasp and eased back a step. Calmly, she said, "You'll start by having a talk with those men?"

Keller backed away uncertainly. "Yes, exactly," he said, though he'd lost some of the intensity he'd felt a minute earlier. "I—I'll go after them right away. Chances are they're the bastards who took the map."

"Well, I've got to talk to them, too," said Jane. "It's a logical place for both of us to start."

Caught off guard, Keller said, "Both of us? Wait a minute. You're not going to suggest we—that you and I become partners?"

She dusted off her hands as though she'd just dirtied them. "You have a better idea?"

"Jeez, yes! I don't need a woman along to—"

"Hold it," she commanded, stopping him short with the force in her voice and one finger aimed at his nose. "Don't start with this woman crap, Keller. I caught up with you guys, didn't I? After you'd had a two-day head start! Don't think you're better at this than me, buster! Besides," she added, taunting then, "I'm not so sure I even want to be on your side."

"What? Why not?"

"Why not?" she demanded, pretending to be amazed by his stupidity. "You betrayed me once already, remember? Don't expect me to trust you now!"

"You want to discuss trust?" Keller cried. "After what I learned from Pompowsky, lady, you haven't exactly been upfront about things. This trust stuff has to go two ways, you know."

"Forget it. I don't owe you any explanations. You'd probably go to Pompowsky and blab."

"He's got a right to know. If national security is at stake—"

"National security! What bullshit!"

"Pompowsky said—"

"Pompowsky's an idiot!"

"He said your husband is selling military secrets."

"My husband Roger," Jane explained with profound contempt, "wouldn't know a military secret if it bit him."

"Well, the Colonel says—"

"I don't give a damn about your chum the Colonel—or my ex-husband for that matter!" Jane whirled around and kicked at stone. "I hate them both."

Things just didn't add up. Baffled, Keller said, "Why are—Jeez, what the hell are you doing here if you don't even like your husband?"

She started away from him and snapped over her shoulder, "I don't have to tell you anything!"

"I know, I know." Doggedly trailing her, Keller said, "But hey, if we're going to be stuck with each other for a while, I thought you might at least—"

"Oh, shut up!" She stopped at the edge of the ridge and shoved her hands into her pockets.

Keller waited. Tentatively, he said, "Are you looking for your husband or not?"

"No," she said shortly, without turning around. "In fact, I hope Roger is dead and buried."

Keller said, "I don't—it's just—what are you doing if—"

"I'm looking for my son," said Jane, blunt and angry.
"What?"

She turned to look at him then, and her face was taut.
"I'm looking for my son, not my husband. Roger stole him
from me nearly a year ago. They came here and crashed and
I—I've got to know if he's still alive." Suddenly she was
trembling. "I've got to find my son."

Chapter 12

"JESUS CHRIST," JANE SAID, DESPISING HERSELF FOR BAWLING. "I hate women who are wimps!"

Keller turned insufferably sympathetic. He even scrunched his face into a sappy expression. "It's okay," he said. "Maybe a good cry would help."

"If you put your arm around me, Keller, I swear I'll bite it off!" Jane swung around on him, her anger renewed and the unhelpful emotions securely under wrap once more. "The only thing worse than a wimpy woman is a man who encourages her to be one! If you haven't got anything intelligent to offer, just keep your mouth shut. Have you got any tea or cocoa mix? I'm starving."

Keller recovered fast. "All right, sure." Pedaling backwards, he retreated toward the temple. "There's plenty of stuff to eat. I'll make a fire, how's that? We'll have breakfast. Anything you want."

"Good," she snapped.

Jane turned her back on him and untied the neckerchief from around her throat with a series of vicious yanks. When Keller was far enough away, she wiped her face with the neckerchief and allowed herself the luxury of leaning against an enormous rock by the side of the trail. The stone had absorbed the morning sun, and it radiated a comforting heat through the seat of her pants. Wearily, Jane climbed up and sat on it. Her fatigue was bone-deep, aching in her muscles and fogging her brain. She closed her eyes and held the neckerchief against her face.

She hadn't meant to blurt it all out like that. Until now, everyone thought she was looking for a missing husband, and that had been her plan all along. She had been afraid to broadcast that Roger had kidnapped Robbie. If Roger heard the baying of bloodhounds, heaven knew what he might do to the boy. Roger was not one to let himself get caught holding evidence against himself. Jane knew her former husband well enough to guess what he'd do to protect his precious reputation. Jane intended to find Roger herself and take Robbie on her own. She could do it, too. If only guys like Pompowsky didn't get in the way from now on.

She might have fallen asleep sitting there with the warm sun beating down and a fresh breeze rising off the mountain path. But listening to Keller as he roused the Sherpas and set them to work, Jane found herself mulling over the fact that she had waited until she found that ridiculous yuppie and his beer-guzzling cohorts again before she let herself succumb to exhaustion. She barely had enough energy left to be irritated by the realization that—unlikely as it seemed —she found herself feeling safer now that Keller was around again. What stone-age idea could have put that notion in her head? Did the simple presence of a man give her license to let go? Jane hadn't shed a tear since the whole mess got started, and one note of sympathy from Keller had suddenly rendered her a quivering nitwit.

She opened her eyes and glared at him. Perched on the rock, she watched while Keller coaxed the Sherpas out of their blankets and proceeded to scuttle around getting bits of firewood from the pack baskets himself. He was an improbable hero, all right. The last person on earth even a truly desperate woman would want to hook up with. A rumpled suburbanite on a goose chase. As she watched, he laid the firewood in a precise Boy Scout–approved arrangement and then dug a foil-covered matchbook from his trousers. Monogrammed matches from some spiffy restaurant in Washington, D.C., no doubt. Carefully, he crouched, struck a match, cupped one hand around the flame, and blew lightly on the twigs until they began to smoke. His concentration on the simple task was intense.

It did not escape Jane's attention that Keller had also managed to stay clean during his trek through the mountains. His expensive twill trousers still held a crease and were barely dusty. After he'd slept in it, his Georgetown sweatshirt looked a little wrinkled, but the white collar that peeked from underneath remained crisp. Judging by the small dusting of whiskers on his baby face, the man had obviously found time to shave each day. His hair, more blond now that he'd spent several days hiking under the intense, high-altitude sunlight, blew boyishly against his forehead.

The fire caught. Keller sat up, shook out the match, and made sure the rest of the twigs had caught and were burning. Then he glanced up and found Jane watching. He smiled at her shyly. An overgrown Boy Scout, all right, she decided. On the loose without his patrol leader.

Jane got up and dusted off her backside. She strode up the trail to him. "Keller?"

"Ready for something to drink?"

"Keller, listen. Maybe we can work something out."

Those words struck a chord of fear in Keller. He braced himself for what was coming from the indomitable Mrs. Parish.

Fortunately, she was interrupted by Yamdi before she could propose her next idea.

The young Sherpa came bounding up from the back side of the temple where he'd gone to perform his morning ablutions. He shouted gleefully and pointed upwards, fairly dancing with delight. "Here, sah! Look who I have found for you! The lama is at home!"

"Thank heaven," said Jane, sounding as if she meant the prayer. "Maybe we'll get some information."

She led the way up to the temple again, and they entered.

The Sherpas had cleared all the trekking gear off the temple floor. Keller didn't see any lama.

"Well?" he asked.

"Up," said Jane, and she pointed.

The Sherpas had apparently not allowed him to sleep in the temple proper. It seemed that the ground floor of the building was simply a lobby of sorts. From a corner, Yamdi pulled a heavy ladder made of logs. The Sherpa braced it on the stone floor and propped it against a narrow hole in the ceiling.

"You go first, Yamdi," Jane directed. She hung back, demonstrating shyness for the first time since Keller had laid eyes on her.

Yamdi obeyed, motioning them all to ascend behind him. Jane climbed next, and Keller followed.

The second floor was much more interesting than the waiting room below, Keller soon discovered. The first sight that greeted his eyes was a small fresco over the upper doorway. The carving depicted two naked, grinning human beings engaged in energetic copulation. The man's penis was exactly the same size as his chubby leg and most of it was buried inside the equally enlarged and detailed genitalia of his partner. Upon reaching the second floor, the Yamdi steadied himself by touching his hand on the buttocks of the frolicking woman. Jane pointedly did not glance at the carving, but Keller took his time. Local art deserved some appreciation, after all.

The main chamber of the second floor was a low-ceilinged platform of stone that jutted out over a cliff without benefit of a banister. The view of the mountains was spectacular. At once, Keller experienced the sensation of soaring out over the mist as if on a magic carpet. The valley seemed distant enough to be another world. The highest snow-covered peaks of the Himalaya loomed above, blocking the sky and wreathed in clouds. The clear air that rose from the valley was clear and biting in Keller's lungs.

By comparison, the room was small and cluttered as a Victorian parlor. An altar of sorts, rugs on the floor. Along the uneven walls were lined a series of crooked shelves that had been packed with scrolls. When he could find no more erotic carvings to study, Keller joined Jane, who stood looking at the array of scrolls with a kind of rapture glowing in her face.

"These are prayers," she explained, her fingers hovering over a scroll as if a single touch could crumble the ancient paper into dust. "There must be hundreds of them."

Her voice was hushed, and Keller stole a look at her face as she turned away from the shelves. To him, she looked as if the sight of the place had enlightened her soul. She studied the rest of the room with concentration, clearly trying to absorb every detail. On the walls were hung two tattered cloth paintings, both depicting humanlike figures in various poses of religious ecstasy. A stone altar stood center-stage and was littered with brass and bronze figures, all small and looking old indeed. A statue of a seminaked god with a Cheshire cat smile on his face and an abbreviated jockstrap clasped around his loins had been placed in the middle of the altar. Offerings had been left at his feet. Cups of grain, a necklace, some crude carvings.

Jane pointed to the floor. "Look at all these prayer stones, Keller. I've never seen so many. This temple must be eight hundred years old at least, judging by the number of stones here. Think of how many lamas have dedicated their lives to solitary meditation in this place." She shook her head. "It awes me."

Solitary meditation did not turn Keller on. He made a polite murmur just the same.

Suddenly, one of the stones on the balcony moved. Keller stepped back, then realized before he made a fool of himself that the stone was not an inanimate object but a man. The man stood up.

"The lama," whispered Jane.

The holy man was a wizened little fellow with skin the color of mahogany. He wore a thin and tattered toga with great dignity, and his feet were encased in a pair of wool booties that reached halfway up his skinny shins. His hair was black and tied up in a braid, and its color and coarseness intensified Keller's first impression that the man looked like a miniature American Indian. His cheekbones were high and flat, his eyes were wrinkled and heavy-lidded, and his expression was noble. But he stood barely five feet tall.

The diminutive lama shuffled into the temple. He stopped before Keller and regarded him with watery eyes.

Keller felt edgy. To Jane, he whispered, "What does he want?"

Jane had begun to rummage swiftly through her many pockets. At last she whipped out a small, flat paper packet. She unwrapped it quickly and stepped forward, elbowing Keller aside. Her hands were shaking as she presented the gift to the lama. To Keller it looked like a white handkerchief.

"What does this mean?" Keller asked as the lama accepted the gift with a sedate smile and bow.

"It's traditional," Jane replied, still whispering. She bowed her head over prayerful hands for the old man, then backed up a respectful pace. "One should bring a *kata,* a white scarf, for the *tulku.*"

"The who?"

"Tulku, the reincarnation of the lama who has lived here for centuries. After each lama dies, the people hereabouts start looking for his replacement, the same spirit in a different body. Within a few years, a child will make his presence known, and the people test him to see if he's really the reincarnation. Show some respect, Keller. This man's spirit has been around for centuries."

"How do they know this guy is the genuine article? What kind of test do they give him?"

"Not multiple-choice," she said. "They lay out the old lama's possessions mixed with—well, with some decoys. If the boy chooses the right things, he's obviously the tulku. The least you could do is bow."

He did. Then the Sherpas gathered around the lama, bowing and muttering. Keller found himself grinning at the pious performance put on by men who just the night before had caroused and sung obscene songs at the top of their lungs.

To Jane, he said, "Aren't you going to ask him about your son?"

"Soon," she said, gazing with something akin to rapture at the old man. "This is a big moment for me, Keller."

Yamdi had apparently gone back outside to rescue the precious fuel that Keller started to consume with the fire outside. The youngest Sherpa entered the temple, carefully carrying a few smoldering twigs in his hands. He laid them with great care into a small brazier in the corner and stood back. The lama took over from there. He added a little more fuel to the fire and proceeded to make tea. Jane and the Sherpas arranged themselves on the floor of the room to wait.

Keller didn't feel like wasting time with a damn tea ceremony. They had things to do. But Jane and the Sherpas sat Indian-style on the floor, and all of them looked ready to go into some kind of community trance. The lama shuffled around the brazier making preparations. He lit some incense. With resignation, Keller sat down, too. The floor was cold. If he tried to sit cross-legged, he'd cramp up for sure. He put his back against the wall and settled himself with legs outstretched in a spot where he could pass the time by studying the erotic fresco in greater detail.

The wait was interminable, of course. At such a high altitude, it took the better part of an hour for the water to boil. Keller eventually got bored with looking at the carving over the door. Everyone else seemed content to mutter and rock and generally look like a bunch of gurus in the wafting smoke of the incense—Jane included—but Keller grew bored and finally annoyed. Not to mention starving. He forgot his manners and was glad when the lama turned from the fire and offered him the first cup of tea before anyone else.

He reached for the cup eagerly, but found himself looking up into the weathered, but strangely ageless face of the lama. The old man did not release the cup, but gazed into Keller's eyes.

"Timi kaha gani?" he asked.

Baffled, Keller looked to Jane for help.

"Where do you go?" she translated, watching peacefully.

Keller frowned. "What does that mean? I've come here. I'm looking for my father."

She shook her head. "That's not what he means, Keller. It's a spiritual question."

"A—?" He let go of the cup, exasperated. "Oh, Christ, Jane, this isn't my thing at all. What am I supposed to say?"

The lama spoke again, addressing Keller so directly that it

was impossible not to look up at the old man. He talked at length in that odd, rhythmic language, then closed his eyes and pronounced some kind of benediction. He handed the tea down. Keller accepted the cup then and took a sip, as if commanded. He felt mesmerized by the old man's gaze. The lama watched expectantly, so Keller emptied the cup. The liquid was warm and felt good going down. But the aftertaste—herbal and very bitter—came as a shock. Keller coughed and his eyes filled with water. He knew right away that something was wrong. And it wasn't just the tea.

Jane said, "It's bad news, Keller."

Still choking on the tea, he looked at her, hardly aware when the cup was lifted from his hands.

"The lama says you've got a test coming," she said. "You're going to have a tough time on a long journey."

He coughed some more. "What?"

"There's danger and a spiritual crisis coming."

"What is this?" Keller clambered to his feet. "Predicting the future with tea leaves? What's going on?"

Jane was biting her lower lip anxiously. "He's been given a message for you, Keller. Your father's been kidnapped."

"Oh my God."

I'll kill him, Keller thought. A flash of rage like a hot bolt of lightning went searing through him. The Professor had done this to him. On purpose! The son of a bitch!

Seeing Keller rendered into a statue, Yamdi pitched in with the translation. "Papa is not here, sah," he explained earnestly. "He has gone with other men far north from here. They want you to bring a prize, sah."

"A prize? What the hell kind of prize—?"

"Not a prize," said Jane. "Ransom."

"Ransom?" Keller turned on her. "Then they're serious? Somebody really has kidnapped my father?"

"Take it easy, Keller. It looks like kidnapping, yes."

"Who?"

Jane questioned the lama and turned back. "The lama doesn't know. He received a message, that's all. He hasn't seen anybody. You're supposed to go to a checkpoint Kang-Mo."

"But who would do this?"

"I don't know, Keller." Jane reached for his arm to calm him. She held on tightly. "What are you going to do?"

He clutched his head and tried to think. "I don't know. I don't. Where the hell am I supposed to go again?"

"Kang-Mo."

Yamdi said, "A border checkpoint."

"Jesus. Where is it?"

Yamdi pointed. "North, sah. Very cold there. Snows aplenty, sah. The Forbidden Land."

Keller swore, then swore some more. Worse and worse. They might as well have chosen the North Pole, that's how accessible Tibet was. "God, we're going to have to meet the police."

"If we do, they'll arrest us for no permits."

Keller moaned. "What do they want for ransom? How much money?"

Jane let go of his arm. "The lama didn't mention money."

"What?" Keller looked at her. Then suddenly it dawned on him. "I get it," he said. "They want the map. Don't they? Jesus Christ. That's why he called me in the first place! He was in trouble."

He walked to the edge of the jutting stone and stared out at the mountains.

Jane came up behind him. The rest of the Sherpas hung back. She said, "What are you going to do?"

It took all his strength, but Keller steeled himself. "Find the map, I guess. No other choice."

She nodded and put her hands in her pockets. "We start with the bandits, right? If they stole it, they'll probably try to sell it someplace. And soon. All we have to do is follow their trail, get the map back, and head up to this Kang-Mo place."

Keller turned toward her like a man underwater. "We?"

"Well, sure," she snapped, bristling at his implication. Her eyes flashed. "I'll help. Hey, I've got to talk to exactly the same guys you do. And I speak the language, remember? We might as well go together."

"Jesus," he said, clearly appalled by the cards fate had chosen to deal to him. He should have stayed at home.

Chapter 13

MOHAN DOK WAS THE LAST DESCENDANT OF THE INFAMOUS Mohir Dok, Scourge of the Himalayan Plateau, and he was proud of it.

"I am the last of my breed!" he often shouted at his wife Didi. "Honor me!"

"Buzz off," said Didi, who had once slept with an American anthropology student, a young man who was supposed to be studying snow leopards, but spent most of his time wrapped up in blankets with the village women. He had taught Didi many uncouth things. She no longer tolerated her husband's habit of every afternoon dozing away in the sunny doorway of their humble home.

Resting in his favorite spot while Didi visited her sister, Mohan once reflected that in the eighteenth century, a great leader of men would not have put up with that sort of behavior from a stranger. Mohan's ancestor would have cut off a piece of that busy student! Put an end to his studying, that's what Mohir Dok would have done! Mohir, the Scourge, rode his marauding troop of bandits up and down the mountains, alternately pillaging or fornicating whatever he pleased. He particularly made a name for himself by stealing horses, riches, and fertile women from the Chinese.

"You are no hero!" his wife shrieked on regular occasions —usually when he roused himself from a chang-induced stupor long enough to knock over her spindle or make a mess of her cooking fire. "You are useless!" she railed.

Which was true. With a good deal less glory than his ancestors brought upon themselves, Mohan Dok supported his family like most middle-aged men in their settlement, not by banditing anymore, but by trading. Once a year, Mohan took yak-hair rugs made by his wife to a rug dealer at Kang-Mo who paid a few rupees for each rug. Mohan's wife Didi, a highly shrewd and industrious woman, was the creative force and financial supervisor of the family, and Mohan was painfully aware that he merely provided the labor of taking the rugs to market. So, in order to obtain some respect from his wife and her many relatives—most all of whom had turned up as Mohan's neighbors in their mountain settlement—Mohan learned to make the most of those trips to the outpost. He told tall tales of adventures he encountered along the way and spent a great deal of time resting up after his arduous journey. During those early winter months, the menfolk were coddled like babies, and even Didi didn't start nagging again until springtime.

The patience of the community wore thin when the snows stopped, however, so to deflect rising annoyance with their prolonged respite, Mohan and his compatriots began promoting their next journey. They sat in the sun all day, ostensibly planning the next foray to Kang while nipping from their pots of chang. Since the trip didn't change much from year to year, of course, these strategy sessions were mostly for show.

"What is there to plan?" Didi demanded when Mohan stumbled in for his evening meal. "What do you do out there all day?"

She was a suspicious she-goat, that Didi. "We make plans," he insisted.

"I think not!" She snorted. "You men get drunk and dream about girls. You dream about Dasain, you filthy man. She's a child! Your head is full of that girl! It shows on your face!"

"Shut up, she-goat!"

As usual, Didi wasn't far off. Rather than planning his next trip to Kang-Mo, Mohan had instead spent the summer plotting the seduction of the nubile daughter of his neighbor, Wim. Dasain was very pretty, but an exceedingly virtuous girl, however. One of the few women whose skin was not blacked by soot, she hid behind her veil and allowed men to see only glimpses of her luminous dark eyes. Mohan was particularly taken with the delicate orange bead that she wore on a golden thread pierced through her right nostril. Oh, she was a temptress! A suitable mate for the descendant of barbarian conquerors.

Driven to distraction over the girl, Mohan set out to win her love properly. Since he was past the age when romance occupied his every waking thought, his clumsy efforts occasionally backfired. From his wife's collection of woolen goods, Mohan stole a pretty shawl for Dasain. His beloved shyly refused the gift, but unfortunately, Didi discovered the theft in no time and—guessing her husband's adulterous purpose—punished Mohan by flinging him out of their tent.

"You and your penis can go freeze together!" she screamed for all to hear.

Oh, how the neighbors laughed at him for that! After months, they still brought up the incident as if it was a good, bawdy joke.

"Remember, Mohan, when your wife threw you into the snow?" asked his neighbor, Wim. "Your fingers were blue by morning!"

Not only his fingers.

By autumn, Mohan was happy to leave the settlement and head off to Kang-Mo with the yearly load of yak rugs.

He was happy for three reasons. First he wanted to get away from Didi. And, after many years, Mohan had finally managed to talk the rug dealer into giving him an extra three rupees apiece for the rugs. That gave Mohan money enough to buy a gift for Dasain without arousing Didi's suspicions. An expensive gift was sure to change Dasain's mind about him.

"She will adore me!" Mohan whispered, hugging himself into his blanket that night. He imagined Dasain's lovely slender arms winding around his neck in gratitude and nearly cried out with the pleasure of such an image.

He had found the ideal gift, too. It was a paper umbrella, painted in bright colors and made in a faraway land called Taiwan. The wily shopkeeper who sold him the splendid thing said it was perfect for a young lady who wanted to protect herself from the sunshine. Shading a woman's skin from the sun was a new concept to Mohan, and it sounded mightily exotic—just the thing for Dasain. Filled with excitement, he paid twenty rupees for the umbrella, and then carried it himself, not wanting to risk a pony stumbling and ruining his present.

On the way out of Kang-Mo the next day, however, disaster struck.

The caravan of men, ponies, and dogs rounded a bend on the high pass and came face to face with that damned American again. Mohan hated Americans in general, but this one reminded him distinctly of Didi's student—fair-haired and growing that bristly stuff on his face. Disgusting.

They had encountered this pesky tourist once already—at the cost of one valuable dog and a great deal of pride—and Mohan groaned when he saw the same American standing on the trail. He even had his stupid pet goat with him. A man who treated a goat like a dog was crazy. And craziness made Mohan nervous. When he stopped on the trail ahead of the American, the goat pranced right up to Mohan and bleated playfully.

A crazy American with a goat was bad enough, but this time he had a woman with him too, an immodest blond creature who wore tight trousers that outlined her legs to show every detail of her lower body. Like the other men in the caravan, Mohan muttered about her indecency, but he couldn't drag his eyes off her, either. She was an eyeful, all right. Pink lips and flossy hair. But tough. If she and Didi ever combined forces, there would be no safe place for a man to hide.

The woman stopped on the trail, blocking the path of the

lead pony. "Keller," she said, "these are the guys you met before?"

The American man didn't look too pleased about finding himself face-to-face with a caravan of hostile faces, but he stayed on the trail and didn't move aside. "Yeah," he said. "These are the ones. That's Edward G. Robinson over there."

"What? Who?"

"Never mind. Just let me handle this, will you?"

Mohan bustled to the front of the pony line, his right hand ready on his dagger. He grimaced ferociously to counter the fact that he carried the pretty paper umbrella in his other hand.

"Calm down, now," the American said to Mohan. "Yamdi, how about translating for us, huh?"

The young Nepalese boy, who'd been with the American before, scuttled nervously forward. "Yes, sah. Tell me anything."

The American cleared his throat and addressed Mohan directly. "Well, Ed, how was your trip? Successful, I hope?"

"Oh, for heaven's sake," said the woman. "Ask about my husband! Ask if they've seen him."

"Will you let me handle this, please?" the man insisted. "We don't stand a chance of finding your old man unless we get my map first. Ask if they've got it, Yamdi."

The woman protested. "You'll alienate them if you start with that! My husband first, Yamdi."

Yamdi gulped, then looked at Mohan and attempted to muster an ingratiating smile. "You mentioned seeing American before, *babu*," he said in Nepali. "Can you tell us where he is? When did you see him last?"

The boy addressed him as "father." Mohan was outraged by the insult. How old did the kid think he was, anyway? He drew his dagger and snarled. Assembling behind him, his men snarled, too. Together, they all bristled like a pack of wolves.

Yamdi scuttled backwards and collided with the woman. She wrapped her arms around him protectively and stared. "Good grief! They act like they're really going to use those weapons!"

"Shut up, Jane," said the American. Then to Mohan:

"Cut the Little Bighorn stuff, guys. I want to know what have you done with my map. Where is it?"

Yamdi's tremulous voice squeaked when he repeated the American's words.

Mohan didn't even listen to the question. He recognized a tough position when he saw one. Already he was sorry he had pulled his knife. His men actually believed all the stories about his daring bandit ancestors, and anything less than a complete victory over these hikers would disappoint them terribly. Wim hefted a rock, and Daw had his stick poised. Chances were good they'd spread the word of Mohan's cowardice all over the settlement if they didn't go through with the fight. On the other hand, Mohan knew if he outright attacked the tall American, he could very well get himself hurt.

"Well?" asked Wim in Nepali, sidling up behind Mohan. He asked, "What are you going to do?"

Scare tactics, that was it. Maybe he could frighten the American away. With a howl that would have done his ancestors proud, Mohan leaped forward and flashed his dagger. His men were so startled by his offensive that they stumbled after him, ready for a fight. Wim opened fire by hurling his rock.

Yamdi yelped, hit on the forehead by the flying stone. The woman jumped to his aid. "My God!"

The American dived sideways to avoid getting tackled, and he took refuge behind one of the ponies in the caravan. He grabbed the harness and spun the startled animal so that its body protected him. The pony's head swung around quick as a snake's to bite the American, but he seized the bridle and jerked the animal to a standstill. The Tibetan men froze, knowing exactly how much a good pony was worth. None of them wanted to kill the animal by accident.

Keeping one eye on Mohan's knife hand, the American proceeded to rip through the pony's load.

"Keller," the woman cried, "are these guys out of their minds?"

"What does it look like? Listen, Jane, I know these characters. They're not the Welcome Wagon."

"Maybe I should try to explain our situation to them. I could—"

"Jane," he said irritably, "these guys hate me. Get it? They aren't going to stand still and listen to my girlfriend try to—"

"I am not your girlfriend!"

"I only meant that they won't stand still for a lot of chitchat."

"What are you doing?"

"I'm looking for the map myself." He thrust the first pony aside and turned to the next beast. "Come on, you can help."

"That animal is going to bite you, Keller."

"It's just playful. Come on, will you? I—*Ouch!*"

"That's playful all right." The woman looked at Mohan and the men behind him. She was frightened, he could see. Her eyes were enormous. When Mohan took one threatening pace forward, she raised her voice in a musical singsong. "Kel-ler, I think you better watch yourself."

Warned, the American wheeled around. There was nothing for Mohan to do but attack. His men would respect nothing less. Mohan leaped on the American and tried to wedge his knife up under the American's throat.

The American was big, though. He was at least five inches taller than Mohan was, but neither one of them realized it until Mohan threw himself at Keller and found he could barely get his arm around the American's neck. The American reacted by ducking his head, getting his shoulder hooked under Mohan's chest, and rolling him sideways off his hip. Mohan went flying. A pony squealed and lashed out with his hooves, someone shouted, and the woman yipped, but all Mohan knew was that one second he was on the attack, and the next he was on the ground.

When he landed, he heard a crackle.

Mohan sat up and looked. When he realized what caused the sound, he screamed.

"Jesus," said the woman. "Keller, you squished his umbrella."

Keller wasn't sure what exactly went wrong. He had spent four days hiking across the most treacherous trails in the world and learned firsthand about survival in the wilderness without loss of life. Suddenly he again found himself face to face with the Tibetan Edward G. Robinson look-alike who still had his silver-handled knife. Until the broken umbrella sent him into a frenzy of rage, he hadn't looked serious about using the weapon. But suddenly he went berserk. Old Ed attacked Keller as if he had committed an atrocity punishable only by instant death.

"Keller! Watch out!"

Keller backpedaled frantically, but Ed tackled him with a technique that would have impressed any NFL scout. Keller's heart contracted before the blow, then all the air was driven out of his lungs and he whuffed a strangled *"woooof!"* Next thing, he was airborne and accelerating, but the ground came up fast. His mouth was soon full of dust and Keller realized—in quite a detached way, actually—that he was about to get the crap kicked out of him by a bunch of wild-eyed Tibetan gypsies.

They enjoyed it, too. They grunted and swung their arms and legs like windmills. Bursts of pain exploded along Keller's ribs and legs. Next, the inside of his head got very noisy, which was annoying because he couldn't think with the ocean suddenly whooshing around between his ears. He tried to roll, then felt the handle of the leader's dagger dig into his belly. Thank God it was just the handle. By some miracle Keller had the wits to stay on top of it. He'd be stabbed to death if he let them have it. They kept up the blows, but knowing he was outsmarting them about the dagger gave Keller comfort for a few seconds. Then the men started using their boots to realign his ribs, and he forgot about comfort. Keller flung both arms over his head and tried to curl up. It didn't work.

In a little while the kicking stopped. Keller's body went on throbbing in the same rhythm as the kicks, though, and that sort of threw him at first. Yes, the beating was over. Jane hovered around somewhere. He could hear her—talking fast and angrily, as usual. Probably she was nursing Yamdi's bruise while he himself lay dying. Typical.

Gradually, her voice got closer. "Keller? Oh, my God. Keller, wake up. Keller? Paul?"

Well, at least she arrived at his side before he made the big journey to the netherworld. He wasn't going to die alone. When Jane rolled him over onto his back, Keller heard a groan. It sounded like his.

"Oh, dear, oh, God." Jane pulled his head and shoulders into her lap, which was an even more agonizing position than laying on the ground, but he couldn't manage a protest. She rocked Keller like a baby and moaned. "I don't believe this," she said. "Oh, dear, oh, God."

Keller moved his left arm. Stiff already, but not broken. He tried flexing his jaw and learned another definition for the word *pain*. His legs throbbed. His head felt like it was moving inside—his brain spinning around inside the cranial cavity. Then by accident—and he would swear it was just an accident pure and simple—he somehow managed to close his mouth around a hunk of Jane's shirt. On the other side of that particular square inch of shirt—and honest to God, it was an *accident*, for crying out loud—was one of Jane's rather nice, round, female breasts.

Jane wrenched free. "Cut that *out!*" She dumped him in the dust again. "Trust you to think you could get away with *that* at a time like this! You're just fine, you son of a bitch. Open your eyes!"

She was right, of course. Keller risked opening his eyes and saw that the sun and sky were still in the right places. He hadn't gone to heaven. Gingerly, he slipped one hand along his side to see if his ribs were stable. He winced.

"I think you'll live," Jane snapped.

He sent a glower up at her and was surprised to see that somehow she had changed in the last ten minutes. In spite of her anger, Jane looked scared. She was pale, and her features looked stark—as if she'd just aged about ten years. Sounding not at all like herself, she asked, "Can you sit up?"

He did it by himself. The effort caused him to suck in a great big breath of air, and the resulting pain jabbed him in the ribs again, but he managed. He soon discovered, of all things, that his face hurt terribly. That was a new experience. Keller touched his cheek with the palm of his hand and tried moving his jaw laterally. There was grit on his tongue, and he gathered himself to spit it out. A splotch of blood landed on the ground along with the spittle. Keller stared at it.

Jane said, "Are you okay? Enough to walk?"

"I think," he said carefully, "I'll just stay here for a while."

"What if those guys decide to come back?"

Keller glanced around swiftly. The wool traders and their ponies had vanished. In fact, everything at all had vanished except for Yamdi, who sat wide-eyed on the ground nearby hugging his pack. The rest of the porters had disappeared. All that remained of the wool traders was a pile of pony dung and the silver-handled knife, which both lay in the dirt beside Keller.

He picked up the knife.

"They stole everything," Jane reported when she saw he still had all his wits. "Everything is gone except my pack and Yamdi's."

"What? My gear, too?"

She nodded. "Stolen. The rest of the equipment and firewood is in the packs that the porters were carrying, but they ran away. So—so did Lambchop."

"The porters *ran?*" Keller sat up and scanned the desolate countryside for signs of fleeing porters.

"Yamdi is still here, but the others—"

"Those no-good bastards! What do they think I'm paying them for?"

"They were scared. Give them time to think, and maybe they'll come back."

"They damn well better."

"If they're smart, they won't." Jane scanned the surrounding rocks. "Let's not panic until we know what we're up against," she said. "Come on. We have to find a place that's more sheltered. We're sitting ducks here. Can you stand up?"

He could, but not without her help. When he got to his feet, Keller paused to slide the dagger piratewise into his belt. He felt better having it there.

Jane put her arm around his waist. "If we bathe those bruises soon, you won't look like you're going trick-or-treating. Yamdi, is there water near here?"

Yamdi clambered to his feet, jabbering in his own language. He was scared, which rendered him incapable of speaking English.

"Okay, okay," said Jane, soothing him. "Let's get out of here."

Keller couldn't seem to get his legs working without her

help. Leaning on Jane, he stepped carefully, squinting at the ground to be sure of each foothold. His right knee didn't work properly, and he limped. Yamdi, muttering nervously in Nepali, led the way back up the trail and across an outcrop of rocks. In a few minutes, Keller saw where the Sherpa was headed. On a small ledge above the rocks lay a small spring of water. Keller heard bubbling first, but he couldn't see it. Yamdi made straight for the sound and soon brought them upon a hidden pool.

Keller paused to catch his breath after the climb, but Yamdi quickly sat down on the flat rocks that surrounded the pool. The stones looked as if they had been carefully placed there by human hands, but heaven only knew how long ago. A misty steam rose from the smooth surface of the water.

"A hot tub!" said Jane, and she assisted Keller to a sitting position opposite Yamdi. "A natural hot spring. Just what we need. Good thinking, Yamdi."

Yamdi plunged his hands into the milky-colored water of the spring and then splashed his face. "Warm, warm!" he insisted, smiling.

Warily, Keller tested the pool with his hand. He wasn't eager to inflict any more discomfort on himself, but the water was warm indeed. Cautiously, he splashed some on his face and was relieved to feel the soothing begin at once. The heat was sure to help his knee. He untied his boot laces, slowly removed the boot and sock, and proceeded to roll up his trouser leg. When he submerged his aching knee, he released a sigh.

Meanwhile, Jane had unstrapped her backpack and slung it on the ground. She crouched down and got busy sorting through the contents. In a few minutes, she sopped some bit of fabric in the pool, wrung it out, and climbed over to Keller.

"Here," she said. "Let's have a look at you."

With surprising gentleness, she tilted his face up to the sunlight and began to sponge his bruises. At first it felt good, but her hands were shaking. Keller winced.

"Ow!"

"Come on, this will help."

"It hurts, dammit. What are you using? A bristle brush?"

"It's a sock. Yours, in fact. I must have been carrying the pack with the dirty laundry in it."

"Give me that!" He snatched it away from her. Sure enough, it was one of his own dirty socks, but in her hands it had felt like a scouring pad. He glanced at her and observed, "You're shaking like a leaf."

She sat up stiffly. "I am not!"

"You are, too." He applied the wet sock with care to his aching left eye. Right-eyed, he looked at Jane. "What's the matter? I'm the one who got pulverized."

Jane's face tightened stubbornly. "I was scared, damn you."

"Scared? You?" Keller laughed shortly. "The woman who escaped the United States Army and climbed the Himalayas by herself is scared?"

"I wasn't—I didn't expect this." She stood up and paced away, then spun around and faced him, pale and quite abruptly trembling all over. "I knew this expedition was going to be tough," she said, "but—those men were *violent*! They're supposed to be Buddhists!"

"Looks like they missed a few Sunday school lessons lately."

She glowered. "Don't make jokes, please."

Keller shrugged. "It wasn't so bad. You're still alive, aren't you?"

"But *you* aren't! Not completely, anyway. You could have been killed. They're supposed to have respect for life!"

Keller waved off her objections. "They were mad at me, that was all. It was a personal thing. You probably would have done all right with them if you'd been alone, but they have a thing against me." For some reason, Keller found himself belittling the fact that he had narrowly escaped execution by stabbing at the hands of a frenzied bunch of barbarians, but he couldn't seem to stop. "It probably looked worse than it really was."

"It's not enough to be brave, is it?" Jane asked, staring at him. "You've got to be cool, too."

"Honestly, Jane," Keller said, suddenly very, very tired, "it's no big deal. I don't even have any broken bones."

She clamped her teeth, struggling inside. "Look," she said evenly, "I've been training and planning and preparing for this trip for months, but I wasn't ready for—I didn't think . . . Just seeing you on the ground down there made me realize something very important for the first time, Keller."

"What's that?"

Jane stood very still and said in a low, scratchy voice, "I think we could die up here."

Keller laughed. He just couldn't help it. The whole situation was just ridiculous all of a sudden. She'd come this far without even considering the concept of death looming around every rock in this godforsaken place. It hit him as funny. Keller chortled drunkenly and threw his head back to really let it out when he realized that in spite of the fact that she was glaring at him, there was a quick sparkle of tears glistening in Jane's eyes. He coughed, choked down his laughter, and tried to reassemble a somber expression, but it was all too late. Jane turned away.

She yanked off her parka.

"Hey," said Keller, "I'm sorry. It struck me funny, that's all. Up till now you've been Mata Hari and Amelia Earhart and Margaret Thatcher all rolled into one, and I—well, I've been a terrified jerk most of the time, but now—"

"Shut up," she said and threw the parka on the ground. "I'm human! Maybe I'm not as tough as you think. Yamdi," she said, putting her back squarely to Keller, "we need food and shelter for the night. Keller won't be able to walk on that sore leg of his. Are there any supplies left?"

"No, missus." As Yamdi gazed up at her, his expression was both apologetic and full of curiosity at the same time. Clearly, he was fascinated by the subtleties of their dialogue, not to mention Jane's uncharacteristic emotion, but he rallied to answer Jane's questions. "No food in any of these packs, missus. And only two sleep bags left. No tent. No tea."

"Then you'll have to go to Kang, I suppose. It's only a few hours' walk, isn't it?"

"Yes, missus."

"Can you go alone?"

Yamdi stood up eagerly. "Oh, yes, missus. And be back before night comes! I will bring food and more porters, maybe." He blinked uncertainly. "Is there money?"

"Sure." Jane shoved her hand into the pocket of her jeans and came up with a neatly rubber-banded roll of paper money. "There isn't much left, but here." She handed it to the young Sherpa, and he tucked his fingers around it. "I'll trust you to get as many supplies as you can for that."

"Very good, missus. You can trust me very well. I will hurry back."

Jane squeezed his hand and released him. Formally, she said, "Thank you, Yamdi. You're a brave fellow."

Overcome with the pleasure of hearing such praise from her, Yamdi backed up and bowed again and again. "The sahib will take care of you, missus, until I come back. Do not worry. His leg is not bad. Do not worry about anything."

The young Sherpa took his leave. Keller waved goodbye and settled back to relax. Jane hunkered down again and unlaced her boots—first angrily picking at the laces and then jerking them loose. She kicked them off, and her socks came next. Barefoot, she sat back and pulled her sweater over her head. By the jerking swiftness of her movements, Keller could see that she was still upset. She threw her sweater on the stones.

"Hey," he said, figuring he'd better try to make friends again. "I'm sorry."

"There's nothing to be sorry for."

"I'm sorry I made fun of being scared." When that had no effect on her, he said, "I was scared, too. I was just joking around afterwards. If I can't make fun of what happened, I'd be quivering like a rabbit."

She looked at him, eyes narrowed. "Like me."

"No, not like you. You've been brave from the start."

"Only when there wasn't anything to be brave about. I can walk up hills just fine, but those men—that was something I wasn't ready for." Jane hugged herself. She wore only her cotton turtleneck shirt and shivered suddenly. Ducking her head, she said, "They might have killed you."

"No, they wouldn't have. Buddhists probably get eternal damnation if they murder stupid Yankee tourists."

She frowned. "There you go again. Making fun."

"Only on the outside."

"True courage," she said, only half-mocking and studying his face. "We all can get through something really scary on adrenaline. But afterwards when—well, some people can get casual about what they've done and others fall apart. You—" But she shook her head, lowered it again, and didn't finish. In a moment, she asked quite humbly, "What should we do now?"

"You want to give up?"

Her head snapped up. "No! No, I don't want that. But I—look, seriously, if anything happens to you or Yamdi or any of the porters because of my plans, I—I'd never forgive myself."

"Nothing else is going to happen." Keller tried to smile encouragingly. "Really. Tomorrow we'll go into Kang-Mo ourselves and ask around about your husband and the map. Maybe those guys talked or sold the map to somebody. We won't quit just because I got roughed up a little."

She seemed glad to have someone else say that. "All right," she said finally. "What do we do now?"

"Recuperate," said Keller.

And he went back to soaking his face. With the wet sock plastered on his eye and the sunlight beating down on the stones around him, Keller didn't become completely aware of Jane's actions until she stood up again. She stripped off her cotton turtleneck and dropped it on the stones. Keller stared at her and let the sock drip down his shirt. Next she unfastened her bra and let it fall, too. Mind-bogglingly barebreasted, she unsnapped her jeans and shucked them down over her haunches. Her panties followed, and Jane was suddenly very, very naked.

Keller didn't move or breathe. She walked straight into the hot spring and lay down on her back in knee-deep water, her eyes closed. She floated, and the tension seemed to leave her body with the steam that rose from the pool.

Oh, Keller had seen his share of naked women before, all right. It wasn't the bare female skin that startled him so thoroughly as he sat there on the hot stones. It was *Jane's* bare skin that rendered him speechless. With her small bare breasts and long, curving belly pointed straight up at the wide open sky and the sun pouring down on her like the gawking stares of a thousand astonished men, Jane was more naked than any woman Keller ever saw before. She had no tan lines, she had no tan. Surely he was dreaming.

The water slipped around her thighs in little currents and lapped at her breasts. Ripples eddied from the erect points of her nipples. Her pale skin shimmered beneath the water's cloudy whiteness. She was a vision.

With her eyes still closed, she whispered, "Are you staring?"

The husky whisper caught him off guard, and he couldn't help himself. He jumped.

"You are, aren't you?"

"Of course not. Think I've never seen a naked lady before?"

She kept her eyes shut. "It feels good."

He swallowed. "I'll bet."

Then, in a voice that had turned positively dreamy, Jane said, "I'm glad you're here, Keller."

Things change, he thought.

She opened her eyes and rolled over onto her belly. With her slender legs floating out behind and her beautiful, water-slick bottom bobbing on the surface of the water, she caught the end of her long braid in her hands and began to unfasten the rubber band on it. Watching Keller's face, she unbraided her hair. She ducked her head and let her hair fan out around her. Her body was only partially concealed. On her lashes clung droplets of water, but Jane's eyes didn't waver as she lay there and looked at him.

Cupping her chin in her hands and frowning a little, she studied him. "You know, with a few bumps and bruises on you, Keller, you look kind of dashing."

"Dashing," he repeated.

"Sure. They're your first battle scars." Jane smiled. "And they're not bad at all."

That was a cue if he ever heard one.

Chapter 14

HE GOT OUT OF HIS PANTS WITHOUT TOO MUCH HOPPING around on one foot and left his clothes in a heap on the stones. The water was very warm, and he sloshed through it to stand over her.

Jane raised one eyebrow at his alert penis and then looked into his eyes and started to grin. "Well? Coming in?"

Keller splashed down and gathered Jane into his arms, all the compact leanness of her. She wasn't surprised, but she laughed unsteadily. The water made her skin feel taut, her curves subtle, and he took a quick inventory of them all, hurrying in case she decided to nix the whole idea. Her hips were rounder to the touch than they were to look at. Then Keller slid around to fill each of his hands with one of her buttocks. He closed his eyes and squeezed.

Jane laughed. "You've wanted to do that."

"Oh, yes."

She lolled her head back into the water, and floated, at ease with her nakedness and his. "Maybe I'm crazy, Keller," she said, blinking up at the revolving sky while he concentrated on the massage of her luscious bottom, "or maybe this whole mess is getting to be too much for me."

"Maybe," he agreed, only half paying attention to her words.

"And maybe this isn't the right time," she said thoughtfully, "but we'll never get a better place, will we?"

"Let's not take the chance," he agreed. His voice didn't sound right anymore, so he decided to skip any attempt at conversation and kissed her.

She seemed to like that idea, too. She wound her arms around his neck and drew him down until their lips hovered within an inch of each other. Her eyes were smoky, and her voice went whispery. "Let's," she said.

He hesitated for about a microsecond and then put his mouth on hers. Their lips met and ground together almost at once, then parted and seemed to melt into one fused, breathless, intoxicating unit. She tasted sweet and hot, and her tongue was like molten candy. She touched him to sort of get acquainted, and then she cupped him, and her thumbs started tracing exquisite patterns on his tenderest parts. Keller held still, ground his teeth, and hung on, for in spite of Jane's chaste serenity up until now, she sure knew a thing or two about tumescence. When she bent and opened her mouth and swallowed him down to his roots, Keller must have let out a groan, because she giggled, and the vibration of her laughter just about ruined him.

On top of the world, exposed to the sky like that, with no living thing stirring for mile after desolate mile and the enthralled essence of his manhood captured in the mouth of a ripe and lustful woman, Keller felt as if he was living the last-man–last-woman-on-earth scenario. They were alone together, primordially naked and bathing in the lava-heated juices of the inner earth. The sun alone acted as witness to their rampant desires. To make the fantasy complete required a primal fuck, and—miracle of miracles—that's exactly what Jane seemed to have in mind. Maybe it was stupid—definitely it was impulsive. Maybe it was the culmination of days of terror and exhaustion, but the feeling was glorious just the same. With her mouth and tongue generating an almost overwhelming pandemonium in his scrotum,

Keller knew somehow that Jane, who held back nothing when it came to survival, was also capable of intense and probably demonic sexuality.

He seized a handful of her hair and pulled her head back. Fiercely, he began to nuzzle her long throat, but her breasts were too close to ignore, and he bent closer to suck them—first one, then the other, harder. He licked the water off her belly, rubbed his face between her breasts, gnawed her collarbone, and inhaled the scent of her body like an aphrodisiac. Her nipples were in his mouth after that, and he made the most of their succulent texture.

"Easy," she said, laughing again. "There's lots of time."

He couldn't slow down, though. He wanted to try everything, touch everything. Her bottom fit his hands perfectly, and from that grip he pulled her thighs apart. Foreplay was in order, but there just didn't seem to be time. He found a hot cleft between her soft thighs, and Jane gasped.

"I'm sorry," he said. "I'm really sorry. I can't, I can't—"

"Don't fuss," she said. "It's great."

She pulled him down by his shoulders and gave a quick hitching kind of hump that buried him deeply inside her. He gasped too and she murmured to him—words he couldn't decipher but understood nonetheless. He went into action and got some momentum going in no time. It *was* great. With each thrust, Keller felt indescribably potent—more of a male animal than he'd ever been before. It was superb! Jane struggled to keep pace with him, but she finally gave up and threw her head back to the sky, her mouth open to breathe great gulps of cold, cold air.

She looked mindlessly ecstatic that way—like the faces in the erotic frescoes of Buddhist temples. Her expression was filled with energy and pleasure and lust for more. Her cheeks were flushed, her half-closed eyes fiery. Her excitement entranced him, and suddenly Keller wanted to see her even more so. He pulled out of her and, clutching her bottom in his hands, he lifted Jane's hips above the surface of the pool and pressed his mouth against the open flower of her vagina. With his lips and tongue, he set out to probe the limits of her self-control. Jane squirmed and cried out, warm water streaming across her body and down between her legs. She seized his hair in her hands and cried out.

Laughing madly, Keller reared back and rolled her over onto her knees. She panted and laughed with him breathlessly. She met each of his thrusts with one full-throated cry after another. He milked her nipples, caressed her underbelly, squeezed her clitoris, all the while thrusting deeper and deeper into her, into the dark passage of Jane's most mysterious soul. Suddenly she began to moan, and it quickly escalated into a groan that sounded almost as if it was being torn from her throat. Every muscle of her body began to shudder. Keller withdrew from her, wanting to feel the contractions with his fingers when she came. He held her belly with one hand and dove inside with the other. Her spasms were strong and wracking, and he coaxed them rhythmically until she let go a cry of pure exultation.

Hearing her hoarse voice, and with an almost primeval steam rising from her flesh and his own still-vital arousal, Keller experienced a moment in which he recounted every erotic act he had ever contemplated. From every wet dream and written *Playboy* fantasy to the crudely graphic images of the X-rated movies of his adolescence, he saw them all in a flash. And he wanted them. Suddenly, here on top of a mountain at the top of the world with a heady woman such as Jane, he thought he could have them.

Perhaps she heard his unshouted wish, because she turned to face him. Her eyes were bright, her features taut. "Not yet," she said.

With her lips, she explored every inch of him. His ears, his neck, his mouth all withstood the inspection. But when she bathed his erection and took it in her mouth, caressing his thighs and in between with feather-light fingernails, he nearly died.

"Shout," she whispered when she came up for air. "Let it out."

He grabbed her arms and pinned her on her back at the water's edge. He pushed inside her again and found he was overjoyed to be there. In no time they were splashing and screwing the daylights out of each other. He shouted like a fiend and so did she, and all the while the sun and clouds wheeled in the sky around them, and the earth pulsed with the joy of life. They were on top of the world, an offering held up to the sky like a human sacrifice, only they were not dead—no, far from that. Keller felt wild and primal. Life had never been so intense. His veins were seething, his brains on fire. He fucked and fucked and learned to love the word, and Jane struggled and bucked and yelped until she was drained, but he bullied her to the edge time and again, wringing one more orgasm and then more again.

"Enough!" she cried. "I can't anymore!"

But he laughed and plowed relentlessly until at last in one glorious explosion, he spurted all the raw fire within him, the stuff that began life and drove men to madness. He howled and reveled like a beast—a triumphant, bedeviled male beast, happy to be alive, happy to have exhausted a seemingly tireless woman, happy to be at the summit of the world with his penis buried like a staff in the fertile richness of a sated female vessel.

Jane collapsed weakly, barely able to hold onto his shoulders to keep from drowning. She panted and looked at him with a wild-eyed kind of wariness, as if she didn't believe he was really finished. The mist from the water wafted up around her face, and she looked like an angel. A bedraggled, tired, and earthy angel who had just been thoroughly ravaged. Her lips looked ripe and rich, and he kissed her.

When she had caught her breath and could speak, she said, "I never guessed you were the type."

He grinned and humped her a little, still stiff inside. "What type?"

"The uninhibited type. The type to *enjoy* it so much."

"I don't—not usually, I mean. This was great, Jane. I felt like the whole world was right here." He squished in and out of her one last time and watched through the water, fascinated all over again by the interplay of bodies and the mysterious sensations that drove men and women to throw away their learned inhibitions and behave like the rest of the animals in the kingdom. "I like sex, but this was more, wasn't it? I feel like I've just been going through the motions until now."

"Then you've learned something."

"What?"

"That sex can be an affirmation of life, I guess." She yawned and stretched her arms over her head. "I had forgotten that myself. There's a moment when the physical body doesn't matter and your soul can fly and unite with the cosmos, a state of grace. What makes it truly beautiful is that there's someone to share it when it happens. You went beyond yourself, and the result was intense pleasure."

Dubiously, he said, "Well, maybe. Or it could have been the altitude."

She had enough strength left to dunk him.

"You're a jerk, Keller," she said, laughing. "A closed-minded pig."

"Oh, come on," he said, finding a place to settle in the water. He wallowed pleasantly there and splashed water at his bare feet sticking up. "Do you really believe that stuff?"

"Certainly."

"That one-with-the-cosmos junk?"

"Of course. You said yourself that you felt it. There has to be more to sex than—than, well, feeling good and making babies. It's a chance for us to learn more about our place in the universe."

Keller sighed and lay down in the water. The air was too cold to be sitting up discoursing on the meaning of life.

"You've never felt it before," Jane continued earnestly, "but I have. There is a greater system—one we don't understand completely yet, but it binds us together."

"It sounds like The Force."

She sat up and hugged her bare knees. "You can make fun because you don't understand it. But I know it exists. There's a special bond—I've felt it only with my son, but it's there. It's like telepathy, but not so specific."

"What are you talking about?"

"The feeling that exists between me and Robbie," she insisted. "There's a link between us—I can't describe it. I just—well, it's still here," she said, vaguely gesturing at a spot halfway between her breast and her throat. "It's here, and that's how I know he's still alive."

Keller sat up and stared at her. In an instant he forgot all about sex and primal yelling. Had he heard right? "What do you mean?" he asked.

"I know he's alive."

"Are you saying," asked Keller, "that you came all the way up here to look for your kid because of some kind of ESP message? Did you go to a seance or something? Are you *crazy?*"

"No," she snapped righteously. "I am not crazy. I *know* he's alive, that's all. I don't need any more proof than what I carry inside. He's a part of me, and I'd know if he were dead."

"My God," said Keller.

"It may sound strange to you, but you'll learn what I mean. There's hope for you, Keller."

"You expect me to start believing in hocus-pocus?"

"I think you're a thinking man—in spite of the act you put on. You're like my ex-husband in a lot of ways, but you have potential."

"Potential? How do you figure?"

"You've changed since you came to this country. You've already learned a lot about yourself, haven't you?"

He eyed her. "What did you mean by that crack about your husband? How am I like him?"

She shrugged and toyed with the end of her hair. "Lots of ways. Maybe all men are the same—"

"How?"

"Acting brave when you're really scared shitless. What's so terrible about being afraid? It's an emotion like all the others. There's no shame in it. But you men think it's a blow to your image if you show the least bit of fear. It's ridiculous. I'm glad you're not a fanatic about it."

"What do you mean?"

"You haven't minded looking like a fool now and then."

With care, he said, "Oh, yeah?"

She continued blithely. "Roger would face Armageddon like a combination of Errol Flynn and Bubba Smith—with his sword drawn in one hand and a crushed beer can in the other. But you're more sensible."

"I am, am I? I suppose you think that makes me less of a man?"

Jane sat up and blinked at him. "What?"

"I didn't turn you over to Pompowsky without a fight,

you know. And I did my best against those bandits, but
there were three of them, and they had weapons—"

"Hey, I meant to compliment you!"

"By calling me a fool?"

"Look, I only meant—"

"You think I haven't got the guts to go after those guys?"

"You *shouldn't* go after those guys! That would be stupid.
Keller, I'm on your side! You're *smart* not to chase them."

"Smart," he snapped, "isn't everything!"

Jane sputtered a laugh and choked on it, and Keller
decided to make a stomping exit from the pool as a grand
finale. The drama of the moment was spoiled by the fact
that the afternoon had waned, and the temperature of the
air was nearly freezing. By the time he dried himself with
his shirt and clambered into his pants, he was shuddering
with cold.

"Listen," said Jane, still sitting in the warm water, "I
divorced the man because he was a pompous, gun-toting
maniac. Every time we made love, he wanted to tie me up
and put a gag in my mouth. Does that sound like an
admirable kind of guy, Keller? I mean, just think about the
reasons why he felt he had to overpower his wife, who was a
teenager and half his weight. The guy was nuts. He still is.
Don't compare your manhood to his, Keller. It's not worth
the effort."

"I suppose," said Keller through chattering teeth, "that
he'd be hot on the trail of those bandits by now, though,
wouldn't he? If somebody hassled him, he wouldn't take it."

"Nobody," said Jane, "ever hassled Roger."

For some reason, that information infuriated Keller immeasurably. He jammed his feet into his boots. "Old Roger
is a real man, is he?"

"*He* thinks so."

"You must have, too. Once, at least."

"Sure," said Jane, splashing composedly in the water. "I
thought he was pretty neat once. He was a big, swaggering
Navy man with money in his pockets. At one time, that was
exactly the kind of man I wanted to be around."

"Yeah?" Keller challenged.

Jane lay down in the pool, and when she spoke again, it

was to the sky. "Keller, my life's story isn't especially romantic. I was fifteen when my father practically sold me to Roger Parish, and I've done a bunch of dumb things since then, but I'm learning, okay?"

Keller sat down on the stones beside the pool. "He sold you?"

"What?"

"Tell me the rest. What do you mean your father sold you?"

She sighed, then looked at Keller. "It's not—all right, I grew up in a podunk place in West Virginia. Things were still pretty rustic there when I was growing up. My daddy farmed, and he—after a while he needed money to buy the place where we lived. Roger Parish came along—he was visiting relatives in town, or something—and he came out to buy whiskey from my grandad. He—well, he loaned my father the money for the farm."

"And?"

She looked at him. "And I was the collateral."

Keller didn't say anything.

"Okay, I was stupid," she said roughly. "I was fifteen and knew only that I wanted out of that place. I didn't have any idea what kind of man a woman ought to look for. I saw a chance to get off that farm and see the world with a good-looking Navy man."

"What happened?"

"I saw the world, all right." Jane grinned. "Looking out from behind the fences of Navy bases. We lived in Germany and the Philippines—you name it. Roger saw the countries from the cockpits of Navy fighters, and I sat in dingy apartments and got fat."

"Fat?"

"Pregnant."

Keller murmured something that must have sounded like a sympathetic remark, because Jane sat up and glared at him, her eyes narrow all of a sudden. "Does this wonderful story surprise you, Keller?"

"No, no. Well, sure, I guess. I didn't expect—"

"Don't I look like a barefoot hillbilly girl to you?"

"No," he said with all honesty.

"Well, then," she said with some satisfaction. "I must have managed all right."

All this was very, very interesting to Keller. Unable to stop himself, he asked, "So what happened? To your marriage, I mean?"

"It didn't work, of course. It did for a while, because Roger liked me. I was young and not bad looking and didn't give him any lip the way the other wives did. I was dumb, and he liked it that way. And of course, he liked—" Jane caught herself, glanced at Keller, and surprised him by blushing. In a rush, she said, "But I wised up. I met some interesting women along the way—women who really taught me things like—well, self-respect. Lana Briskine was my friend and a—a big influence on my life. Roger spent most of his time with the other guys, and I had time to read and talk to people like Lana and—really grow up, I guess. He didn't like what I turned into, and after a while, I didn't like him very much, either."

"What about the kid? Didn't Roger—"

"Oh, Roger liked the idea of kids at first. They were proof that he was a man, I guess. But I had two miscarriages before Robbie was born, and Roger didn't like the ordeal of those at all. When Robbie lived, Roger preferred to ignore him. In case he died, I guess. Roger didn't mind divorcing me when the time came. I think I was too old to suit him after I hit voting age, and Robbie didn't interest him either."

"But if he didn't care about the boy, why has he taken him? Why bring the kid clear up here if he didn't even like him?"

"Oh, Roger just didn't like Robbie when he was a baby. After the divorce, when Robbie was about six or seven and old enough to be fun to play with, Roger took an interest in him. Roger didn't change diapers or teach shoe-tying, but he wanted Robbie to learn about guns and military maneuvers and oh, all that stuff. The older Robbie gets, the more Roger wants to—to influence him."

"What do you think about that?"

"I hate it, of course. Roger is a warmongering crazy man who—who probably looks forward to the day he can take his son to his first prostitute. He's that kind of guy. He knows I want to keep Robbie as far away from him as possible."

"So he kidnapped the boy? In hopes of taking over his education?"

Jane didn't answer. Not at first. She lay down in the water. "Probably."

End of interview. Slowly, Keller tied his boots and brought Jane's clothes to the edge of the water.

"Okay, listen," he said, "we've got to keep moving if we're going to find this kid. I'll see if I can scrounge up some wood for a fire, all right? You stay in there till I get it going. Then we'll eat when Yamdi gets back, and decide where we're headed next."

Jane seemed relieved to get off the subject of her past. "To Kang-Mo?"

"Yeah. If we don't find what we're looking for there, we'll backtrack and find Pirim again. I have a feeling he knows more than he's saying. I'll find a way to make him talk."

"What if those bandits are with him?"

"They will be."

Jane said, "You'll have to face them all over again."

"Well," he said, thankful that his voice didn't crack, "we'll cross that bridge when we come to it."

"All right," said Jane. She looked up at him, and there was trust in her face.

Keller looked down at her naked body and wondered what had provoked him into leaving her alone in there. There were lots of things to do, but the one he considered the most interesting meant getting out of his clothes again.

"Anything else?" she asked innocently. Maybe a shade too innocently.

"No," he said, pulling on his hat. "You stay there. Let me take care of things."

Jane eased back in the water and sighed. "Uh-oh."

He hesitated. "What does that mean?"

She opened one eye and looked up at him, smiling a little. "Has one fuck turned you into a hero?"

"Maybe," he said, trying not to leer. "Got any objections?"

"Not yet," said Jane, relaxing. "Not yet."

Chapter 15

WHEN HE GOT THE FIRE GOING, JANE MODESTLY STEPPED OUT OF the misty pool and dried herself by the flames before she got dressed. Keller decided he was watching like a Peeping Tom, so he wrapped his sore knee in a spare sock and went off to look for something to eat. He found nothing, not surprisingly, and when he returned, Jane was dressed.

She sat on the smokeless side of the fire and dried her hair, combing her fingers meticulously through it. The long strands steamed and smelled like wet dog, but she made an attractive picture sitting there.

"I've been thinking," she said.

That didn't sound so ominous. Not after what had just passed between them. But they were interrupted before she could propose her idea. Yamdi's voice called out from the bottom of the hill, and when they looked around he waved exuberantly, calling up to them. The delighted Sherpa started up the hill at a trot. Both Jane and Keller stood up to greet his return.

"Who's that with him?" Keller asked.

"My God," said Jane, putting her hand up to shield her eyes from the glare of the low-hanging sun. "I think it's a yeti."

Either that or the forward for Nepal's Olympic basketball squad. Keller said, "We aren't going to need any more porters if we've got him."

Yamdi called cheerily, "Hello, hello, Missus! Hello, sahib! Look what I have found! An American like you! A man from your own country!"

He wasn't the Abominable Snowman, and he wasn't a basketball player, either. He didn't walk softly, but he carried a big stick—a pole he carried the way a Watusi warrior carries his spear. Wearing traditional Nepalese garb of loose trousers and a swaddling of shirts and vests, he might have passed for a native except for his mountain man's beard and his size. He was probably eight inches over six feet tall. He was skinny, but still had bearlike shoulders and big hands. Weather had beaten his face considerably, but Keller guessed the man's age to be close to forty.

"Gawldang," he said, looming over the crest of the slope. "I said I wouldn't believe it till I saw it. Americans! Howdy, folks."

Keller put out his hand automatically, dazed by the appearance of this gangly apparition. "Hello. This is a surprise."

"Dang right, it is. My name's Calvin Cahill. How do you do?" He pronounced the words *"hayow dew yew dew"* in a drawl straight out of *Gomer Pyle* and his handshake could have crushed Christmas chestnuts into pulp. Lumbering to a stop, he surveyed them with bright-eyed interest. "This here feller says you two are Americans. I could hardly believe him, but it's true, I can tell by lookin'. Whatever happened to your face, friend? It looks mighty mean. Hello, miss. I'm Calvin Cahill. My friends used to call me Coot."

"Hello," Jane said faintly.

"You're out pretty far from where trekkers usually hike, arncha? Yamdi here tells me you're not on a vacation at all. You're looking for people! 'How about that?' I asks myself. 'I gotta see this.' So I came along to find out what's going on, and here I am." He had a huge, toothy smile. "Who you lookin' for?"

"My husband," said Jane, still awed by his size.

"Ex-husband," Keller corrected.

"He's Roger Parish," she went on, warming up. Perhaps she recognized Coot as a source of information and decided to be charming. "He might have a little boy with him. That's really who I'm looking for. They either landed or crashed a plane up here somewhere."

"Dang!" said Coot, marveling.

"Have you seen them? Or heard anything about them?"

"Not a thing," Coot replied with regret. "I'm sorry to say that, Mrs. Parish, but it's the truth."

She smiled a little and finished shaking his hand. "Well, thank you for caring enough to come with Yamdi. I'm Jane. Since we're going to be friends, you'd better call me that."

"Jane," he repeated, caressing the syllable. When he gazed into her eyes, he looked like a schoolboy just smitten by a new teacher.

Keller stepped in forcefully. "I'm Paul Keller."

"Paul," said Coot, shaking himself out of his trance. "I'm glad to meet you."

"That's some stick you've got there. I thought every bit of wood in this country was burned for firewood."

Coot's face glowed as he held up his walking stick. "Ain't that a fine one? I cut this for myself in Cambodia an' kept it ever since then. Reminds me of whackin' woodchucks back home." He took a couple of practice swings as if the pole was a Louisville Slugger, then grinned at Keller. "Hit a man with a stick like this, and it's more lethal than any weapon I know."

"Uhuh," said Keller. "Listen, Cahill, maybe you can help a little. My father is Professor Randall Keller, and he was up here doing some fieldwork. He must have fallen in with some criminals, because we've heard he got himself kidnapped. You know anything about that?"

"Boy, oh boy, you two sure have your share of troubles!" Coot wagged his big head. "No, I don't believe I've heard a thing about any foreigners except you folks. I only get into Kang-Mo once a year myself, but I generally hear about most of the Americans who come through." He grinned shyly at Jane. "The folks around here think they ought to keep me in touch with my old country."

"That's nice," said Jane, and she was smiling, too. A big, friendly kind of smile. "You mean you live here?" she asked. "All the time?"

"Sure!" Coot's face split into another big, loopy grin. "Not here here, but here in these hills. Been here sixteen years."

"Sixteen!"

"Heavens," said Jane. "Why did you choose to come here, Calvin?"

"Well," he said agreeably, "it's a long story. I brung along some cocoa and some cheese in my pack. If you want to sit down and share a bite with me, I guess I could tell you. If you really want to know, that is."

"Of course, I do! I'm fascinated already. Keller can heat some water."

"Oh," said Keller. "Sure."

Keller and Yamdi were relegated to making preparations for the meal, and Jane and Coot sat down and got friendly immediately.

Jane was clearly curious and pleased to have found herself in the company of a genuine hermit. She asked, "Are you here for spiritual reasons, Calvin? Is that it? Are you studying Buddhism with these people?"

"Oh, no!" Coot chuckled. "Nothing so highfalutin' as that. No, my reasons for bein' here aren't very noble at all, to tell the truth, Jane. Why, I'm a deserter, you could say."

She sat forward. "Why, Calvin, whatever do you mean?"

It turned out, Keller soon learned, that Coot had been living in the Himalaya since the final days of the Vietnam War.

"No shit," said Keller when the word was out.

"Heavens!" said Jane, equally startled.

"Yes, ma'am," Coot replied. "When my hitch was up and we was all pulling out of 'Nam in defeat, it just broke my heart. We'd made a mess of that war, and I heard all about the hippies back home kicking up a fuss, and I—well, Jane, I just couldn't face goin' home. My momma and daddy were gone, so I figured I'd just start walkin' and see where I ended up. I deserted my country because I didn't want to see it, well—"

"Compromised?" Jane suggested.

"Contaminated, I was thinking."

"Do you mean," said Keller, trying to get a bead on Coot, "that you haven't left Asia since the end of the Vietnam War?"

"That's right."

"Because your own country wasn't what it used to be?"

"Yep."

"Amazing," said Jane.

Crazy, that's what it was. Keller plunked himself down on one of the stones around the fire and stared at Coot while he told his story to Jane. Keller could hardly believe it. This man had been out of circulation for almost two decades because he didn't like progress. He probably didn't know about light beer or heard about the G spot. What he had missed! Captain Kirk's midlife crisis and the renewed popularity of Ravel's *Bolero!* The guy was a modern Rip Van Winkle.

"I just didn't want to go back to a country that had forgotten what made it so great," said Coot. "Kids smoking dope and politicians growing their hair long and—well, I just didn't like anything I heard from back home."

"Not even about the nuclear power protests?" Jane asked. "You didn't want to get home to lend your voice to that?"

"Or for a last look at miniskirts?" Keller inquired.

"None of it," Coot declared. "I figured I was better off alone. I wanted to keep my memories pure. So I came up here to the mountains. They kind of reminded me of where I grew up."

"Where was that, Calvin?"

"Boone County, West Virginia."

Jane lit up. "Why, Calvin! I was born just forty miles from Boone County!"

"No kidding? Isn't that the dangedest coincidence? Who'd have thought we'd meet in a place like this?"

"It's incredible! Don't you think so, Keller?"

"Incredible, all right." The guy was a nut case. Just the right ingredient, Keller thought, to make the trip complete.

"Calvin, I'm so glad we found you," Jane was saying.

"Fate must be working in our favor for once. You must come along with us for a few days. You'll be good luck."

"Well, sure," Calvin said. He gave Jane a puzzled grin. "I got nothing better to do, but do you really want me along?"

"Of course we do!" Jane cried. "Don't we, Keller?"

Keller couldn't help noticing that it had begun to snow. While Jane rapidly explained their circumstances, tiny flakes of snow filtered down from the sky and began to stick to the crannies on the rocky ground. Good luck? By nightfall there would be an inch of snow on the trails, maybe more. That was luck, all right. The farther north they traveled, the deeper the snow would be, too. And the whole time Coot Cahill would be thumping along with his stick—the one like he used to use to whack woodchucks with. Keller wondered how long it would take for a guy like Coot to start seeing a few woodchucks in the snow.

"I might be able to help," Coot suggested when Jane had finished their story. "I don't talk their lingo so good, but I can understand enough to get by. And I know a thing or two about gettin' around in these hills. I can tag along until you find your husband, Jane. And your daddy, too, Keller. Are they together, do you suppose, Jane?"

"I can't imagine why," said Jane. "Keller and I are only traveling together because we think those bandits have information about my son and his father. Once we learn something concrete, I imagine we'll split up. Right, Keller?"

"Right," he said, though probably not loud enough for anyone to hear even if they were listening. And they weren't listening—not to him, anyway. In fact, he stopped paying attention to them, too.

He had just noticed that the snow did not stick to the water of the hot spring. The flakes struck the warm water and melted. Their blissful fall from the sky was fleeting. Like lovemaking. When it was over, it was over. He put his hands into his pockets and watched the snowflakes disappear on the surface of the warm pool. How quickly they melted.

"Who are you going to see now?" Coot asked Jane. "Where are you headed exactly?"

"Into Kang-Mo to see what we can learn."

Calvin's expression loosened kindly. "Honey, you've got a strange idea about Kang-Mo. It ain't a city. It's one house and a store—sort of. Basically, it's a police station."

"A border checkpoint," Jane said, frowning.

"Yes, ma'am. The cops there will arrest you soon as look at you if you've got a fishy story to tell. Believe me, I didn't hear a word about any map or lost airplanes or kidnapped professors. The border police keep things tight. You'll waste your time going there."

Jane sighed. "Well, then, I guess we'll head back to talk to a man called Pirim. Right, Keller?"

Coot asked, "Pirim? Who's that?"

"Pirim's an innkeeper and a pal of Keller's. He used to be a bandit, Yamdi says, but he's got a lot of kids now and has to behave himself. Because of his old contacts, he may know something. We're counting on that, anyway." Jane paused and glanced at Keller. "We haven't got much choice when it comes to informants, actually. We don't know anybody else to ask. Keller, are you awake?"

"I see," said Coot. "Well, I hope this Pirim guy has what you want to hear."

"Oh, me, too. And I hope he's alone. Some of the people we've met so far are awfully unpleasant." She explained about the bandits who had beaten Keller. Her description of the event uncannily renewed Keller's aches and pains.

"Well, now," Calvin soothed, "don't you get nervous, Jane, honey. I'll be with you now."

Jane said, "I feel better. I really do. You've renewed me, Calvin."

Coot grinned shyly. "Why, your company is a pleasure for me, too, ma'am."

"I feel safe."

"Well, I'm a big fella," Coot admitted. "And I know how to handle myself. If you get into real bad trouble, I got a gun, too."

"A gun?" Jane repeated.

Terrific, Keller thought. Great. Exactly what they needed. Keller made up his mind. Under no circumstances was he going to trust this guy.

Watching the snow fall, he asked of no one in particular, "Do you think we're being watched?"

"What?" said Coot.

Keller shrugged. "I have a feeling, that's all. Like somebody's watching us."

Coot was silent. After a minute, Jane said, "Don't worry about Keller. He'll be okay. He got a bump on his head."

Chapter 16

PIRIM, ONCE AN INFLUENTIAL UNDERWORLD BOSS WHOSE PROMIS-
ing career had fallen victim to improved law enforcement,
was surprised to find as the years rolled along that he had
grown fond of his new life as an innkeeper. Not only were
the financial rewards of snookering tourists greater, but the
parade of guests was enormously entertaining as well.

"I have yet to meet a man who is cleverer than I am," he
often boasted to his wife. "The more men I meet, the more I
am convinced I should have been a king."

She agreed. After all, if he turned out to be a king, she'd
become a queen. Or at least the concierge of the beautiful
hotel Pirim dreamed of owning one day. He was saving up
for that. It was going to have rooms with curtains and beds
and a pot with water that passed through it like the
Australians spoke about and—oh, it was going to be wonderfully decadent.

After the last of his relatives departed for their winter

homes on the plateau and there was no word of trekkers in the area looking for lodging, Pirim decided to slaughter a goat to reward his family for their hard work during the guests' stay. It was hard keeping up the appearance of abject poverty—for that was Pirim's way of extracting a little extra money from the tourists—and the family deserved a treat for their performance.

Just as he had trussed the goat and prepared to sharpen the knife, however, his youngest daughter rushed into the settlement and interrupted the task.

"Father, Father," she cried, dancing excitedly around the hobbled goat. "A bad man is coming!"

Pirim chuckled, for the girl was best known for her bizarre daydreams. She had once told her brothers and sisters a story about a snow leopard who ate stones and regurgitated them into mountains of white rock. Crazy stuff. If she had been a boy, she'd have made a holy man. In fact, Pirim often wondered if underneath her earthy guise, she really *was* a boy and a priest. So in order to protect his own spiritual future, Pirim set aside his knife and indulged the pesky kid. "Daughter, how can you see that a man is bad?"

"I just know, Father," the girl insisted. "Come have a look."

Sighing, Pirim left the goat and followed his daughter. A man had to make a few sacrifices for his immortal soul now and then. Together they crawled up onto a ledge that overlooked the trail from the south, and sure enough, a big American man with feathered hat and an entourage of uniformed Nepalese police was making his way up the mountain. He was fat, and his progress was ponderous, but by the set of his jaw, he looked as determined as a bull in rut.

Laying flat on his belly on the dusty ledge, Pirim studied the man and decided at once that the girl had pegged him correctly. The man looked belligerent. Capable of using the gun he had strapped to his hip.

"Go," Pirim muttered to his daughter, making an instinctive decision. "Take your brothers and sisters and find the trail of Mohan Dok. Go with him to your relatives on the plateau. Stay there until I send for you."

"But, Father—" said his daughter.

"Go!" Pirim ordered, and he shoved the girl by her shoulder.

Then he went down to meet the American man alone.

"Greetings, my friend!"

The big American stopped on the trail and lit up a big cigar. His eyes passed insultingly over every inch of Pirim's person. He puffed smoke a while and finally spoke.

"Hello, there, Gunga Din," he said. "My name's Pompowsky. Let's have a talk."

For Jane, meeting Calvin Cahill was a lucky twist of fate.

She was mostly glad he'd turned up because after the fight with the bandits, Keller suddenly got very queer in the head. If he was going to have a major crack-up, she was glad to have a man the size of Calvin around to subdue him.

Besides, Calvin was such a nice man. He hadn't argued a bit when Keller insisted on hiking into Kang-Mo to ask about the map himself, and he had cheerfully accepted their late start back to Pirim's place. He knew everything Yamdi did about survival in the mountains, and he willingly threw his supplies in with their meager provisions so they could all eat enough to keep going. His instant cocoa was a godsend.

Jane couldn't understand why Keller was so rude to Calvin. Perhaps rudeness was a manifestation of his injuries.

"I hope he isn't permanently hurt," Jane confided to Calvin.

"Oh, honey, things aren't too peachy for him just now. He's lost all his gear, remember."

"You haven't had any gear for years," Jane pointed out. "And you're not depressed."

"But things are important to a fella like Keller. He wants a change of duds now and then. A shave, too. A sleep in his own sleeping bag."

Jane found herself blushing. Keller had spent the night wrapped against the cold in a dirty blanket and sleeping so close to the fire that the last embers singed the nap of his blanket. But she was not going to share her sleeping bag, no sir, even though she knew he was hoping she'd suggest it.

"And a'course," Calvin added, "I imagine he's worried about meetin' up with those bandits again."

Of course, Jane agreed. But fear didn't give Keller the right to get surly. Certainly not after he and she had—well, shared a moment of oneness. Immature, that's how he was acting.

Calvin was just the opposite.

"Jane, honey," he called to her from the fireside the next morning. "If you wake up and talk to me, I'll fix you a nice cup of cocoa. How about it, sugar? Does that sound like a nice way to greet the morning?"

How could Jane refuse sweetness like that? The poor man was starved for human companionship, and Keller was a brute for being so short with him.

Maybe Keller started to suffer from some kind of altitude sickness in addition to his bruises from the fight. Jane noticed a change in Keller almost from the moment Calvin joined their merry band. Keller developed paranoia.

"I think we're being watched," he said that first morning at the campfire.

"Oh, nonsense," said Jane.

"I will have a look, sahib," Yamdi offered, not ready to see a shift in leadership yet either. "Should I scout around before we leave today?"

"No, no," Keller had said, obviously annoyed that Jane dismissed his observation. "No, no, forget I mentioned it."

So Jane did. Until that afternoon when she noticed Keller wasn't hiking along with the rest of them, and she doubled back and found him standing still in the middle of the trail looking back in the direction from which they'd come.

"Someone's following us," he insisted. "I just know it."

"Have you seen someone?" Jane asked, taking a look for herself.

"No, not yet."

"Well, you've heard them, then?"

"No," he said stubbornly, "but I know someone's back there. I can feel it."

He was making her nervous with that kind of talk—as if she didn't have enough on her mind already. Jane jiggled his arm and tried to josh him back to common sense. "Don't try to get on my good side by pretending to develop telepathy, Keller. Come on, let's get going."

"I am not developing anything!" He wrenched out of her grasp. "I *know* something's out there."

"Keller—"

He got angry. "Oh, go play with your buddy Calvin! He's probably lonesome for you already, anyway. I'll catch up when I feel like it."

"Keller, for God's sake, are you jealous or something?"

"Jealous!" He hooted at such a ridiculous suggestion. "Jealous?"

"You heard me. You've been acting like a bigger jerk than ever since Calvin came along. Do you really dislike him?"

"I don't dislike him. I don't trust him, but I—"

"Are you pissed off that you can't be cuddled up next to me every night? Is that it?"

"That is not it!" Keller snapped. "I prefer to forget I ever cuddled up with you, thanks just the same. It was one of my more stupid moves."

His tone infuriated Jane immediately. "You want to forget it, do you?"

"Entirely!"

"Why? Because every sexual encounter for the rest of your miserable life will pale by comparison?"

He flushed bright red. "No, because it was a mistake, that's why. It should never have happened. I—you—we both were under a lot of strain. We acted rashly, and now—"

"Now we've got more important things to think about," she cut in, glad she could be the first to say it.

He glowered. "Exactly."

"Well, I couldn't agree more," Jane replied. "We should save our concentration. Rest assured it won't happen again! I've got my son to worry about, and I presume you are concerned about your father, so—"

He pounced. "What's that supposed to mean? You think I don't give a damn about my father?"

Jane regarded him coldly. "You said it, I didn't."

"Why, you little—"

"I have seen no evidence that you love anything but yourself, Paul Keller, so don't get on your sanctimonious horse about rushing ahead to rescue your father! You're only looking for him so you can prove something, and personally I don't think you *can* prove it because it doesn't exist!"

"Oh, *yeah?*"

"Yeah! So if you want to pretend that nothing happened between us back there in that pond, I'm perfectly happy to agree. A love affair right now would be disastrous!"

"You're telling me! You've been nothing but trouble so far, anyway." Sticking his face down to her level, he sneered, "Maybe I should warn your mountain man before he makes the same mistake!"

"Calvin," she said coldly, "can take care of himself."

"What the hell is *that* supposed to mean?"

Jane spun away from him. "Oh, stop being so paranoid about your precious manhood! If you ask me, all men are idiots when it comes to proving how big and brave and strong they are." Over her shoulder, she shouted, "You're all nitwits in the first place!"

She shoved past him angrily and stomped up the trail after Yamdi and Calvin, leaving Keller—she hoped—standing with his mouth dropped open. Chances were good that he fumed, at least.

"Jane, honey," Calvin said when she caught up with them. "What's wrong?"

"Nothing," she snapped, rubbing both hands on her face as if that might erase her expression. "I just stopped to listen to a moron rave for a while, that's all."

"Huh?"

"Never mind, Calvin. Let's just keep moving."

"Shouldn't we wait for Keller?"

"He'll catch up," she said grimly. "And if he doesn't, maybe a wolf will eat him."

Amiably, Calvin shrugged and set off hiking after Yamdi. The three of them traveled several miles more before the afternoon began to wane, and Yamdi suggested they make a camp early.

"If the sahib has a pained leg," explained Yamdi, "he may need to walk slowly."

"His knee!" Jane exclaimed, and she clapped her hand to her forehead. "Oh, my God, I forgot!"

"What?" Calvin asked. "What's the matter, honey?"

"I didn't—I forgot how hurt he was," she babbled. "Oh, I

should have remembered and done something! Maybe he was getting delirious back there!"

"Delirious?"

Jane grabbed Calvin's shirt. "Oh, Calvin, Keller and I had a—well, a fight earlier today, and I said some mean things to him when he was probably just—just having a hard time recovering from his injuries. He was badly beaten up, you know. No wonder his mind is wandering!"

"His mind is wandering?"

"He kept talking about being followed and—oh, Calvin, I have to go back and look for him! He could have fallen and—and it's all my fault for not insisting that he stay closer to us. I'll be back soon, I promise—"

"Hold it, little lady!" Calvin caught Jane's arm and hauled her back to him. "Hey, if Keller is lost, I think me and Yamdi better be the search party. We know the terrain a little better, right, Yamdi? We'll find him in no time."

"But it's my fault, don't you understand? If he—"

"Calm down," Calvin insisted, soft-voiced and kind. He patted her shoulder. "Keller may stroll into camp any minute, and if we're all out looking for him, we'll miss each other. You stay here and fix up the camp for the night. Build a fire so's he can see it. We'll be back in a jiffy."

"Are you sure? Do you really think he's all right?"

"Keller's made it this far," Calvin said, "so it'll take more than a slip on the trail to put him out of commission. Don't you worry your head, Janey. We'll bring him back. You just stay here and fix me up some supper, okay?"

"Okay," said Jane, "but . . ."

"Scared to be alone?"

"No, it's not that." Jane stopped herself. Yes, she *was* afraid to be alone. Ever since her arrival in Nepal, she had been in the company of someone, and the thought of waiting by the fireside for their return as darkness fell around her was suddenly quite unnerving. It didn't seem right to admit such a fear, though.

Calvin interpreted the look on her face and smiled. Patting her again, he said, "There, there, you'll be fine. We won't be gone long. And the wolves will stay away from you if there's a fire."

"Wolves!"

"Here," said Calvin. "Maybe this will make you feel safer."

He pulled his gun out from inside the tied waist of his trousers and pressed it into her hands.

Jane had never held a handgun before. The thing was very heavy, and the metal, having been warmed against Calvin's skin, gave off heat like a living creature. Jane stared at it. Then the revulsion swelled up inside her, and she fumbled the weapon. Calvin caught it before the gun dropped, and he carefully wrapped her fingers around the handle.

"It's easy to use." For all the fatherly kindness in his voice, the weapon might only have been a slightly complicated Christmas toy. "This here is the safety, and you flip it this way. Then just point and pull the trigger. It'll give a little kick, but—"

"Calvin," Jane said, shaking, "I can't use this thing!"

"I'm not askin' you to use it, honey," he coaxed. "Just keep it till we get back. Use it on a wolf, if you have to. You won't have to kill anything. The sound will scare most any animal away."

She gave up trying to argue, mostly because it would be dark soon, and she didn't like the mental picture of poor Keller lying in raving agony at the bottom of a cliff somewhere.

"Be careful!" she urged Calvin. "And come back soon!"

"Just knowin' you're here waitin' for us, Jane, honey, is enough to bring any man back to this place." Calvin smiled. Yamdi looked dazed, but he followed Calvin.

Both men set off in the direction they'd come, and Jane could hear them discussing the best way to split up. Jane watched until they were out of sight, and then she dropped her gaze to the gun in her hands. Hastily, she put it on a rock and busied herself with setting up camp.

The routine she knew by heart, and because their supplies were so few, it didn't take Jane long to get everything organized. Using the sticks of wood they carried in their packs and collected along the trail, she got a fire going in no time and poured a precious portion of water from their goatskins into the teapot. She set the teapot in the fire, knowing that at such high altitude, it would take nearly an hour to heat the water to boiling.

Then she sat down, wrapped her arms around her legs, and began to stew. Poor Keller. What a fool she had been to let him get so far away from the rest of them. What if he had gotten hurt even worse than before? What if he had gone completely crazy? Had his head wound been that bad? Or had his knee given out? He could have hurtled down the mountainside without a sound. Oh, poor, poor Keller. Maybe he'd been attacked by wolves.

As if on cue, a howl sounded very faintly in the distance. Jane scrambled to her feet and stood craning her head around, trying to figure out where it had come from.

"Oh, God," she whispered. "Keller, if you're getting mauled by wolves, I'll never forgive myself!"

The wolf howled again, sounding closer than before. Was it up the hill? Or down below? The mountain was so steep, they had only managed to find a few square yards on which to camp, and it was exceedingly difficult to figure out from exactly where various sounds came. From down in the gorge to Jane's left, the wind whooshed very softly. Already, the sunlight was fading and the gorge was dark.

A few pebbles rattled eerily along the edge of the trail. Gasping, Jane backed up to the fire and stood stiffly, listening.

Suddenly every sound around her seemed amplified a thousand times. She could hear the faint rustle of grass. No birds stirred the air, but she listened intently for the whisk of wings. Nothing. All the birds had fled.

She picked up Calvin's gun. Sitting down again, Jane put her back to the fire and propped the weapon on her knees. She could be prepared, at least.

How much time passed? Jane was afraid to look at her watch. The sun slipped lower, though, until it hung closely on the horizon for an agonizing moment. Abruptly, then— and silently, too—the world was dark.

Jane took the safety off the gun.

Before she came to Nepal, she had prepared herself mentally, she thought. She had told herself that the time might come for her to behave in ways she would not normally allow. If she was to find Robbie, she needed to climb mountains and learn to survive under the most grueling conditions. She might even, she decided, need to use a gun. Killing appalled her. Heavens, she had even become a vegetarian because she couldn't bear the idea of eating the flesh of a creature of the earth. Perhaps Roger's bloodthirsty side had disgusted her most about her marriage to him. His pride in murder frightened her at first, then gradually sickened her to the point where she couldn't look into his eyes without thinking of his lust for killing. But now, faced with killing an animal in order to survive—and in order to find Robbie—Jane steeled herself for the worst.

The stones rattled above her on the trail. Their sound was louder than thunder in her ears. Jane bolted to her feet and stood trembling, squeezing her jaw and listening with every fiber of her body. Another sound? Breathing, perhaps? A panting animal?

The gun dangled in her hands, and Jane tightened her grip. She brought the weapon up and pointed it into the darkness. With both thumbs, she drew the hammer back.

More stones shifted above. Then one dropped and fell squarely at her feet. Jane swung the nose of the pistol toward the sound. She couldn't breathe, but sound was rushing in her head like crashing floodwaters.

Suddenly a clatter, then a thump, a growl. Jane pointed the gun and pulled the trigger.

The sound exploded. Rock blasted into shards. Jane cried out, thrown backwards by the unexpected recoil.

Then Keller's voice.

"Jesus Christ, woman!"

Somehow she had ended up plunked on her ass on the ground, and when Keller stepped into the firelight, she could only gape stupidly at him. He, on the other hand, had enough wits left to be furious. He looked awful—gray-faced and shaky and exhausted—but he had enough steam left for rage.

"Damn you, you really carry a grudge!" he cried. *"You* were the one who took your clothes off first! It was your goddamn idea in the first place! Jesus, now you're trying to *kill* me! Are you *crazy?"*

He was carrying a goat.

"You're a menace to mankind! The first chance you get, you shoot me! Where's all that one-with-the-universe bullshit you were spouting before? All that respect-for-life crap? Give me that thing before you kill somebody!"

She handed him the gun, but he didn't have any hands to take it with. He was holding a *goat*.

He glared at her, then blinked, seemed to come out of his rage, and must have figured she was so shocked she couldn't manage a syllable. Still angry, he said, "Here. I found your stupid goat. I *told* you something was following us!"

"L-L-Lambchop?"

He dumped the bleating animal into her lap. "You're goddamn right, it's Lambchop. I spent the whole afternoon chasing her around this godforsaken mountain. She's been following us. She just didn't want to get caught. You don't know what I went through to get her back!"

"Lambchop!" Jane hugged the little goat and pressed her face into the matted hair. "Lambchop!"

"I like that," said Keller angrily. "You shoot me, but all you can get worried about is a fucking goat!"

"It wasn't my fault," she said finally, lifting her head to look up at him. "I thought you were a wolf."

"A wolf?" He got the wrong idea and blew up. "A wolf! Hey, *you* started that whole scene back at the pond, lady. It was *your* idea to screw our brains out, and now you call *me* a wolf—"

"I mean I thought you were a real wolf! Yamdi and Calvin went off to look for you, and—and I was here alone, and I heard the howls, and I thought they were eating you—the wolves, not Yamdi and Calvin, and then they came closer, and I heard—I heard—I thought you were a wolf, that's all." Angrily, Jane finished, "So I shot at you."

"You could have called out, you know!"

"To a wolf? That would have brought him closer!" Jane dumped Lambchop and scrambled to her feet. She could get mad, too, blast it! She pointed a finger at his face. "Listen, Keller, all this wouldn't have happened if you hadn't wandered off today."

"I was rescuing your *goat,* lady!"

"You were supposed to be taking care of yourself!"

"*You're* telling *me?*"

"Goddammit, Keller!" Jane shouted. "What am I supposed to do without you?"

Red-faced with rage, he bellowed, "You almost found out!"

"Goddammit!" she shouted. She stamped her foot. "God*dammit!*"

"Hey—"

"You're such a son of a bitch!"

"Jane—"

"An idiot! You had to go after a stupid *goat,* for crying out loud—"

"I thought you *liked* the goat!"

"Not enough to get you killed! Goddammit, things are different!"

He stared at her, panting and furious, but also confused. Mostly confused.

"God*dammit,"* said Jane, and she grabbed him.

For a kiss, it was pretty quick and probably too impulsive, and maybe she'd regret it in a while, but when he quit being surprised and put his arms around her, Jane felt much better than she had in days.

When he broke the kiss and held her away from him, "I've learned a lot since I got to this country," he said, breathing fast. Things *were* different. "And some of it I learned from you. I wish—I wish I knew how to tell you some of it."

Blankly, Jane looked up at him. What had she done?

They could hear shouting then, Calvin's voice ringing in the darkness like the bay of a bluetick coonhound. "Jane! Jane, honey!" he called. "Jane, you all right?"

She wasn't sure.

Chapter 17

PIRIM WOKE UP ONE LAST TIME, FEELING VERY, VERY COLD AND tasting blood. Only this time there were people standing over his body, blocking out the sunlight and making him colder still.

"Oh my God," said the woman, staring down at him as he lay on the ground at her feet.

"Get back," said one of the men.

Pirim opened his eyes and recognized the man. "Killer," he said, smiling as best he could.

"Jesus Christ," said the man called Killer. "Coot, get her away from here! Pirim, what happened?"

He put his hands on Pirim, then drew back as if the awfulness had reached out and struck him. Then he swallowed and steeled himself, anger passing over his face as swiftly as a breeze. More gently than before, he asked, "What happened?"

Pirim tried to talk. He wanted to tell the story. But the

only sound he seemed to be capable of making was a gurgling noise. Killer frantically ripped some material out of his backpack and tried to press it against Pirim's throat. Or at least to the spot where Pirim's throat used to be. The knife had cut him deeply, but not enough to slaughter him. No, he wasn't dead. Killer's bandage soaked up the blood that had already spilled, and then seemed to start drawing blood from inside, too. Like oil drawn up on a wick, his lifeblood was going.

He was glad he was dying, for the pain had started to go away, but now there was just a cold, black hole where his chest had been, and it frightened him. He did not want to die in fear. Nor in cold. Let death come quickly and warmly.

"Easy," said Killer, trying to cover up the hole. "Take it easy, Pirim. Your children. Are they here?"

"Gone," Pirim said. "To Mohan Dok."

"They're safe?" Killer asked.

Pirim nodded. Nice of Killer to be so concerned. Pirim didn't remember treating Killer especially well when he had come before. In fact, Pirim had suggested that they all steal Killer's gear and clothes.

Killer pressed the cloth gingerly into his wound. "And your wife? She's safe, too?"

Pirim motioned with his hand to indicate that she had made her escape. The motion turned into a shuddering shiver. Killer tore off his parka and tried to tuck it around Pirim's chest. It didn't help.

"Who did this?" Killer asked. "Who did this to you, Pirim? Bandits? Those men who were here before?"

For an instant Pirim thought about telling Killer about the crazy American with the gun. Americans had a good grasp of the concept of avenging death. But a good Buddhist didn't think like that. No, Pirim figured he ought to come up with a better exit line. If he was going to depart from this earth any minute, he had better leave a better mark on it.

He made a feeble grasp for Killer's shirt. The American bent closer, and Pirim whispered, "Father."

Killer's gaze sharpened. "What do you mean, Pirim? Your father?"

Pirim shook his head. "Find father."

"*My* father?"

"Go to Suli," said Pirim, but his voice didn't quite form all the syllables. His throat was dry. His eyes were dry. His whole body felt cold. His feet had already disappeared. Frozen, he thought. All these years of mountain life, and he had to die with frozen feet. "Suli," he said.

Keller held Pirim until the big man died. In the movies, holding a dying person always seemed like a noble thing to do.

Keller didn't feel noble when Pirim died. He felt sick. He felt dizzy and hungry and tired, but not noble. In a little while, he became aware of Coot talking.

"Gawldang," said Coot. He had come and was hunkered down just a few feet away, examining Pirim's hacked throat and chest from a safe distance—as if the wound might be contagious. He shook his head with something like admiration. "That's a real mean way to die, if you ask me. Who did it?"

Keller gently let Pirim slide back to the ground. Awkwardly, he arranged the dead man's hands, on top of his parka. His own hands were shaking pretty badly. To Coot, he said, "He didn't tell me who did it."

"What did he say?"

Keller's mouth felt thick. He wasn't sure he could speak, but in an effort to appear as if none of this had really happened, he said, "Pirim told me to go to a town called Suli."

"Suli? That's no town, that's like a—well, a territory, I think. It's Tibet. Man, that's some bad country up there. What's he want you to go to Suli for?"

"To find my father."

"Wow," said Coot, wide-eyed. "He told you where to find your old man before he kicked off? Lucky."

"Yeah," said Keller. He stood up.

Suddenly he wanted to talk to Jane. He wanted to hold her. Well, not that, exactly. He wanted *her* to hold *him*, but it could at least look like things were the other way around. He got up and headed down the hillside where she stood with Yamdi, hugging herself and trying not to cry.

"Is he—?"

Keller nodded. He took her in his arms, and she hugged

him back, putting her face against his chest so he could bury his nose in her hair. She smelled like firewood, not like blood. And she was warm. When Billy died, Keller remembered feeling awful, but not like this. Billy had simply disappeared. His had been a long-distance death. But Pirim was truly *dead* dead. The stickiness of his blood and the smell of his breath when he died—those were details Keller would never forget.

Breathing warmly into his chest, Jane said, "Things are getting bad now, Keller."

"Hey," Coot called from up above. "We'd better get out of here, y'know. Those guys may come back."

"Oh, God," said Jane, and her voice shook.

"He's right," said Keller, glancing up at the surrounding ridges. "The bandits might be watching us, even now."

"I'm not afraid of them!"

Keller held her off and stared down at Jane. Her face was blotchy with tears, but the firmness of her jaw bespoke the fortitude never far from the surface of her personality. She hiccoughed and said, "It wasn't the bandits who did this, Keller."

"What? How do you know that?"

"Because you've got their only knife."

He glanced at his own belt, where the silver-handled dagger rode against his side. Sure enough, it was the only weapon the bandits had possessed, and he had it now. "Maybe they used Pirim's own knife to do it."

She pushed her hair back from her face and pointed to the last remaining wall of Pirim's house. "His knife is hanging right over there on that peg. See? It hasn't been used. Not unless somebody cleaned it afterwards."

Keller saw her point. The rest of Pirim's property had been torn apart. His fence had been ripped down, the walls of his home had been smashed. The bits and pieces of his cooking pots lay scattered on the ground. Somebody had ransacked the place in search of something valuable, all right. Keller nodded. "Judging by how they left everything else, they wouldn't bother cleaning the murder weapon."

"Exactly. So your bullying bandits didn't kill Pirim. Somebody else did."

"Who?"

"Didn't he say?"

"Nope. He just told me to go on to a place called Suli. He says my father is there."

Jane looked surprised. "How did he know that?"

"If I were to venture a guess," said Keller, "I'd say he learned it from whoever killed him."

"Oh, God," said Jane, and she put her hands on his arm for support.

He knew what she was thinking. Pirim might not have died if he hadn't gotten unwittingly mixed-up in the affairs of a couple of troublesome Americans. Like Billy, he had died simply because he had offered his services to the wrong people.

From across the rubble-strewn yard came a voice. A loud, pompous, and commanding voice.

"That's a good idea, friends. Go back to civilization where you belong."

Keller turned, instinctively putting Jane behind him. "Pompowsky!"

The Colonel marched across the yard, flanked by a small patrol of Nepalese officials in uniform. Pompowsky was dressed in his bush attire, complete with a military-issue plastic rain cover that fitted over his cowboy hat. Under the plastic, his little fan of erect feathers bristled importantly, and the gleam in the Colonel's eye was undimmed by days of hard trail life. Keller had a feeling that a man like Pompowsky actually enjoyed the rigors of outdoor survival. Just two yards from Keller, he halted, paused, and smiled.

"Well, my boy. We meet again."

"Hello, Colonel. You got here just in time."

Pompowsky didn't blink. "For what?"

Keller gestured at Pirim's inert form laid out on the ground near the open door of the shack. "There's been a murder here. This man has had his throat cut."

Pompowsky appeared to be surprised. "Balls afire," he said mildly. "Is that true?"

"Have a look for yourself."

With a flippant gesture, Pompowsky dissented. "No, thanks. I've seen enough dead gooks to know what one looks like. Who did it?"

Warily, Keller shook his head. "I don't know. We just got

here. We've been following some bandits, though. They would have stopped here before heading west into their own country. If you can send these fellows of yours ahead, they may be able to catch them and find out——"

"Maybe that won't be necessary. Is that a knife you're wearing there, boy?"

Keller stopped and dropped his hand to the dagger. "This? Well, yes."

Continuing to smile, Pompowsky put out his hand. "Give it over, son."

With the entire patrol of Nepalese police concentrated on staring at Keller, just then didn't seem a like a good time to start defending his innocence, so Keller withdrew the knife from his belt and handed it over.

Pompowsky hefted the knife expertly and examined the weapon, even running his thumb along the blade. No blood appeared, the blade too dull. "This couldn't have done the job," he said finally, tossing it end-over-end back to Keller. He grinned when Keller bobbled the catch. "You're in the clear, I guess."

Pompowsky turned and finally laid eyes on Coot. Until then, he had pretended not to see anyone else at all, which was quite a trick since Coot looked a lot like Larry Bird, if Larry Bird ever put on a burnoose and flying goggles. Coot stood still with his long arms hanging at his sides while Pompowsky looked him up and down like an enormous side of USDA prime.

Squinting, Pompowsky said, "Do I know you, boy?"

"No, sir," said Coot, ducking his head and peeking at the Colonel like a shy teenager facing his future in-laws. "No, sir, we never met before."

Pompowsky frowned. "You sure, boy?"

"Yes, sir, I'm sure."

Pompowsky nodded. "I recognize your type, though. Seen combat, have you?"

"Not for sixteen years, sir."

"Still," said Pompowsky, "it's in your blood, I'll bet."

Then he turned to Jane and stood grinning at her for a long while, his hands braced comfortably into the cinched belt of his parka. She glared back.

Her undisguised opinion of him didn't seem to bother

Pompowsky. He reached into his pocket and came up with a cigar, which he proceeded to unwrap. "Well, little lady, you've turned out to be a bit of trouble for me."

"You don't know how happy that makes me," she retorted. She took a stalking pace toward him, and Pompowsky reacted by tightening his jaw like a bulldog and standing his ground.

"Now look," Keller began, and he stepped between them before the biting and snarling started. "Let's settle this like adults, can we?"

"One problem," snapped Jane, and she hooked her thumb at Pompowsky. "He hasn't grown up yet."

The glitter in Pompowsky's eye intensified. "Lemme tell you something, girl, you're no picnic. I had to get the United States of America to pay for the damages you inflicted on that shack they call a jail back in Kathmandu."

"I'll reimburse the United States," she snapped.

"Your country isn't gonna be real happy with you for causing all this ruckus, y'know."

"My country," she replied, "could have done something about this ruckus long ago."

"Okay, okay," said Keller, striving to be the peacemaker. "Just shut up a minute, both of you. Maybe all of us ought to put our cards on the table."

Pompowsky growled, "See here, boy—"

"Just a minute!" With growing confidence, Keller said, "It strikes me that we're all here for almost the same reason, guys."

Jane began, "Keller—"

"No, I mean it," he said. "Jane's looking for her husband, I'm trying to find my father, and Colonel, you're trying to lay your hands on some airplane blueprints. Now—"

"Christ's crackerjack!" Pompowsky exploded. "I trusted you with classified information, Keller! Have you blabbed this story all over Nepal? What does this crazy woman know about—"

At that, Jane blew up, too. "Watch who you're calling crazy, you lummox! If you think I'm going to put my feet on the same trail as General Patton, Keller, you're—"

"Hold it down!" Keller shouted. "We're all headed in the same direction through some very rough country. Why

163

can't we forget our differences, combine our supplies, and cooperate?"

"No way," said Pompowsky, and he jammed his new cigar between his teeth.

"Forget it," said Jane.

"All right," said Keller. "Have it your way. Let's all split up. Let's all go alone and see which one of us comes back alive."

"What?" said Pompowsky.

"From what Pirim told me just now," Keller went on, "we've all got to head north and west. That's where my father is, and that's the direction the bandits went, and they're our only link to Parish. We're headed into the roughest, most uninhabited terrain in this whole country. Hell, this might be the most remote part of the *world* for all I know. It's full of murderers, thieves, wolves, unmapped trails, and there's very little water and certainly no food. Do any of us really want to try this trip alone?"

"My God," said Jane. "You're suggesting we team up with Colonel Cluck now?"

"Yes," Keller said, glaring dangerously down at her, "that's exactly what I mean."

"I won't do it, Keller!"

"Yes, you will. It's a question of survival, Jane. He can probably scare off those bandits in a way neither of us can."

"I won't do it!" she repeated. "He's slime, Keller! He's a sneaky rat who—who—my God, he's already tried to kill me once!"

"Oh, come now!" Pompowsky protested.

"You shut up!" she shouted. "Keller, I—"

"See here, boy, she's—"

Jane seized his jacket, her face pinched and white. "Don't listen to him, Keller. This man planned to murder me in Kathmandu. I escaped just in—"

Keller grabbed Jane's wrists, half to calm her down and half to protect himself from her in case she let go. Trying to be sensible, he said, "A minute ago you said he *did* try to kill you, and now you say he only *planned* to do it. Which is it, Jane?"

"It's all nonsense," Pompowsky muttered. "She's got delusions. What time of the month is it for you, girl?"

It was a good thing Keller was holding onto her, because Jane wheeled around and swung a lethal kick at the Colonel's groin, and judging by her momentum, she would have inflicted some serious damage if she'd connected with her target. Keller hung on and wrestled with her while the Colonel prudently retreated a pace and then watched with disgust.

"Let go!" Jane panted. "I mean it!"

"Stop it," Keller commanded. "This isn't going to help, Jane. Pompowsky can do us some good. He's got supplies and manpower, not to mention some government clout if we get stopped by the border patrol. We can't make it just the two of us, Jane. Listen to me!" She stopped struggling, and he said, "If we're going to succeed, we're going to need some help. I don't like him any better than you do, but we're stuck."

"See here—" said Pompowsky.

"Shut up," said Keller. He released Jane, and she dove out of his grip, then spun around and faced him like a cornered animal, panting and quivering, but with fire in her eyes, ready for a fight.

When he was pretty sure she'd accept the facts, Keller said, "We've got no choice, Jane. We've got to join forces."

Chapter 18

JANE DIDN'T CARE WHAT KELLER SAID. SHE WAS DAMNED IF she'd put her life in Colonel Pompowsky's hands. For all she knew, *he* had murdered Pirim, not the bandits from Tibet.

He was certainly bloodthirsty enough. The first thing he had wanted to do was kill Lambchop. When he found the goat nibbling at his gunbelt, he swatted her away, took one look at the gnawed leather, and burst into a rage.

"We've got our dinner walking around like it owns the whole camp!" He pulled an enormous knife from one of the many pockets on his fatigue jacket. "I'm gonna slit that little sheep's throat and have roast mutton on my plate tonight!"

Jane blocked his path, placing herself between the Colonel and the innocently cavorting Lambchop. "Over my dead body!"

Pompowsky smiled and lifted his knife a quarter of an inch. "Glad to oblige."

"Oh, for Pete's sake!" Keller intervened. "Put that thing away, Pompowsky. The goat is off-limits."

Pompowsky put his knife away. "You may not catch me in the act, Keller."

The next problem to deal with turned out to be the Nepalese police that Pompowsky had brought along as an entourage. They refused to go to Suli. The leader of the police lectured Pompowsky at length. Then the Colonel began yelling back.

Yamdi translated. "They will not go, Missus. Suli is too far and near China. And weather, Missus. There will be snow coming. See? We may get lost and our families will sue the government for allowing such dangerous travel. They will report us to the border police if we go. The Pompo is angry."

"Yes, I can see. What can the border police do to us, Yamdi?"

"Arrest us," Yamdi said simply.

"That doesn't sound bad to me," she remarked to Keller, who was also hanging around the fringes and listening. "They have to catch us first."

Keller was prepared to ignore the threat of bad weather, too. "But what about Yamdi?" he asked her. "We're putting him in jeopardy, too."

"I go with you!" Yamdi said quickly. "I want to go."

"Why?" Jane asked the boy. "It's kind of you to offer, Yamdi, but—"

"My job," Yamdi explained. "I promised to be your guide, and I will do my duty."

"Yamdi—" Jane began.

Keller touched her arm. "Let him do what he has to do, Jane."

The Colonel finished with the police and strutted over to Keller. He plopped himself on a rock and stretched his legs comfortably. "We should hit the trail as soon as we eat, Keller."

"We should leave now," Jane said. "Get off your rear echelon, Colonel. The food is ready, and we can walk while we eat. It'll save an hour."

"She's right," said Keller after casting a look up at the gathering clouds. "Let's go."

"Wait a minute," the Colonel objected. "Is she going to countermand every order I give?"

Keller looked him rather grimly in the eye. "She might."

On the trail later, Jane fell into step with Keller.

"Trying to get on my good side?" she asked as they hiked up the hillside.

"What?"

"By standing up to Pompowsky back there. You think you're going to get back in my good graces that way?"

Keller looked at her. "I haven't the slightest interest in getting into your good graces, Mrs. Parish. From now on, I'm going to stay out of trouble, thank you."

"Why are you pissed off all of a sudden?"

"Why?" asked Keller. "You ask why? Because I'm stuck on a wild-goose chase with a fanatical Army officer, a woman who will probably get me sent to an early grave, and a goddamn nanny goat with a penchant for causing trouble just by staying alive. Now with a blizzard coming, I'm climbing the most treacherous mountains in the world in the company of all of them, and you want to know why I'm pissed off?"

Jane sniffed. "Just asking."

She kept away from Keller after that. She concentrated on putting one foot in front of the other and keeping up with the pace. Coot took the lead, with Yamdi and Keller behind. Pompowsky trailed farther back, and Jane preferred to keep up the rear so she would know what everyone was doing. She maintained a steady pace, but finally overtook Pompowsky after about three hours. He had been gradually slowing down all afternoon, and finally, when the snow began to fly, he plunked himself on a rock beside a trickling stream and loosened his shirt collar to get more air. His face was the color of canned beets.

Without speaking, Jane stepped by him to continue up the trail. But he stuck his foot out, and she tripped.

She heard herself cry out as she lost her balance. And the next thing Jane knew, she was sitting squarely on her rump in the water.

"You son of a bitch! You tripped me!"

Pompowsky's expression was the picture of wounded pride. "Tripped you? Lady, you plain fell on your ass."

She came up boiling mad. "You lying rat! You *tripped* me!"

"I did not!"

It was Keller who flew down the creekbed and managed to wedge himself between them before Jane enjoyed the supreme pleasure of punching Pompowsky's lights out. She lunged, struggling to get past Keller, but he grabbed her in a body lock, and she couldn't escape. She kicked him, but he hung on. "C'mon, Jane," he panted. "Hey, it was an accident."

"It was no accident!" she shouted, spitting snow away from her mouth. "He pushed me!"

Pompowsky dusted snowflakes off his jacket, acting as if her rage had caused an unpleasant dust on his clothing. "I wasn't anywhere near her," he said mildly. "The clumsy bitch slipped and fell."

"Why, you overgrown—"

Keller subdued her, but not without effort. He had to wrestle her to the ground, and even then, Jane wasn't ready to give up. Keller sat on her stomach and pointed his finger at her nose. "Now settle down, Jane. Getting mad isn't going to solve the situation. We'll make a fire and dry out your things."

She quit fighting him. "That will take hours!"

"That's okay," said Keller, and he eased up on her. "You can't walk in wet boots."

"Oh, yes I can!"

"Be sensible for once, will you? Let's just—"

She shoved him off and sat up. "I'm not going to be the one who wastes time, Keller. If we blow half a day getting my damn boots dry, we'll just be that much farther away from our destination. We've *got* to keep moving!"

"Jane—"

"Don't argue," she snapped. "I'm not stopping."

Keller sighed, eyeing her sopping boots. Then he gave up with a heaven-help-us gesture and got to his feet. "Have it your way."

"I will," she said.

And she did. Jane took the lead and set a blistering pace after that. Her boots squished and oozed, but she ignored them and concentrated on putting one foot in front of the other on the winding trail. Soon she was wading ankle-deep in snow, too. The mountain got so steep they had to string

lines from pitons at several points, but she made sure she
was the first one to reach the top of the hill. She was
exhausted and longed for a rest, but seeing Pompowsky pant
was too gratifying. She wound up the line, threw it over her
shoulder, and kept going until darkness threatened. That
night, Jane rolled up in her sleeping bag and fell into such a
deep sleep that she didn't budge until Yamdi came and
shook her shoulder in the morning.

"Missus? Missus?"

She bolted out of sleep and didn't know where she was at
first. The earth around her had been completely blanketed
in snow during the night. "What—?"

The smiling Sherpa pressed a steaming mug of tea into
her hands. There was even snow clinging to his eyebrows.
"Good morning, Missus. Time for tea."

She accepted the mug without getting out of her sleeping
bag. Without moving, she knew she had a problem. Her feet
ached like hell. When she checked her boots she realized
they had dried and stiffened during the night. They didn't
feel right at all.

By way of sheer willpower, Jane kept pace with the men
that morning. They made good time, but in the afternoon,
Jane's determination flagged. She slowed down. Oh, she had
plenty of wind. Her metabolism had adjusted to the altitude
very well, and she didn't feel breathless as much as she first
had. All her training and mountaineering practice paid off.
Skills and endurance weren't her problem. Her carefully
chosen boots didn't fit anymore.

"For months I worked up to this," she muttered to herself
when the pain got so bad she had to sit down and rest. "And
one stupid mistake screws me up!"

She had a terribly painful blister on her left foot. Calvin
set the pace in the afternoon, and as the expedition wound
its way up the knee-deep snow of the next mountain, Jane
gradually let all the other hikers pass her. At nightfall, she
trailed into camp long after the others, and she had a
genuine limp going. Everyone noticed right away.

Coot hurried toward her, plunging across the snow from
the campfire. "What's wrong?" he asked anxiously. "Honey,
did you have a fall? Why didn't you blow your whistle?"

"I didn't fall," she retorted irritably. "I've got a blister, that's all."

"A blister? Oh, darlin', that's bad news. Do you have any Band-aids left?"

"I used the last one this morning."

"Oh, honey," soothed Calvin. He took her arm gently. "Here, let me help you."

She jerked out of his grasp, determined to walk into camp under her own power. The rest of the men were sipping soup from their mugs and watching through the steam. Pompowsky actually smirked.

Jane sat down as far away from everyone as she could get without leaving the warmth of the fire. Her relief was so great she almost sighed aloud. Rest was all she needed, she decided. In the morning, her foot would be fine.

But in the morning, she wasn't fine. Not at all. When she put on her boot, she could hardly walk.

"Let me carry you," Calvin offered. He had come over to help her wrap her heel and gazed at her with infuriating pity when an unintentional gasp of pain passed her lips. "I can manage, honest. Honey, you can hardly move."

It was infuriating. Maddening! Horribly female. And Pompowsky enraged her further. His smug smile was the only motivation she needed to stalk out of camp and head up the trail through the unbroken snow.

But anger wasn't enough to keep her going all day. At noon, she had to give in and sit down. The men surrounded her and stood looking down while she unlaced the offending boot. The laces tangled, and Jane jerked at them angrily.

Calvin knelt down to help untangle the knot. "Here, honey—"

"Get away from me!" she yelled at once. He looked like a wounded puppy when he backed away, but she didn't apologize.

Stifling a cry of pain, Jane pulled off her boot and looked at her foot. The blister was huge and bloody now. The sight of it caused Jane to gasp. Her skin was rubbed so badly that it looked like raw meat. She closed her eyes and let out an unsteady breath. She was in a real fix now.

In a few minutes, Yamdi came over and sat down in the

snow beside her. He opened his pack and unwrapped some food and water. Jane was grateful that he didn't speak. He handed her a hunk of clotted cheese and took bites of his own portion while using the water from his pouch to dampen a strip of cloth. He must have torn his own shirt to get the fabric, but he didn't mention the sacrifice, and Jane kept quiet, too. Yamdi was the one person on this trip who knew when and how to keep his mouth shut. He passed the wet cloth to her and said, "Here, Missus. Clean the wound. Then butter is what you need."

Jane accepted the bandage and began to dab at her blistered flesh. The combination of cold air and cool, wet cloth was actually soothing, and she felt a sting of tears in her eyes at the relief. "Oh," she said, voice shaking, "this helps, Yamdi. It's marvelous. But skip the butter. I'm not really hungry right now."

"No, no, Missus," Yamdi protested, laughing. "Butter is for the feet!"

He proceeded to demonstrate by unwrapping a smear of rancid butter and dipping his fingers into the mess. "In this country, everyone rubs butter into their feet. It keeps us warm and—and smooth so no hurt places come from walking. You try before your whole foot gets sore."

Game for anything, with Yamdi's guidance, Jane cleaned off the dried blood and began to massage the rancid butter into her blister and the rest of the skin of her foot. When the job was done, she did feel better, and she sat back to rest. Wearily, she shook her head and muttered, "I hate this, Yamdi. I wanted to be strong. I *can* be strong. This kind of trouble is so humiliating!"

Yamdi stayed beside her and smiled a little. "You are a proud lady, Missus."

"Not proud. Just determined."

"Proud, too," Yamdi argued amiably. "You think you will conquer everything with no trouble. That is dangerous sometimes. Your foot may be a warning."

Jane smiled at the young Sherpa. The concept of *hubris* was apparently universal. "Why, Yamdi, I didn't realize you were a philosopher."

He ducked his head shyly and grinned. "Just a guide."

"A very good guide," she assured him. "You'll deserve a vacation after this trip, won't you?"

"Vacation, Missus?"

When she explained, he shook his head firmly, "Oh, no, Missus, I will find more jobs, more walking with sahibs. This is better work than what my friends have."

"Still," said Jane, "we shouldn't exploit you. Your help has been above and beyond the call of duty, Yamdi. We'll see that you are paid for your effort."

He smiled, and by the relief showing in his face it was apparent that Yamdi had started to doubt that there would be enough money to pay him when the expedition was over. "Thank you, Missus," he said gratefully.

Jane made a mental note. At all costs, she must see that Yamdi was very well paid.

Her train of thought was interrupted by a shadow that fell across the snow between them. Jane looked up to see Pompowsky standing there. With a cigar clamped in his teeth, he took his time examining Jane's bare foot.

"Well?" she asked finally. "What are you staring at?"

Pompowsky's grin didn't change. "You know what's gotta happen now, don't you, little girl?"

She glared. "What are you talking about?"

"About you. We're gonna have to leave you."

"Leave me?" Jane spat out. "Look, you son of a bitch—"

"It's gotta happen, girl," said Pompowsky, practically glowing with triumph. "You're slowing us down too much. It'll take a week for that wound to heal enough for you to walk, and by that time, I intend to be long gone."

Jane scrambled to her feet, holding onto the last sliver of her patience by a fingernail. "If it hadn't been for you, you moron, I wouldn't have this in the first place!"

Pompowsky scoffed. "Oh, I wasn't anywhere near you when you fell! You've been crying about that ever since it happened, but you and I both know it was you tryin' to look pretty while you jumped that stream that caused—"

She hit him.

Perhaps she lost her head, but Jane knew the swing was perfect the moment she brought it up from the ground. She socked Pompowsky right across the cheek, heard fist and fat connect with the power of a triphammer. Pompowsky's head snapped backwards, and by sheer force of momentum, he fell back, lost his footing, and went down like a felled steer. Fluffy snow exploded around his huge body.

"Jane!" Calvin seized her arms to stop her from throwing herself down on Pompowsky and beating him senseless. Yamdi and Lambchop bleated together, and Keller strode over and went down on one knee beside the whalelike lump of the Colonel. Pompowsky didn't move. Keller felt for a pulse, then sat back on his heels and glowered up at Jane.

"Now you've done it."

She thrashed in Calvin's grip. "I hope so! Let me go! I want to smash his face!"

"You've come close," said Keller. "Jesus, what'd you have to do that for, Jane? The man's a fool."

"He's been pushing me, Keller!" She yanked herself out of Calvin's hands and pointed down at Pompowsky's spread-eagled body. "From the start, he's been trying to get me to screw up. He's put every obstacle in my way for no other reason than I'm female! If I'd been a man, he wouldn't have found my problem so *inconvenient!* Well, I'm not going home, dammit! Not just because he's afraid I'm tougher than he is! I'm not giving up until I find my boy!"

"You think that's going to be possible now?" Keller shouted. "If you'd taken a couple of hours to get dried off after you fell into the creek, we might—"

"I did not fall into that creek! He *pushed* me!"

"Whatever the hell happened," Keller went on ferociously, "doesn't matter anymore! The point is that your stupid pride kept you from doing the right thing. You're acting no better than he is, for crying out loud! You've jeopardized the whole trip, Jane, because you thought you had to prove something."

"Look who's talking!"

He flushed. "We're in real trouble now, lady. Don't go making a lot of unnecessary accusations."

Teeth clenched, Jane said, "I'm not quitting, Keller."

"Well, then, I suppose you've got a good plan up your sleeve? Something simple and straightforward, I hope! What's next, Mrs. Parish?"

Jane shoved her hands into the pockets of her jacket. "I don't know," she mumbled.

He feigned being hard of hearing. "What?"

"I don't know!"

Calvin edged forward cautiously. "We could make a litter. You know, like the Indians did? We could take turns pulling—"

"Oh, Christ!" she cried, fending off the last humiliation. "I refuse! I won't be dragged along like some kind of helpless papoose!"

"For crying out loud, look at yourself!" Keller shouted suddenly. "You can hardly walk! You'll have an infection by nightfall! And gangrene is the next step. Use your head, woman!"

Jane felt herself trembling, but she couldn't stop it. "I won't," she insisted. "I won't do it!"

"Yes, you will," said Keller, immovable and gruff. "Or else you'll stay here and rest until we come back." When she glared at him anew, he added, "You've got no other choice, Jane."

If he had taken her into his arms just then—and it looked for a second like he might—Jane would have bitten him. Or burst into tears. But he didn't, and Jane was glad. He stayed mad. Pompowsky started to come around again, moaning faintly, and Keller turned his attention to the Colonel. Calvin took Jane's arm and pulled her away.

"C'mon, honey," he said. "You can help me make the litter."

She helped him, though her hands were shaking with the anger and shame she kept inside. In less than an hour, they had constructed a slinglike carrier out of a blanket and some length of climbing rope. With the men standing around silently waiting, Jane finally had to climb into it. Calvin volunteered to pull her first. Nobody objected.

The sling wasn't hard to pull across the deep snow, but when they set off again, Jane felt as if she weighed five hundred pounds. Calvin didn't complain, not even when he plunged into the hip-deep drifts of a pass, but Jane found herself counting his steps—measuring in her mind in inches exactly how much she was going to owe him when it was all over. When Yamdi led the way up the next slope, Calvin threw himself into pulling her the way a draft horse puts its shoulders into the harness.

As if they had crossed some kind of line between civilization and no-man's-land, the cold took their curious caravan in its teeth after that. Bitter wind blew down off the peaks, carrying razor-sharp bits of snow and ice into their faces. Everyone wrapped their mouths and noses against that onslaught, but it wasn't enough. Without proper food, their bodies couldn't keep warm and keep moving at the same time. The world seemed made up of rock and ice, with heavy washes of snow that were hard going until a crust formed on the top. Only Lambchop could scamper across the crust without breaking through.

Calvin sounded like a freight train as he plunged step by step through the mess. Jane sat still, wrapped tightly against the chill in all her clothes and her sleeping bag to boot. Around her, the mountains no longer looked like travel posters. The steely black rocks looked as if they were crouched down together, purposely barring the way northward. The swirling snow bit deep and bogged every step of the way.

After several hours of exhausting progress, Yamdi spotted a sheltered ledge, and they all struggled to reach it before the storm obliterated their vision entirely. They camped. Swirling snow and screaming wind prevented conversation.

The next couple of days were equally blurred by weather and exhaustion.

On the fourth day, Jane sensed they were approaching a settlement. There were signs of human life—a few tracks, a pile of prayer stones, a spindly tree wrapped in tattered flags. The flags looked old and worn, however, as if the people who had placed them reverently there had forgotten the prayers that accompanied the symbols. The desolate terrain looked like the kind of place even the most sympathetic gods might overlook.

Then, they came over the crest of a ridge and approached the narrow entrance of a gorge, and Jane sat up on her litter. The air was different somehow. The silence was not complete. She wanted to call to Calvin, who walked before her with the traces of the sling in his hands, but she wasn't sure what to say.

At the head of the expedition, Yamdi halted.

Keller plowed through the snow to the Sherpa's side. "What is it, Yamdi?"

The Sherpa guide did not answer. He remained frozen in his tracks, and in another instant, a human head rose from behind a tumble of rocks. Keller stood still.

They came silently, but quickly. In a moment, the entrance to the gorge was blocked by four men, all dressed in the same grubby garb as the Tibetan bandits who had beaten Keller and stolen his map. Only these men hefted weapons. They carried small, lethal-looking swords, and the leader had a rifle in his hands. Jane knew enough about guns to recognize a standard M16.

"Calvin," she said.

Coot dropped the sling. He had kept his walking stick, tucking it into the belt of his clothing so that it ran up his spine like a giant antenna. He reached back and pulled it out.

"Hold on," Keller warned, one hand outstretched.

Too late. One of the Tibetans leaped down from the rocks and landed squarely in front of Calvin, brandishing his long-handled knife. Without warning, the man charged for Calvin's throat.

It was no contest. Calvin parried with his stick, sidestepped, then caught his attacker smartly on the back of his skull. *Whump.* The man fell flat on his face and Calvin looked down at his victim in mild surprise. He hadn't expected the fight to be over so quickly.

"Oh Christ," said Keller. As a group, everyone turned and looked at the Tibetan leader, the man carrying the M16. Nobody moved.

Except Lambchop. The little goat skittered out onto the trail and looked beguilingly up at the newcomers, twitching her little tail like an anxious-to-please chorus girl. The Tibetans did not spare her a second look. Their deadpan stares were fixed on Calvin and his stick.

"Uh," said Keller. "Hello. We're friendly. Honest."

No response.

Pompowsky blustered his way to the front of the procession and stood beside Keller. He took the stub of his cigar out of his mouth and gestured with it. "Attention, you men. I have come on an important mission to look for an American named Roger Parish. Where can I find him?"

The man holding the rifle nodded once. "Par-reesh," he said thickly, and he sketched a salute, adding a sentence in dialect.

Yamdi translated. "Parish is their leader, sahib."

The Colonel grinned hugely. "He's your leader? Well, Keller, that was easy, wasn't it? Take us to him, if you please. Take us to Par-reesh."

The man with the rifle didn't obey. "Par-reesh."

Instead of leading them, though, he lifted the muzzle of the rifle and took aim at Lambchop. Before anyone could protest, he pulled the trigger. Jane cried out. The blast exploded, then echoed, and Lambchop shrieked, kicked high, and landed on her side in the dust.

The goat twisted, struggled, and lay dead.

"Well," said Pompowsky, when the shattering noise had faded into silence, "it looks like we have a gift for our host now. Pick up that animal, Yamdi. And bring it along. I'm hungry."

Chapter 19

THE RIFLE-BEARER LED THE WAY, AND KELLER FOLLOWED. The rest of the expedition trailed him. There wasn't much choice but to do whatever the Tibetans demanded. Keller climbed up the stony hillside and arrived on a flat plateau that was blown free of snow and overlooked a huge gorge. At the bottom of the gorge tumbled a clear stream, but the distant sound of rushing water did not rise to the top of the cliffs on either side. It was too far away. The distance from the plateau to the water below felt like a mile.

Gratefully, Keller noted a bridge that had been constructed across the gorge. Though it looked weathered by at least a century of Tibetan winters, the guides headed toward it. The structure had been built of hewn wooden slats and poles, with balustrades of stones meticulously laid and cemented with mud. There was no handrailing for lesser men to hold onto. Keller took a deep breath, vowed not to look down, and inched across the creaking bridge. One foot in front of the other, just like the high wire act at Barnum and Bailey's. Pompowsky followed without qualm. Yamdi and Coot helped Jane pass over the bridge next, and all of them shot nervous glances over the sides of the bridge. Wisely, they left the litter on the far side of the gorge, and Keller guessed that was not just for safety's sake. Jane had no intention of facing her ex-husband lying down. She gritted her teeth and hobbled along with the sole aid of Coot's walking stick.

As they mounted the snow-dusted slope that rose from the plateau, Keller had to admit that even he was anxious to meet this Roger Parish, too. He'd certainly heard enough about the guy to become intrigued. What kind of man snatched his own kid, crash-landed in Tibet, and made himself the leader of these surly people?

Before he could form an opinion, the trail wound around a spiked peak of rock and leveled out. Suddenly, it seemed they had arrived. Keller stopped on the trail. There above lay a palace.

Not a true palace made by human hands, but shards of rock thrust up from inside an angry earth formed the towers and turrets of a forbidding medieval fortress—one that seemed to challenge the heavens. Only the most violent forces of earth and sky could have created so awesome a structure. It *did* look like a castle—in ruins perhaps, but forever magnificent. The visual effect was as spectacular as the monuments around the Grand Canyon, but an eerie aura hung around this gigantic phenomenon as well. Keller sensed it so intensely that the cold fingers of Shiva might have come and clasped him in an inexorable grip. On the towering walls of stone, a dying sunset shone rays red as blood, and the rubble of snow-covered stones that lay everywhere around looked like the bleached and broken bones of cannibalized beings. Without thinking, Keller zipped his parka closer around his neck—protecting his jugular from whatever evil lurked in this place.

It was not deserted. Though the structure had been created by the most powerful forces of nature and might very well stand long after mankind had destroyed itself, a curl of smoke from a cooking fire spiraled up from behind the stone walls. Men had made use of this natural wonder, making homes for themselves behind the protective walls.

Though his own knowledge of military matters was minute, Keller understood the concepts of defense and aggression. This natural fortress was unconquerable. The army of a nation could hide behind those walls and nothing short of starvation would drive them out.

Pompowsky arrived beside him and stared up at the mountain castle. "Christ in a crabtree," he said, never at a loss for words. The Colonel took off his bush hat and squinted at the impregnable rock formation. "He's found a place to set himself up like a Chinese warlord."

Their guide did not pause, but continued up the rocky path toward the stone fortress, hefting his rifle on his shoulder. The last man carried the carcass of the goat. Lambchop's limp head hung down over his back, and her blood was leaking out of her mouth and onto his legs as he made his way toward the settlement.

It wasn't just the dead goat that got to Keller. Though the place was wildly beautiful, there was definitely something bad here. It even smelled wrong. Though few Nepalese people were Hindus, they rarely slaughtered animals for food, and the stench of roasting flesh hung pungently in the air. Where were the children? Everywhere in Nepal there had been bright-eyed children popping out from behind rocks and crags. Was this place some kind of bandit hideout? A haven for criminals and murderers? Or just the castle where a renegade American made himself the emperor of all he surveyed? The old Marlon Brando in Cambodia routine.

There was still time to turn back. But Keller motioned everyone forward. He and Pompowsky went first. Yamdi followed, and Jane and Coot came last.

Puffing, the Colonel asked, "You think we're in China yet?"

Keller took a last look around. "It sure doesn't feel like Nepal anymore."

A country unto itself, that's what it felt like. Roger Parish had found the one place on earth that came under no outside jurisdiction. There were no police here. No government officials. No embassy diplomats to come to the rescue of wayward tourists. This was the last outpost, the final frontier. The guides pressed upward and through the arched peaks of stone that formed a kind of entrance. Keller and Pompowsky followed, side by side and cautious. Their boots rang on the pavementlike rocks underfoot. The sound alerted the inhabitants of the fort. One by one, a handful of human beings showed themselves. Their sooty faces were wary and hostile. In their hands, they clasped a variety of weapons. A stout stick here, a hand-fashioned spear there, a rifle. Unconsciously, Keller conducted an inventory of the weaponry. The appearance of a sawed-off shotgun brought him up short.

He didn't have to point it out. *Sotto voce,* Pompowsky murmured, "I see it."

They walked up through the middle of the settlement and arrived on a natural loggia, a flat expanse of stone that ran fifteen feet in either direction and faced an opening in the facade of solid rock. A cave, Keller guessed. He and Pompowsky stopped there, and soon the others arrived behind them. Their guides split up. Two remained outside —not exactly holding their knives at the ready, but conveying the message that the Americans should wait. The rifleman ducked through the cave's entrance and disappeared. Keller waited in prudent silence, and soon the man returned. He came out of the cave and stepped aside, making way for a greater personage.

The man who strode out of the cave needed no introduction, but Pompowsky did it, anyway. "Parish!"

Roger Parish paused on the stone loggia like a great ham actor making his entrance into Elaine's after an opening night. He halted, shoulders thrown back, head high, legs straddled as if a bracing wind was about to sweep lesser beings off their feet. Tyrone Power, Keller thought at once. If Parish had been wearing a silk scarf, he'd have flung it over his shoulder.

Keller figured Parish had been expecting them. Nobody could make an appearance like this without some preparation. His costume consisted of a sheepskin-lined leather flight jacket carelessly unzipped to show an open-throated shirt, which was quite a show of strength, since the air temperature was probably all of twenty degrees. His belt buckle depicted a bucking bronco, and his twill trousers looked like standard issue from the Air Force. His cowboy boots were made of snakeskin. Maybe Parish even killed the snakes himself. His blond hair was whacked off in a military crewcut. He looked tough and in command. His expression was a haughty smirk. Only the faint Charles Manson glitter in his eyes gave any clue about what was going on behind such a dashing outward appearance.

Keller was gratified to note also that despite all his efforts to look like a movie hero, Roger was going slightly bald.

"Mercy," Parish said mockingly. "Look at this. Company stopping by."

"Parish," growled Pompowsky, "I've been looking all over for you!"

"I've been right here all the time. Did you go to much trouble, Herman?"

Keller looked at Pompowsky. "Herman?"

Parish came down the steplike rocks, his gaze roving among all the members of the expedition to figure out who was who. Yamdi he dismissed at once, and Coot received only a second glance. Finally, though, Parish stopped and connected with Jane.

"I'll be damned," he said. "This *is* a surprise. Hello, Janey."

Jane looked like a woman who was about to confront all her demons at the same time. Her jaw was firm, her body was stiff, her eyes didn't flinch. But she was pale, too, and if her hands hadn't been stuffed into her pockets, Keller knew they'd be visibly trembling. Coldly, she said, "Hello, Roger."

At the sound of her voice, Roger Parish began to smile. It was an eerie expression on his face. "I can't say it's a surprise to see you here."

"Nothing could have kept me away," she said.

He laughed. "Animal magnetism, huh? I've still got it."

She shook her head. "You know what I'm here for."

He laughed again and managed to avoid her unasked question. "Well, I'd say this calls for a party. What do you say, Herman?" He clapped Pompowsky on the shoulder. "Will you and your merry men stick around for a while? We're about to have an important ceremony here. Having you join the festivities would make a real occasion out of it."

"Parish—" the Colonel began.

"Now, now, let's not get right to business, please. Let me make you welcome first! Introduce me, will you?"

Keller decided not to depend on Pompowsky or Jane to do the honors. He stepped forward and put out his hand. "My name's Keller. I assume you're Roger Parish?"

Parish hesitated only an instant before smiling broadly and accepting Keller's handshake. "That's exactly who I am. Keller, you say? Where have I heard that name before?"

"Perhaps my father," said Keller, smooth and collected. "He's been traveling in these parts recently. You've run into him, maybe?"

"No," said Parish, and he frowned politely. "I can't say as I have. Is he a tourist?"

"No." Keller smiled politely. He knew in his bones that Parish was lying, but short of accusing him then and there, there wasn't anything to do but swallow what he said. Keller gestured. "These are our friends. Calvin Cahill and Yamdi, our guide."

Parish acknowledged the two of them with a short nod, then perked up. "Well, unless anyone else is likely to wander in, why don't you come inside and make yourselves at home? You've brought your own provisions, I see. You needn't have done that. We've got plenty of food. Meat's scarce, though. The goat will be welcomed."

Keller decided not to make a fuss about Lambchop's demise. "You have someone who can cook it?"

"Oh, yes." Parish waved his hand, and the man bearing Lambchop's carcass nodded and silently took the beast away, presumably to be roasted. "Come along," said Parish. "I'd like you all to join me for dinner. It's a special occasion. I'm about to be married."

From behind him, Keller heard Jane choke.

Chapter 20

KELLER FOLLOWED ROGER PARISH THROUGH THE CAVE'S ENtrance. Jane was right behind him, and Pompowsky, Coot, and Yamdi brought up the rear, side-by-side like the Tinman, the Scarecrow, and the Cowardly Lion entering the forest of the wicked witch.

The cave was wide, but low-ceilinged and very cold. A series of flickering torches had been jammed into crevices along the jagged walls, and they provided plenty of light, which was lucky. The floor of the cave was uneven and provided poor footing. Keller's boots broke through a puddle of ice and then tracked the brackish water along the rock-strewn ground. They climbed over stones.

Finally, however, the ceiling rose, and the stone underfoot smoothed out, and Keller followed Parish into a huge, vaulted room. It was, Keller could see, a man-made structure that had been incorporated into living rock. Walls had been fashioned out of stone and mortar by human hands, perhaps a thousand years ago. Instinct told him that the primitive chamber had once functioned as a monastery or a temple, not unlike the temple at Kol. A collection of beautifully cut prayer stones lay in a mosaic along the floor, having been set like pavement to provide solid footing. But other religious carvings lay scattered around the walls, discarded like rubbish. A hot fire had been built in a raised hearth, and the smoke curled upwards and through a hole in the roof. The waste of firewood caused Jane to shake her head. The air in the room was warm and smoky. Keller unzipped his parka.

The only furniture in the enormous chamber was a long, rough table built Chinese-style just eight or ten inches off the ground, but stretching perhaps fifteen feet in length. Its scratched and gouged surface had been decorated with plates and earthenware bowls, and three butter lamps cast pools of golden light through the haze of smoke from the fire.

Two female figures dressed in tattered black robes had been administering to the lamps, but when Parish entered the chamber, they hastily bowed and scurried away from the table. They disappeared through one of two passageways that led out of the ceremonial room, and Parish shouted after them.

"Come back here!" he bellowed. When they did not obey, he snorted with annoyance. "Those stupid women run away as soon as they hear me coming. I hope they have enough gumption to serve the meal tonight. Sit down, sit down. We might as well get comfortable. Take your coats off. Yo, take their coats, will you? We're having a party!"

A pan of tea had been prepared and stood steaming at the head of the table. Parish began pouring. "How about a drink? Have you learned to drink the local stuff, Keller?"

"I didn't have much choice," Keller remarked, having given up his parka to the obsequious servant, Yo. Pushing his sweatshirt sleeves up comfortably, he said, "In this country, you learn to like what's offered to you, or you starve."

Parish laughed. "Not me, pal. Around here, you got to learn to take what you want. Tonight, for instance. I'm gonna show these folks a party. I've had men scavenging the neighborhood for all kinds of treats. Pass this to Janey. You want some chang, Keller? I've got a whole barrel of the stuff. Best brew this side of Milwaukee."

"All right."

"Herman?"

"You're pouring."

Parish turned to his lackey, who was already burdened with coats and his weapon. Parish said, "Yo, bring the chang. Bring all of it, in fact. The whiskey, too. My guests are due any minute."

"Wedding guests?" Jane asked tartly.

Parish smiled. "Exactly. I met a prince from Pakistan not long ago—he was passing through—and he mentioned he had a sister of marrying age. Can you believe it? A guy like me marrying a princess?"

The others uncertainly began to find places along the low table. Keller found himself more interested in his host and lingered near him, hands in his trouser pockets. "You really mean to marry this woman? Without meeting her?"

Parish grinned. "No harm in lookin' over the merchandise." He clapped his hand onto Keller's shoulder. "Sit here by me. I have a feeling you're going to enjoy this party."

Keller started out by making an inner vow not to get drunk, which wasn't an easy task. The chang that Parish's men brought into the chamber was sweet and good. Cups were filled, drained, and refilled within minutes. Next, the berobed women returned with cheese, an unleavened pancake, and potatoes, all heaped rather unappetizingly on large, flat plates. They offered the food to all the guests without speaking, but there was enough noise going on in the room so that their silence was not readily noticeable. Parish kept up a running monologue as he described exactly how he had acquired the food. It seemed that a nearby village had been raided by Roger's gun-toting servants in order to provide enough food for the visitors from Pakistan.

As one of the servingwomen bent over and offered him the tray of food, Keller was startled to recognize her face. The woman was Pirim's wife, he was sure. Her expression was blank, however. She stared dully at the floor and showed no signs of recognition. Prudently, Keller decided not to speak familiarly to her. In Parish's camp, she had become a slave. Keller wondered what had become of her children. The youngest girl, in particular.

Despite the presence of Pirim's enslaved wife and the sad story of a hungry village nearby, Keller accepted a portion of food and ate it quickly. After days on the trail with little to eat but well-soaked lentils, the carbohydrates tasted like manna with honey. Pompowsky dug in with gusto, and Coot shoveled potatoes happily, only half-listening to Roger's patter.

Only Jane did not eat. She sat stiffly on the floor on Keller's right, listening coldly while Parish talked. The anger practically radiated from her like heat from a fire.

At last a noise from outside the chamber alerted everyone to new arrivals.

"Ah!" Parish cried, and he leaped to his feet. "My guests!"

They had all heard the sounds of an approaching party, but Keller was unprepared for the sight that next greeted his gaze. With a great fanfare of bells and beating drums, a procession of gaily dressed men paraded into the room from the cave entrance. Politely, Keller stood up as they entered.

At the head of the procession came two small boys. Both were dressed in ragged shirts and the traditional jodhpurlike trousers, but their appearances were jazzed up by elaborately embroidered sashes and fancy dress turbans. Threads of gold and silver had been expertly woven into the scarlet fabric of the sashes, and the material was pinned with jewelry at their shoulders. Behind the boys came a stocky little fellow with a strut like Napoleon's and an upturned nose that registered complete disdain. His dress was also flamboyant—not like the Nepalese at all. He wore an Afghan turban and was, no doubt, the Pakistani prince.

Behind the prince was his sister. The princess was half-concealed behind four panels of silky fabric that were carried around her by four blank-faced young men who apparently pretended they could not see through the sheer curtains that separated them from the lovely young woman within. And she *was* lovely, Keller decided.

The girl's skin was nearly luminous, and against it, her black eyes shone like jet. She was outfitted in a flowing robe made of silvery brocade festooned with tufts of feathers and draping silk. Her brown-black hair was smooth and carefully swept back from her face into a serpentine coil that had been clasped with jeweled combs. There were rings on her fingers and bells on her toes, too. She even jingled as she walked, though her stride was more like a regal glide than a human gait. The girl was composed and elegant, but Keller saw past the carefully contrived appearance she projected. Judging by the jut of her pouty lower lip—not to mention the underlying baby fat that still puckered her otherwise exquisitely feminine features—Keller guessed that the princess was no more than fourteen years old. Roger Parish's perfect mate, if Jane's story of his predilection for youth was true.

Beside him, Jane expressed disgust. Quite audibly, she said, "Good grief, Roger. Even you couldn't sink this low."

Parish pretended not to hear. Or maybe he really was caught up in the fantasy. He strode forward, passing between the two boys to bow deeply before the prince. The prince returned the politeness, though his bow was a little less emphatic. He spoke in a language Keller did not recognize. It wasn't Chinese, though, and it wasn't Nepali. Whatever did they speak in Pakistan? Whatever it was, Parish apparently didn't understand it either. The host gestured, however, pantomiming that the newly arrived guests should come to the table. Neither of the men acknowledged the presence of the girl.

But the princess appeared to be accustomed to being ignored. With her head tilted high and her pert little nose lifted into the air, she skirted the table with her entourage of curtain-bearers and arrived at the spot directly across from Keller on Parish's left. When her slaves stepped back, she raised the hem of her royal robe and settled on the floor like a butterfly landing on a rose petal.

Once seated, she allowed her royal gaze to rest impassively on Keller for a split second, during which time she appeared to sum him up and spit him out of her conscious mind like an unclean thought. She studied Coot and Pompowsky, too, and then turned her eyes to Jane.

Jane returned the girl's cold scrutiny with equally chilly aplomb. Though dressed in the same tough jeans and shapeless sweater that had served her for more than a week's worth of hard traveling, Jane looked just as female as the luxuriously garbed girl from Pakistan. Her simple hair, the clean lines of her lean body, and the homespun simplicity of her rugged clothing compared quite favorably to the princess's elaborate appearance. Keller wondered if perhaps he had just gotten used to Jane's unadorned plainness, but he found himself siding with her—preferring her unaffected ways to the feigned sophistication of the visiting princess. Jane didn't need jewels, Keller decided. Apparently, the princess felt the same way, for she bridled visibly. For thirty seconds, the two women conducted a stare-down. Jane won. Demurely, the princess directed her kohl-rimmed eyes toward the ceiling.

Jane turned to Roger, who had remained standing and appeared to be gloating over his prize. Jane was not impressed. Distinctly, she said, "You can't be serious."

Parish laughed. "Janey, are you jealous?"

"Don't be stupid. She's a baby."

"She's older than she looks."

"She *looks* twelve!"

"And you look forty. What the hell happened to you, anyway?"

"As if you didn't know," she snapped. "Roger, I didn't come all the way up here to—"

He waved his hand to interrupt. "Pleasure before business. Those are my rules, and as you can see," he said, "I am the boss around here. Let's have a drink, shall we? Prince, how about some chang?"

"If he's a prince," said Jane, "then I'm the Queen of England."

The prince, Keller observed with great relief, did not speak English. He smiled and bowed at Jane when she spoke, and seated himself beside his so-called sister so that he could appreciate Jane's presence more completely.

Roger said, "Watch out for the prince, Janey. I hear he's got an eye for older women."

Jane sent him a freezing look, but Keller put his hand out and touched her. Jane jerked out from under his hand, and Keller shrugged. The princess had observed the whole unspoken exchange, however, and when Keller turned back she fixed him with a wide smile. She had decided upon a method to make Jane jealous, it seemed. She batted her eyes at Keller.

Jane watched the girl's efforts for a moment and finally said, "You can't be serious about this girl, Roger."

"Hey," said Roger, chuckling, "the prince came looking for me, Janey. Was I supposed to spit in his eye?"

"He's no prince," said Jane. "And Pakistan is hundreds of miles from here. Neither one of you has any kingdom to unite. You're both con artists."

The prince smiled and nodded.

Roger set about pouring more chang into Keller's cup and his own. "The prince heard I was in the neighborhood and came looking for me. These folks have been waiting for somebody special to come along, and I just figured it might as well be me."

"Waiting for somebody special?" Keller asked.

"Yeah." Roger put his elbows on the table and lounged there, smiling. "Some relative of theirs used to pull raids and come back with all sorts of loot. That's why they could afford to build a place like this I guess. Some hideout, don't you think?"

Keller had been thinking that the cave and interior chamber reminded him of the stories he'd heard about "Hole-in-the-Wall" and various outlaw hideaways in the Old West. He pushed his plate aside and leaned toward Roger Parish, interested in hearing more. "You mean these people used to be bandits?"

Roger speared a hunk of cheese with the knife at his place. "Bandits, that's it. They stole from India and China. Their leader died eventually, and they've been looking for his replacement ever since. They expect to be led to the land of plenty again by a great leader. A son, they say, of some character called Mohir Dok. If they think I'm their man, why should I argue? I like the idea of leading people into prosperity."

"Have you seen any proof that the legend is true?"

Roger grinned at Keller. "You like fairy tales? No, I haven't seen any proof, but I been told there was some pretty fancy stuff that came up here on the backs of stolen ponies. Gold and jewels. But all that was a long time ago."

"How long?"

Roger shrugged. "Couple hundred years. Hell, these people are dirt-poor now. Until I came along, they were living on an occasional scrawny goat and melted snow."

Jane looked at the food heaped on the plates before her. "And now?"

Smiling, Roger said, "Now we steal what we want."

"Roger—"

He held up his hand. "It's not so bad for anybody, believe me. We eat, and the people we steal from gradually end up here with us. I'm starting a whole new country."

"By starving people into joining you?"

"Janey," he chided, "you always were a bleeding heart."

"What will you do when you run out of people to steal from?"

They looked at each other, and the rest of the roomful of people might as well have disappeared. They focused on each other exclusively. Parish said, "You know what happens next, Janey."

"You go to China," she said.

He nodded. "I've got some trading to do there. But when I'm finished, I'm coming back here. With some cash, right?"

Pompowsky had been stuffing his face with cheese and pancakes and rice beer. His cheeks were bright red, and he sat forward. "See here, Parish. Is it—"

"Shut up, Herman," Parish commanded. He did not take his gaze from Jane. "You'll get your cut. First I've got to square things with the little lady here."

"Yes," said Jane.

"Did you bring it?"

She said, "I have to know about Robbie."

"I'll tell you," Parish promised. "After I have the microfilm."

Keller asked, "What microfilm?"

Pompowsky's mouth fell open. He swung on Jane. "God's mustard!"

Firmly, Jane said, "I have to know about Robbie, Roger."

Parish smiled. "You sure kept that boy tied to your apron strings, didn't you?"

"Roger," she began, voice rising.

He put his hand on the table, palm up. "The film, Janey. I want the film first."

Pompowsky sputtered. "You—you bitch, you had it all along, didn't you?"

Jane answered the question by calmly reaching down through the gaping neck of her ragged sweater. Inside her shirt somewhere, she found what she was searching for and brought out a rectangular box no bigger than a cigarette pack. Perhaps she had kept it next to her from the beginning. She could have concealed it in her clothing when she undressed to bathe in the hot spring. Keller hadn't seen the case before, but he didn't doubt that Jane could have kept it a secret. She laid it on the table in front of her.

Parish reached past Keller and put his hand on the plastic case. He pulled it across the table to himself and put it next to his ear before giving the container a shake. It gave off a satisfying rattle.

Jane said, "Tell me now, Roger. Is Robbie alive? Is he here?"

Pompowsky turned apoplectic. His face grew redder and redder. "You," he choked, staring at Jane as if she had been transformed into the lowest form of life on the planet. "You bitch. You rotten, spying bitch. Do you know what you're doing to your country? Do you know what this information is?"

"I didn't look at it," Jane said steadily, watching Parish without a blink. "I did exactly what you told me to do. I brought the film, and now I want Robbie back. It was a deal, Roger."

"You stupid female," Pompowsky growled. "The balance of power is maintained by—"

"Oh, Herman," said Parish, "shut up. You're just pissed off because you didn't find the plans on her. Were you ready to double-cross me?"

"No!" Pompowsky's head shot up. "Nothing like that, Roger. I just—I wanted—"

"To bring this to me yourself? How loyal." Parish appeared to be amused. "Keep your mouth buttoned a little longer, will you? Maybe the prince doesn't speak English, but we have our uninvited guest to consider, don't we?"

It took Keller thirty seconds to find his voice. "I don't understand what's going on here."

Parish grinned hugely. "You never thought you'd witness a transaction among spies?"

Keller stared at Jane. "You, of all people."

But she ignored him. Jane sat forward urgently. "Roger, quit stalling. I want to see Robbie at once."

Parish sighed then. With care, he tucked the case into the inside pocket of his flight jacket. His guests watched his every move, and he enjoyed heightening the drama. Finally, he reached for his cup, took a sip of chang, and replaced the cup on the table. He looked at Jane.

She said, "Well? Where is he?"

"The boy," said Roger, "is dead."

Jane didn't budge.

Roger shrugged and said, "The plane crashed, that's all. I survived, but the boy sustained incredible injuries. There was no way to get a message to you."

"No," said Jane.

Her voice was very small, though. As the fact sank in, she became incredibly still and barely audible. "No," she said.

"Yes," Roger replied. "The boy died after the plane crash."

Chapter 21

KELLER DECIDED THAT ROGER PARISH WAS AN EVEN WORSE PIG than Jane had described. There had been a certain gleam of triumph in the man's eyes when he announced the news about their son. Jane had been too blown away to notice, but Keller saw the look and felt hatred of a magnitude he'd never experienced before.

Pirim's wife and the other robed woman took Jane away—presumably to a place where she could grieve in peace. As she was led out of the chamber, Jane could hardly walk.

Roger Parish didn't notice and appeared not to care.

"Well," he said, when she was gone, "let's have a party, shall we?"

And he proceeded to entertain them. The scene was so familiar that Keller thought he was experiencing one of Jane's "feelings" until he realized that he'd seen the same scenario in every James Bond thriller. Agent 007 was always lavishly wined and dined and frequently womaned before

195

the villain finally lowered the boom and sent James to an ingenious form of execution.

The prince and princess, if indeed they were royalty at all, enjoyed their food and drink with gusto and spent a great deal of energy bestowing compliments on their host. Using Parish's right-hand man as a translator, they exchanged exaggerated pleasantries while Pompowsky got redder and redder. Yamdi looked uncomfortable, and Coot looked belligerent.

"Just how," he blustered suddenly, interrupting the prince in midsentence, "do you think you're going to get away with this, Parish?"

Roger Parish turned on Coot, blinking mildly. "Away with what?"

"Taking good American know-how to the Chinese! Somebody'll come after you!"

Roger toyed with his drinking cup and smiled. "A posse, you mean?" he asked. "What d'you think old Herman was supposed to be?"

Coot glared at Pompowsky. "You! I'd never have thought this of you."

Pompowsky shrugged. "I got my reasons, boy."

"Like what?" Keller asked. "I'm really curious. Why are you two taking information to the Chinese?"

Roger continued to smile and hunched forward on his elbows, getting chummy. "Because it's there," he confided, and he winked.

Keller knew he wasn't going to get a straight answer out of Parish. Not now, anyway. He turned to the Colonel. "How about you, Pompowsky? What's in this for you?"

"You mean besides the money?"

"There's that," Keller agreed. "But what else?"

Pompowsky cleared his throat with a rumble. "Because for a man like me there's no glory without a war, boy. A foot soldier's got to make his own place in the world."

"And outside of combat you see no chance for fame and glory?"

Parish said, "You hit the nail on the head, Keller. Some of us need glory—a place in history. This is how Herman and me are going to get that. We're going to be remembered. Not just for this Chinese maneuver."

"Afterwards?" Keller said. "You plan to live here among these people?"

Parish lifted his cup in salute. "Genghis Khan did."

"Khan?" Keller repeated. "You intend to cash in on the legend these people believe? You'll live with them—?"

"Train them, too," Pompowsky put in. "Betcher ass. In time, boy, we'll be a military force worth mentioning!"

"The plans are still in the early phase," Roger said, "but yes, that's like a clear explanation of what we have in mind. Nice way with words, Herman."

Pompowsky accepted the praise with a belch.

The princess burst into giggles, and Parish bent closer to her, as if thoroughly charmed by her behavior. They laughed together at Pompowsky's expense, and the prince launched into a fresh spate of gushing.

Keller escaped by feigning a call of nature. He slipped a pancake into his pocket for Jane and then pushed away from the table while the others were occupied in an uproarious two-language conversation that nobody really appeared to understand, and he managed to duck into the passage where he'd seen Jane go with the other women.

The corridor was dark except for a single torch. By its light, he found Pirim's wife. She had been lurking in the rocks, and she came out hurriedly when she saw Keller. She seized his sleeve.

"Hello," he said, catching her in his hands. "What are you doing here? I thought—"

She silenced him, glancing cautiously in the direction of Parish's grand chamber to be sure they were safe. She looked up into Keller's face with hope shining in her eyes. "Pirim?"

Keller clenched his teeth. "I'm sorry," he said. "He's dead."

Whether she understood his words or not, he couldn't tell, but the woman clearly comprehended his message. She slumped sadly in his arms, emitting a tiny wail in the back of her throat.

"Steady," said Keller, conscious suddenly that neither of them ought to get caught just now. "Tell me, ma'am. Do you know who killed your husband? Who did it?"

He pantomimed, and she nodded. "Big man," she said,

using her hands to draw his frame in the air. She tucked in her chin and pretended to march.

"Pompowsky," Keller guessed. "Pompowsky killed the innkeeper."

The woman nodded.

"What about your little girl?" Keller asked suddenly. "Is she—? Is she all right? The one I saved?"

But the woman did not understand. No amount of pantomime could coax an answer from her. They were startled once by the sound of approaching footsteps, but Keller drew the woman back into the shadows of the cave, and they were not seen. Then she pulled him out into the light again and pointed. Urgently, she thrust him down the corridor, whispering and pointing.

"Go, go," she said. "Missus."

Keller understood. He went looking for Jane. With the woman's help, he soon found a rough opening in the cave wall. A small ladder made of poles and twine led up to it. The woman pushed Keller toward it. He turned to thank her, but she put her face into her hands and hurried away from him. She didn't look back.

Steeling himself, Keller climbed the ladder and pushed past the goatskin that had been hung across the entrance to the cavelike room beyond.

It was a room, too, with stone walls that had been built by men a long, long time ago. The ceiling was low, but a cut in the roof allowed the smoke from a pathetic fire of twigs to curl up and out of the room. One of the women had tossed a sprig of juniper on the embers, and the sharp scent wafted in the chamber. By the meager light of the fire, Keller saw no furniture, only Jane who was huddled into a coarse blanket and sitting with her back against the furthermost wall. She gave no sign that she heard him enter.

He ducked to avoid bashing his head on the ceiling and crossed the small floor.

"Jane?"

She looked catatonic. With her body curled up tight, she stared at the stones of the wall and showed no signs of consciousness except for her dull open eyes.

Keller hunkered down beside her. "Hey," he said. "I'm sorry, Jane. I'm sorry things turned out this way."

She shook her head a little.

Keller sighed. He wasn't good at this sort of thing, but he put out one hand and patted her shoulder.

She pulled away and muttered something. It was probably "Leave me alone."

He couldn't, though. A week ago, he could have gone away and let her sit in that cold room all alone. Now Keller sat down beside her with his back against the wall. "How about a pancake?" he asked, reaching for his pocket. "I snitched one for you. They're not bad."

"I don't want anything."

He extended the food to her. "Jane, you ought to eat something. C'mon."

She put her face into her hands. "I—" Her voice quavered, then broke. "I only want my little boy."

"Jane," he said.

She started to cry.

The best thing to do was take her into his arms. Knowing she'd probably punch him unless he did it fast, Keller grasped her shoulders and held Jane against his chest. She resisted for an instant and then just gave up and sobbed.

Coming from Jane, it was an awful sound, too. Keller had coped with weeping women before, but this was something different. Other women cried because movies were sad or the wedding was mushy or because sex had been terrific or terrible or he hadn't said the right thing or *had* said the right thing. Women cried for a variety of reasons, and Keller had learned that if a man just shut up and hugged the weeping female long enough, she'd eventually settle down before he had to actually say some words that might commit him to anything.

But this kind of crying was something totally different. Jane, who possessed the serenity of a monk at the worst of times, just let loose. She had lost her son, perhaps the center of her universe, and she was positively wracked with grief. The depth of her emotion was a terrible thing, and it galvanized Keller into babbling.

"Hey," he started, talking fast. "Easy—you'll get sick. Jane, c'mon. It's—there's nothing we can—Jesus. I'm sorry. Darling, I'm really sorry." Helpless and angry, he muttered, "That son of a bitch. What a bastard! He could have

199

said it differently. He just—damn it! I could strangle him myself!"

But Jane wasn't angry at Roger. She was devastated by the loss of her boy and had no energy to spare for another emotion. She pressed her face against Keller's chest and choked on incoherent words. "He was a part of me," she finally cried. "I can't—I don't think I'm alive anymore without him."

"Of course you are." Keller rocked her, holding her tightly, as if he could lessen her pain by squeezing.

"He was *my* son," she said, weakly grasping at Keller's shirt. "From the minute he was born, I knew he was *mine*. Not Roger's—not even ours together. He was mine alone. He was *me* all over again—just in a different body. I *felt* him living. That's why I came. I knew he was alive just the way I know my own arm is living!"

"I know, I know," Keller soothed, stroking her skinned-back hair. He remembered the day Jane had talked about the feeling—that oneness with her son. It had been the afternoon they'd made love, he recalled, jolted by how long ago it seemed. The boy had been dead then, and she hadn't known it.

As if she heard Keller's thoughts, Jane said, "He was alive, you know. I felt it. I *knew* he was all right."

"And now?" he asked softly.

"Now—now I feel *guilty.*"

"Guilty? Jane, I don't—why guilty?"

"Because," she said, choking on her tears, "I worked so hard to get here, and I—I had to use all my resources and my money and—and everything, and it was tough—tougher than I ever imagined, but I had *fun.* I enjoyed being by myself—alone. I liked not being a mother for a while—not being responsible for anyone but myself, and I—it's horrible! It was selfish and mean, and I was horrible to let myself feel that way!"

"Jane—"

"I—I used to have awful dreams," she raced on. "Like what if Robbie was drowning in a pond, and I had to—to run through a field full of rattlesnakes to get to him—I *hate* rattlesnakes, Keller—but I knew I could do it if I had to. I'd do anything to save my son. But now—now I've done everything I thought I could do, and *it wasn't enough!* I am supposed to learn something from all this—I'm sure I am—but what kind of world is it that makes a little boy pay for his mother's stupid thoughts?"

Keller put his arms around her and rocked her gently. He could feel her shivering uncontrollably. She couldn't feel angry yet, but he could. It swelled in his throat, clamping his voice. His rage at Roger Parish was overwhelming. The son-of-a-bitch had been gloating! Roger had actually looked forward to telling Jane the news. He had enjoyed making her suffer.

Without thinking, Keller said, "He's lying."

The thought occurred to him at the exact moment he said it. As soon as the words were out, he realized he shouldn't have spoken them. Giving Jane any shred of hope seemed more cruel than anything her former husband could do to her. Keller touched her face and smoothed the tears from her cheekbones. Gently, he said, "If he is gone, Jane, I think you can take some comfort in knowing that Robbie died happy."

She wiped her own face. Her hands were trembling, but the initial bout of tears was over. "What d'you mean?"

Keller shifted, sitting with his back to the wall and cradling Jane against his chest once more. He said, "When I was a kid, I idolized my father. He was larger than life to me. Not just to me, but to the world! Roger must be like that for Robbie—a big man with a reputation that—well, it's just not possible to compete with a father like that. If my dad had taken me on one of his adventures when I was Robbie's age, I'd have been happy to die afterwards. No kidding. Just being with him when he was doing his thing would have put me in heaven."

"Were you afraid? Of your father?"

"Not afraid that he'd hurt me, no. Just afraid that I wasn't—that I wasn't the son he wanted. But if Roger took the boy, that must have made Robbie feel as if he was important. He surely knew you loved him, but fathers—they're different."

Jane sighed wearily. "That's such bullshit."

"All right, it's bullshit," Keller agreed. Male bonding was trendy. But he felt right in guessing that Robbie had probably been delighted to be a part of his dad's big adventure.

In a while, Keller said, "In these mountains, nothing seems absolutely gone. Maybe that's how all that reincarnation stuff got started. It just feels like what you're looking for is hiding over the next peak."

"Like your father?"

When he didn't answer, Jane looked up at him. "He's never felt dead to you, has he?"

"No," he said slowly. "But I guess it's likely that he is, isn't it?"

Jane went on looking at him, saying nothing.

A creepy chill passed over Keller. "I—I never considered that," he said. "Like you, I just had to keep going—assuming he was okay. But he—the old man could be dead, couldn't he? Maybe he isn't just hiding from me."

Jane put her arms around him. She didn't hug him, just held on. They sat like that for a long time while Keller mulled the possibility of Randall Keller's mortality. Fathers like the Professor just didn't die. Keller couldn't quite grasp the concept. He felt dazed.

Finally Jane said, "I'm glad you're here, Keller."

That should have been startling news. He fondled a tendril of her hair and said, "I didn't want you to be alone."

He kissed her then. Lightly on the forehead. It seemed an okay thing to do.

She tilted her face, and so it seemed all right to kiss her on the mouth then. Lightly. Then more firmly, with more feeling. The feeling wasn't one Keller could identify right away. It wasn't lust. Not exactly. Lust was there, though, roiling around inside him with a few other emotions he didn't completely recognize. How did he feel? After all this talk of life and death—and maybe he was muddled—Jane transcended mortality. The waters of life rushed inside her, all right. She was the kind of woman from whom life sprang. Even grieving, she was alive and vital, warm in his arms. If ever there was a way to immortality for a man, it would be through a woman like her.

Keller held Jane tighter and kept on kissing her.

She kissed him back. Maybe she was looking for nothing more than a little comfort. When she parted her lips, though, the whole picture changed. Keller put his hands under her sweater and found her warm skin. In return, she began to unbutton his flannel shirt.

When he broke the kiss and looked into her face by the flickering light of a dying fire, she looked back solemnly with tears sparkling on her eyelashes and said, "Stay with me. Make love with me."

Chapter 22

Chapter 22

LATER, DRUGGED WITH A POTION OF RICE BEER, FILLING FOOD, and satisfying sex, Keller fell into a soundless sleep, conscious of little more than Jane's entirely naked body curled warmly against his own in a bed made up of a scruffy yak-hair blanket and their own discarded clothing. The dreams that drifted in his mind that night blended confused images of his own father with those of the child he imagined Jane's should look like—steady-eyed and firm of jaw.

Perhaps in response to his dream, Jane rolled into his arms during the night, and languorously—half-asleep—they made love again with her long, flaxen hair tangled around both their necks. Making love. Making children. It all meshed together in his dream. With beautiful Jane. Quick, stubborn, hell-bent Jane.

When morning came, it was she who woke first. Not gently.

She convulsed out of sleep and sat up, hugging the blanket and tilting her head to listen. "Oh, God," she said.

"Huh?" Keller climbed laboriously back to consciousness. His brain was fogged, and he didn't want to be awake. It was too nice where he'd spent the night.

"Quick," she said, grabbing his shoulder.

"What's—huh?"

"Paul," she hissed. "Wake up! It's Roger!"

He almost said, "Roger who?" but he remembered in time. He was in the act of sitting up when Roger Parish barreled into their cozy room like a maddened water buffalo.

"The wedding's off!" he bellowed.

"Roger," Jane began.

"The bitch slapped me!" Roger shouted. He came to a straddled halt above the two of them and stood glaring down at Jane with fire in his bloodshot eyes. "I could have made her a queen, and she slapped me! I won't have a woman like that! What do you think you're doing? Get out of there immediately!"

"I'll do nothing of the kind," retorted Jane.

He seized her hair and hauled her up out of the blankets, naked. "You slept with him! A *librarian!* What kind of woman are you?"

"Divorced!" She fought her way loose, crying, "Let me go!"

Keller found himself on his feet and between them—shivering Jane and an enraged ex-husband. "Hey," he said, not in top verbal form just yet.

Parish glanced down Keller's undressed frame with a sneer of disgust twisting his features. "You're a pathetic specimen, Keller."

"Can this wait?" Keller asked. "At least until we've had our morning coffee?"

"There'll be no coffee for you," Roger snapped. "Get your pants on, for God's sake. And you," he said to Jane, "get your things. You're coming with me."

"I will not," said Jane. "You have no hold on me, Roger."

"You're a guest in my house," Roger shot back. "And you'll obey my orders."

Keller tried intervening again. "Look, just because—"

"Shut up!" Roger shouted. "Yo! Rabia! Come in here!"

Jane caught up the blanket and wrapped it around herself

in the instant before Roger's henchmen entered the small room. They avoided looking at her and instead gazed like expectant hunting dogs at their master. Roger indicated Keller with a gesture.

"Take him to the cave below," Roger commanded. "See that he doesn't escape."

"Look here!" Keller started.

He fought, but he didn't have a chance from the beginning. The two thugs grabbed his arms, and Roger swung a punch. It caught Keller on the jaw. The thugs let go, and Keller fell. The air was suddenly filled with pinprick stars. Keller took pleasure in his last coherent thought, which was that Roger had to have broken a knuckle.

"Roger!" Jane's voice cried out from very far away. "Don't! Oh my God. Paul!"

Blackness swam up then.

He was freezing cold after that. *Freezing* cold. In fact, it was probably the cold that brought him around again. Keller remembered a lot of voices—some of them real and some of them out of his past. They babbled together like the instruments of an orchestra warming up, finally all melding into one single voice. His father's.

"Boy? That's a respectable goose egg you've got there. You awake?"

Keller blinked hard, and the darkness melted back enough to reveal a face. Then a whole head and shoulders. With bushy white hair and huge, hawklike eyebrows.

Keller blinked again. "Dad?"

"By God, you're alive after all."

"Dad!"

He sat up, but the world began to spin, and he eased back down on one elbow and squinted into the semidarkness. Indeed, the apparition that swam before him was his own father, Professor Randall Keller. The old man's craggy face and piercing blue eyes hadn't changed in twenty years. He was gaunt and bony as an underfed stork and dressed in a field jacket that had probably been purchased at Abercrombie and Fitch during the days of Teddy Roosevelt. It was stained and filthy, which surprised Keller, who knew his father to be mildly bizarre, but always fastidious. His trousers were worn thin, and dirt encrusted his boots, which were cracked from lack of maintenance. The white mane of his hair hadn't seen a comb in weeks, he had straggly whiskers all over his chin, and his teeth desperately needed the attention of a good toothbrush and floss.

The Professor smiled quite happily, however, and the light of pleasure shone brightly in his eyes. He appeared to be content—even pleased—with his situation. "Well, good to have you aboard finally, boy. Took you long enough to get here, didn't it?"

"Jesus," said Keller. "It is you! I had started to believe you were dead."

"Me? *Dead?* What put that damn fool idea into your head?"

"I hadn't heard from you since that night you called me!" Keller cried. "What the hell did you expect me to think? You son of a bitch, you could have dropped a few more clues, you know!"

"Steady, steady," said the Professor, patting Keller's shoulder. "I'm delighted that you made it, boy. You look healthier than I expected, in fact."

That typically two-edged fatherly praise gave Keller the strength to sit up and gingerly feel the lump on his head. The lump caused a little surge of nausea, too. "What did you expect?"

The Professor grinned. "Touchy, aren't you? How about if we get you dressed before we go into the specifics? Freeze your pecker off in a minute."

He was right. With his father's help, Keller sat up. "Where are we?"

"A worse place than where you spent the night, from what I hear. I understand you just got caught dipping your pen in the wrong inkwell this morning, boy. You got more spunk than I thought." He assisted Keller to his feet and winked.

Keller did not wink back. At least Parish's henchmen had kindly brought along his trousers and boots. He reached for them and discovered no shirt or sweater. Shivering, Keller pulled on his trousers, and while stepping into his boots, he looked around himself to get his bearings. Shadows wobbled on the walls. Or maybe the wallop on his jaw was causing things to waver. Gradually, however, things came into focus.

"Where the hell are we?"

"Too cold for hell," the Professor replied pleasantly, sitting back on a rock and folding his arms over his chest. "I think we can correctly call this place a dungeon."

A *dungeon* was perhaps too formal a term. The cave in which Keller found himself half-crouching was hardly six feet high and ran a length of perhaps fifteen feet before narrowing down to a space hardly large enough to accommodate a squirrel. This was no cave like Becky Thatcher's. Jagged rock jutted inward from all directions and gave the chamber the look of a medieval torture chamber. The place also smelled horribly of sulphur and human waste, contained no dishes or furniture whatsoever, and was blocked off from the rest of Roger Parish's fortress by the two broken halves of a carved stone that had been rolled across the only entrance. A sliver of light penetrated the sizable crack between the two stones, providing the sole illumination for the cave. By that poor light, Keller finished with his boots and looked at his father.

"It's time," he said, "for you to do some explaining."

"Well, what would you like to hear first?"

"What you're doing here, I think. Unless I'm hallucinating, Dad, you're a prisoner."

"Hmm," said the Professor, nodding. "I suppose it might look that way, yes. But I'm not. Not really."

"You're being held for ransom," Keller reminded him. "The map, right? You're stuck here until I give—"

"Oh, well, yes, that part's true, I suppose. But I'm staying willingly."

Keller held his head, hoping it wasn't going to crack into two pieces. Inside, his arteries were thumping. "Dad," he pleaded, "just tell me what's going on."

"All right, all right. You've met Roger Parish, I guess? What a character he is!" The Professor shook his head admiringly. "He's got some plan to take some information over the border to the Chinese."

"Yes, I know all about that."

"Oh? Well, it's not an easy trip, as you might imagine. Bad weather is due any day now. And the border is patrolled. There are some other chaps Parish would like to avoid."

"I'll bet."

"So he's asked me to take him across."

"You?"

"Yes. We could hike our way across the plateau to the mountains, but that's tundra, you know, and it would be like walking across a desert, only colder. Then we'd have a hell of a climb over the hills to get into China after that. But you see, there's an easier way."

"What do you mean?"

"I mean I know a better route to take to China."

"I think you'd better elaborate."

The Professor leaned closer. "Have you studied the map?"

"Sure, I took a look."

"Then you know about the Black Bridge."

"The—? No, I don't."

The Professor glanced toward the cave's entrance to assure himself they could not be overheard. No life-forms with more sense than a centipede would willingly remain in such a stinking hellhole, but the Professor had to be certain. Reassured, he dropped his voice anyway, and Keller leaned closer to hear. He said, "The Black Bridge is an ancient route, first discovered and used three hundred years ago by a Tibetan renegade called Mohir Dok. Have you read about him?"

Keller shook his head.

"It's not likely that you would," the Professor went on. "He was small potatoes, considering the successes of Genghis Khan, but he was the same sort of fellow. Robbed from the Chinese for a while, and then he discovered that stealing from the Indians was a great deal less trouble and certainly more profitable."

"Robin Hood without the philanthropic bent."

"Precisely. Dok made a practice of swooping out of the Himalaya, stealing whatever struck his fancy, and then retreating to his fortress in the mountains."

"This place," said Keller.

The Professor grinned, pleased to have heard the correct answer. "Very likely. This castle doesn't look like the monasteries hereabouts, does it? It's a bloody fort. Mohir Dok had an extraordinary knowledge of the mountains. He found and built this place, and he knew ways in and out of the hills that no one could follow. He was not, however, a mapmaker. One of his relatives attempted to map some of his routes, but few of the papers survived, and even fewer were accurate."

"I'm beginning to understand," said Keller. "The map you had in the safe at home is one of Mohir Dok's routes."

The Professor beamed. "Exactly. The map depicts one of Dok's earliest forays into China. He used a land bridge across the seemingly unpassable ridges to the north of here—ridges that go around the desert to the Chinese border. From the point where this land bridge comes out, there's easy access to China."

"The Black Bridge," said Keller.

"Yes, a solid mass of black granite that stretches for perhaps twelve miles across some of the most desolate ground on the face of the planet. The bridge was untouched by glaciers, but ice activity in the surrounding areas has rendered it practically invisible to explorers. Hell, because of weather and the political conditions right now, we can't even fly a plane over that territory without risking lives. I had to pay for a satellite sweep of the area. That's how I came to meet Roger Parish. He was mixed up in that high-tech surveillance stuff with the Navy."

"And a Navy satellite picked up the bridge?"

"Plain as day," he declared with triumph. "Only a few westerners know about the Black Bridge, and even fewer have actually looked for it. None have succeeded."

"And you," said Keller, "think you can find the bridge."

"I'm sure I can. All I need is the map."

"Why didn't you bring it yourself?"

The Professor sucked on his lower lip a moment, regarding Keller. "I thought it would be wiser not to show it to Parish just yet."

"Oh?"

"I had some doubts, I admit. I wasn't sure Parish was trustworthy. But now I know."

"What do you know?"

"That he's misguided. But determined! I want a partner who won't turn back. I want that bridge at all cost! I've spent years studying this, boy." The Professor stood up and stripped off his jacket. Kindly, he put it across Keller's bare shoulders.

He accepted the jacket, knowing it wasn't going to make him feel any better but at least he'd be warm. "Since when have you been studying this bridge? This whole thing is news to me."

"I have never kept anyone abreast of my activities." Sitting back down on his rock, the Professor said, "Since before you were born. I read about Mohir Dok in the journals of a Buddhist mapmaker. I was hardly into my thirties when I came here and hiked all over this plateau in search of evidence to corroborate the story. I bought a map from some hill people who claimed to be relatives of Mohir Dok and spoke with them at length about his travels. We made friends with the people."

"We?"

Relaxed, the Professor nodded. "Your mother was here with me."

That *was* a surprise. As far as Keller knew, Charlotte rarely ventured beyond the District of Columbia unless it was out to the suburbs to shop at Bloomingdale's. *"Mother was here? Here?* But she's never gone on any of your expeditions—"

"Not since that one," the Professor agreed. He stroked his whiskers and mused. "You were born the next year, if I remember correctly. Why, yes, I'm certain of it. She never went with me after that. We did not," the Professor added, "exactly enjoy a second honeymoon on that trip. We left before I was finished with my work."

"You fought with her," Keller guessed.

"This place," the Professor explained, "is not conducive to romance."

"I can't argue with that," Keller muttered. "So thirty-five years ago you came out here and listened to some cockamamie stories and bought a tourist trinket, and now you've come to find the bridge they told you about?"

Grandly, the Professor nodded. "Once and for all."

"With Roger Parish."

"Parish," explained the Professor, "is paying for the expedition. All I have to do is lead the way."

"I hope," said Keller dryly, "you didn't give him the Super Saver rate."

"Now see here," the Professor began.

"No, just answer a couple more questions, Dad. Do you know why Roger Parish is so interested in going to China?"

"Of course. He wants to avoid customs."

Keller laughed shortly. "You bet he does! He wants to avoid government intervention entirely. Any government. The man's a spy."

"I know."

"You *know?* Then why in God's name are you taking him?"

"Because I want to go, and he wants to go, and he's willing to pay for the supplies and manpower. It's a simple business arrangement."

"Dad, listen to yourself. The man is selling military secrets to the Chinese."

The Professor made a noise of exasperation. "What do I care about military secrets? This isn't the Cold War anymore, you know. We're friendly with the Chinese. Tip O'Neill sang on the Great Wall, for heaven's sake! After that, maybe we *owe* them a few secrets."

"Dad," Keller insisted, "you can't get mixed up in this. This is international politics we're talking about."

"I'm not interested in politics," said the Professor, waving his hand airily. "I'm looking at the larger picture. The story of humankind! Finding the truth! Exploring the story of a real man! This is the opportunity of my lifetime, boy!"

"To make an international ass of yourself? Dad, you— you'd be an accessory to treason! They can probably hang you for that in *any* country."

Impatient, the Professor said, "This discovery is the chance I've been working toward all my life. I want to relive a part of history and bring it to the modern world. Think of it! It's immortality."

"Immortality?" Keller was appalled. "That's ridiculous! It's not just foolhardy and stupid, it's silly! You've gone around the bend." He started to pace, but bashed his head again. He eased back down again and fumed. "Maybe it's the Stockholm syndrome. That's it. Has Parish been brainwashing you? Forcing you to do whatever he says?"

"Of course not! I want to go. I *am* going. It's as simple as that."

"Why? For the fun of it? For the adventure? Why risk your life for glory, Dad?"

"If you have to ask that question," said the Professor, "you aren't man enough to understand the answer."

"That," snapped Keller, "is B-movie bullshit!"

"Then B movies have a lot of truth in them."

"You're acting like a fool. You're letting Hollywood dictate how a grown man ought to act in a damned dangerous situation!"

"I'm a man of action. I always have been, and I always will be."

"Oh, for God's sake! You're going to be seventy years old soon! This is life and death we're talking about!"

"Good," he said. "I'll be happy to die on this trail. You won't catch me wasting my life in a dusty library, boy."

Keller pointed his finger at the Professor's beaky nose. "Listen, you son of a bitch, I'm sick and tired of having my manhood put on the line for a bunch of stupid ideas. I came all the way up here over mountains and through blizzards to help you, and all you want to do is lecture me about courage and the manly art of dying."

" 'This thing of being a hero,' " quoted the Professor, " 'is knowing when to die.' "

"Who said that?"

He frowned. "Will Rogers, I think."

"Doesn't *that* tell you something? For crying out loud, Dad, being a hero is nothing more than being an egomaniac. You and Parish are exactly the same! Both of you are busy trying to prove how tough you are, but you're only succeeding in showing everybody that you're *crazy!* The bravest, toughest person I've seen in the last two weeks isn't either one of you; it's a woman who spent her entire life's savings, trained herself to survive in the worst conditions, and fought her way up the highest mountains in the world to find her lost child. Now, if you can be tougher than that, I'd like to see it."

"You'll get your chance," said the Professor, not missing a beat. "Because I'm taking Roger Parish across the Black Bridge to China."

He gave Keller a frosty no-more-arguments stare and then said, "Now where's my map?"

"Map?" said Keller.

"You heard me. The map I told you to bring. Parish won't let me out of this pit until I have it in my hands and can show him the route. Where is it?"

"The map," Keller said again.

"Good God," said the Professor, staring at him. "You haven't lost it, have you?"

Chapter 23

JANE GOT DRESSED WHILE ROGER DRAGGED HER DOWN THE corridor. She'd had some practice doing things like that. It was especially easy if he hauled her by her hair, because she had both hands free. They arrived in the enormous chamber where dinner had been served the night before, and Roger swung her around and let go. Jane crashed onto the table, but she didn't make a sound. Crying out only made him worse. The table cracked and broke at impact, but Jane rolled free—another trick she'd learned after years of practice—and scrambled out of Roger's range. Scrambling away from him was like riding a bicycle. She'd never forget how to do it.

It seemed that he wasn't interested in hitting her, however. He spun around and proceeded to pace, muttering and snorting like a corralled rhino. Jane hustled into her clothes while he ranted.

"The silly bitch! It wasn't like I was after sex. All I wanted was a—she actually hit me! And scratched my face! Look at that! Blood!" He swiped his palm down his cheek and showed Jane the result. Nothing showed on his hand, but he didn't appear to notice. Eyes agleam, he shouted, "I smacked her back, though! Nobody hits me and gets away with it!"

"You're no slouch when it comes to diplomacy," Jane agreed, tucking her shirt into her jeans.

Roger snorted. "Yeah, well, she's leaving this morning. Her and her fag brother. Pompowsky's rounding them up now." He pointed. "I want you here when she leaves."

"Me? Why?"

"To show her I don't need her," Roger snapped. "It's not like I'm desperate to hook up with the first female without a thousand wrinkles. Why are all the women in this country old? You sit down right here and smile like you're glad you're here, got that?"

"Do I get an Academy Award afterwards?"

"Shut up," he said. "Here they come. Do something about your hair."

It wasn't the princess who entered the chamber, but rather Calvin Cahill. He spotted Jane, and his hound-dog face lit up with joy and relief. He rushed across the chamber and crashed to his knees beside her.

"Jane, honey! You all right?"

She touched his face to calm him. "Fine, Calvin. You? And Yamdi?"

"He's out getting some air. We're okay, though." He peeled Jane's hands off his face and clasped them hard between his own. He was staring at her, searching her expression for some sign of her old self. Alarmed by what he saw, he began, "Oh, Janey, you look—" But he caught himself and stopped. "Did you get something to eat?"

"No," said Jane. Oddly enough, she didn't feel hungry, either. Her stomach felt numb. Her whole body felt dull, in fact. Trying to explain that to Calvin would be a mistake, though. "Maybe later," she said, making a poor attempt to ease the concern she read in his face. "I don't—"

"Cut the chatter," Roger commanded. "Here they come."

Calvin put his arm around her. Mystified by Roger's rage, he whispered, "What's the occasion?"

"Exit princess," Jane murmured.

"She didn't measure up?"

Barely audibly, Jane said, "I'm betting she was too much to handle."

The both of them fell silent and watched as the prince and princess entered, complete with entourage, for a final audience with Roger. Colonel Pompowsky brought up the rear, driving the procession like a smug shepherd.

The prince appeared to be most distressed by their imminent departure and his subsequent loss of profit. His blubbery face was puckered into a pout, but the princess held her head up high as she strutted in and halted in front of Roger. Her posture was perfect, putting her young breasts into perfectly detailed relief against the draping silk of her sari. Her perfect face registered nothing but disdain. Roger returned her haughty stare with a glower, but tapped what was left of his stick against his leg in a nervous rhythm.

The prince began to make a speech in his native tongue; he was ignored by everyone, who seemed to be transfixed by the unspoken messages flashing between Roger and the princess. The prince's voice rose petulantly, but even his sister disregarded him. She and Roger appeared to be locked in a stare-down.

Roger lost. He broke the contest of wills by gesturing impatiently at the luggage-bearers. "Get this crap out of here!"

As the boys bent over their loads again, Pompowsky stepped forward and grabbed the prince by his elbow. The prince halted his tirade at once. Clearly offended, he shook off Pompowsky's grasp and sketched a hurried bow at Roger. He made a scuttling exit.

The princess, however, took her time. She feigned the beginnings of a bow at Roger, then turned it into a far from reverent shoulder dip complete with a searing Joan Crawford look calculated to terrify lesser men.

Perhaps it worked. Hoarsely, Roger said, "Clear out!"

The princess allowed a triumphant smile to curl her lip.

To shield himself from any spell she might see fit to cast on him, Roger hastily stepped behind Jane, who was making every effort to look as if she was minding her own business. Roger clamped one of his hands possessively on Jane's shoulder. Calvin also tightened his grip on her.

The princess's dangerous black eyes fell on Jane and filled with rage.

Jane tried a smile. "Good-bye," she said, and waved.

The princess reacted with a high-pitched screech. She dived into the folds of her sari and came up with a long-bladed knife that caught the firelight with a glitter of steel. Flinging herself at Jane, she slashed the air with her weapon.

"Man alive!" Calvin shouted. "Stop her!"

Jane yelped and fended off the girl's first stab. Together, they crashed over the broken table and landed in a heap on the cold floor. On her back and helpless, Jane grabbed the princess's wrist and held on tight. The infuriated princess shrieked and fought, hampered by her voluminous garment for just an instant. Then she gathered her strength, tore free, and plunged downward with the knife. Jane rolled in the nick of time, and felt the sting of the blade along her forearm. She gasped, and the princess reared back, knife poised high for maximum momentum.

Jane cried out, "Somebody *help!*"

Calvin came to her rescue. He grabbed the princess from behind and lifted her into the air. She howled and struggled, kicking him, but Calvin hung on determinedly. Pompowsky arrived in time to wrestle the knife out of the girl's hand. Then he stepped back to avoid her slashing fingernails.

"Take her outside!" Roger ordered. "Dump her in the nearest snowbank!"

Panting with the effort of holding the writhing princess, Calvin gasped, "Whatever you say," and made his exit.

Jane checked her arm. The knife had broken her skin, and a tiny thread of blood appeared. The wound didn't hurt, but the sight of her own blood made Jane feel strangely dreamy. The blade had torn the sleeve of her shirt, too. She examined the material, trying to puzzle through how she could fix it. Her mind seemed to be functioning very, very slowly.

"Crazy female," Roger muttered.

"A nut case," Pompowsky agreed, wiping the blade on his trouser leg.

Roger turned to the Colonel, and his face was shining with perspiration. "I think it's time to clear out of here, Herman."

"I'm just waiting for the order to move," Pompowsky said staunchly. "Did the Professor come through?"

"His son was supposed to bring the last of the information he needed. By now, they've had a chance to confer. We should be ready to move."

"What about her?"

Jane looked up from her torn shirt to find both Roger and Pompowsky studying her as if she was a piece of artillery that needed moving. She did not speak. Her voice probably wouldn't work, anyway. Everything seemed to be going in slow motion, as far as she could tell. She was numb.

Pompowsky said, "She's been a pain in the A from the beginning, Parish. You could have *told* me she was bringing the goodies."

Roger gave his coconspirator a thin smile. "If I'd told you that, Herman, you might have decided to complete the mission on your own."

Pompowsky flushed. "Well, now she knows what we're doing. We can't exactly turn her loose. She's got a big mouth."

Roger gazed down at her, but Jane knew he wasn't seeing her. Not really. She was baggage, that was all. Another item to be checked off his list of things to do. She didn't mind just then. He could do whatever he pleased. It didn't matter anymore.

As was his practice, Roger made up his mind with a quick nod. "We'll take her with us."

"Take her with us!" Pompowsky clapped his palm to his forehead and groaned. "She'll be dead weight! She can't even walk! She's got—"

"We'll take her," said Roger. He bent down a crooked forefinger under Jane's chin. Smiling, he tickled her. "I might have a use for her later. When we settle down."

Jane didn't have the spunk to lift her chin away from his caress.

"Why?" Pompowsky demanded.

Roger stood back, still grinning down at Jane. "If I'm going to be an emperor, I'm going to need some heirs. One good thing about Janey is that she's a proven mare."

On any other day, Jane might have reacted with rage. But today she didn't have the spirit. Today she couldn't hate his stupid barbs. That would have taken too much energy. She didn't feel a thing. Though her arm continued to ooze blood, she didn't care. She didn't even have the strength to return Roger's look. She let her head loll forward.

Roger laughed. "See, Herman? What a nice girl she is. I'll have a use for her."

Pompowsky grumbled and stuck the princess's knife into his belt. "All right, what about Keller?"

"The Professor's son?"

"Yeah. I can guarantee he won't cooperate like his old man. And he won't tag along peaceably like the girl. What do you figure to do about him?"

Roger shrugged. "You've got your gun."

Pompowsky blinked. "What?"

"Use it," said Roger. "You were so red-hot to dispose of little Janey here a minute ago. Divert some of that thirst for blood onto Keller. Kill him."

"But—"

"He'll go straight to the authorities, if you don't." Calmly, Roger explained, "Any country can arrest us now, Herman. We've broken a whole bunch of laws, not the least of which is the way you commandeered the Nepalese police and had them running around like chickens with their heads cut off. If Keller gets loose, he'll lead them straight to us. Hell, he might even call in our own people to nail us. He's got to be stopped, Herman." Roger clapped Pompowsky on the shoulder. "And you're just the man to do the job."

Pompowsky didn't move.

"Herman," Roger chided, "you're not getting squeamish, are you?"

Straightening manfully, Pompowsky said, "Hell, no. Just thinking things through. I'll take care of Keller."

"Good." Roger gave him a friendly pat. "Go down to the cave now, will you? Send the Professor up to me. I'd prefer that he not know what happens to his son for a few days, understand? I'll be in my headquarters."

"Gotcha," said Pompowsky. He turned to go, then paused. "What about the girl?"

Roger glanced down at Jane. "She's not going anywhere."

And Roger was right. Jane didn't feel like going anywhere. Both men left the chamber, each taking a different exit and marching off into the labyrinthine corridors. Jane listened to their footsteps, but felt no urge to follow them.

She wasn't sure how long she sat there. But in a little while, she became aware of whispering. Perhaps she had fallen asleep and was dreaming. Yes, that was it. A woman in a black robe was bending over her, and tugging Jane by her arm. If it was a dream, Ingmar Bergman was definitely directing.

"Missus," whispered the woman. "Missus!" She spoke in Swedish—or maybe it was Nepali. In either case, Jane didn't understand her words. The woman pulled and pulled, however, until Jane was standing.

Then she became aware of another woman in the chamber, too, also dressed in a black wrapped robe. She had a little girl with her, holding her hand. The little girl was pretty and wore huge dangling earrings. She blinked at Jane wonderingly. The woman holding her hand looked fearful, however.

"What?" Jane asked, finally gathering enough energy to speak. "What do you want?"

The first woman spoke in Nepali again, and continued to draw Jane out of the chamber. They walked together and whispered. Jane couldn't make out what their message was, but it was plain to see that the women were agitated.

"Killer," said the first woman. "Missus, Killer!"

"Killer?" Jane repeated. "You mean Keller?"

The woman nodded frantically and began to point down the winding cave. The rocky corridor seemed to melt into a long, black tunnel. The woman gave Jane a push, then stood back and mimed that she and her friends would hide where she was, behind the rubble of rocks.

As though acting in a dream, Jane obeyed. Slowly, she set off walking down the long corridor. The air temperature grew colder and colder, but Jane did not gather her shirt around her body. She walked into the darkness and felt the wind at her back. She felt as if she was walking into a hellish place.

Soon footsteps sounded in front of her. Jane stopped, then slid instinctively to one side of the tunnel. She saw a man approaching and crouched.

The man held a small butter lamp in front of himself to

see his way along. He was very tall, lanky-legged, and white-haired, wearing an American-made jacket. His expression was tense, wild-eyed and filled with excitement. Chances were good that this was Professor Keller. He was so intent on making his way up from the cave that he did not see Jane huddled against the rocky floor. He went past her and up into the light.

When he was gone, Jane stood up and felt her way farther down into the tunnel. When she heard voices, she stopped.

"Hey," said Paul Keller's voice. "You're not gaining a thing by killing me, Herman."

And Pompowsky said, "Kneel down, boy. This will just take a second."

Chapter 24

THOUGH THE CAVE WAS FREEZING COLD, KELLER BEGAN TO sweat. Pompowsky had killed Pirim, and all evidence pointed to the conclusion that he could kill again. "Herman," he said, trying his damnedest not to beg shamelessly, "let's discuss this."

"Discuss?"

"Yes, exactly. You don't really want to—to murder me, do you?"

Examining his gun before he used it, Pompowsky sighed. "It's the way it's got to be, son. Parish says you'll squeal, so—"

"Squeal? Me?" Keller hugged his naked chest to keep from shivering. "Hey, I'm just going to be relieved to get out of this godforsaken country! Do you think I'm going to hang around and get mixed up in a Third World version of a sheriff's posse? Herman, Herman, I thought you knew me better! I just want to get the hell home! Come on now, don't you believe me?"

Pompowsky eyed him frostily.

Keller sensed a hesitation in the man, and he jumped at his chance. "Honest, Herman. I just want to go home to my condo."

Pompowsky went on studying him.

"I'm an American," Keller pleaded. "You wouldn't kill a fellow American, would you? Let me go, Herman."

"Well, now," said Pompowsky, "how do I know that's what you'd really do?"

"I'm a man of honor," Keller promised at once. "Cross my heart, all I want to do is go home. I've got a promotion coming, did I tell you? I have to get back, or they'll give it to somebody else!"

"You work for the government," Pompowsky pointed out. He snapped the magazine into the pistol and stood back. "All you have to do is walk across the hall to the CIA and tell them what you've seen up here."

Looking down the barrel of a loaded pistol had a galvanizing effect. Keller started talking very fast. "Herman, I work in a *library*. That's hardly across the hall from anybody! I study maps all day. What do I know about spies? Please, Herman. Let me go. I'll keep quiet. Honest, I will."

Pompowsky smiled. He lifted the muzzle of the pistol. But he kept smiling.

Weakly, Keller smiled, too. "You don't really want to do this, do you? I'm one of your own. If this was wartime, why, I might have been one of your very own boys. Think of it, Colonel."

Pompowsky lowered the pistol and appeared to consider matters. "You could have been," he admitted.

"Exactly. I could have looked up to you. Admired you. Wished I was just like you."

The trick almost worked. Then Pompowsky began considering some possibilities. "What about the girl? She's going with us, you know. Parish wants her."

"Good!" Keller exclaimed. "Terrific! She's been a pest from the beginning. Maybe Parish can handle her. I just— well, I just took advantage of a good thing when it was offered to me, that's all."

"You won't make any effort to get her back?"

"Are you kidding?"

"What about your old man?"

"What about him?"

"He's going to China, too. And he won't be coming back, you know. Parish won't let him go Stateside after this trip."

Keller shrugged, except he was so cold that the gesture turned into a shudder. "Okay by me," he said, teeth chattering. "The old coot is crazier than Parish, anyway. Take him, he's all yours!"

A noise scraped outside the cave. Pompowsky half-turned and listened. Suddenly, he was nervous. With the gun held at the ready, he went out into the tunnel and squinted into the darkness there.

"What is it?" Keller asked.

"I thought I heard something."

Whatever form of little mouse had been listening outside had obviously escaped before being discovered. With a satisfied grunt, Pompowsky came back into the prison and got down to business. "Listen, Keller, are you serious about all this?"

"About keeping my mouth shut?" Keller could hardly keep his voice from squeaking. "Oh, you bet, Herman!"

Pompowsky frowned. "You're sure? You'll go straight home and not say a word?"

"Absolutely!"

"I hate the thought of killing an American."

Keller almost wept with relief. "I understand, Herman. I really do."

The Colonel considered matters, then looked sharply into Keller's face. "You'll have to clear out without getting spotted. I can't have Parish know I let you go."

"Can I have the rest of my clothes first?"

"Too risky. You'll have to jump one of the guys on watch outside and steal his stuff."

Desperately, Keller said, "A weapon, then? I'm not good at this stuff, Herman."

Warily, Pompowsky withdrew a knife from his belt, one he had obviously stolen from somebody. It was a pretty bejeweled blade, and Keller accepted it eagerly. "Oh, Herman, you're a peach!"

Pompowsky growled. "Let's not advertise that, all right? Listen, I want your promise as a man of honor that you'll start down the mountain and not look back. Do I have your word?"

"Oh, absolutely," said Keller. "I'm looking out for my own skin from now on!"

Chapter 25

JANE STUMBLED BLINDLY BACK THROUGH THE CORRIDORS OF THE cave, sick with distress. First Robbie, and now Keller. He was leaving! She had heard every word. He had a chance to run away, and he was jumping at it. Jane tripped and caught herself on the rocky wall. She put her forehead against the cold stone and wished she could freeze to its surface.

"Why, Janey!"

It was Roger. He sounded smug and cheerful at finding her clinging to the rock face. Jane didn't bother to move.

He pried one of her hands loose and chided. "You're not running away, are you? Bad girl." He laughed. "Come with me. We've got things to do."

Docile, Jane allowed him to take her hand and lead her along the cave. She didn't care anymore. Going with Roger was just as easy as lying down and waiting for death.

"This is my headquarters," he explaining, drawing her into an open-air cave.

For the first time since her arrival at Suli, Jane found

herself standing in the sunshine again. The cave's stone ceiling had long ago collapsed, leaving only three standing natural walls and a fourth barricade constructed by man out of rocks and mortar. Weak sunlight poured down from between patches of fog and clouds. Roger had chosen his headquarters well. From the center of the room, Jane could see the hillside fall away below to the wooden bridge they had crossed to get here. From this balconylike vantage point, a commander could observe attackers and direct his own defense with ease.

To one side of the headquarters, a chunk of the fallen ceiling did service as a table, upon which a large piece of paper had been spread out and pinned down with pebbles. Standing over the paper was the tall, raggedy white-haired gentleman, who looked up when Roger entered.

"This is Professor Keller, Janey," said Roger. "Sit down there and listen to what he says."

She had nothing better to do. Jane slid into a sitting position and stayed there.

Smiling, the Professor toyed with the stub of a pencil he had and regarded Jane. He appraised her, in fact, with bright eyes. "You must be the inkwell!"

Roger scowled and finished the introduction bluntly. "She's Jane. My wife."

Delighted, the Professor laughed. "Wife? Ho, ho! *Now* I understand! You tossed my boy in jail for canoodling with your better half!" He crowed like a rooster and flapped his bony arms. He looked like a demented crane.

Roger was not amused and turned toward the table. "Shut up, Professor."

The Professor went on looking at Jane, but archly needled Roger. "She's not bad to look at, is she? I figured you'd marry a big, loud commandeering hausfrau. The take-no-prisoners sort."

Roger, busily rattling the paper, ignored him.

The Professor looked Jane over some more. "What's the matter with her, anyway?"

Roger shrugged. "Moody, that's all. You're too old to be looking at women, anyway. Is this the map?"

"Never too old to look, my boy."

Roger pointed at the paper. "You going to be able to get us

where we want to go, Professor? Or do I leave you locked up here?"

"I've been making final calculations," said the Professor. "This map is my own draft, a combination of all the information I have gathered."

"I thought your son was supposed to bring a map?"

"Oh, that!" The Professor waved his hand. "That was an antique—a product of hearsay. We simply used some of the suggestions on that map to formalize my theory. Here, this is what you're looking for."

Roger studied the page, but he did not look convinced.

"Believe me, Rogey," said the Professor, "this trip is the culmination of my life's work. I'm staking my reputation on it."

"You'll stake more than that," Roger snapped. He looked at the Professor. "I'm going to assemble my people. Be ready to leave within the hour. And Professor, if you back out or lead us into the wrong territory or somehow manage to get us ambushed, I will see that you die for it. Understand what I'm saying?"

"To the letter." Professor Keller smiled politely. "I mean it."

"So do I."

"I am not the kind of man who lowers himself to threatening bodily harm, my boy, but please note that if my expedition fails because of anything you have done to spoil it, I will see that you do not escape punishment, either."

Roger looked tough, but he didn't respond, just spun around smartly and made his exit.

Jane stayed on the ground. No sense getting up if she didn't have to.

The Professor turned back to her, and he continued to look blithely amused by Roger's threat. "Unpleasant chap, isn't he?"

Jane didn't answer.

"A bully," the Professor decided. "But I behaved in an equally uncivilized way, didn't I? Tch, tch. Did I surprise you, Jane, dear? I apologize. I'm an educated man, really— a scholar, even. But sometimes I break out of that character and act like a thug, I suppose. I hope I didn't offend you."

Jane did not speak, and her silence appeared to intrigue

him. The Professor hunkered down beside her again and peered at her. His smile was encouraging, but Jane didn't feel like talking. Not to him or anybody else. Funny how she felt detached from everything now. He patted her leg, however, and the contact was sufficient enough to jolt Jane partially out of her daze. She looked at the Professor. Although he had a kindly tone of voice, his appearance was hardly sedate. His hair was wild, his eyes too bright. His smile quivered at the corners, as if he teetered on the edge of exhaustion. Or sanity. At another time, Jane might have felt afraid of him. But not now. Now he couldn't hurt her. Nobody could.

Perhaps the Professor understood her lack of conversation. He patted her again and sat down beside her and then proceeded to muse aloud, talking about what Jane decided was probably his favorite subject. Himself.

He said, "If you married little Rogey, I suppose you understand men like me. We're nice enough on the home front, but ruthless in our own fields of expertise. I'm a scientist, but I've been known to sacrifice men's lives for my science, just the way a good military man gives up a few men for every victory. You think I went too far threatening him? Oh, I don't. He needed proof that I'm going ahead with this plan come hell or high water. Right now he thinks I'm a nutty old man. He needed reassurance that I'm on his level."

Jane listened.

The Professor relaxed and kept up the monologue, apparently happy for an audience. He said, "I've worked around men like Parish before, you know. Tough-minded types. Gung ho and all that rubbish. Usually they're a lot of hot air, and I don't trust fellows like that. But he and I are going to find some genuine glory when this is all over with. That's what I've been looking for, you know." He allowed his hand to fall on Jane's thigh, and he began to caress her there, as if appraising her flesh while he talked. "All my life I've been adventuring around the world, but I want to be remembered for one glorious act—one supreme discovery that will put me in history books forever."

Jane looked at him.

"Oh, I know what you're thinking," he said quickly,

putting up one hand to silence her objection. "You've already heard of me, haven't you? I've been doing big things all my life! Why, I've discovered some of the most historically important ruins in all of Southeast Asia! And I was the first man to climb all of the five highest summits in the world. Did you know that? Well," he said, nodding firmly, "it's true. I've had some of the grandest adventures in the world!"

He chuckled. "Yessir, I've had excitement like no other man alive. And since you're so talkative, little lady, I'll tell you a secret. I'd give up all my adventuring in a minute! What for? I'll tell you." He gazed out at the mountains with a dreamy look in his eye, as if deciding once and for all if what he was about to say was true. At that moment the panorama of the Himalaya might have represented all the triumphs of his lifetime. He surveyed them with dignity, weighing their value.

Finally, he nodded, mind made up. With a ringing voice, he declared, "I'd give it all up for a woman!"

Jane sat still, but her expression must have reflected surprise, because he laughed.

"That sound funny?" he asked. "It's God's truth. I haven't had a woman in forty years, my dear. Not for lack of wanting to, mind you. I'm no fruitcake! I've been a goddamn dud nearly all my life, that's all. Even a gumdrop like Marilyn Monroe herself couldn't get a rise out of me. Humiliating, is what it is. I've spent my life making up for it. I've got to have *something* to leave behind me in this world. I'm making history."

The Professor shook his head with regret. "But I'd trade every bit of the fame and glory from this last expedition for one lousy erection."

Chapter 26

CASHING IN HIS CHIPS, CUTTING HIS LOSSES, THROWING IN THE towel—whatever it might be called, Keller decided to run. When Colonel Pompowsky showed him the exit, he bolted. The caves were dark, and he encountered no one until he arrived at the entrance of Roger Parish's hideout. Beyond the mouth of the cave spread the mountains, gleaming beautifully in the sun. Funny how they looked so pretty at a distance. Knowing firsthand how hellish they could be on closer inspection, Keller wondered about his sanity for an instant. Only a crazed person would want to go dashing off all alone into those hills.

But dash he must.

He flattened himself against the rocks and peeked outside to check for lurking henchmen. Immediately, he dodged back inside. Yo, the gunman who had escorted them into Roger's fortress in the first place, sat dozing in the sun with the rifle cradled on his lap and a cup of no-longer-warm tea dribbling from his mug onto the ground.

Cautiously, Keller peeked again. Yo appeared to be soundly asleep. With a few quiet steps, Keller could sneak past him, surely. But the snoring guard was wearing a *chupa*, a thick sheepskin coat with assorted insulating rags tied from his wrists to his elbows. The garment was tied over one of Yo's shoulders and bound at his waist and looked incredibly warm. Gazing at the chupa, Keller almost salivated.

Controlling his shivers, Keller began making calculations. The knife wasn't his kind of weapon. He chose a rock from the rubble at his feet.

Forty-five seconds later, he charged out of the cave and flung himself onto Yo. With the rock, Keller promptly rendered Yo harmless. The Tibetan flopped into a heap on the ground, and his gun rolled harmlessly out of his hands.

Keller resisted the temptation to release a Tarzan yell.

Within two minutes, however, he had confiscated the clothing from Yo's upper body, stolen the rifle, and drained the last of the tea from the mug. Then, like a rabbit with the fear of buckshot foremost in his mind, Keller hightailed it down the hillside to a scattering of glacier-tumbled rocks. He hid behind the largest one and got dressed as quickly as his frozen fingers would allow.

When he had swathed himself in Yo's somewhat aromatic clothing, Keller spread his arms and examined the new duds. He looked like Dan Rather masquerading in Afghanistan.

But he had no alternatives. Warm is warm. Keller snatched up the rifle, poked his head above the rocks to reconnoiter, then took off in a half-crouch, dodging from rock to rock until he was within a few bare yards of the wooden bridge.

He had learned what he needed to know about the surrounding countryside from his father. After the Professor's initial temper tantrum about the lost map, they had gotten down to business like the pair of trained cartographers they were and pieced together what they knew and remembered about maps of the area. On the walls of their prison, they had sketched out landmarks and trails. Armed with that information, Keller thought he could make his way over the wooden bridge and back to the place where he had last camped with Jane and Pompowsky before arriving at Roger's place. He had a good sense of direction and remembered terrain easily. If he could find food, he believed he could find his way to a settlement.

Before Yo woke up and turned in some kind of alarm, Keller decided to hustle across the bridge. He did so, and no shots were fired. Free at last. He headed for the lower ridge and didn't look back.

He soon realized, however, that he was being followed.

At first, the feeling was just that—a feeling. Paranoia at work, he assured himself. His imagination was in high gear, and no wonder. But in a while, he definitely heard the soft *shush* of footsteps on the trail above himself. And a little later, some stones came rattling down to him, certainly dislodged by someone who was hot on his trail.

Breathing hard, Keller first tried to outrun his pursuers. He stumbled down the trail, gasping if he lost his footing, leaping over a gully and once sliding perilously close to the edge of the trail and the chasm beyond. He sat down hard, panting, and had to scramble to his feet and keep going.

At that altitude, however, he soon lost his will to run. He found a niche in the rock and prepared to do his Butch and Sundance impression. Surely the whole Bolivian army couldn't be on his trail. With his back to the stone, Keller took the safety off Yo's rifle and put the weapon to his shoulder. He squinted down the barrel. On the trigger, his forefinger was slippery. He waited, trying not to breathe. In a minute, his head turned light.

He inhaled a big breath, spotted his target rounding the trail, and started to squeeze the trigger.

Lord knew what stopped him.

"Eieee!" cried the woman in the lead. She reeled backwards and snatched up the child who had been following.

Keller put down the gun and stood up. "Jesus Christ!" His knees quaked so badly he had to lean against the rocks to stay upright. "I could have killed you!"

The woman railed back at him, and it wasn't until she quit shouting and spat an enormous wad of spittle at his feet that Keller recognized her. Pirim's wife!

She brought her two companions forward, apparently for introductions. One was a round-faced woman, the other was a child. The child, Keller recognized immediately, was the little girl he had saved from the wool traders' dogs. She smiled brightly at him, and her earrings twinkled in the sunlight.

Keller picked her up, and she wound her little arms around his neck. "What's this about, then?" he asked her mother. "Why are you following me?"

It was a stupid question, really. The woman didn't speak much English, and he didn't speak any Nepali. She gesticulated back toward the fortress, and began to complain loudly. She ranted, in fact, gesturing at her little girl, then pointing up the trail again with rage. It took Keller several minutes to figure out her drift. Then he realized he should have seen the whole thing coming.

"Oh, I get it. You want to keep your little girl away from Roger."

She blinked, not sure she understood, and Keller tried to pantomime. That took a while. In the end, she agreed. She didn't want Roger to get his hands on her pretty child.

"But," Keller explained, shaking his head and pointing from his own chest to the mountains, "I can't take you where I'm going."

The woman cried out, then angrily began to argue.

"No, no, I can't," said Keller. "Look, lady—"

She screamed at him, doubling her volume, until Keller set the little girl on her feet and tried to reason with the mother by putting his hands on her shoulders. "Hold it down, will you? They could figure out I'm alive any minute and come looking for me. Just—oh, hell. I want to travel fast, don't you get it?" He walked his fingers rapidly through the air. "I have to hurry. I can't take women and children along." He rocked a pretend infant in his arms.

She got the point. With an outraged look, she gathered up his rifle, put it to her shoulder, and set off walking down the trail. The other woman and the little girl followed. They moved fast, and as surefootedly as goats.

Keller got the point.

"Hey!" he called. "Wait for me!"

They made very good time, in fact. Going down the mountain was a hell of a lot faster than going up. In another hour, they reached a flat spot where a small pool of water provided drinks all around. Keller sat on the rocks and tried to form a plan. He wasn't sure exactly how to execute what he'd had in mind ever since Pompowsky suggested he could go free. Now might be a good time to consider the options.

The women had been more thoughtful before escaping Roger Parish's fortress. They had the foresight to bring along food. They hunkered down and proceeded to chew on some tough marbles of yak cheese. The little girl brought Keller a portion, which he accepted gratefully. While he chewed, he tried to think.

Suddenly, however, the women were as alert as a herd of antelope that had scented a stalking lion. They sat up stiffly, with their eyes open very wide, as if they could hear better that way. For a full minute, nobody moved.

Keller listened hard.

And gradually, he became aware of the sound. Human voices. Not too far away and whispering urgently among themselves. Keller looked around at the rocks.

"Perfect place for an ambush," he muttered. In a split second, he was on his feet and had the gun. The women stood, too. He put his fingertip to his lips to keep them silent, and motioned for them to precede him down the trail. Noiseless as ghosts, they obeyed.

With Keller at the rear, they hurried downward, scuttling along the steep trail as fast as they could safely go. From time to time, Keller paused to glance over his shoulder, but he saw nothing. Once he thought he spotted the tassel on someone's hat, but he wasn't sure. He drove the women downward and didn't allow them to stop and rest. Though he could have used a breather himself, he kept going.

In the late afternoon, everyone was exhausted. They hadn't had enough to drink and needed rest. Keller tried pushing them farther, but the little girl fell and cried out, and when he scooped her up to carry her, he stumbled, too. They had all reached their limits. And behind them, the sounds indicated that a whole posse was on their trail.

Keller tried forcing the women into a cul-de-sac for protection. They balked like mules, but he shoved and shouted, and they went. He backed in, too, and readied his rifle.

And then the posse descended. With horrible banshee

shouts and brandishing weapons, they jumped up from all sides. There were too many of them! The little girl screamed. Keller jerked the rifle to his shoulder.

"Sah!" cried a joyous voice from among the crowd of men who surrounded them. "Keller, sah! Oh, happy day!"

In the nick of time, Keller avoided pulling the trigger.

He lowered the gun and stared at the little man who was thrust to the front of the attacking horde. He couldn't believe his eyes.

"Billy?"

Billy Bhim, smiling ear to ear, stood big as life on the trail.

"My God, *Billy?*" Keller tottered forward. "Is it you?"

"Yes, sah, thank you, sah. It is I!" Billy grinned happily and took a jaunty bow, hands outstretched like a ringmaster's. In the middle of a scowling bunch of desperadoes, two of whom still held him by the scruff of his neck, Billy looked desperately pleased to see a friendly face.

"You son of a bitch, you're *alive!*"

"Oh, yes, sah!" he exclaimed. "Alive I am. A little banged up, sah, but alive. You see my head, sah?"

Billy pulled back the edge of his tasseled hat and displayed with pride a black bruise the size of a saucer. It covered half of his forehead and most of the side of his head. By the looks of the wound, there had also been some blood involved, but that was cleaned off. His face was scratched, his arm bandaged, and he seemed to be favoring his left leg, but Billy's pizzazz appeared to be undiminished by his assorted injuries. His foxy smile was as wily as ever, and his eyes gleamed with as much energy as before.

"I have terrible fall, sah," Billy explained. "Fall down and down and down. You remember?"

"Vividly," said Keller. He remembered so vividly, in fact, that he found he had to sit down to hear the rest. Seeing Billy alive again made him feel very queer inside.

"I fall and fall," said Billy, using his hands to show how his body tumbled. "And hit my head at the bottom, sah. When I wake up, it is daylight, but I do not know which day! I am alive, though, and not too bad hurt. A bird showed me the way up from the bottom of the hole." With a huge smile, Billy asked, "Is that not strange, sah?"

"Yes," Keller said weakly, "very strange."

"I was very happy not to be killed," Billy confided. "When I climb back to the top, though, sah, I find nobody has waited for me! I was alone!"

By that time Keller had grasped the fact that Billy had indeed not died because of his stupidity, and the knowledge had a strange effect on him. "My God," he said. "Do you know how awful I felt about you dying?"

"But sah!" Billy protested. "I am alive! See?"

"Yeah," Keller growled. "I see, all right. How the hell did you get up here? Why didn't you just go back to Kathmandu?"

Billy swallowed. His confidence sagged momentarily.

"Don't lie to me, Billy," Keller warned.

Billy decided to be honest, it seemed. He glanced furtively at the men who stood around them. "You see these chaps, sah?"

How could he miss them? He and Billy were surrounded by a pack of bristling bandits. They carried spears, for heaven's sake, and knives. Their clothing consisted of rough animal skins, yak-hair boots, and very bright fabrics. Their long black hair hung out from underneath filthy turbans. They looked like genetic throwbacks to American Indians with a little Turkish influence in their apparel thrown in. They were the Tibetan bandits he'd heard so much about, Keller was willing to bet.

At the head of the pack was none other than Edward G. Robinson.

"This, sah," said Billy, swinging around to make a dramatic presentation, "is Mohan Dok. He is—I am his guest, you see, sah."

"His guest?"

"Well, in a way, sah, yes. He found me, you see, and—well, he—"

Eyeing the gloating expression on Edward G. Robinson's face, Keller guessed, "You're his prisoner."

Chapter 27

CALVIN CAHILL HAD SPENT THE LAST SIXTEEN YEARS OF HIS LIFE
living out in the wide-open spaces where he didn't have to
answer to anybody, and nobody cared if he took a bath or
brushed his teeth or remembered how to multiply numbers
above seven. He could sing under the moon or eat beans for
six days running—anything he liked. What he didn't like
was being locked up. And Roger Parish had just about done
exactly that.

Oh, Parish hadn't exactly *said* that he was holding anybody a prisoner, but telling his guests to stay in one place
until they were sent for didn't sound like Southern hospital-
ity. Coot did as he was asked for a couple of hours, then he
gave Yamdi an elbow nudge.

"We're bustin' out of here, amigo."

Yamdi woke with a start. *"Yie?"*

"C'mon," said Coot, and he clambered to his feet. "Let's
go find Jane. Something doesn't smell right."

Yamdi obliged, though he kept sniffing the air as they left

the small cavern where Roger had bid them to remain until called. Coot led the escape. They picked their way out through the biggest of the caves and avoided two Nepalese men who were laughing together in a niche along the way. Only when they arrived at the entrance of the fortress did they encounter anyone else.

The whole company had been motivated, by the looks of things. Roger Parish strutted around giving orders to a dozen or so porters who obeyed his commands and appeared to be getting ready for a big expedition. Baskets of supplies lay on the ground, ready to be picked up and carried. A single yak had been found and was being tied up with an enormous load by two men. Pompowsky, chewing gum ferociously, watched them work. Only Jane didn't seem interested in the proceedings. She sat calmly on a stone in the sun, staring at nothing.

Coot forgot to be cautious and walked right out into the sunlight. "Jane, honey! You all right?"

She turned to look at him, but her face didn't register any emotion. She looked like the battle-fatigued footsoldiers Coot remembered from his Vietnam days. Dully, she said, "Hello, Calvin."

"Honey, you look tired! They treating you okay?" He looked around at Roger, who was too caught up in his preparations to notice anything. "What's going on? These guys headed somewhere?"

She nodded. "In a few minutes."

"Gawldang," said Coot, sizing things up pretty fast. "You going with them?"

Jane nodded again, still blank-faced and creepy silent.

"Where's Keller?"

She lifted her shoulders. "Run away."

"Run—? What d'you mean by that? He's still here, isn't he?"

She said, "He went home. Tired of everything."

"He went and left you?" Coot couldn't believe it. "He deserted you?"

Jane didn't respond. She was spacey.

"Gawldang," said Coot, unable to believe that Keller had actually deserted Jane when she really needed someone. "I'm gonna have to get him for this," he said. "You want me to come along with you, honey? Keep you safe from these horse thieves?"

She blinked, only half-comprehending his offer. "No, Calvin. You go on home."

Her blankness scared Coot. He'd seen the look before—on men who'd seen too much and done too many things they wanted to forget. Jane looked like a woman who had shut herself off for a while. Coot touched her arm and gave her a jiggle. She didn't react.

He stood up. "Yamdi, let's clear out of this place."

The little Sherpa bounded up like an excited rabbit. "Where to, Mister Coot?"

"We're gonna look for that Keller fella. I've got a bone to pick with him."

"Bone, sah?"

"He oughtn't left this nice lady here when she needs a friend. Man like that oughta have his head punched."

Yamdi looked doubtful. "You punch the sahib's head, Mister Coot?"

"And a few other things," Coot replied. "Let's leave these folks to their packing, Yamdi. We're gonna go hunt ourselves a woodchuck."

Chapter 28

AS ORDERED, KELLER STOOD UP AND PUT HIS HANDS ON TOP of his head. The Tibetan bandits commanded Billy to do likewise. Together, they were marched out into an open patch of ground.

They walked in step and Billy began his story. "Well, sah, I looked for you for many days. I followed your trail to the house of Pirim, but I arrived after you left. I started after you, but—well, sah, I met these men on the trail instead. I asked about you, sah, and the mention of your name was enough to—well, sah, this man Mohan Dok does not like you very much."

"I'm sure," said Keller. He glanced at Mohan, who grinned back, clearly enjoying being in charge. Keller halted and stood facing Billy, both talking with their hands still clasped on top of their heads while the bandits surrounded them once more.

Billy jerked his head toward Mohan Dok. "He would like to kill you, sah, for insulting him, I think."

"No doubt," said Keller.

"But what he would like more, sah, is riches from you." A spark of hope gleamed in his terrier eyes.

Wearily, Keller said, "Billy, I hate to say this, but I'm flat broke. No lie. I can't pay him a cent. Or you either, for that matter."

"Sah!" Billy cried, pained by such an idea. "I would never ask for a penny! Not after all that has befallen you!"

"I paid you in advance, remember?"

"Naturally," said Billy, exhibiting some asperity. "I meant that I would not charge you more for helping when you are in such terrible—"

"Helping!"

"These men mean to kill you, sah. Unless you pay them."

"I *can't* pay them!"

Billy's sly smile deepened. "What about treasure, sah?"

"Treasure?"

"The treasure on the map."

"I *told* you, Billy, there is no treasure on the map. That map was just a drawing of—"

Billy widened his eyes to shut Keller up. Softly, he said, "Maybe it is wiser to let Mohan Dok *think* there is treasure, sah."

Keller glanced at the men surrounding them. Mohan Dok appeared to be sharpening a new knife on a nearby rock. He made quite a show of testing the blade, and was dissatisfied when it didn't draw blood on his thumb. He looked at Keller with narrowed eyes and carved the air with the knife. Keller must have blanched involuntarily, because Mohan Dok laughed and went back to grinding the blade against the stone.

Keller said, "I see what you mean, Billy."

"These men, sah, will not accept an empty hand from either one of us."

Their predicament didn't look good. Keller had managed to escape from one villain with murder on his mind only to land himself in the hands of another who looked as though he would enjoy committing the crime himself. Judging by the look in his eyes, Mohan Dok was ready for blood. Which gave Keller an idea.

Thoughtfully, he said, "I don't think I want their hands to be empty, Billy."

Billy frowned. "Sah?"

Keller straightened his posture, galvanized by the idea growing in his mind. "I need a few good men, Billy! These men!"

"Need them, sah? For what?"

Keller began to count heads. "To get Jane back from her ex-husband."

Billy's confusion grew. "From her husband, sah? He is alive?"

"Oh, yes, very. He's got her, and we've got to get her back."

"Is that wise?"

"Probably not," said Keller, as confidence in his hatching plan grew within him. "But you know what, Billy? With these men behind me, I think I could beat that son of a bitch Parish!"

"Sah," Billy said nervously, "maybe you do not understand. These men do not want to follow. They want to disembowel."

"Then we've got to win their confidence! Billy, with all these men, we could stop Roger Parish before he gets to China! We could rescue Jane *and* prevent the exchange of top-secret military information! We'd be heroes!"

"But sah," Billy said plaintively, "they are going to kill us."

Mohan Dok finished sharpening his knife. He turned around and signaled to his men. Instantly, Keller and Billy were seized from behind and held fast. Billy gulped and his eyes darted fearfully towards Keller. He choked out a whisper: "If you can win their confidence, sah, I wish you would do it now."

"I'm thinking," said Keller, watching Mohan Dok advance with his knife glittering in the rays of the setting sun. "I'm thinking. What we need is an eclipse."

"A what, sah?"

"Mark Twain used that. *Connecticut Yankee.* How have you escaped being murdered up until now, anyway? How come they haven't killed you already?"

Billy's neck was being stretched, and he had difficulty getting his words out. "I have promised them the treasure from the map, sah. But I could not lead them to it. I cannot read your map, sah."

"You—" Keller craned around as best he could and stared at Billy. "You can't read the map? You mean you *have* the map?"

"Oh, yes, sah. I took it from your pack before I fell into the hole."

"You have the map?"

"Yes, sah. It is in my shirt."

Mohan Dok lifted his knife and prepared to plunge it directly into Billy's chest. Keller had come to this hellish country in the first place to deliver that stupid piece of paper, and now the one man who could probably help him was about to destroy the map completely and murder Billy in the process, which didn't seem like such a bad idea to Keller.

"You stole my map!" he shouted.

He couldn't control his rage. Suddenly a scream of tortured agony rose in Keller's throat. He couldn't stop it.

Chapter 29

HIS SCREAM CAME OUT LOUD. SO LOUD THAT ALL THE BANDITS practically jumped out of their skins and began to babble with fear. Keller thought he stopped screaming, but the noise kept coming, and he was momentarily confused. Then he realized that the scream of rage had not been his own.

From high above them on the mountain, an inhuman cry rent the air. It sounded so animalistic, so frightening, that the bandits dropped Billy and dodged behind Keller. Mohan Dok, equally startled by the horrible scream from above, fumbled his knife into the snow and retreated backwards.

"Yeti," he murmured, staring up the mountain. "Yeti!"

On cue, a huge white creature bounded down from the boulders, yelling and waving a terrifying stick.

"Good Lord," said Keller.

"Bad luck!" Billy screamed. "Very bad luck to set eyes on a yeti! Quickly, sah—"

"That's no yeti! It's Coot!"

The bandits scattered anyway. To them, Coot looked exactly like the most abominable of snowmen. Even Billy dove for cover. Yelling at the top of his lungs, Coot roared down the hillside, waving his stick like a madman. Yamdi was right behind him, looking terrified.

"Coot!" Keller shouted in delight. "Coot, you big lug! Am I glad to see—"

Coot swung his stick, and it whistled past Keller's ear with the momentum of a rocket-launched missile. He snarled, "Shut up, you sniveling son of a coward! I ought to shove this stick—"

"Coot!"

Keller leaped up onto a rock to avoid receiving the stick into a sacred part of his body, and he danced on the rock for an instant, not sure which way to jump. In one direction lay a wide open gorge, and in the other was Coot's woodchuck killer. "Calvin!"

"You left her, you chickenshit! You ran off and left her!"

"What the *hell?*" Keller cried. The stick zoomed past his head, and Keller felt the whisper of its vapor trail against his face. He grabbed his nose to make sure it hadn't been whacked off.

"She's all alone!" Calvin shouted. "Her boy is dead and you—you—! I'm gonna kill you!"

Calvin clenched his teeth, gripped the end of his stick with both hands, and swung it with all his strength, aiming to cut Keller's knees out from under him.

"Jesus *Christ,* Calvin!"

A swan dive over the edge of the cliff was the only answer. Keller dove. For a split second, it seemed the better of two choices. Spread-eagled, he flew out and over the edge, then realized he'd made a mistake. A big mistake. But there was no stopping himself. He sailed out over a huge space of emptiness, then dropped like a stone and crashed into solid rock. He rolled, thudded against more rocks, and plunged through a wall of snow. Head over heels, tumbling out of control he went. The earth became a blur of snow and pain and rock.

Keller lurched the final yard and bashed his head. A huge flashbulb exploded in his head, and he sprawled on the surface of the snow, senseless. It felt good.

After several minutes, however, the pain returned and the sky began to brighten. By then, Billy had reached his side.

"Sah, sah, are you alive? Bloody good, sah, you are!"

Keller's voice was hardly more than a croak. "Billy?"

"Sah!"

"Is he—? Am I—?"

Coot said, "Move outta the way, boys. I'm gonna fix him."

"Wait!" Billy cried.

Keller wasn't quite sure what happened next. He felt himself get frisked and a bunch of voices were clamoring in Nepali. Yamdi and Billy babbled together. The bandits shoved their way into the rapid-fire conversation. Coot got muscled out of the way, a fate he accepted with surprisingly good grace. He didn't hit anybody, at any rate. The surroundings quit moving and settled into shape—Keller had landed in a snowbank at the bottom of a hellishly steep hillside. The bandits and their leader had obviously scrambled down after Billy and Coot, and they all gathered around and bent over Keller's snowbound body.

Keller didn't try to sit up. Inside, his head thumped like a marching band was on parade. Tentatively, Keller put up one hand to investigate. His skull seemed to be in one piece.

But Billy prevented a full examination by hauling Keller by his shoulders into a very painful sitting position. He and Yamdi supported Keller.

"Sah, they want to know. Where did you get this knife?"

Keller blinked hard. "Knife?"

"This one, sah. With the jewels."

Keller shook his head to clear his vision. Edward G. Robinson stood before him and dangled the jeweled knife six inches from Keller's nose. "That knife?" he said, trying to focus his vision. "The Colonel gave it to me, I think."

Coot said, "I came from the princess. Pompowsky took it from her."

"A princess!" Billy cried. "Oh, bloody good, sah!" He translated for the bandits, who were awestruck by this news.

"What's going on, Billy?"

"Sah, these men know this knife! It belongs to their relatives!"

"What?"

"The knife is a sign, sah, given once by Mohir Dok to his favorite mistress in a faraway land. You have brought it back! They think—"

"*I* didn't steal the thing, Billy. It was *given* to me! I—"

Billy patted him. "Do not worry, sah. These men are happy that you bring them the bloody knife. You have returned their rightful property! You are a bloody hero, sah!"

Keller realized that all the bandits had begun to smile, and they bowed to him, muttering in their own language. Even Edward G. Robinson appeared to be happy. If Keller could trust his own powers of observation, it even looked like old Ed was relieved not to have an execution on his agenda.

"Hero?" Coot shouted, raising his stick once more. "This guy's no hero! He just abandoned a helpless woman back there!"

Keller broke from Yamdi's grip and scrambled backwards like a crab. He needn't have tried to escape. As soon as Coot lifted his stick to strike, the bandits leaped forward, weapons bristling. Even Billy flung himself in Coot's path.

With Yamdi's help, Keller got to his feet. "See here, Coot, I haven't abandoned anyone. I just came looking for reinforcements."

With his stick at the ready, Coot hesitated. "What?"

"I mean it," Keller insisted. "I figured I had a better chance of success if I was on the outside. Parish wanted me killed. He'd have gotten around to you, too, I'll bet."

Coot put his stick down. "You think so?"

"I know so!" Keller pushed through the crowd and pumped Coot's limp hand. "I'm glad you're here, old buddy. Now that we're both free agents, we'll have a better chance of raiding his camp and getting Jane back."

Frowning, Coot said, "He left."

"Parish?"

Coot nodded. "And the Colonel and Jane. They've started for China. With the old man who is their guide."

Keller swore softly. "My father. Do you know which way they went?"

"No. Yamdi said—"

Yamdi spoke for himself. "The trail we may be able to

follow, sah. They have many porters and will make many tracks in the snow."

Keller glanced up at the sky and the snowflakes swirling in the air. "Not likely if this weather keeps up. We're going to have to find our own way, I'm afraid. It's just—Billy!"

Billy snapped to attention. "Sah?"

Keller grabbed him. "Billy, hand over the map. If we study it, we may be able to head off my father before he gets across his Black Bridge. Will these men come with us? I can promise them no money when it's over, but I could sure use their help."

Billy grinned. "They will follow you anywhere, sah."

Chapter 30

JANE DIDN'T MIND BEING PULLED ALONG IN HER SLING ANYMORE. She didn't care where she was going, she didn't care how long it took, and she didn't care that she was a burden to anyone. The whole expedition could take place with or without her. Passivity was her new way of looking at life, she decided.

That was her idea at first, anyway. But her attitude changed in less than twenty-four hours. The first night, Roger came to her tent and made every effort to resume the conjugal rights they had legally terminated years ago. That did it.

"Out," she said, feeling a surge of gumption at the first sight of him.

"Aw, Janey, it's only me." Roger crawled into the tent and proceeded to pull her sleeping bag apart.

She grabbed it out of his hands. "Get away from me!"

"Janey, I'm the father of your child. I'm Robbie's father. That ought to give me some—"

She hit him across the nose with her boot, which settled matters for the time being. He smacked her back, but left. Jane knew Roger well enough to guess he'd try again. Roger was not a man to give up on any idea. He'd just spend some time thinking up a way to sneak past her defenses, and he'd return tomorrow night. In the meantime, he'd have figured out a way to cripple her enough to get what he wanted.

Keller was escorted into the camp of the Tibetan bandits. They insisted he be their guest of honor at a tribal feast that night.

"Gawldang," said Coot when they were ensconced around the campfire and drinking chang with the other men. "These fellas sure know how to travel!"

The nomads' camp consisted of several swooping tents made of colorfully striped yak-hair fabric, a few pieces of pottery and cooking pots, two vicious mastiff dogs, a half-dozen ponies, and three placid yaks which—Keller soon discovered—supplied the whole traveling caravan with the fuel to cook and keep warm by. Like the men, all the women and children had soot-blackened faces, long wild hair that they braided into stringy plaits, and multiple-layered clothing with lots of aprons and belts and cloaks.

Pirim's wife had been accepted into the group. She acknowledged Keller with a bow and went about her business.

Together, the women prepared food for communal consumption, all chatting companionably while their menfolk hunched at the fireside telling stories and generally getting in the way. Soon after nightfall, all the men were given portions of cheese and a thick lentil- and potato-based soup—all exceedingly satisfying after days of too little food. Keller accepted his clay bowl with pantomimed thanks. The meal was nicely washed down by chang, which also served to loosen tongues.

After the women collected the bowls and set about refilling them for the second wave of diners, Edward G. Robinson came and draped himself affectionately across Keller's shoulders. With great melodrama, he proceeded to make a speech. Billy translated the chief bandit's remarks.

"Sah, this is Mohan Dok, and he has hated you bloody well much, sah, until today."

"I'm glad he had a change of heart," said Keller, trying cautiously to dislodge his sloppy-drunk host.

"Mohan is pleased to travel with you now, sah, because you have returned the knife of his ancestor."

"It was my pleasure."

"This knife," Billy went on, "was the property of his exalted one. Do you know of this man, sah?"

"The Scourge of the Himalaya," said Keller. "Yes, of course."

Billy translated, and the entire camp stirred, suddenly interested that Keller should have heard of their ancient relative. They muttered and elbowed each other. Billy said, "They want to hear, sah, how you know about this ancestor."

"I know all about Mohir Dok. My father told me the stories. He mapped parts of the world that have never been seen since. These people are really his descendants?"

"The tribe of the same Mohir Dok, yes, sah. They await the return of Mohir's blood to lead their people. He was tall, like you, sah. And not so—so like these people in his looks. Do you understand? They say he was half-western, sah." Curiously, Billy asked, "Do you really know about this man, sah?"

"Why, yes. Not all of this stuff, mind you, but some of it." Keller smiled. "Why? Don't they believe me?" The men around the campfire were grinning, he noticed. "Don't they believe the fame of Mohir Dok might have spread to the West?"

Billy chuckled. "No, sah, they do not smile about their own importance. They smile, sah, because . . ."

"Why?"

"Because—well, sah—"

"Come on, Billy. Tell me."

Billy came clean hastily, smothering a laugh. "They do not think you are very smart, sah. They do not believe you *truly* know about their relative."

"They think I'm lying?"

Billy tried to look sympathetic, but his grin broke

through. "I am afraid so, sah. To these men, you are a very ignorant westerner."

"By God, Billy, I've got a Ph.D.! I work for the Library of Congress! And dammit, I'm up for a promotion soon!"

His outrage was apparently hilarious. The men gathered around the fire burst into laughter. They laughed loudly and long. It was contagious, in fact. Even Yamdi and Coot joined in.

Even Keller laughed. All his degrees and promotions didn't amount to a hill of beans in this part of the world.

Soon, he actually felt his smile fading on his face, however.

He'd spent his life looking for ways to recognize himself —ways to measure his success. Here and now nothing mattered except—well, the here and now. Keller sat back and drank his beer. The men had finished eating, and at last the women and children came close to the fire to enjoy their food. Everyone seemed pleased to share the fire and companionship. The children did not sit, but snatched their food and walked around the circle of light munching, giggling, or sometimes addressing one of the adults in their own language. The conversation shifted into smaller groups, and the nomads forgot their guests for a few minutes. The family groups settled down together, fathers holding a child on one knee, a cup on the other, women smiling in the firelight.

In a little while, the children finished eating and began to play again. They jumped up with the kind of before-bedtime energy that children everywhere seemed to summon after dinner. Keller watched. They appeared to be reenacting a battle their ancestors must have fought, for some of the stronger ones wielded make-believe swords and cried wild oaths into the night air. The combined steam from their breathing and exertions created a misty cloud around their play area. In their midst, Keller spotted the young daughter of Pirim, the little girl he had rescued so long ago. She dodged among the others with the agility of a deer. One of the boys—the tall, fair-skinned one—raised his pretend weapon and threw his head back to deliver a genuine war cry. He even pounded his mouth like a matinee Indian.

The boy who had war-whooped dashed out of the mist

and into the light of the fire. In the split second that it took for him to race past, Keller noted the boy's lively face. The kid's expression was full of vitality. In his imagination, he was a marauding Indian brave, and his face reflected all the excitement and pleasure a little boy could bring to a role like that.

An Indian? Here?

Keller got to his feet. When the kid came dashing around again, Keller grabbed the boy's arm. His momentum swung him around, but he planted his yak-hair boots on the packed snow and stopped, then turned his face up to Keller. His expression froze. Hostility and fear clamped down on his features—on his narrow little mouth and very blue eyes.

"I'll be damned," said Keller, suddenly breathless.

The boy said, "Let me go!" In perfect English.

"My God," Keller said. "Robbie?"

Chapter 31

NEXT MORNING, WITH JANE'S SON FIRMLY IN TOW AND THE MAP brought out of its case and thoroughly studied and discussed with the Tibetans, Keller and company set off through the snow toward China.

"I can hardly believe it," Coot declared, marching by Keller's side at the head of their ragtag army. "All this time Miss Jane's been thinking her boy is dead and now here he is—big as life!"

"Parish lied," Keller agreed.

"Or else he really didn't know Robbie got away."

"Fat chance."

"You don't believe the kid's story?"

"That he crawled out of the wreck and wandered off? Sure, I believe him. He probably got a knock on the head and was delirious—didn't know he was leaving his father. I even believe that he got himself accepted by these people."

"Accepted!" Coot shook his head. "The kid's a natural here. I never noticed he was any different than the rest."

Robbie's fair hair had come to light only after Keller

ripped off his cap and scrubbed his face to make sure of the resemblance to his mother. It had taken several minutes to convince Robbie he could safely speak English, but even then he hadn't chattered. The boy had a lot in common with Jane.

Keller said, "What I can't believe is that Parish didn't go looking for his own son." He glanced over his shoulder to be sure Robbie wasn't within earshot. The boy happily gamboled between Billy and Yamdi, practicing on the two guides the Nepali he had already begun to learn. To Coot, Keller said, "I think Parish had no intention of giving the boy back to Jane. The bastard."

"Then you're looking to settle a couple of scores with him," Coot observed.

"Maybe so."

"You really think we can catch him? They got a day's head start."

"But we," said Keller, smiling a little, "have got the map."

"But your old man knows the way, too. If he's leading Parish—"

"He *thinks* he knows the way," Keller corrected. "He and I drew sketches of the map from memory on the walls of a cave. We had a few hours to kill. He copied our final draft on paper, and he intends to use that to guide Parish across the mountains. Fortunately, neither of our memories is perfect. He's going to miss the Black Bridge by several miles."

"So? How'll we find 'em?"

"He'll find another way across the plateau, but it'll take him a lot longer. If I know him and Roger Parish, they'll make it out of stubbornness. And, Coot, my friend, we're going to beat them to China."

"Head them off at the pass, you mean?"

"At the bridge, at any rate. Let's just hope Parish isn't going to be greeted by an official welcoming committee. I really don't want to run into the entire Chinese armed forces."

"Oh," said Coot, admiring his walking stick as he stumped along the winding trail, "I wouldn't mind a scuffle."

Keller sent him a wry look. "I've had enough rough stuff, thanks."

Coot grinned, still walking. "Yeah? I thought you were getting a taste for it." He shrugged. "I could be wrong."

Coot walked on ahead, and Keller allowed himself to fall back a little, ostensibly to check on the progress of Mohan Dok and his bandits but actually taking a few minutes to ponder. Maybe he was getting a taste for fighting, after all. He wasn't dreading the encounter that lay ahead. Rather, Keller found himself almost looking forward to seeing Parish again. And Jane, too, and his father, but Parish was the one Keller really wanted to face once again. Maybe Coot was right.

For the trip across the Black Bridge, Keller had finally gone native in his dress. If Chinese border officials did come along and see the caravan of travelers, they would probably not recognize Keller for being different than his companions. He took his cue from Robbie and covered his hair and face. Dressed in his own trousers and boots along with the shirts and jacket he'd stolen from Parish's guardsman, he pulled on a turbanlike cap that Mohan had pressed upon him along with a pair of the traditional baggy white jodhpurs that fitted warmly over his own pants. To a casual eye, no doubt Keller blended nicely with the other men.

But Keller needn't have worried. That whole day the expedition met no other travelers. The mountains appeared to have been deserted by all humans. Wind echoed in the labyrinthine valleys. Snow gleamed on the peaks.

On the third day, the expedition struggled up a huge incline of perhaps a thousand feet and landed on a long, wide plateau that had been blown clean of snow. Black rock shone in the sunlight, looking like a gigantic rooftop. "The Black Bridge," Keller said aloud, staring at the expanse of solid granite that had been his father's goal.

The view took Keller's breath away. In the distance, a few misty peaks gleamed, but they were so far away and picturesque that the Black Bridge truly did look like a route across the roof of the world. The unbroken expanse of granite stretched ahead like a highway into a lost kingdom.

"This is it, sah?" Billy asked. "The Black Bridge?"

"It is indeed," Keller replied, surprised to hear a catch in his own voice.

Billy released a sigh. "It looks like everything else, sah. Nothing special. No treasure here."

Keller smiled. "Maybe not for you, Billy."

Keller slithered down a pebble-strewn slope and landed at the bottom, where he was the first to set foot on the black granite. The rest of the caravan followed him. They set off walking northward.

"Sah," Billy panted, catching up after a quarter of an hour. "Sah, if we find these men who kidnap Missus Jane, what will we do?"

"What do you mean, Billy?"

"Well, sah, I do not think that bloody husband will want to let Jane come with us, will he, sah?"

"Probably not, no."

"So?" Billy asked. "What will you do, sah? Have a gunfight?"

"Only Coot has a gun," Keller pointed out. "We wouldn't get very far that way, I'm afraid. We can't just waltz in and ask them to let Jane go either. No, we've got to come up with a plan."

Billy agreed. "We don't want a bloody botch-up, sah."

"Right. We won't get a second chance."

"Sah!" Billy's eyes lit up. "What we need is a bloody diversion!"

"A diversion."

"Oh, sah, I am bloody well trained in diversions!"

Keller grinned. "Like every good con artist. Okay, Billy, what do you suggest?"

After a little thought, Billy told him.

Even though they were probably lost, Jane didn't care. Not exactly. She meditated as much as possible. She had completed her journey, why wasn't it over? What should she have learned about herself? The answers did not come, and Jane experienced clear moments during her meditations which should have facilitated the coming of those answers. She could only surmise that her journey was not over yet.

On the fourth or fifth day, Roger's shouting brought Jane

abruptly out of her meditation. Though she was sitting a hundred yards or so from their stopping place on the trail, she could see the whole exchange.

Roger punched Professor Keller and knocked him to the ground. "You stupid bastard, you haven't the slightest idea where you're going, do you?"

The Professor tried to speak, but Roger kicked him in the side and walked away.

An idea came to Jane at the moment Professor Keller got up off the ground and dusted himself off. The thought of stealing the precious microfilm from Roger made Jane feel absurdly happy for the first time in many days.

Before dawn, just as she had expected she would, Jane woke and lay listening quietly for a while. All quiet. She pulled her parka into her sleeping bag to warm it up, and in a few minutes, she slipped it on. Once dressed, she slid out of her tent and stole across the campsite. It was dark.

The fire had gone out, and no one had risen to tend to it yet. None of the porters had awakened. The soft sound of snoring emanated from Colonel Pompowsky's tent; no noise came from Professor Keller's. Cautious, however, Jane crept across the snow, careful not to step too close to the sleeping porters.

At the entrance to Roger's small tent, she paused. No sound came from inside.

Slowly, Jane crouched onto her hands and knees. With fingers that were so cold they hurt, she began to unfasten the zipper on the tent flap. She slid it up and up until the opening was large enough to admit her head and shoulders. Cautiously, Jane eased inside.

The blinding beam of a flashlight stabbed her square in the eyes.

"Why, Janey," said Roger. "You have a change of heart?"

Jane swallowed her genuine cry of pain. The light hit like a knife thrust. She clapped her hand to her face. "Roger!"

He kept the beam trained on her, pinning Jane in the entrance. Jane felt his hand on the zipper of her parka. He said, "Trying to surprise me, were you?"

"Turn that damn thing off, will you?"

"Sorry. Don't want to wake up the others, do we?" He snapped off the light and in the resulting darkness that left Jane dazed he grabbed her arm and pulled.

Awkwardly, Jane sprawled across his sleeping bag. She couldn't gather her balance sufficiently to resist and felt Roger's breath against her cheek. She had failed. Now she was in trouble. "Roger—"

He laughed softly, put one of his hands into her hair, and kneaded her head, pulling her closer. Jane braced her knees like a stubborn mule, but Roger was stronger. She took a deep breath and prepared herself for a kiss, squinching her eyes closed so tightly she saw stars.

But the kiss didn't come.

Roger said, "What's that?"

"What?"

"That noise."

Jane, frozen on all fours, opened her eyes and listened. In the darkness, she heard nothing at first. Then the sound drew closer. Weird cries, it was. Animal yelling. Outside the tent, the porters stirred in their makeshift beds. They muttered, then began to call to Roger. "Sahib!" "Sahib!"

He flung off his sleeping bag and shoved Jane down and out of his way. He grabbed his gun, but not his boots. Sockfooted, he scrambled out into the snow.

"What the hell?"

Jane followed hastily. Dawn had begun to lighten the sky. By that light, the awakened porters looked down the mountain and pointed. Roger joined them. The strange wailing continued to grow in volume. More voices rose. Pompowsky came blustering out of his tent, wearing his long johns and waving his gun. "What the hell is that?"

On the other side of the campsite, Professor Keller crawled out of his tent. On hands and knees, he asked, "What's that shouting?"

Jane said, "I don't know."

Roger buckled on his gun and stomped back to his tent. "I don't know either," he snapped, "but I'm going to find out." He seized his boots, plunked down on the snow, and shoved his wet feet inside. "Sounds like some kind of animal."

Without thinking, Jane suggested, "Maybe it's a yeti."

At that word, the porters stepped into tighter formation, murmuring with agitation. Roger said, "Shut up, woman. You want them all to run away?"

He shouted for Yo and commanded his men to follow him and marched them off down the hillside. Pompowsky, still in his long underwear and boots, trundled after them, and the Professor brought up the rear, taking time to pull on his parka against the cold. They left Jane to guard the camp alone.

Standing there listening to the eerie voices and the whisper of an early-morning wind suddenly gave Jane the creeps. She shivered and hugged herself, wishing foolishly that she had asked one of the men to stay behind.

From behind her, she heard a scrape. She turned toward the sound. "Oh my God!"

Two Tibetan bandits jumped down from the rocks and landed in the campsite, crouching warily. Both carried long knives and covered their faces against the cold with the tails of their wrapped turbans. Instinctively, Jane turned and ran.

The bigger man tackled her from behind, bowling Jane into the snow and landing hard on top of her. She landed facedown, wind momentarily driven out of her. Then she kicked and flailed with all her strength. He grabbed her left arm and pulled her up. Jane cried out. He clapped his rag-wrapped hand over her mouth at once, then wound one very strong arm around her waist and pinned her against his body. Jane bit his hand. He stifled a yelp, but backpedaled up the hill, dragging Jane with him.

She fought him every step of the way, gagged into silence, but screaming with rage behind his hand. His assistant made a quick and furtive inspection of all three tents, then joined the first thief and lent a hand with Jane, hefting her up the rocky hill to a series of boulders. Against two of them, Jane struggled all the harder. The bigger man kept her head jammed against his coat, so she couldn't hear their words. In breathless undertones, they exchanged exclamations. They dragged her up into the boulders.

When the sunlight at last poured down over the ridge of the mountains, the big thief fell down, dragging Jane with him. Quick as a cat, she rolled free and tried to scream.

"Goddammit!" Keller hissed. "Will you shut up?"

"Keller!"

Jane grabbed his mask and pulled it down. Sure enough, he was Keller. A little smudged, bruised, dirty, and bewhiskered, but definitely Keller. "You son of a bitch! You scared me to death!"

"Shut *up*," he insisted. "They'll hear you! Yamdi?"

The little Sherpa, peering over the boulders to the campsite below, turned and smiled delightedly. "No trouble, sah. Mister Coot and Billy lead those fellows long way down the hill!"

"What's going *on*?" Jane demanded.

"This," said Keller, standing up and dusting himself off, "is what's called a rescue."

"Rescue?" Jane repeated. Inside, her heart was pounding like a freight train. "It looks more like costume night on the Love Boat!" she snapped. "What's that you're wearing? It smells like yaks."

Keller glowered. "I didn't have time to slip into my tuxedo. Forgive me. Now let's—"

Shaky enough to make herself furious, Jane said, "Do you realize what you've done, you idiot?"

Keller halted in the act of turning up the hillside and looked at her. "I *think* I've just snatched you away from a maniac, but—"

"I was about to get the plans back, you fool! I was in Roger's tent and—"

"I know where you were," Keller retorted testily. "We've been watching the damn place for the better part of two hours."

Jane flushed. He had seen her go willingly into Roger's tent. "Well, I almost had the microfilm! If you hadn't come along, I'd have—"

"I know perfectly well what might have happened," Keller snapped, "and it had nothing to do with microfilm!"

She clambered to her feet. "What the hell are you talking about?"

"Didn't take you long to climb into Roger's sleeping bag, did it?"

"Why, you—!" Action was better than words. Jane slapped him.

Keller grabbed her wrist. He dragged her close and glared deeply into her eyes. "Listen, damn you, we've worked out one hell of a rescue here, and if you don't mind, we'd like to make sure all the loose ends are accounted for. Go with Yamdi, do you hear me?"

Trembling even harder than before, Jane managed to control her voice. "Where are you going?"

"To get my old man." He flung her away. "Yamdi, take her now. Show her our little surprise. Maybe that will lighten up her mood a little!"

One look at Keller's face told Jane that now wasn't a good time to argue with him. He left without another word, anyway. Looking positively expert in his bandit gear, he leaped over the boulders and slid noiselessly down toward the campsite again. Jane almost followed, but Yamdi held her back.

"Missus? The boss says for you to come now."

"But he—Roger might—"

Yamdi didn't let go. "Come now, Missus. The boss knows what to do next."

"But—"

"Come, Missus. Come up higher, we have found a safe place. There is a surprise for you."

"What surprise?" Jane followed Yamdi up the hillside. She scrambled for handholds and climbed quickly after the Sherpa. Stones and chunks of ice rattled from her hands. Her boots slipped perilously. There was hardly enough sunlight to see where she was going, and she didn't dare look back to see where Keller had gone. "What surprise could be more than this?" she muttered. "The crack of dawn—he accuses me of—of—Yamdi, how on earth—? Wait! Can you—?"

Yamdi put down his hand to help her up the last yard. She cleared the rocks and hesitated, panting with fear and exertion, poised there on the top of the highest boulder with the sun shining over her right shoulder to gleam on the upturned face of the little person crouching behind the stone.

"Here, Missus, is the surprise."

Robbie smiled. He looked up at her and put out his hand to help her down. His touch hadn't changed, his voice was the same. He might have been jumping off the school bus to greet her. "Hi, Mom."

Chapter 32

THOROUGHLY ANNOYED WITH THE FEMALE OF THE SPECIES IN general, Keller slithered down the mountainside in his bandit costume, staying as close to the ground as he could. No telling what the men on the trail below might be able to see. Keller could only hope that Coot and Billy and their traveling yeti act had successfully lured Parish's men into an ambush.

What Keller hadn't counted on was his father going off and joining the party! What did the old man think he could do? Why hadn't he just stayed curled up in his sleeping bag and let himself get rescued?

The Professor wasn't the type to stay in his sleeping bag when there was adventure to be found, that's why. Cursing the old fool, Keller slipped and slid down the hillside.

The report of a gun stopped him. Panting, Keller jammed himself between two rocks and listened. Two more shots echoed in the hills, followed by a yell of pain. He couldn't stop himself and peeked over the rocks. By the early morning light, he spotted a few of Parish's men hiding in the rocks below. They cowered there sensibly, waiting out the gunplay. Like characters in a spaghetti western, however, Parish and Pompowsky had taken up positions in the rocks and were shooting at targets lower down on the hill. Keller only hoped they couldn't actually see anyone to shoot. A third gun answered their shots with a couple of very loud blasts. Coot's handgun, Keller supposed. The one with only six bullets.

Footsteps drove Keller back down into hiding. He hugged the rocks and held his breath.

"Goddamn blasted fools," muttered a voice. "Can't see or hear a thing and go shooting off like it's skeet season at the rod-and-gun club! I'll never understand in a million years why grown men—good God!"

"Dad!" Keller rolled aside and narrowly avoided getting stepped on. He reached up and grabbed his father's arm and hauled him down to safety behind the rocks. "Wow, am I glad—"

"What the hell are you doing here?" The Professor struggled to sit up and then glared with equal parts of surprise and outrage. "I thought you had gone home!"

"Are you kidding? And leave you with this maniac? I came to get you back."

"Get me—? What in the name of almighty damnation are you talking about?"

"I'm taking you home!"

"The hell you are!" The Professor scrambled to stand up. "I'm on expedition here, boy! I'm not going anywhere except over the border."

"You're already over the border," Keller retorted. "Which just goes to show how scientific this trip really is."

"I'm going to find the Black Bridge. It's here. I know it is."

"Dad—"

"Boy, don't you try bullying me." The Professor pointed a long and bony forefinger at Keller's nose. "I may be getting old, but I can whip you—"

"Dad, I'm serious." Keller struggled to maintain his patience. "You can't stay with these people. For crying out loud, they're shooting at each other! Come with me. We've got to find the nearest border checkpoint and turn in Parish and his pals. After that—"

"Are you this much of a moron?" the Professor shouted. "The border police will arrest us, too! There won't be anything after that!"

"Dad, we've got to stop Roger Parish. That has to be our first priority. Afterwards we can walk the Black Bridge. I've got the map."

The Professor's craggy face slackened, then filled with excitement. He seized Keller's coat in both his hands. "Where is it? Where's the map?"

"Shh! First we get Parish," Keller said. "Then the map. Understand?"

"Give it to me!" With all his strength, the Professor shook Keller, as if trying to jangle the map loose. "Give it to me now! It's mine!"

"Dad, be quiet, will you? Let go! We haven't got time for this! For God's sake—"

"You have no right to keep it from me! It's mine! This is my expedition. I won't have Parish or you or anybody ruin it—"

"I hate to do this," Keller muttered.

He brought the punch up from down low and struck his father right across the jaw. The Professor's head snapped back and his knees buckled. Even though his eyes were open, Keller saw the lights go out in the old man's head. Keller caught him before he struck his head on the rocks, but lost his balance and together they tumbled a few feet down the slippery hillside.

Keller braced his legs and stopped their slide. He wrestled with his father's dead weight and finally struggled to his feet. Puffing with exertion, he managed to sling the old man's body across his shoulder in a precarious fireman's carry. The old maniac weighed a ton. Keller started uphill, staggering, toward the rendezvous point he'd established with Yamdi.

Jane followed Yamdi's directions, heading around the side of the mountain before heading downward. She kept Robbie's tight little hand clasped in her own and couldn't help looking back at him as they clambered down the hill. He grinned back at her. He had grown! She was sure of it. And he glowed with excitement. To him, the whole ordeal had been a great adventure. It wasn't over yet, and Robbie looked as though he was glad.

Jane didn't feel the same way exactly. But finding Robbie alive had given her a boost of adrenaline so intoxicating she could hardly put one foot in front of the other.

"You okay, Mom? Want me to lead? I know the way, honest."

"I'm sure you do." Jane smiled, though shakily. "But I'm taller and can see who's coming. When we slip past the others, you can be the leader."

Robbie followed obediently, and Jane climbed down through the snow to a ledge. They edged along that narrow trail and came out on a rocky hillside. Jane led the way across the field of stones. She stopped to negotiate her way down some rocks, reaching back for Robbie's hand to steady her.

He said, "M—mom!"

Jane nearly cried out. Standing just six feet below them was Pompowsky. He looked like a lost and angry bull, not able to find the barn but belligerently unconquered so far. His face was red and his body looked flabby under the insulated long johns he wore. He wasn't wearing his parka, but he had remembered his gun. It was thrust down into the waistband of his underwear.

Jane collected herself and faced the Colonel without speaking. She didn't trust her voice.

"Who's this?" he demanded, looking suspiciously at Robbie. Something connected in his exertion-fogged brain, because he snapped his attention back to Jane and his right hand automatically reached for his sidearm. "Where are you going, girl?"

"I heard shooting. I thought I'd make sure everyone was okay."

Pompowsky pointed. "The shooting's that way."

"Well, I didn't want to *get* shot. I only wanted—"

"Who's the kid? Where'd he come from?"

Jane prayed Robbie's disguise looked authentic. "I found

him wandering. He's—I don't know. He must be from around—"

"He's your boy, isn't he? The one you've been looking for."

"Listen, Pompowsky, I don't—"

The Colonel drew his gun. "Shut up and listen. You're not going anywhere till we regroup. You're not leaving my sight."

Jane dropped Robbie's hand. "All right, I won't. But I have to know if Roger's all right. Just let me—"

"Stay where you are," Pompowsky barked. Jane had sidled to her left, and Robbie, bless him, began moving in the opposite direction. The Colonel swung the barrel of his gun back and forth between them. "I mean it," he said. "Both of you stop!"

Jane obeyed, but put up a feisty front. "I don't have to listen to you. Put that thing away."

"You'll listen, sister! Now—Goddammit, stop moving!"

"If you shoot me, Roger will murder you. Listen to reason for once, Pompowsky." His face was sweaty, and he looked frazzled—just off-balance enough to fool. Jane feigned a stumble, drawing his attention completely onto herself. Still moving, she cried, "Robbie, run!"

The boy dove for cover, dodging like a bolting rabbit until he was safe behind a rock. Pompowsky instinctively pointed the gun after him, and Jane flung herself at it. She hit the Colonel full force with her shoulder, and they both lost their footing.

Pompowsky went down like a sack of sand, and Jane landed on top of him. She drove her knee into his belly and grabbed for the gun.

He grunted something obscene, then wrestled the gun free. He clubbed her with it. Jane saw stars dance. Panting, Pompowsky said, "I've been looking forward to this, girl."

Keller struggled uphill, breathing as if he'd run a marathon and trying valiantly not to drop his father on the rocks. "Jesus Christ," he said, starting a rhythm. "Jesus Christ."

Suddenly a rock four feet away exploded. Keller staggered. Another rock blew up. He shouted and turned, stumbling under his father's weight. He hardly had enough breath left to speak. "Parish!"

Roger Parish had come up behind him and stood just several yards down the hillside in knee-deep snow. He pointed his gun away from the rocks and directly at Keller. When he spotted Keller's face, his own expression turned to surprise. "You! You're supposed to be dead!"

There didn't seem to be a good response to that. Keller couldn't catch his breath anyway.

Roger's eyes narrowed. "I should have taken care of you myself the first time." He took aim.

Keller dumped his father. Looking down the barrel of a loaded gun tended to force a man back on his instincts. The Professor's body thunked on the rocks. Then guilt took over, and Keller grabbed the Professor's arm and dragged him to the nearest cover, a stone about the size of a large pumpkin.

"You had your chance, Keller," Roger said. "But you blew it. You should have run for home."

He pulled the trigger. The bullet zapped the ground under Keller's left boot. The second bullet zinged through Keller's trousers. He felt a searing heat crease his right thigh. By that time, he was moving, though, and the third bullet made a lot of noise against the rocks above. Keller ran. Unfortunately, his right thigh seemed to have something wrong with it, and he stumbled. He fell across the slithery rocks and tried to scramble up even before he hit. Roger quit shooting and started laughing. A clump of many pumpkin-sized rocks lay just four body-lengths away. Keller gathered himself for a run toward them.

Roger took aim and fired, and the clump of rocks scattered. Then a softer shot echoed on the hillside, and Roger stopped shooting. He looked up the hill toward the sound of the other gun. The air reverberated with the noise of gunfire. It sounded like thunder.

"Who's up there?" he shouted. "Pompowsky!"

Jane was up there, Keller knew. He'd sent her there himself. She didn't have a gun, though, and neither did Yamdi. Who was shooting? And at whom? A second report resounded in the mountain air, followed by a scream. A distinctly female scream that sounded high and clear above the rumble of the echoing shots. Keller had never heard Jane cry out like that, but he recognized her voice anyway. Jane was screaming!

Not for long. Her voice died out, and then they could hear a younger voice shouting—protesting. A third gunshot silenced him.

Robbie and Jane.

Roger didn't move.

Keller did. But for some reason he couldn't make himself run away from Roger Parish. In a split second, he was flying through the air and tackling Roger with all his strength. They connected, hit the ground, and rolled together. They tumbled over and over and finally stopped. The hillside fell away to a cliff, and the chasm yawned at them.

Keller didn't notice. "If you've killed her," he panted, seizing Roger's left arm and the collar of his in his fists, "I'll—"

Roger wedged his gun between their two struggling bodies. He pulled the trigger. The sound was incredible, and burned powder cut the air. But the bullet went wild. Keller punched him. Roger grunted. Keller grabbed his throat and rolled so he'd have leverage. Underneath, Roger fought, kicked, and then shoved the nose of his gun directly into Keller's lowest rib. He looked into Keller's eyes and squeezed the trigger.

Keller froze. The gun coughed. That was it. No explosion.

"You're empty!" Keller shouted gleefully. And he smashed a punch into Roger Parish's cheek.

An empty gun didn't deter Roger, however. He bucked and threw a punch that glanced off Keller's chin. Keller fell over, rolled, and leaped to his feet, dizzy but prepared.

Roger got up, too. He looked sweaty and angry and hurt, but also balanced. The way he weaved and held his body let Keller know that he was in for the kind of fight he wasn't ready for. Roger hit him with a fist. The next thing Keller knew, he was sitting on the ground.

And a rock near his hand blew up. A bullet ricocheted off into the air with a whine.

Roger stopped moving. He looked up the hill.

Jane stood there. She had Pompowsky's gun and she pointed it at Roger. "Stop it," she said.

Roger shook his head, meeting her stare. "No, Janey."

"I mean it, Roger. Forget everything. This is over now."

"All right," said Roger. "You can go. Take Keller—you can even take the old man. Go on, all of you. I won't try to stop you anymore."

From his spot on the ground, Keller said, "You don't get it, Parish. We mean to stop you."

Roger looked down at him, then back up at Jane. "Stop me? From what?"

"From taking anything into China," said Jane. "We're all going home."

"You can't stop me," said Roger. "Why should you? What does my trip have to do with any of you? Go ahead and leave. But I'm going ahead with my plans."

"I don't think so," said Jane. "And I've got the gun. I'm pretty good with it, too."

Roger smiled a little. "But you haven't got the heart for it, Janey. I know you haven't. You and your respect-for-life crap. What was that screaming we just heard? We thought you'd been hit."

"I shot Pompowsky," said Jane. Keller suddenly realized that she was very pale. Her hands were steady, though, and her voice sounded strong. She said, "I shot him in the knee, so he's alive. I can do the same to you."

"A bad knee won't stop me," Roger argued. "You'd have to kill me, Janey, and I don't think you can."

To prove his point, he started up the hill toward her. One step at a time, he walked up and up. Jane didn't move, didn't step back. She held the gun steady. When Roger stepped into her sights, she squeezed off the shot.

Nothing happened. Her gun was empty, too.

There was nothing for Keller to do but try the tackle again. He scrambled up and ran hard, then hit Roger just as he was reaching for Jane's hair. The two of them crashed to the ground, slid dangerously close to the edge of the hill, and stopped, both flailing at each other's faces.

"Watch out!" Jane cried.

They struggled, wrestling, then Keller dodged Roger's

best punch and fell back. When he released Roger, Parish lost his precarious balance. He grabbed for the rocks and slithered over the rim. With his legs, he hunted frantically for a foothold. Panting, he shouted, "Hey!"

Keller, on his hands and knees, started to grab him. But he didn't reach Parish in time—Keller missed his chance. Roger Parish plunged over the edge of the hillside and slammed into the rocks many yards below. He screamed and kept falling. His body hit again and once more, then disappeared.

Jane reached Keller and seized his hands. Together, they strained to hear any sound below. But the only sound that rose to them was the wind.

"Dear heaven," Jane whispered.

Keller couldn't make his voice work. He hugged Jane hard, wishing he could snatch back the last sixty seconds. Jane began to weep, and Keller felt a knot tighten in his own throat.

"Gawldang," said Coot at sunset that night. "I didn't think everything'd turn out so neat as this. You okay, Miss Jane?"

"Yes, Calvin." Jane smiled weakly. She held Robbie in her lap and rocked him, even though the boy squirmed and objected, "Mom!"

"What're you going to do now?" Coot asked. "Go home?"

"Yes," she said. "Exactly. Back to the States." She tugged at Robbie's ear. "Back to school for you, young man."

Robbie squinched up his nose, but grinned.

Coot turned to Keller. "How about you, Paul?"

Keller allowed Yamdi to apply a soaked sock to his bruised face, but winced just the same.

Billy answered for him. "Not back to your old country, I hope, sah! You cannot go back there! Not after all this adventure!"

With his unswollen eye, Keller glowered at Billy. "Has it occurred to anyone that maybe I've had enough adventure?"

"Sah, you cannot go home! Mohan Dok, sah, is giving you all the maps of his people! They expect you to lead them, sah, to great wealth and glory once again. It is your destiny, so they say."

"My destiny?" Keller snorted. "Wealth and glory?"

He could have objected more. But sitting there with Yamdi fussing over his wounds and with Jane and Robbie and Coot and all the gathered clans of Mohan Dok expectantly watching his every move, Keller couldn't quite summon the right arguments. Wealth and glory, huh?

"Keller's right," Jane said suddenly. "He ought to go home where things are nice and safe. Life and death is too—well, a person shouldn't have to face questions like that every day."

"Ain't that the truth," said Coot. "Some peace and quiet sounds good to me."

The Professor, sitting slightly apart from the rest of them, was already studying the cache of maps that Mohan Dok had bestowed upon "Boss Killer." As the fireside conversation lulled, the old man said, "This map shows a route to Afghanistan! Imagine how valuable a route over the Himalaya into Afghanistan might be today! Do you suppose that fellow Dok could really have found a negotiable trail? I'll have to get started on some research right away!"

Keller got up and strolled over to his father. In the firelight, the collection of tattered maps looked intriguing indeed—mountains and hideaways and secret routes of a long-dead marauding bandit. Softly, Keller said, "Why start research when you can just start the journey?"

The Professor stayed on the ground and looked up at his son with watery eyes. "You—you think it's possible?"

Keller shrugged. "The Black Bridge existed. Why shouldn't these trails also?"

Clutching the maps to his heart, the Professor said, "Should we? I mean, do you think—?"

"Well," said Keller, "what have we got to lose?"

The Professor grinned, and Keller found himself smiling back. He sauntered off into the darkness then, feeling the need to think, some time to absorb everything that had happened. He'd come a long way, and not just in the kind of distance measured in miles. The snow whispered under his boots as if predicting tales of adventure to come. Keller shook his head. A little adventure could go a long way. What he wouldn't mind now was a long trip—an easy one—during which he could reach a few more conclusions about himself.

Behind him, Jane murmured, "You okay?"

Keller turned toward her. "Yeah, sure."

Her face was a pale oval, and her gray eyes looked clear and luminous. She paced closer, her hands in her pockets, her head lowered. In the darkness, her hair gleamed with distant starlight. Softly she said, "A lot of this is my fault, Keller. I'm sorry."

"I made my own decisions," he said.

She looked up at him, and a trace of a smile crossed her face. "Yes," she said. "You have. What about the one I heard just now? Are you really thinking of going to Afghanistan?"

He smiled, too, and shrugged. "Why not? I hear there's a little excitement going on up there. Maybe I ought to have a look."

"You made the Professor very happy," she said. "If he really is your father, you've made him proud."

"If he—? What do you mean?"

Jane shook that off. "I talked with him, that's all. I wondered if—well, with all this talk about Mohir Dok's descendant and your father not—I mean—"

"My mother was here," Keller said suddenly. "She came with him the first time he studied these mountains."

Jane's gaze didn't waver. She let him think.

Keller obeyed an inner wish and took her into his arms. Jane came willingly, wrapping her arms around his body until they were hugging lightly, standing in the snow. He said, "No matter where I came from, I think I know where I'd like to go."

"That's Afghanistan?"

"Yes. Yes, I think so. I only wish . . ."

She tilted her face up to his. "Yes?"

"Nothing. I just thought—well, you've got Robbie. He'll have to get back and—"

Toying with the collar of his shirt, she said, "Robbie and I can't go into Kathmandu. We've lost our passports and everything. We'll get arrested for sure."

"I hadn't thought of that," said Keller. "You'll have to find another route back to the states."

"Exactly what I was thinking." Gently, Jane drew his head down to her level and kissed Keller very lightly on the mouth. She was smiling.

Keller grinned, too, and pulled her close. "Isn't it amazing," he said, "how we've started to think alike?"

"Amazing," she agreed. When she kissed him again, Keller held her in his arms and said, "I could get used to this hero stuff."

Outstanding Bestsellers!